For Joey

By Jaclyn M. Hawkes

Spirit Dance Books

Be sure to read Jaclyn's other books

Journey of Honor A love story
An entertaining historical romance set in
1848 in the American West

The Outer Edge of Heaven
A rollicking contemporary love story set
on a beautiful Montana ranch

The Most Important Catch
A tender and intense modern day story
of devotion set against a backdrop of
pro football in North Carolina

Healing Creek
A heartfelt and fun tale of love and trust

Rockland Ranch Series
The epic saga of a Wyoming ranch family
Peace River
Above Rubies
Once Enchanted

Warrior's Moon
An intrepid tale of adventure and devotion set in the medieval
kingdom of Monciere'

The Sage After Rain
A sweet love story set in Colorado about finding what truly
matters most.

What readers are saying about Jaclyn's books:

This book held a great combination of romance, adventure and peace. I will always recommend Jaclyn Hawkes books. I love them all and this one is no exception.

The descriptions of the people and places were so good I couldn't help wanting to move in next door. I can't wait to see more of them. Another clean, fantastic read. I'm waiting anxiously for the rest of the series!

Great story line, I enjoyed the story and mystery from the beginning, I couldn't put it down. Will look for more by this author.

I loved Outer Edge of Heaven and would recommend it to all readers. Grab a pack of Oreos and some milk then head out onto your porch with this one!

I liked that the heroine fought hard and made thoughtful, difficult decisions, but still crumpled in the arms of the man she loved. She was brave and strong, but still cried. Sir Peyton was any girl's fantasy hero. I really enjoyed Warrior's Moon. I will read it again. Can't wait to read Hawkes' newest.

I love, love, loved this book!!!!!! It was clean, and wonderful from beginning to the end.

For Joey A love story
By Jaclyn M. Hawkes
Copyright © April 2014 Jaclyn M. Hawkes
All rights reserved.
Published and distributed by Spirit Dance Books. Spiritdancebooks.com
855-648-5559

Cover design by Roland Ali Pantin
Printed in USA
First Printing April 2014
LOC 2014936094
ISBN: 0-9851648-7-4
ISBN-13: 978-0-9851648-7-4

Acknowledgements

Thanks to the many people behind the scenes on my team who make my books come together. I could never do all of this without you.

And thanks to my dad for buying my mother a grand piano and giving all eleven of us kids the gift of beautiful music in our home. And of course, thanks to Mom for putting in the countless hours to become a gifted pianist. Even now, when your fingers are looking a little grandmotherly, your music brings joy whenever you sit down to play.

I know I gave you gray hair over my own lessons, but I regret that now and have insisted my own children take music lessons, just like you did. Please try to forget how many times I threw my piano books under the snowball bush and ran away every week when I was supposed to go to Mrs. Simmons for lessons. And we are not even going to talk about those dance lessons.

Thank goodness my children take after you in music and not me—although my hearing will never be the same after that time I had the entire high school marching band trumpet section practicing in my living room, because it was pouring rain outside.

True story. Best kids ever. Today's youth are awesome!

Jaclyn

Dedication

This book is dedicated to my four brothers, Lane, Shaun, Charlie, and Jon Jon. Just like Joey's brothers in this book, my brothers loved me and watched over me and teased me and occasionally made my life miserable. I'm sure I deserved it. (Hey, but now we're adults and we're supposed to be mature, so stop already.)

It's also dedicated to my fantastic husband. He's survived 23 years of marriage with me. That can't have been easy. He is incredibly durable.

He is also a musician in his own way. He refuses to sing in the ward choir, but he sings to me in the truck when we're off on adventures and you should hear his La Vida Loca late at night when he's tired! Once you've heard it, you will never forget it! Marriage to him has always been entertaining. I'm sure it always will be.

I love you dearly, hon. Thanks for loving me back,

Jaclyn

Chapter 1

Michael James Morgan stood under the canopy that shielded him from the pouring rain and watched wordlessly as they lowered the casket that held his father's body into the muddy hole in the ground that was draped with green carpet. There had been no words spoken at all and no formal funeral. It was what his father had wanted and was somehow fitting for the heart wrenching pain of this moment.

Michael didn't think he could have handled a service. His unbearable sadness was such that he couldn't face the media circus that would have ensued and he'd never even released an obituary. At least he had avoided the press and could lick his wounds in relative privacy.

The only other people there were the man his father had asked weeks ago to handle the burial arrangements, and Doc, the man who had become Michael's good friend through the process of helping his father die of liver cancer with as much dignity as possible, and Doc's kind wife, Ashley. Michael hadn't wanted anyone else to be there. He hadn't even wanted anyone else to know. For some reason, his grief sought privacy.

Michael waited as the man his father had referred to as Brother Jones quietly picked up a nearby shovel and began to drop the watery dirt piled to the side on top of the striking spray of white roses that covered the casket. It was only a token smattering of dirt. The cemetery people would finish closing the vault and filling the grave, but it symbolized that his father was indeed gone and buried.

He reached up to brush aside the one tear he'd been unable to contain. It rolled down from beneath the dark sunglasses he wore despite the low, gray clouds that hung on the misty hills here north of New York City. With the muffled sound of the shovel full of dropping dirt, Michael tipped his head back and tried to gather his emotions and stow them away enough that he could get himself back to the low slung black Ferrari that waited at the curb without shattering.

A gentle hand touched him on the arm and Brother Jones looked into the dark sunglasses and quietly said, "I don't know what you believe about the hereafter, Michael, but I want you to know that I believe your father has gone on to a joyous work on the other side. I didn't know him well, but what I did know, I had the greatest respect for. I'm sorry you lost him."

Michael nodded, unable to answer. He'd had the greatest respect for his father as well. He had been his best friend. One of the few that he'd known was a true friend in the circles they moved in.

As far as a hereafter, Michael wished desperately that he could take this man's opinion and hold it in his heart, because the idea that his father was simply gone was killing him. He'd been trying to picture seeing his father again in some other estate, but so far, the idea of a hereafter kept getting swept away by nightmares of a nondescript gray void that his father had simply disappeared into. It was the most frightening and discouraging thing he'd ever dealt with in his life.

He turned away and was heading toward the sports car when Doc interrupted him, "Where are you headed? Would you be interested in coming with Ashley and me and getting a late lunch?"

Shaking his head, Michael stopped. After a moment he was finally able to answer this man who had befriended him when he'd needed it most, "Thanks, but no. I'm not really up to eating."

"What are you going to do?" Somehow they both knew Doc wasn't asking about what he was planning for the afternoon.

Again it was a few moments before Michael answered with a bitter laugh choked by tears, "Honestly. Drop off the face of the earth for awhile. Write the score for a movie somewhere far from banking and the teeming masses. When I have it figured out, I'll call you."

Doc stuck out his hand and when Michael took it, he held on for several seconds. Finally, Doc said with a sad smile, "My great uncle just left me a little house out in Wyoming somewhere. I've never been there, but they say it's miles from the nearest paved road up in the mountains. It's yours for as long as you want, if you're interested. I think that's considered still on the face of the earth, but just barely."

The best Michael could summon was, "I'll think about it. Thanks for coming today. See you around." With that, Michael turned and walked to the beautiful car with the incredibly racy lines and climbed in as the late March rain turned to snow.

He started the car up and drove, turning north out of the cemetery without even consciously making the decision. He just drove, pulling over occasionally to clear his eyes of the moisture that clouded his vision and made his head ache. Finally, when the road ended on a bluff above the sea, he turned off the car and bowed his head onto the steering wheel and closed his eyes, trying to shut out the overwhelming sense of loneliness and loss.

He could have had people around him. He knew that. There were always people who wanted to be included into his world of money and power, but there honestly wasn't anyone he trusted inside this bubble of pain and emptiness. Well, Doc maybe, but Doc had been there almost constantly these last few days of waiting and dreading. Of mentally trying to get ready for something that you could never truly be prepared for.

No, the choice had been his. There was no one who would really understand the bond between his father and him. And he certainly hadn't wanted to bare his pain to anyone else. It was too hard to face it himself, let alone trying to maintain a stoic face for all those that society would have decreed be involved.

None of these thoughts filled his head at the moment. Just now there was only a deep and wrenching sense of something vital in his life that was gone forever, leaving a gaping hole where his heart and his energy should have been. Not only was he deeply sad and alone, but he'd lost any sense of future. Any interest in actually getting out of bed in the morning and pressing on with this life. How was he ever going to drum up the initiative to actually keep on living?

He got out of the car and walked over to the edge of the sea wall and looked down at the pounding surf crashing into the rocks below. The never ending rhythm of the waves was comforting somehow. It was reassuring to know that the world could seem to come to an end, but the waves would still roll up onto the shore, time after time after time.

There was no sun to go down, just low, forlorn, charcoal gray clouds, but the light slowly drained from the wet air and left him and the racy car and the crashing black ocean in the darkest of dark. Still, he stood there in the soaking rain, listening to the surf until his teeth began to chatter, and he turned again to the car. When a set of headlights pulled onto the deserted overlook, he was glad to be back in the safety of the car and heading on his way. That's all he needed tonight was to be mugged here at the end of the road to nowhere.

At a little after ten o'clock that night, he knocked on the servants' quarters door of his maternal grandfather's imposing estate home on Long Island. When the surprised elderly gentleman who had been his grandfather's butler for as long as Michael could remember let him in, Michael smiled for the first time in what felt like years. "Hello, Gerard. Is Warren in and still up?"

The butler quickly covered his surprise and became the picture of correctness, in spite of the fact that he was in pajamas and robe and slippers. "Why certainly, Michael. I believe he's in his study. Let me take that wet jacket and then come with me, I'm sure he'll be more than thrilled to see you." He headed off into the interior of the house and Michael followed, grateful that the older man was far too polite to ask what he was doing dropping in at this hour.

His grandfather did indeed seem glad to see him, but Michael had no doubt that he knew something was wrong when he got up from his massive desk to walk around and shake Michael's hand. "Michael, it's good of you to drop in. Is it still pouring cats and dogs out there?" Michael nodded and his grandfather went on, grumbling, "Nasty weather. Makes my old football injuries ache and I never played football. I was a band geek, as you know."

He smiled gently at Michael and Michael had to wonder once again how this wonderful, rock solid man had ever produced a woman as shallow and unproductive as Michael's mother. He took Michael's arm and led him over to the leather arm chair beside his desk. "I'd offer you a drink, but you'd only turn it down, thank goodness." When they were sitting, he turned back to Michael and asked soberly, "All right, now tell me what it is that brings you to Long Island in the middle of the night in the rain."

Michael was hesitant. He respected this man so much and knew what he was going to say to him was going to let him down. After struggling to find the words, he finally

5

Jaclyn M. Hawkes

started in, "Actually, I've been thinking, Warren. I've been thinking of making some changes in my life." He paused and his grandfather's gaze sharpened and he wished he'd brought the sunglasses he'd been wearing earlier.

At length, Michael looked away and went on, "I'm going to resign my position on the board of the bank, Warren. I'm sorry to disappoint you, but my heart isn't in it anymore. Someone should be there who has his wits about him. Someone who has a passion for it."

His grandfather didn't answer right away, just watched him for several moments and Michael was surprised when he asked a completely unrelated question that cut him to the quick, "How is your father these days, Michael? He had a cold last time I saw him. I trust he's doing better."

Now Michael truly wished for the sunglasses. As he struggled to be able to answer, he reminded himself that his grandfather would never intentionally hurt him. They had worked together on the board of the bank these last six years since Michael had turned twenty-two and graduated from Columbia University, and he'd never told anyone his father was even ill, let alone dying. When he was finally able to speak, he was honest with his grandfather, knowing he would honor Michael's wish for discretion and privacy.

With every bit of self control he had, he admitted softly, "He's dead. Last night. He's been battling liver cancer."

Warren Heinz leaned forward abruptly in shock when Michael finally got the words out. The gray haired man before him repeated the words in a whisper, "Dead? Liver cancer? Oh, Michael. I'm so sorry. I had no idea." He reached across and put a hand on his grandson's knee. "Please forgive me for not realizing."

Michael rubbed his eyes to control the burn of tears as he shook his head. "No one knew. He'd become very private. And there wasn't much point in making a big deal of it. What he wanted; what we both wanted was peace and to be left alone."

6

His grandfather got up to come and stand beside his chair and put a hand on his shoulder. "It's good to have peace and privacy, Michael, but one must also have support when they need it most. I wish you would have told me. I would have honored your privacy, but I would also have listened when you needed to talk. No one should have to tell their dearest friend goodbye without that. I know that it's human nature to want to turn away and grieve, but it's too hard to bear that alone."

Michael simply shrugged and rubbed his eyes again and his grandfather went on, "I know I'm your mother's half of the family, but you know I had only respect for your father. He was the best thing that ever happened to Marilyn. I have always wished she had stayed with him."

Shaking his head, Michael answered, "He was the one who asked for the divorce, although she had been gone in principle for years." Bitterly, he admitted, "She decided he wasn't any fun anymore when he quit carousing like she did. When he found out how sick he was, he formally filed for divorce. In some strange way, he wanted to spare her the pain and hassle of it all. She has no idea he was even sick, let alone that he's gone."

The older man grimaced sadly. "I'm sorry about your mother. I'm sorry she didn't end up with more substance. I always hoped that one day she would grow out of the superficial stuff." He sighed. "It was my fault. Her mother never grew out of it either 'til the day she died. I should have chosen better, but she was so beautiful." He smiled sadly. "When you go looking for a wife, shop well. That's the key. And then I'm sorry to admit that I let Meredith spoil your mother shamefully."

Michael sighed. "What's done is done, Warren. There's nothing that can help my parents' marriage anymore." He paused while he struggled to contain his emotions. "I'm sorry to resign my position, but I can't do it. Not right now. Today I don't even care if the bank were to be blown to smithereens."

"Which is exactly why I'm not going to accept your resignation. My wonderful businessman father, who had his own issues with beautiful but shallow women, always said, never make big decisions on bad days." Warren sat back down in his desk chair, studied Michael and then got back up and reached for his hand. "I do believe that I need a bit of something to eat. Would you be willing to join me for a bite? We'll talk while I make my famous grilled cheese sandwiches."

Michael let him lift him from the chair. "I never knew of any famous grilled cheese sandwiches."

Warren grinned. "Well, they're not really famous, but it's all I know how to make for myself anymore, and I don't believe you want to visit with the staff right now. Have you had dinner?"

Michael shook his head and admitted, "I haven't even had lunch. I haven't felt much like eating. I've been driving around all day trying to find one thing that I'm interested in enough to consider doing and so far it hasn't worked. I'm afraid I don't have a very good attitude in general."

His grandfather turned toward him as they entered the kitchen. "I don't blame you, Michael. Losing your father is tragic. But you should know that I have absolute faith that eventually the grief will fade and you'll figure it all out. You are the strongest charactered man I know, and I have a great respect for your wisdom and your ethics. That's another reason why I can't agree to letting you go. Maybe your heart isn't in banking right now, but we desperately need your good judgment, whether it's full time or even long distance."

He began to dig through the huge kitchen. "Now where is that griddle?"

He opened a few more cupboards, found the elusive griddle and then opened the mammoth fridge. "I know music is your passion, Michael. It was mine as well and I didn't have one fiftieth of your talent, but that doesn't mean you
8

can't still be a banking genius. Especially right now when the financial industry the world over is making foolish, short sighted decisions. If we're not careful, we're going to be in even worse trouble than these politicians have us in at the present. And I also need your wonderful diplomacy to keep the rest of the board from wanting to cash in on all these government bail outs. Your great grandfather would have had a coronary."

Michael smiled sadly. "We all might make a huge chunk of profit right now if we did ask for government bailout money."

Warren made a sound of disgust deep in his throat. "On the backs of the taxpayers? No. I know that sometimes our family has used poor judgment and I know that at times we've let our children or our mothers," he winked at Michael, "pull some stuff. But we've always been able to sleep at night for being honest with our fellow man and we're not going to stop now. If we did, I'd throw in the towel and resign with you."

He was thoughtful as he slathered mayonnaise on bread. "Heavens, I might just throw in with you anyway for the fun of it. You usually have a pretty good time at whatever you're into. What are your plans, may I ask? Here, help me stack this ham and cheese would you?"

Coming to stand next to his grandfather at the stove, Michael reached and turned down the stove under the smoking griddle just as Gerard appeared in the kitchen doorway. "Oh, good, it's just you, Warren. For a moment there I thought we were on fire." As he turned around to go back out, he said to Michael, "You will keep him from setting off the smoke alarms, won't you, Michael? It's his ritual when he's making those things, I'm afraid."

Michael couldn't help smiling down at his grandfather and it felt good. "You did say they were famous." He paused for a moment, sobering and then answered the older man's question, "I have no plans beyond eating grilled ham and cheese. I have the score of a movie to write in the next few months, but even that's not critically urgent. A friend of mine recommended Wyoming for some bizarre reason. Actually, it's intriguing. Not a soul knows me in Wyoming that I'm aware of. I could fly completely under the radar and compose to my heart's content."

Warren flipped the slightly blackened sandwiches onto plates and then opened a cupboard to get glasses while Michael took the plates to the nearby bar at the counter.

With the glasses in hand, Warren commented, "Wyoming is nice. I've spent some time there on the Rockefeller's place near the Teton Park. It's quite beautiful. They're a little rough around the edges, and there's not much of our ridiculous pomp and folderol, but it was very refreshing, actually. If Meredith hadn't insisted we return to the smog and traffic, I would have stayed longer. I loved it. You would probably really like it there under happier circumstances."

Michael bit into a sandwich and tried to blink away the moisture in his eyes. "My dad loved the mountains. He changed in some ways lately. I suppose knowing you're dying does that. He'd never been terribly religious, but toward the end he had so many questions. He'd begun to wonder whether there was a God almost desperately."

Michael's grandfather watched him with quiet eyes and then asked, "And what did he find out? He was always so good at figuring things through. I trusted his judgment."

Michael paused while he considered this question. "I don't know for sure. He would search and then settle on one thing and then change his mind and start over again. I'm afraid I was struggling too hard to just try to deal with the fact that he was dying to want to take on anything else too deeply important."

He brushed at a cheek that had a wet streak down it and admitted, "I hope there's a God. I hope that my dad's truly gone to heaven and that someday I'll get to see him again. It's awful to think he may just be gone. That his existence is over."

A gnarly hand with age spots and a touch of arthritis covered Michael's on the countertop. "I hope that too, Michael. There should be a point to it all, shouldn't there? Maybe after all these years I should make that a priority. Finding out for sure. I've always told myself that if He was out there, He'd be kind enough to understand that I was busy, but tonight that sounds silly, doesn't it?"

Struggling to swallow past the lump in his throat, Michael answered honestly, "I'm a little mixed up right now. I don't know what to think or believe. If there is a God, why would some of the stuff that goes on in this world be allowed? And if He's out there and I've basically ignored Him for twenty-eight years, He might be pretty ticked off at me."

"Don't sell yourself short, Michael. You've always chosen to do what you believed was right and honorable, when even your own mother didn't necessarily teach that. You've always followed your conscience and encouraged others around you to do their best as well. With that in mind, you followed what I would guess would be God's chosen way without even knowing for sure if He existed. Isn't that all we can do in this life? What we believe to be right? Other than finally getting to the other side and actually seeing for ourselves, I don't see how you'd ever truly know for yourself whether He exists."

Michael chewed thoughtfully, thinking back to Brother Jones at the cemetery. He hadn't seemed unsure of what he believed in the slightest. Michael tried to stem the sadness of thinking of the burial as he thought out loud, "I don't know. There are some who seem pretty sure that He's out there. It would be interesting to ask someone like that just how they know. Or think they know. If there is a God, you'd think

11

He'd have found a way to let us know about Him conclusively."

Warren stood up, turned out the light and walked to the window of the kitchen and looked out into the darkness of the night, broken by all the lights of the city and then the abrupt blackness of the ocean and the sky. "Maybe he did, Michael. Somehow it doesn't seem possible that all of that," he nodded toward the window, "is just coincidental. Somehow, the intellectual in me doesn't buy the happenstance theory."

Michael came to stand beside him with his sandwich. After a long quiet moment he asked softly, "Then where do people go when they die, Grandpa?"

Chapter 2

Joey Rockland leaned her head back against the seat of the luxurious sports car and sighed silently. She'd been home from her mission for almost fourteen months and she never lacked for dates, but sometimes she wondered if this whole social game wasn't a gargantuan waste of time and money.

Bryan had come clear from California to Wyoming to see her again, and she appreciated that. She really did. He was very nice and fun and good looking and she wondered just what was wrong with her that even a country music star did nothing to her heart.

At least she had been honest with him from the beginning. She had met him almost three years ago when her sister-in-law Kit had gone out to L.A. to work at a studio as a musician. Under the circumstances, Bryan had been so good to Joey that it made her feel guilty for not feeling something for him in return.

Well, she did feel something. He was eminently likeable, she just didn't feel the fireworks that led to wedding bells that Bryan seemed to be experiencing. She had to hand it to him; he kept after her even when he knew she wasn't in love with him.

When they made it back to the ranch, she smiled at him at her front door, thanked him for a fun evening, then leaned across and lightly kissed him and turned around and went inside without looking up into his eyes. She knew she'd see disappointment there, but she couldn't help it. She just didn't feel it.

In her living room, she kicked out of the heels she'd worn to go to dinner and the concert at the Jackson Hole Ski Resort and fished her phone out of her purse to check her messages. The family ranch was just finishing the last of the calving season. Everyone tended to work the clock around and she wondered if she was going to be needed tonight. If she was, one of her six brothers would text her.

There was nothing from her brothers, but Dr. Seth Hendricks had left her a quick hello and a smiley face. She thought about him. He was very good looking and brilliant and would probably be wealthy some day when he got medical school paid for.

She had met Seth when he was working his way through medical school as an EMT and she had been stuck in the middle of a huge traffic accident in a canyon up north. Seth had delivered her sister-in-law's baby in the back of her dad's Suburban and Joey had assisted. It was probably because of what they went through together that day that they'd become such fast friends, but still, no fireworks.

She checked through the last of the messages that had been left while she was with Bryan and sighed as she closed her phone. There were three more from other guys, but none of them did anything to her pulse rate.

She leaned down and snagged the pair of shoes and petted her old Australian Shepherd that was her shadow whenever she was home. "What do you suppose, Blue? He's out there somewhere, isn't he? What have you been up to tonight, huh? Have you made the rounds and is all clear out with the cows?" The old dog wagged his whole back half and loyally padded behind her to her room, where he flopped down on his bed just inside her French doors out to the balcony.

She walked into her bathroom and unpinned the blonde hair that hung an inch or two past her shoulders and took off her jewelry. In the mirror she glimpsed the poster of a bright

14

red Lamborghini that she'd hung on the back of the bathroom door. Now that was a car!

She turned and touched the poster with one long, French manicured finger. She really loved cars, but sometimes she thought her passion for cars was completely misplaced here in the mountains of southwestern Wyoming. A working ranch at this elevation was no place for a sports car buff.

She'd gotten a degree in automotive engineering, thinking she'd go back to Detroit and design cars when she grew up, but after being called there on her mission, it had only taken her a few days to know that no matter how much she grew to love the people of Michigan, she couldn't stay there forever. She was a mountain girl, born and bred, and the flat, industry choked cities where cars were usually designed were not for her on a permanent basis.

Even though she'd been up early helping with the cows, she was still wide awake and glanced out the window toward her parents' house across the field from where she rented this apartment over her brother's garage. There were still lights on and she slipped into a pair of sneakers and went outside to walk across to talk to her mom.

Upon letting herself in the patio door of the deck, she laughed at the motley crew that was gathered in various stages of sleep in the great room. Three of her brothers, one of their wives, two other ranch hands, her dad and two dogs were scattered in chairs and on sofas in front of a TV that was just now starting to roll the credits from one of the Pirates of the Caribbean movies.

All of them but one of the ranch hands was asleep and Joey picked up the remote and clicked the TV off with a laugh. Her mother, Naomi, was standing at the kitchen counter wiping it down and loading the dishwasher and she looked up and smiled and said, "I didn't even hear you come in. How was Bryan?"

Joey put a piece of popcorn in her younger brother Cooper's nose as she went past to come around and give her mother a hug. "Bryan's good. Dinner was wonderful, the concert so, so. How did you guys do here? Who's out with the cows if these guys are all here?"

"I think Slade and Rossen are out there with them. Rob thought two was enough for tonight. Could you go out at first light and take a shift? Where did you eat?"

"At Jenny Lake Lodge. It was marvelous. Some French thing with fish and a cream sauce. It was to die for. Sure, I'll take a turn in the morning." The various zombies in front of the TV began to wake up and Joey was aware that the one ranch hand was watching her every move as she helped her mother finish straightening the kitchen. Cooper woke up and sneezed popcorn clear across the room and the others laughed.

Joey innocently asked him, "You getting a cold, Coop? That was a record for distance with the popcorn, by the way. Good job, buddy!" Twenty-one year old Cooper got up and picked up the popcorn bowl and began to walk around the couch toward her. Backing up, Joey said, "Don't even think about it. Coop. Mom, Cooper's coming after me with a whole bowl full of popcorn. He's gonna make a mess."

Naomi placidly wiped down the sink. "You're going to have to be quick about it, Cooper. She's pretty fast. Is that buttered popcorn? Don't spill it on the carpet."

Cooper set the popcorn aside and went to come around one end of a couch and Joey made a run for the other end, but he switched gears and went right over the couch and caught her in midstride on the backside. Their momentum carried them into the nearby chair where the attentive hand sat watching and Joey landed right in his lap with a thud with Cooper on top. The hand groaned and when Cooper and Joey backed off, he doubled over, gasping for breath and Cooper offered heartfelt condolences, "Oh, Lee, dude. Sorry man. You okay?"

Joey tentatively went to Lee, not knowing what to say or do. She touched him gently on the arm and said guiltily, "Sorry, we really didn't mean to land on you. Are you okay?"

Lee started to answer, but his voice cracked the first time and he had to start over, "I'm fine."

He wasn't and everyone in the room knew it, but that didn't stop Cooper from jovially slapping him on the shoulder and laughing and saying, "Oh, good. For just a minute there, I thought we'd have to call the vet."

Joey's dad, Rob, laughed from across the room and then reprimanded Cooper, "Coop, show a little empathy. I swear, you're like a bull in a china shop. Don't add insult to injury. You'd better help him up and out to the bunkhouse, you goofball." Then he laughed. "But I would say that you definitely caught Joey. Speaking of which, shouldn't you be just a little bit more gentle with your sister?"

Cooper looked up, honestly stumped. "No, why?"

Rob sighed and looked at Naomi in mock resignation and the rest of the room laughed as Cooper made another mad grab for Joey, tackled her on the rug and this time licked a piece of popcorn and put it in her ear. She shoved him off in utter disgust. "Oh, Cooper! You are so gross! Get off me, you big oaf. I so owe you for that."

"No way! That was just my paybacks. Now we're even."

Lee came over and extended a hand to help Joey up off the floor. "You all right, Jo?"

She was still digging damp popcorn out of her ear and hair. "I'm fine. Are you?"

The young cowhand gave her a lopsided grin. "No, but I would never admit that to you. I'll be fine in a couple weeks, I'm sure."

Cooper laughed again. "Oh, quit whinin', Lee, and come on. Dad says I gotta help you out to the bunkhouse." He laughed again. "Come give me your arm and let's get to hobbling out there."

The two of them went out the kitchen door, followed by the rest except for Rob and Joey. Naomi shook her head. "Poor kid. You really landed on him, Joey. Cooper is completely incorrigible." She finished in the kitchen and came around and began replacing throw pillows and folding the throws that she kept in the ottoman. "So how was your date, really? Still no fireworks?"

Joey was on her hands and knees fishing stray pop corn kernels out from under the arm chair. She shook her head. "Don't you think if I was ever going to feel fireworks for Bryan, they'd have started by now?"

Naomi and Rob glanced at each other. Rob grinned and Naomi admitted with a smile, "Yes, I think when you finally find him they'll start immediately, but we can always hope. At least Bryan has joined the church because of you. When is he leaving to go home?"

"Late tomorrow morning. I agreed to return his rental car, if he'd agree not to ask me to marry him again before he goes. The car was great! This time he rented a darling little Corvette with a t-top. My hair will be a complete mess by the time I get it back!"

Rob shook his head as he leaned down to help her with the popcorn. "He's trying to buy her with sports cars, Naomi. That's pretty underhanded, and with her it might work."

Joey laughed and Naomi reassured Rob, "She might be tempted, but she's holding out for fireworks. She knows better than to be bought off with a simple Corvette. Now if it were a Ferrari or a Tesla Roadster." She winked at Joey. "Then we'd be in trouble."

With the overboard popcorn finally contained, Joey stood up and dumped the strays into the garbage and hugged both of her parents in turn with a smile. "You might be right, Mom. Just don't tell Bryan that. Night. Love you."

On the way across the pasture, she looked up at the brilliant stars in the midnight blue Wyoming sky. Was she wrong to hold out for fireworks? She was only twenty-four, but still it felt like she'd been dating forever and it was beginning to get discouraging. Was she going to end up old and alone because she wouldn't settle for someone she wasn't madly in love with?

In a moment of self-pity she looked up and said, "Come on Lord, I'm trying to do all the things you've asked. Help me out here. I need more than a cute car."

Jaclyn M. Hawkes

Chapter 3

Michael Morgan pulled off the interstate into the non-descript town of Rock Springs, Wyoming and looked around. It was a typical, small western city surrounded by sagebrush and rolling hills and covered in dust, even this early in April. Or maybe it wasn't dusty, it was just dust colored. Even the trees were the color of dust where they hadn't sprouted leaves yet.

He'd never seen a less striking place in his life and began to wonder just what he'd gotten himself into. He'd wanted peace and privacy, but did that have to mean desolation? He pulled over into a truck stop service station and hauled out his map. Maybe he was just tired. Things would look better when he'd had some sleep.

He consulted the map and decided he needed to stop for the night or he'd be arriving in the little town of Hollister, Wyoming at three a.m. And from the looks of it, Hollister had no Plaza Hotel. This was the most likely place to have a room and he decided to stop and rest up. In the morning he'd grab a few groceries and call that tow truck driver Doc had found.

Michael had left New York the night he had spoken to his grandfather and after traveling randomly for a day or two, he'd finally decided to take Doc up on his offer of a house that was only marginally still part of the planet out in Wyoming somewhere. On the three day drive he'd tried to think and plan and had ordered an electric grand piano out of Salt Lake City that had hopefully already been delivered.

He'd gotten all the way into Iowa before it had crossed his mind that arriving in a miniscule town in Wyoming in a

21

black Ferrari wouldn't be all that inconspicuous. He'd once again called Doc to ask him if he knew anything about the town and whether it had a car dealership or a storage facility.

Doc had had no idea what the town comprised, but he'd mentioned that his benefactor great uncle had also left him an older model Chevrolet that certainly wouldn't stand out. He'd offered to let Michael drive it until he was able to get something other than the Ferrari. Then Doc had kindly arranged for this tow truck to plan to bring him the car as soon as Michael found out approximately when he'd be arriving. Now all he had to do was find a place to store the Ferrari.

Because Michael had left without really intending to, Doc had agreed to go to his condo and empty the fridge and turn off the answering machine and ship him a few of his things. In the mean time, Michael had shopped in hotel gift shops enroute and had called his building manager and arranged to have his mail shipped to him general delivery in Hollister.

He got the room and went to the pool and swam laps and then worked on an elliptical to ease out the kinks of these last days on the road. Between the depressing grief over his father and the long hours behind the wheel, he felt terrible.

When he looked in the mirror of the hotel, he had to admit that he looked terrible as well. He had two days worth of razor stubble and his hair had been too long for weeks. Now it had graduated to shapeless and out of control, but he just shook it back when he got out of the shower and went down to the restaurant to find something to eat.

That night, after searching the internet and then making a series of phone calls from one interesting local to another in Hollister, he finally found a place to store his car. Ironically, it was the same towing company that was going to bring him Doc's uncle's car that would store it for him.

When he went to bed, as tired as he was, sleep wouldn't come and when it finally did, he dreamed of his father. He woke with a start with his heart racing and when he came fully awake and realized that indeed the nightmare was true and his father really was gone forever, he was more full of despair than ever.

He turned over and gathered his pillow into his arms and tried to think of the good times that they'd had together over the years. They truly had had some great days, but the ache in his heart made it hard to breathe. He got up and turned on a light. This had happened every single night for the last couple of weeks. Before his dad had died it was to awake to the horror that he was dying and now Michael woke to face the heartbreaking fact that he was dead.

Sitting at the desk, he thumbed through the folder about the hotel and the amenities it offered but it was just a generic listing and he closed it and picked up the remote. Punching the On button, he clicked through three channels and got exactly three different shots of questionable movies ranging from mildly offensive to hard core pornography and he clicked it right back off in disgust. He glanced at his watch. It was three a.m. No wonder everything was questionable.

He considered going back to the pool and seeing if he could get in even though pool hours ended at eleven. Finally, he dug in the desk drawer and surfaced with a Gideon Bible and another blue book that had a gold trumpet player on the front.

He glanced at the blue book and set it aside, then picked up the Bible, and idly opened it and began to page through. It was so huge that it never even occurred to him to start reading it from the first and he turned pages at random. Even though it was written in English, the language was so involved that he struggled to understand the passages and eventually he closed it and put it back down and picked up the other one again.

This one was much smaller and he opened to the first and was less discouraged when he realized that although it was written in a style reminiscent of the early nineteenth century, at least he could understand it. He thumbed through the first few pages and found himself honestly intrigued. It was obviously about a religious fanatic, but at least it wasn't pornography and he took it back to bed and read himself to sleep.

Waking back up in the early hours of the morning, he was surprised that he wasn't still tired after being up in the night, and also grateful that the suffocating sadness he'd woken up with for days didn't hit instantly like it had been. It was a welcome relief. The grief sucked his energy out like a hot, dry wind.

He got up, packed his few belongings and went down to eat again at the little restaurant. Honestly hungry for the first time since he'd left New York, he ordered the rancher breakfast that included an unbelievable amount of food. He was hungry, but there was no way he could make it through that mound of food. The local ranchers must be something else.

Pointing his Ferrari north, he was encouraged when he realized that the closer he got to Hollister, the more beautiful the country around him became. By the time he got to the little town, he could understand why his grandfather had liked Wyoming. The place his grandfather had spoken of staying was only an hour or two north.

The elevation was obviously high. The hills were just barely greening up and the leaves hadn't come out on most of the trees and bushes, but the mountains around him were glorious even in this ungainly season between winter's snow and summer's vibrancy.

The tow company was called Bubba's Towing and Michael wasn't sure what he expected, but it wasn't this clean cut, well dressed, young Hercules with his pretty wife and two young children with him. He met Michael at the tow company offices and drove around back to the building where the Ferrari was to be stored.

Michael drove it inside and the young Hercules came toward him with a canvas car cover and an outstretched hand. "Branden Farnsworth. It's good to meet you. Never stored a Ferrari before, but it's kind of fun. Mostly in this country we just have trucks and SUVs. It's the snow, I think. People around here like to feel like they can take whatever Mother Nature hands them."

He helped Michael pull the canvas cover over the sleek black car and then handed him a set of keys. "It's not what you're used to, but it runs good. I left a map to Merv's place on the seat and the key to the house is under the flat rock in the front flowerbed. And the piano company wouldn't take the piano clear up there. It's here at the Post Office; I'll bring it up tomorrow." He also handed him a business card. "I'll let you in to get your car whenever. If it's after business hours or during deer season, call the cell number and whoever is on call for the truck can help you."

They walked back out front and Branden shook his hand again. "Welcome to Wyoming. You're going to love your stay here." With that, he climbed back into the big shiny gray pickup he had climbed out of and drove out of the parking lot. Michael glanced at the door of the tow company shop and noticed a note taped to the door that read, "I'm at Mert's if there's a problem."

Michael couldn't help the grin that broke out. How had Branden known where the key to his house was? This place was a joke, but it was unbelievably comfortable. Walking around the probably ten year old maroon Chevy Impala with a small ding in the right rear bumper and a rusting spot starting above the windshield, he gave a self deprecating half smile. He was definitely not going to stand out in this baby.

He smiled again when he was a couple blocks down the quaint main street and noticed a sign outside an old, pinkish brick building. "Mert's Cafe". And on a placard on the side walk was hand lettered, "Today's Special Meatloaf". *Well, that explained everything, didn't it?*

Chapter 4

The map was good and the route was straightforward, and Doc hadn't been kidding, the house was in the middle of nowhere. He drove through fields and pastures interspersed between relatively wild areas of woods and canyons and several times crossed a river that ran through all of it. His grandfather was right. Under happier circumstances he would have loved this. His father would have loved it as well.

Thinking of his father brought back that now far too familiar heartache and sense of discouragement he had almost felt like he was getting past earlier this morning. Apparently not. He swallowed past a huge lump in his throat as he looked under the flat rock in the flower bed near the door. His dad really would have loved this.

The key was there, right where Brandon had said it would be. He straightened up and looked all around him. After seeing the car, he had wondered what the little house would be like, but it appeared to be in excellent repair and the yard was neat and well kept even though the snow had only recently melted off from the looks of things. Michael shivered as he looked out across the surrounding valley.

It was obviously a vigorously working ranch and the unmistakable smell of cows drifted on the breeze that blew from the huge herds he could see just across the pastures. It must have been calving season and he could see men walking in and among the cattle with their tiny, newborn young either pressed tightly against them or curled up sleeping nearby while the mother stood patiently over them.

There were five or six houses scattered across the valley and a number of barns and out buildings and what looked like both an indoor and outdoor arena. There was even what looked like a small race track that surrounded the buildings, fenced in with stark white rails.

His own house was of neat white clapboard pushed back up against the hillside and although it was small, it was much more inviting than he had feared when he'd pulled off in Rock Springs. As he unlocked the door, he could swear he smelled fresh baked bread. He shook his head, wondering where that thought had come from.

On walking inside, he was amazed to find that he hadn't been hallucinating. There on the small spotless kitchen counter was indeed a fresh loaf of homemade bread, a pound of butter and a Mason jar of raspberry freezer jam. The jar was still frosty and as he touched the loaf of bread, he found it to be still warm. *How in the world?*

He opened the fridge and found a gallon of milk and a small basket of brown eggs. How had someone known to do this? For a second he wondered if Doc had called someone and then he thought back to Branden's easy going good will this afternoon and knew instantly that Brandon had either done this or told someone else that he was coming this morning.

He grinned again. Even with the heavy burden of heartache, he had a feeling that he was truly going to like it here. It was like being on a different planet from Fifth Avenue.

Even before he went back outside to bring in the single leather bag that held the few belongings he'd purchased along the way, he stopped and dug in the kitchen drawers until he found a cutting board and knife and a butter knife. He cut a piece of the fresh bread and slathered it with the real butter and homemade jam and closed his eyes as he bit into that small slice of heaven.

He had no idea who had made them, but there was no doubt that whoever it was, they knew how to cook! He cut another one and washed it down with a glass of the cold milk and then went back out and brought in the groceries he had bought in Rock Springs. Next to the home goods there on the counter, his box of cold cereal and handful of frozen entree's seemed plastic in comparison.

With the groceries put away, he explored his new house. The whole house could have almost fit into his living room back home, but the style of the little farmhouse and its furnishings couldn't have been more different. There was the kitchen and small living room, one bath, two bedrooms and a small mudroom/entry off the back door that led from the gravel drive and the small garage. The furnishings were all geared toward comfort rather than style and although it wasn't what he was used to, it was definitely welcoming and homey.

There were still several coats hanging on the hooks in the mudroom hall and he wondered for the first time about Doc's great uncle. What had he been like? And had he left a heartbroken son behind as well? That didn't seem likely when Doc had inherited the house from a great uncle and had never even been here. Doc hadn't been close and didn't even know what the distant relative had died from.

Michael wandered back into the living room and sat down in the recliner that was in front of the little TV with a set of rabbit ears sticking out of the top. He'd heard of rabbit ear antennas, but he'd never actually seen anything like them and wondered what television reception would be like here at the edge of the universe on that archaic set up. It didn't really matter. He wasn't much of a TV watcher.

He looked around and mentally tried to picture where the piano needed to go and realized that with it in here, the little TV and melamine entertainment center was going to have to go anyway. There would barely be room for the

29

couch and recliner in here with the grand set up there in front of the big front window. If there was going to be a television in the little house it was going to have to be a new flat screen that would hang tightly on the wall.

Sitting finally brought on the fatigue he'd known was coming after his intermittent night and he got up with a sigh and checked his watch. Four o'clock. He wished his piano had been here so he could throw himself into his work and try to bury the grief. He wanted to go to bed right now, but if he did he'd only be up that much sooner in the middle of the night. He sighed as he went to see what the linen situation was like. It wasn't like it mattered whether he slept at night or during the day. Here alone he'd be able to work whether it was light outside or not, and it wouldn't bother a living soul unless it was a farm animal.

He found clean linens and made up the most promising of the beds. It was only a full size, but it beat the two twins in the other bedroom. When he stripped the bed down, he was pleasantly surprised to find a rather high end mattress. That might help his sleeping issues. He remade the bed and put the discarded sheets into the washing machine that lived in a utility closet just off the kitchen, and then dug through various cupboards and drawers to get an inkling of what he might have available here in the veritable outback of Wyoming.

He'd become a bit of a hermit much like his father these last months. Between his work as a composer out of his home and the fact that people tended to want to socialize with him based solely on the fact that he was blessed to be the offspring of some of the wealthiest old money families in New York, he'd gotten thoroughly burnt out on society. That would help in this remote setting, but still, he was a long way from a department store or even a Wal-Mart. He'd have to learn to make every trip into a town count and order more on-line as far as music supplies went.

Looking out the window toward the herds of cows, he considered the near future. Becoming a hermit in New York City had been a relief from the attention of superficial friends, especially women, but honestly, it had been lonely. The only reason he'd pulled back from society was because it was preferable to being a socialite. As pretty and peaceful as this setting was, it would probably be even more lonely. A lone ranch in the middle of the sticks couldn't provide much in the way of entertainment or humanity.

After taking stock of the house, he decided to bump back over the long gravel road into Hollister and see if the little town at least had any staff paper or another couple of zip drives for his lap top. Then he'd be ready when the piano arrived in the morning. Just sitting around here waiting for it to get late enough to go to bed would make him crazy.

He climbed into the funny old car, hoping that Branden was right in his assessment that it ran well. It didn't look all that dependable. He wasn't sure what a person did out here when they had car trouble. He couldn't imagine that Triple A had any idea that Wyoming existed. At any rate, he had Branden "Bubba" Farnsworth's card if he needed it.

Wondering if the car was dependable must have been bad luck because on the way home to the little house, several miles onto the gravel road, the aging car's battery light began to flicker on and off and within just a few more miles the car sputtered and died, so he coasted it to the side of the road.

When he realized that he also had no cell reception at this particular spot in the mountains, he resolutely gathered his small shopping bag and climbed out to begin walking the last couple miles to his new home, glad that he was in jeans and deck shoes. He gave a half-hearted grin when he left the car unlocked with the keys in it. Maybe someone would steal it and give him an excuse to buy Doc a new car.

When it started to rain on him too, he grimaced and looked up at the sky. Talk about learning how the other half

Jaclyn M. Hawkes

lived. This change of pace back in time into the wilds of Wyoming was giving him a taste of what a lot people probably lived like in a very large spoon.

He'd only been walking for a few minutes when a Jeep Grand Cherokee pulled up beside him with the window down. A middle aged woman with a pretty, cheerful face and dark hair smiled out at him. "Get in quick! You'll catch your death out there." He looked all around in amazement. This woman had never met him in her life and she didn't look like the type to make foolish decisions, but here she was, offering him a ride. At least he didn't think she was a mugger.

Opening the car door, he got in, grateful that she was willing to rescue him, even if it wasn't very safe. He sat down and then realized that he was dripping water all over her car. When he looked up at her, she smiled. "There are some napkins in the glove box. Apparently Merv's car hasn't been driven enough lately. And you probably didn't have cell service right there either. This isn't a very nice way to break you in, I'm afraid. I'm sorry I didn't get here sooner."

She reached a hand across the car toward him. "I'm Naomi Rockland, by the way. I'm the mom of the whole bunch that I'm sure you'll meet soon enough. Welcome to Wyoming."

He shook her hand, still surprised at her lack of concern and wondering how to introduce himself. He'd wanted anonymity and although no one here would probably know him, he wanted to keep it that way. But then again, he was uncomfortable with being less than honest. Quickly, he settled on giving the pseudonym that he wrote music under, "Joseph Michael Blouet. From New York City. It's good to meet you. Thank you for picking me up. It looks like one of the first things I'll need to do is get a good, dependable car."

Naomi smiled, but then she said, "Actually, I'm surprised that that car broke down. It may not be a Porsche, but we

32

tried to make sure it was always running good, especially when Merv was becoming more feeble. We didn't want him out here walking in the rain. I guess it wasn't running as well as we thought. I doubt it's a big mechanical breakdown. One of my kids is a wonderful mechanic. I'll ask to have it looked after. When is Branden bringing your piano?"

Michael was surprised that she knew about the piano. "He said tomorrow, but I'm not sure."

She nodded as if that settled it. "That'll work. When Brandon brings the piano, we'll get your car brought up and fixed. It'll just take him a second to pick it up on his way. Do you have everything you need? My house is the big tan one in the center that usually has all the trucks parked around it at dinner time. If you ever need something and don't want to trek all the way into town, drop by. We probably have it somewhere if we can find it."

"Thank you, I appreciate that. Being this far from everything is going to take some getting used to, but I'm looking forward to it." Something in her direct, blue eyed gaze made him add, "I know absolutely nothing about cows. I'm actually a composer, but if there's ever anything I can do in return, I'd love to repay your kindness. Were you the one who left the bread and things?"

"I was. I was hoping it would make you feel welcome and cheer the place up a bit. It's seemed so lonely these last few weeks since Merv passed away."

They pulled up in front of the little house they were discussing and she turned off the car as he replied, "It was marvelous. It certainly made me feel welcome. Thank you. What happened to Merv, may I ask?"

He saw genuine concern and sadness as she replied, "Poor man. He was healthy almost to the last. He'd been with us for more than twenty years and we miss him terribly. He had cancer, I'm afraid."

Michael's gut tightened wretchedly and it was all he could do to keep his composure as he swallowed and struggled to thank her as he got out. "Thank you so much for the ride, Naomi. It was good to meet you. I'm sure I'll be seeing you around." He shut the door behind him and walked to the back door of the house and let himself in, tossing the plastic bag onto the table. He went into the bedroom and got a change of clothes before heading for the shower. At least in the pounding spray he wouldn't feel so foolish when his eyes watered.

Chapter 5

Naomi Rockland drove away from Merv Harris's little white house slightly sick at heart. She had no idea what she'd said, but she had never in her life seen the kind of pain she had just glimpsed in that young man's eyes. They'd been talking about Merv, but this Joseph Michael Bluoet hadn't even known what Merv had died from, so she didn't think it was speaking of Merv himself that had brought that look of raw pain and grief. It must have been speaking of the cancer. Did someone he know and love have cancer?

Or what made more sense, someone he knew and loved must have died of cancer. Was that why he'd shown up here out of the blue? As soon as the idea came to her, she knew she had to be right. And judging from the haggard look and the haunted eyes that she'd noticed as soon as she'd pulled over to pick him up, it hadn't been long since his loved one had passed.

She pulled into her garage, let herself into the house and began to get dinner, with her mind positively humming over the seemingly lost young stranger who had taken up residency in Merv's cottage. Strikingly handsome even in the soaking rain, he had said he was a composer, but his physique and strong features didn't mesh with the musicians she'd known in her high school orchestra all those years ago.

He'd had a marked New York accent and he'd looked at her like she was crazy to stop and offer him a ride and she smiled. A little good, old fashioned, Wyoming neighborly mothering was just what this obviously heart sick and lost young New Yorker needed. There was no doubt about it.

As she finished getting dinner for the large, happy crowd she knew would show up in a few minutes to eat, she called

Brandon and told him about the car breaking down and asked him to pick it and Joey up on the way to deliver the piano in the morning. Then she called Joey and asked her if she'd mind looking at Merv's car for the new neighbor without mentioning that the new neighbor just happened to be gorgeous and deeply sad. It would be interesting to see Joey's reaction to the man Naomi had just met.

She smiled when she thought about how he would react to Joey. Naomi had five sons of her own and another they'd basically adopted when his family had been killed in a car accident, but the ranch's main mechanic was her one and only, drop dead beautiful daughter. Usually men had a hard time coming to terms with that. At least until she had whatever vehicle she was working on up and running, which she never failed to do.

****

When Joey told her mother she'd go help work on Merv's car, she didn't realize that she'd be called out at two o'clock in the morning to help with calving in a downpour. She didn't mind helping with the cattle, but by the time Branden showed up to pick her up at two-forty-five that afternoon, she was starving and exhausted, not to mention chilled to the bone by the incessant cold spring rain.

She swallowed her whiny attitude, knowing her mother wouldn't have asked if she didn't think this new resident of Merv's house really needed the help. And she was like the rest of her family, willing to do whatever it took to welcome this person who would be living literally on the ranch, to the valley. They'd always tried to promote a big family atmosphere here and so far it had worked like a charm.

Climbing up into the high cab of Brandon's tow truck with a tired sigh, she let the hood of her rain coat drop back so she could refasten her hair that had escaped from the clip she'd pulled it up with.

36

Branden's wife was one of her best friends. He was like a brother to her and he glanced over at her with a grin and said, "You look like heck. You been partying all night?"

"Yeah, me and those party animal cows. Or should it be party cow animals? I'm not sure. My brain has petrified because of all the rain. But thanks for mentioning it."

"Anytime." He smiled. "So have you met this guy?"

"No, why? Mom just asked me to look at Merv's car for him. What's he like?"

Brandon hesitated and Joey sighed again. "Is he bad? This is another one of Mom's mercy missions, isn't it? What? Is he an addict? Atheist? What?"

"Haunted." Joey turned to look at Branden like he'd lost his mind, but he just looked back at her. "You'll see."

"What does that mean? Is he really ugly or something?"

Branden grinned. "No, I'd say he's about the prettiest boy we've had around these parts in a long time. You're gonna drool. And he's probably smart and wealthy as well. But he's haunted. That's the only way I know to describe him."

She didn't know whether to be intrigued or worried, and frankly she was too tired to be either. She was as willing to do a good deed as the next Rockland, but just now she wasn't up to much more than fixing the guy's car and she admitted it, "Yeah, well, Mom is going to have to unhaunt him today. I can't dredge up that kind of energy at the moment. Sign me up for tomorrow's shift, would you? Maybe by then I'll be cognizant."

They pulled into the gravel driveway of the little white house and Brandon backed the wrecker up to the garage and then lowered the old car until the hood was just inside the garage enough that Joey would be out of the rain when she was looking at it. She jumped out with her tool box and a mechanic's dolly and Brandon went on toward the house where she could hear him talking to someone. Then she

37

could hear the sounds of them unloading the huge crate that had been strapped to the back of the wrecker.

They worked with whatever it was as she tinkered with the car for awhile and then Branden poked his head into the garage and asked, "Can you walk home across the field, if I leave? I'm through for now."

Joey looked up absently mindedly. "It was just a loose battery connection. Did you just ask if I can walk home?" He nodded. "Branden, it's like a sixteenth of a mile. Of course I can walk home. I could probably swim home. Are you okay?"

"Just being polite. I'm outta here. Tell Sean I'm going fishing in the morning if he wants to go."

She glanced out at the rain, "The fish are all probably going to be drowned by tomorrow morning, but I'll tell him. Would you take my tool box and dolly?"

"Sure thing. See ya."

He walked off into the rain to get back in his truck with her stuff and she went back to her work. Once she'd figured out what the problem was, it had only taken a minute or two to fix, but she did a quick check over the rest of the car anyway. She was actually a little embarrassed that the thing had quit. She'd thought it was in relatively good repair. Merv had been like a grandfather to her and she'd tried to make sure he was as safe as possible in his funny old car.

Finally satisfied that the car would run fine, barring any new equipment failures, she snapped off the rubber gloves she'd been wearing and tossed them into the nearby dumpster. She started the car up and pulled it the rest of the way into the garage and then taking the keys, she shut the garage door and headed for the back door of the house.

Just as she was about to step up onto the porch, she paused in mid-stride. There was music coming from inside the little house like she had never heard before. It was cliché', but the only word that came to mind to describe it was the same word Branden had used to describe the new neighbor who had just moved in here. Haunted.

Stepping the rest of the way onto the porch, she scraped her boots on the scraper as she glanced inside the screen door. She could see him sitting there at a beautiful shiny new piano, bare footed and wearing only a pair of jeans, his longer dark hair a tousled mess, still damp from the shower.

His back was to her and she couldn't see his face, but still she knew that the plaintiff, soulful notes she was hearing were the tangible product of hopelessly broken emotion. This man was a master at putting his whole heart into his music and the resulting sound made moisture start into her tired eyes as she stood there.

Without thinking, she opened the screen door she had walked through a thousand times in the last twenty-four years. She had always known she was welcome here anytime and it never occurred to her that she was barging into someone else's house as she walked across the kitchen and silently sat on the end of the couch and listened. Branden was right. This man was haunted.

She leaned her head back and closed her eyes, letting the heartache of the music breach her weary spirit and she couldn't help the tears that overflowed her tired eyes. His sadness floated on the melody and filled the small home, while at the same time the music drew her in some convoluted pain filled symphony. It was the depth of emotion that she'd been hoping for for years, but it was a depth of pain, not joy.

She opened her eyes and watched him move over the keyboard and wondered what had happened to have scarred him so deeply that the very air around him shimmered with despair. It felt as if it would consume not only just him, but everyone who came into contact with him. In a way it wasn't just sad, it was scary as well. The sheer hopelessness that emanated from him was so thick it shut out the light.

When she realized just what she was feeling, she closed her eyes again and began to pray. It was the only thing she could imagine to begin to heal the soul-deep sorrow she sensed he was dealing with. Only the Spirit could absorb that heavy, dark heartache and start to let the light in.

Even though she had no idea who this man was or what troubled him, she silently prayed for him with all her heart that somehow he could glimpse a ray of hope that could begin to heal him. She prayed that his despair would ease and he would find the light and hope and joy she had known so much of in her life. She wasn't even sure what to pray for, she just asked God to help him.

Time slowed as she listened and she had no idea how long it had been when he finally switched over to a gentler, more peaceful, almost lullaby in a happier key. Still sad, this time the music softened the heartbreak like one who treasures the sweet memories of a loved one, without the suffocating anguish.

His hands caressed the piano with a touch that seemed too light to plausibly produce sound and the feeling the quiet melody pulled from her was impossible to understand. She loved music, but she had never heard anything as evocative as this. The pain that flowed from his soul into his music flowed back out into her soul and touched her like nothing ever had.

She continued to pray and his music lightened even further, until though not happy, it was at least at complete peace, and she changed her prayer and thanked God for sending the help this man so needed. If only for a little while, some of his sadness had dissipated and she could hear that sweet glimmer of hope come through in the exquisite music that poured from his hands. She yawned, struggling to focus on her prayer and his music in spite of her bone tiredness. Hope sounded beautiful.

Chapter 6

When Branden had shown up with the little old car and the huge piano crate, Michael was unbelievably glad to see him. He never wanted to spend another night like the last one. As hard as it was in the bright light of day to face the loss of his father, the nights were worse. Far worse.

The recurring theme of his dreams had become this image of blurred gray nothing. An awful, yawning, faceless place where his father had disappeared and ceased to exist. His death was one thing, but the hazy, dull, gray emptiness was unbearable, and Michael desperately hoped that with the piano, he could make the gray maw disappear.

Between him and Branden and a piano dolly, they wrestled the monstrous crate inside, opened it and attached the legs and lid and keyboard cover. As Branden refused pay and left with all the packing materials, Michael lovingly touched the silken tops of the new keys and then used the digital tuner he'd ordered with the piano to tighten the cables until it was perfectly in tune. Finally, with it in complete working order, he sat down on the bench and poured himself into the music.

It had been most of a week since he'd really played. Oh, he'd slipped into the conference rooms of a couple of the hotels and played, but it seemed like forever since he'd truly felt the music well up inside him and either sooth the pain, or bring it rushing to the surface with slicing sharpness. He wasn't sure if it helped or hurt, but somehow, even the grief that he felt he would drown in, at least made his father feel real. The pain he could deal with. It was the emptiness that threatened to consume him.

He sat in the half light of the Wyoming rainy afternoon and played, not knowing what he was playing and not even trying to channel the melody. The music flowed and swirled in his head and he felt it to the deepest part of his being. As it poured out of him, he almost willed a catharsis. It was as if somehow the tapestry of sounds could pull the nothingness right out of him.

At first, the raw emotion left him bruised and beaten, but slowly, strangely, he felt something change. He wasn't even sure what it was and then the oppressive nothingness gave way to shafts of light. Small, subtle breaks in his heartache that truly felt like an emotional dawn, breaking through the layers of gray.

He played on, grateful for the outlet of the music, the release that allowed him to come out of the shadow and feel the brightness. He had no idea what was going on, but his relief at this peace was overwhelming. For the first time, he felt like he could escape the hazy, threatening gray.

At length, his hands stilled on the keys and the sound faded and died out. Although he was exhausted, for the first time, he honestly thought he could someday get past this. It was going to take a long, long time, but just as his grandfather had predicted, he would survive.

Standing up from the bench, he turned to go into the kitchen and was floored to realize there was a young woman sitting on his couch in the dim light of the rainy afternoon. Make that sleeping on his couch. She was dead to the world and even out cold he could see the exhaustion in her face. He sighed, wondering what she was doing here, and why the last while had been so excruciating to him, but had managed to put this mystery visitor soundly to sleep only ten feet from him.

For Joey

He stopped short and studied her. This had to be Naomi's daughter. Although blonde, where Naomi had dark hair, she looked remarkably like her mother. And remarkably tired. And sad. There were still tears wet on her cheeks from where she'd been emotional and Michael was completely at a loss as to why this girl had come into his house out of the rain, sat on his couch and cried and then fallen asleep.

Her being here made as much sense as the rest of it, though. The fresh bread and groceries, the key under the rock and being out to lunch at Mert's, Naomi's ride home and offer to have her kid repair his car. Not to mention Branden bringing his car and piano and refusing payment even after taking his time to help him uncrate it. This was an unusual set up no matter how you looked at it. A beautiful young woman showing up in his living room shouldn't really surprise him.

Walking into his kitchen, he cut himself another piece of bread and buttered and jammed it, while he wondered if he should do anything about the sleeping beauty or just let her rest. He took his bread and a glass of milk to the coffee table, sat on the floor and pulled the pad of staff paper there toward him and began to pencil in one of the melodies that had just come to him. At first he'd just been playing to ease the pain, but there at the end some good things had happened seemingly miraculously.

Almost an hour later, he could feel her eyes on him before he even glanced up to realize she was awake. He looked up and into the bluest eyes he'd ever seen in his life and had to smile in spite of himself at her obvious discomfort. She groaned and put a hand to her forehead and then said, "Oh, I'm so sorry. I was listening and didn't mean to fall asleep. Your music was so . . . so . . . " She looked away, embarrassed. "Please forgive me."

Jaclyn M. Hawkes

He looked again at the almost dried tears on her cheeks and asked mildly, "For not being able to describe my music? Or for being bored to sleep by it?" She laughed and eyed his bread and jam and he asked, "Would you care for some thing to eat? I had this welcome fairy who brought me survival food yesterday morning. I'm just going to guess it was your mother. It's very good."

She stood up and he noticed her long, jean clad legs, the scuffed cowboy boots she wore underneath them and the rain coat that had seen a few years of showers. She was almost looking him in the eye when he stood as well and she answered, "Actually, I would love some. It looks marvelous. I'm starving." She extended her hand. "I'm Joey Rockland. My mom asked me to fix your car. It's running fine again by the way. A cable had just come undone."

For a second he wondered if she was teasing him and then he couldn't help skeptically asking, "You're the mechanic?"

She nodded and said patiently, "You can take the shocked look off your face. Women have worked on cars for a few years now. I do most of the work on vehicles around here and I'm very good, thanks. You were going to share your bread."

He remembered guiltily. "I was, wasn't I? You being a mechanic made me lose my train of thought. Thanks for fixing the car." It was hard to take the shocked look off. He'd never even seen another girl that looked like her, let alone one who hooked up cables on old cars for people she didn't know.

He walked into the kitchen and wasn't surprised when she followed him and buttered the slice of bread he offered as she said, "I'm sorry for intruding. I was just coming to give you your keys, but the music . . . I couldn't bring myself to interrupt you. It was . . . " She paused while she considered. "It was so . . . I don't even know what to say. It was like nothing I've ever heard. You have an incredible gift. Thank you."

44

Not sure how to respond, he gave her a sad, half-smile. "You're welcome, although I had no idea you were there. I didn't hear you come in."

She studied him so directly that he almost felt a little uncomfortable with her gaze, and then she asked softly, "If you had known that I was there would you have played like that?"

It took him awhile to answer and he had to turn away before he could. "I don't know." It came out more softly than he intended and the deep sadness he could hear in his own voice embarrassed him. He tried to go on more matter-of-factly, "I don't usually mind an audience, but I probably would have played something different. That couldn't have been very entertaining." He turned back to her.

Shaking her head, she agreed softly, speaking almost to herself, "No. Entertaining is definitely not the right word. It was far stronger than mere entertainment. It was incredibly evocative. Almost searingly so."

After a second she turned to him and added, "I'm sorry I barged in and then fell asleep. I took the night shift calving and it caught up with me. Please forgive me." She reached into the pocket of her rain coat and put his keys on the counter and then looked back up at him, studying him again. "Thank you for sharing. It was good to meet you. I'm assuming you're Merv's great nephew, the doctor. Welcome to Wyoming. I think you'll love it here."

Still watching him, she moved to the back door and then she was gone and he stood there, unmoving, listening to the sound of the rain through the screen door, wondering what it had been about her that had held back the strangling emotions. Whatever it had been, he was grateful.

After a few minutes, when he finally came back to the present, he glanced down at his jeans and bare feet and rolled his eyes to himself. Man, had he made a good first impression this time. He went to run a hand through his messy hair and it caught in the long tangles. Half dressed and tousled and then music that she described as evocative and searing, and he hadn't even paid her.

He put the food away and wandered into his bedroom to pull on a shirt. A mechanic. He shook his head. And what a mechanic! Whether the car ran wasn't the point.

Joey walked across the pasture in the rain in a daze. *Holy Moly! Haunted was right!* She had never seen anyone with eyes that troubled in her life. And his music had almost scared her at the same time it enchanted her. She was even more exhausted after listening than she had been before.

Haunted and beautiful. Branden had said he was a pretty thing. At the time she had thought he was intimating the guy was effeminate. She hadn't realized he was saying raving, drop dead gorgeous. Rain dripped off her jacket hood onto her nose and ran down onto her lip. She shook her head and groaned. She'd walked into the guy's house, sat on his couch and fallen asleep. Her brothers would have a good time with this one.

She walked straight to her mother's house instead of going home to her apartment. It was almost time to start dinner and she wanted to talk to her mom about the new neighbor with the tragic countenance. Her mother could have warned her.

She got all the way to the French doors on the deck before she changed her mind and turned back to her own house instead. She wasn't sure she was ready to talk about what had just happened back there yet. She wasn't even sure what *had* happened back there. Nothing had really happened, but somehow, she felt differently than she ever had and she needed to take that fact out and examine it a bit before she discussed it. Perhaps her mother hadn't even noticed that the guy was so deeply sad.

She shook her head even as she thought that. No, her mother wouldn't have missed that. She was the most intuitive woman on earth. That was exactly the reason she had sent her. She had already started on Naomi's famous mothering of a lost soul back to the fold, and as Joey thought about it, that was exactly what he needed in his life right now. It couldn't have been more obvious. Whatever she had seen in his eyes, hope in Christ hadn't been it.

Realizing that, she quickly showered and changed clothes and headed back to her parent's. She didn't know what her mother had in mind for their new neighbor, but Joey knew her mother would figure it out, and personally, she was on the team one hundred percent. It might take awhile, but if everyone pitched in, they could help this guy. Before he went back to wherever it was that he had come from, he was going to be unhaunted.

****

Naomi had been watching for Joey's return and had almost begun to worry when she didn't show up. When she'd picked him up, this Joseph hadn't seemed dangerous, but where the heck was Joey? Then she saw her walking slowly across the pasture and she could almost see how thoughtful Joey was as she walked. Naomi was looking forward to talking to her to get her take on what was going on there.

Naomi walked toward the patio door to welcome her and then was nonplussed when Joey didn't appear. She glanced out the window and saw Joey headed toward her own house instead and Naomi was puzzled. She'd seen Joey walk clear onto the deck. Why had she changed her mind and gone to her apartment instead of coming in?

Still wondering, Naomi went back to fixing dinner, glancing from time to time toward Joey's apartment and then toward Merv's house. She wondered if she should invite their new neighbor to dinner or if he had come here to find solitude.

Only twenty-five minutes after she disappeared into her apartment, Joey reappeared looking tired, but relatively happy. Naomi walked up to her, studying her face and she smiled when Joey grinned back at her. "Yes, Mother. He was very good looking as well as very thought provoking. You could have warned me, you know. I looked like a drowned rat and probably smelled like a cow. Is he married?"

"I have no idea, sweetie. How was he today?"

"Meaning does he still look like he's lost his very soul? Or worse. What do you suppose? Did he say anything to you?"

Naomi shook her head sadly as she chopped vegetables for her soup. "He didn't say anything, but he asked what Merv died from and when I told him cancer I thought he was going to pass out. The look in his eyes made the hair on the back of my neck stand up. It made me wonder if he'd recently lost someone close from something similar."

Naomi was thoughtful for a moment and then continued, "He actually seems sadder or more lost or something than anyone I've ever seen, even after losing a spouse or a child. What do you suppose has happened to him?"

Joey picked up a potato peeler off the counter and began to peel a carrot and said almost to herself, "Do you remember when Dr. Hedeman died last year? All of his children were sad, of course, but remember that Celia took his death so much harder than the others? Celia was the only one who didn't know exactly where he was going. She had left the church as a teenager, remember?

"She says she's agnostic now. But when her dad died, she was devastated. To her he was simply gone. Had ceased to exist and their relationship as father and daughter was over. She was a basket case while the rest of them were comforted by knowing they would be with him again in the hereafter.

"I remember running into her at the hospital and talking with her a day or two before he passed away. She was an emotional wreck. Maybe this guy lost his wife or mother or something and is in the same boat."

After considering that for a few minutes, Naomi nodded. "You may have hit on something. Only time will tell, I suppose. I was wondering about inviting him to dinner, but then thought that maybe he has come here for peace and solitude. What do you think?"

"I think you can always invite him and he can come or not. How do you suppose he can up and leave his practice back in New York? What kind of doctor did Merv say he was? Can you remember?"

Naomi shook her head. "Oncologist maybe? I can't really remember, but for some reason I don't think he's Merv's nephew. Merv's nephew was named Tristan. This guy introduced himself as Joseph Michael Blouet. And he didn't know what Merv had died of, or sound the same as the man I talked to on the phone about Merv's estate."

Joey was puzzled. "Hmm. That's strange. I just said to him that I assumed he was the grand nephew doctor and he didn't deny it. He's the most amazingly talented musician, Mother. What Branden brought was a piano and you can't imagine how he was playing. It was incredible. I've never heard anything like it."

Naomi stirred the soup. "I wondered why you took so long. I was wondering if I'd made a mistake sending you up there alone. Would you ask Rossen to stop there and invite him to eat on his way in?"

As Joey waited for Rossen to pick up, she reassured her mother, "I was safe. He may be a mystery, but he's trustworthy. I don't doubt that for a minute."

She paused and then admitted sheepishly, "The reason I took so long was that I accidentally fell asleep on his couch listening and he just let me sleep. I was so embarrassed.

49

Don't you tell the guys. I'd never live it down. I hadn't even knocked and been invited in. I just heard him playing as I went to take his keys back. I guess it was just Merv's place to me and I wasn't thinking. At least he was decent about it. He wasn't uptight. Just sad."

Rossen picked up and Joey gave him the message and then began to set out dishes as she mused out loud to her mother, "He needs you, Mom. I don't know what his story is, but I know you're wonderful with those of us who have lost our way from time to time. You figure out how to help him and I'll work with you."

Naomi raised her hand to high five Joey. "Deal."

Just then Rob came in the door with several others and asked, "What are you two making deals about? Dare I ask?"

Joey laughed. "Oh, Mom just agreed to adopt you another kid. This one has a New York accent and sad eyes. It's not a big deal, just another kid."

Rob came and gave Naomi a hug from behind and kissed her neck and then asked, "Another kid? Have I met this one? I don't remember any New Yorkers."

Naomi just smiled. "No, I don't believe you've met him. But you will."

Chapter 7

Michael's grandfather called to check on him and give him another update about what was going on with the bank board. He'd called every other day and Michael knew that although he tried to keep it light, his grandfather was truly concerned about him and the calls always made him feel loved and more hopeful.

His mother called once as well, but her phone call actually had the opposite effect. She hadn't spoken to him in weeks and she had no idea he'd left the city. All she was concerned with was whether he'd finally decided to get serious about Margot Witter, a wealthy New York socialite, who, for some reason, his mother had decided would be the perfect match for him.

Michael got off the phone more than a little disgusted. It was just as his grandfather had warned him. His mother was all of an inch deep, and while Michael believed that Margot was fairly intelligent, she was no more interested in anything of consequence than was his mother.

He stood at his kitchen sink watching the sun set behind the striking pine clad ridges to the west and watching the goings on across the ranch around him. So far he'd met Joey and Naomi and three of the brothers who all looked almost like twins, but he realized there were a number of people he hadn't met yet and they were all quite close. The brothers he'd met were as obviously good people as Naomi and Joey had seemed. The entire family appeared to be wonderful, down to earth, hardworking and clean living.

Usually the whole bunch of them would gather to eat dinner up at the house Naomi had told him was hers and he'd come to understand that it was several extended families as well as a handful of ranch hands. He had been invited up for dinner three times so far, but had yet to accept and felt guilty about that. These people had been good to him. He just wasn't really up to meeting that many strangers at one time. Maybe when he'd gotten his smile back a bit more.

Right now, he was just trying to get through the days and nights. Especially the nights. His internal clock was beginning to be skewed because the nights were so hard that sometimes he'd get up to play the piano to be able to survive and then the next day he'd be dead tired. It was a vicious cycle that left him hammered, but he'd made it through two whole weeks so far.

A scratching sound at his back door made him smile and he had to admit that he probably wouldn't have made it this far without this funny old dog that seemed to have adopted him lately. He'd first seen him the day Branden had brought the piano and then he'd met Joey and he wondered if the old pooch belonged to one of them. He didn't think Branden lived right here in the valley, so it was probably Joey's dog.

As he let the sweet old canine in, he leaned down to pet his white muzzle and the dignified elderly gentleman wagged his tail gently and then flopped down almost on top of Michael's feet. Somehow this dog seemed to know that he needed a friend, just not one that he had to answer any questions for. It was almost a little silly, but the simple companionship of this pooch had been a life saver. He just hoped whoever it belonged to really didn't mind him borrowing him.

He watched the beehive of activity around him, surprised at how much truly went on around the ranch. There were the cows obviously. One couldn't take a breath here without knowing that this was a beef ranch, and then there must have been extensive farming operations as well as there were constantly different farming implements coming and going. There was also something that required a locked gate house that actually had guards in it on the main gravel road in and although Michael hadn't seen any petroleum equipment, from the security he assumed there were oil wells here somewhere.

There was also a small horse racing operation here and early mornings Michael saw a handful of race horses being exercised on the brush track that encircled the perimeter, and he was fascinated by what could be done here seemingly a million miles from a real established flat track of any import. Michael loved to watch the race horses. They were one of the few indulgences he dabbled in.

When he was only twenty he had purchased the Rose Run Farm in central New York and for years now he had taken pleasure in the Thoroughbred horses that were raised and trained there. And he had done well. What had started out as an expensive tax write-off had evolved into a very successful operation that produced winners consistently now.

The last few years he had also begun to play polo and loved it. Too large to ever hope of becoming a jockey, he had tried polo and found that he came by exceptional skill naturally. He'd become an avid competitor until his dad had gotten so sick. He looked out the window now at the horsemen in the arena and felt a touch of melancholy. He wasn't really up to dealing with the people, but he would have loved to do something with the horses. He wasn't very familiar with whatever it was they were doing. Roping of some kind, but from this distance it was surprisingly intriguing.

****

Joey woke up in the middle of the night again to the faint sound of his piano floating softly into her open window. She glanced at her clock. Poor man. It was three-twenty-six in the morning. About every other night lately she had heard him playing in the wee hours.

Slipping on a warm robe and slippers, she went out and sat on her balcony in the dark where the music floated more clearly. It was that serenade of anguish again and she began to pray for him, knowing that whatever had him out of bed and playing needed the Holy Spirit for it to dissipate. She prayed and listened for close to an hour, asking the Father to comfort this lost soul and bring him the peace she knew she'd hear if she kept praying and listening long enough.

As the music lightened, she finally went in and went back to bed with her mind caught up in thoughts of the handsome stranger who had been living in Merv's house for a couple of weeks now. Over that period of time he'd become more and more thought provoking.

She had only seen him outside his house a handful of times. She'd seen him walking in the woods and pastures a couple of times and she'd seen him get in the car and drive away once. And a few times she'd seen him come outside to watch the sun rise or set on particularly brilliant colored occasions.

Often when she glanced toward his house, she knew he was standing in the kitchen looking toward the other houses, but even though her mother had invited him a number of times, he never came to dinner. She had begun to think of him as an antisocial recluse and began to worry that they'd never be able to help him if no one ever came into contact with him.

One afternoon, her younger brother Treyne called her to ask her to go round up the small herd of longhorn cows Merv had begun raising in the last years of his life. He had raised the rope steers the brothers used to team rope and had done quite nicely at it. The roping fees had more than paid for the whole operation and the herd had grown steadily every year until there were almost fifty, if you counted the cow calf pairs and the steers, when Merv had died.

Since his death, the new owner had arranged for the Rocklands to care for the cattle, which they had, but today Joey decided to use the loose cattle as an excuse to get the New York hermit out into the sunshine.

She went prepared with two saddle horses, one of which was her bulletproof old gelding, Wildfire, that anyone could ride, just in case this guy was a complete novice. Riding up to his house, she stepped down from her horse and tied them both to the fence. On walking up to his door, she was surprised and glad to find her old dog Blue calmly lying on Merv's back porch in the shade.

She patted his head and said, "Blue, I've been worried sick about you." The old dog got up and wagged his entire back half at her, but then lay back down as if he were porch security as Joey knocked on the door.

At first, there was no answer and she knocked again, more assertively this time. For some reason, she felt strongly that being a recluse wasn't good for this particular man at this time. He opened the door to her and she took one look at him and knew that he had every intention of telling her to go away and leave him alone. That was one thing she wasn't going to do.

He looked awful, even compared to how he had looked that first time and something had to be done. There was absolutely no question about that. He was still strikingly gorgeous, but looked all but sick and pale.

Just as he went to say something to her, she pushed past him into his house and matter-of-factly stated, "Your cows are out. I've come to help you put them back in." She went from window to window and began opening the tightly closed blinds and drapes and then the windows to let the sunshine and fresh air into the rooms that were so dismal that they felt almost cold.

Once the immediate windows were open, she went into his kitchen and began to rinse the dishes stacked in the sink and load them into the dishwasher while Michael watched her with those haunted eyes.

When he leaned against the counter and asked, "What are you doing?" It was all Joey could do not to say something about saving him from himself.

Instead, she simply said, "Hustle and throw on some shoes. Your cows are going to founder in the Lucerne if we don't go get them right now. I brought you a sweet, gentle, old horse in case you don't ride. But hurry, unless you want to spend the night helping the vet wrestle a bunch of very sick bovines."

He was still standing there looking at her as she opened his fridge and began to dig through it, pulling out anything that was growing and tossing it and putting the dirty containers into the dishwasher as well.

When she hit a particularly bad smelling science fair project and all but gagged, he finally went back into the other part of the house and emerged with a pair of hiking boots and some sunglasses. By then, Joey had tackled the kitchen garbage can. She pulled the full bag out, tied it off and handed it to him as she dug under the sink and into drawers, looking for a replacement bag to line the can with.

When she didn't find one on the first ten tries or so, she finally looked up at him with more than a little exasperation. "Are you enjoying this? Or is there a possibility that you could divulge the location of your garbage bags? Could I get a little help here?"

He gave her a half smile. "You're being a busybody. They're in the far right drawer. Second one down."

56

Pulling out the sought after bag, she shut the drawer just a tad too vigorously and corrected him, "I'm being neighborly. And you obviously need some neighborly. What did you have for lunch?"

He shrugged. "I haven't had lunch yet. Why?"

Glancing at her watch, she said, "It's four-twenty. What did you have for breakfast?"

"Coffee and a Pop Tart. Why? What? Are you the meal police?"

She put both hands on her hips. "What? Do you need the meal police? Your body is a temple. A whole day on nothing but coffee and a Pop Tart will kill you. Do they not know about nutrition in New York?" She dug into the fridge again and after a few minutes surfaced with a yogurt and an apple, then began to dig in his silverware drawer for a plastic spoon. Glancing over at him again, she asked him, "What's your name?"

He gave her that half smile again. "Michael."

Turning toward him, she asked outright, "Then who's Joseph Michael Blouet?"

"That's the pseudonym I write music under."

She put her hand on her hip again. "Why did you give my mom your pseudonym?"

"I don't know."

She looked at him steadily and finally said more gently, "We really do need to go. Alfalfa could kill your cows. Put your shoes on. You can eat on the way."

Sitting on the bottom step, he put his shoes on and Joey was surprised when he volunteered, "I can ride."

Watching him again, she asked, "Well?"

He finished putting the hiking boots on before he said, "Well enough."

"Good. I'll take the old horse then. I'm lighter."

On the way out the door, he leaned to pet her dog and she said, "His name is Blue. Has he been here with you all week?"

"Yes and part of last. He's yours?"

She couldn't help smiling at him. "He was. He seems to have jumped ship. I thought something terrible had happened to him. You're not feeding him coffee and Pop Tarts are you?"

He looked guilty and she groaned. "That's it. You're eating at my mother's. Both of you. Tonight will actually be a good night to break you in. Only about half of us will be there. It should only be mildly chaotic."

In the yard she put the food in his saddle bag and checked both cinches and he automatically went to the younger horse and adjusted the stirrups before stepping into the saddle. It was the single smooth motion of someone who's done it a thousand times and she began to wonder what a song writer from New York did with horses, but she didn't say anything, just headed out toward the renegade cattle over the hill.

As they rode side by side, she quietly asked him, "You didn't know you had cows, did you?"

"Nope."

"Did you know anything about this place before you came here?"

Again he gave her that sad half smile. "I believe I was told it was the edge of the universe and that there weren't a lot of people around." He paused and then said, "That didn't sound very good. Sorry. I wasn't trying to be offensive."

She shook her head and grinned. "That was just a nice way of saying that you didn't want to live near any busy bodies, but I'm afraid you were misinformed. This valley is full of busy bodies. Everybody who cares about you will bother you. You'll have to straighten up and take better care of yourself or we'll drive you crazy." She smiled over at him. "In a nice way."

"Of course."

"What did you do back east? Did you write music full time? I take it you're not the nephew doctor."

58

"No. He's a friend. I was in an office some of the time. What do you do out west? Or are you a ranch hand full time?"

"A part time office guy. Okay. My degree is in automotive engineering. I was going to grow up and design race cars until I lived in Detroit for awhile. I'd been incredibly naive to think I could go from this to that and be happy. So now I'm a ranch hand again. It's not glamorous, but I love it here."

He looked around and softly said, "I think I do too and I've only been here two weeks."

She stopped the horse and got off to open the gate. Walking past his horse, she paused and looked up. "But you're not happy here."

He met her eyes, then looked away and after a minute said, "I'm working on it."

Once their horses were through, she shut the gate and got back on. "There aren't many coincidences, Michael. God knows where you are and what you need. Just be sure that you don't refuse to accept what you need when He sends it."

Gathering the cows was surprisingly easy. Michael could indeed ride "well enough". He was like a part of the horse, even when it cut sharply to go after a couple of cows that tried to dodge him, and the cows were back inside their pasture shortly.

Joey shut the gate and then began to ride the perimeter of the pasture, looking for wherever it was that they had gotten out, with Michael riding quietly beside her. When they found the break, she got off and when he did the same, she dug into his saddle bags and got out the tools to pull the fence back up, tighten it and resecure it to the posts.

Standing there beside him, pulling on the wire, she was quite frankly amazed that being with him was this easy, even when they didn't know each other well and getting him to actually say much hadn't happened. Somehow, she knew he

59

needed tacit, unconditional acceptance, and for her that was a given. He was one of God's children. If he'd have been loud and a showoff, like a lot of the guys she came into contact with, she'd have been miserable. As it was, he was very comfortable. Still haunted, but comfortable.

He hadn't ever fixed a barbed wire fence before, but when she showed him how to stretch the wire and then refasten it to the posts, he caught right on and she moved over to the next section confident that the fence would be fine. She looked up while she was working and watched the way his shoulders stretched the fabric of his shirt and wondered how a musician/office guy who never went to a gym could be built like that. He was definitely a gorgeous man.

On the way back to the ranch, she finally asked him, "How is it that there aren't a whole bunch of ladies from New York beating a pathway to Merv's house since you got here?"

He gave her another one of those sad almost smiles and shrugged. "I guess the women back there just weren't my thing." She pondered that for several minutes as they headed straight toward her mom's house, and when she came to a conclusion, she was thoroughly disappointed. It must have been that he was gay. Why else would he admit to not having a thing for the girls back there? It was a city of millions and millions. There had to be some girls who were okay.

That would explain how he always seemed well dressed and well groomed even in only jeans and with his hair damp and the rest of his life in a mess. She'd met a few men who preferred men. There had even been one in their little local high school. He had been very good looking and had, in fact, been voted best dresser. She shook her head sadly as she glanced over at Michael. What a waste! He was one of the most attractive men she'd ever met in her life.

At her parents' house, she stopped the horses near a hitch rail that ran parallel to their driveway and they tied the horses to it. She saw the barest hint of a smile and had to ask, "What?"

He shook his head gently. "My mother lives on the top floor of a sky scraper. This is great."

Joey laughed. "It comes in very handy. Sometimes she doesn't necessarily care for what gets left behind here, but all in all, my mother is the most wash-and-wear woman on the planet. She's very hard to fluster. Come on in. Right now there are probably only a couple of people here, so you're relatively safe for the time being. The others will show up in awhile."

Jaclyn M. Hawkes

Chapter 8

They walked in the door off the deck and Naomi, standing at the sink in the great room, looked up and smiled. "Hello, Joseph. It's good to see you again."

Joey looked at him quietly and then asked loud enough for her mother to hear, "Do you go by your middle name? Michael? Or Joseph?"

"Usually Michael."

Coming around the kitchen island, Joey hugged her mom and then she went to the big sink in the adjoining mudroom and washed her hands and Michael followed suit. Returning to the kitchen, Joey asked, "What can we do to help you, Mom? He's great with a horse. I'll bet he's just as good with a paring knife."

Naomi turned to smile at Michael again. "Oh, you ride? That's wonderful! Even if you didn't ride, you'd soon learn around here. Would you guys mind making the garlic bread?" She handed them four loaves of French bread and Michael gave Joey that hint of a smile again.

They'd been quietly slicing and buttering the loaves when Isabel, Slade's wife, walked in carrying her baby and said, "Hi, everyone. Sorry I wasn't here earlier." She glanced at Joey and Michael and then did a double take and said, "Hello, Michael."

Without skipping a beat, he replied, "Hello, Carrie."

As she put the baby into the swing that sat just off the kitchen, Isabel asked, "Where did you find him, Joey?"

Joey looked from one to the other of them and Michael answered, "In that little white house there across the pasture. I've moved in over there. What are you doing here?"

Glancing out the window toward Merv's house, Isabel turned back to Michael in surprise and Joey couldn't even begin to understand the look that passed between the two of them before Isabel said, "I married one of the brothers. Slade Marsh. The only dark one. He's sort of been adopted here. And I changed my name when I married. I go by Isabel now. Dante runs the horse farm."

Michael nodded and Joey got the impression that a lot had gone unsaid there. She glanced at Naomi and then wondered, "Isabel, are you going to grill the salmon? We're about through here. Maybe Michael could help you at the grill and I'll make the salad." She wiped her hands and picked up the baby from the swing. "After I play with my little buddy, Cody, here. Sorry, Michael. Aunthood, you know. It's a rough job, but somebody has to do it." She held the four month old baby close to her face and he laughed and grabbed two handfuls of her hair.

Isabel pulled a huge sheet pan piled in salmon out of the mammoth fridge and handed it to Michael and then dug into a cupboard and pulled out several ingredients. "Would you mind helping me, Michael? It's not terribly difficult; it's just the sheer volume of food here."

The two of them went out onto the deck and when the door closed behind them, Joey and Naomi exchanged a pointed glance, and Joey said, "Treyne called and asked me to put Merv's cows back in and I decided to go roust him out to help. He's not doing too well over there. We need to drag him out more. Blue has been over there by the way. He was just laying there on his porch when I got there. And he can ride better than I can."

Naomi looked at her and then said, "I don't believe you."

"Well, okay, maybe not better. But he's good. He stayed on Jammer after two cows tried to get away. Never even lost his balance when he cut straight sideways under him. He's good."

"You put him on Jammer? First thing? Joey, what if he'd not been a good rider? Please don't get sued over loose cows."

Joey shook her head. "He said he could ride. And even though I don't know him well, there's some understated, quiet assurance there that I can't explain. I had no doubt that when he said he could ride that he could ride." She paused and then went on, "He's killing himself in that dark house with the blinds all closed. And he's not eating. All he's had today is a cup of coffee and a Pop Tart and the apple and yogurt I insisted he take with us. He's lost weight even since a couple weeks ago. If he won't start coming to eat, then we need to take some stuff to him."

Naomi glanced out the window to where Michael and Isabel were in a serious conversation and she smiled at Joey. "He's still incredibly good looking."

With a wry smile, Joey returned, "Don't get your hopes up, Mother. He's not a member, at least not an active one if he drinks coffee and I think he was trying to tell me this afternoon that he doesn't like women."

"What do you mean?"

"I mean, I'm not sure, but when I asked why there weren't girls following him to Wyoming, he said that they weren't his thing. Or something along those lines. I could be mistaken, but . . . "

"Joey, that's a terrible thing to intimate if you're not sure. You'd better not repeat that to anyone else. You could be completely off base.

"You're right. I'm sorry. I was just so disappointed. He's beautiful. It's such a waste."

"He's a son of God, Joey. Not a waste. Don't write him off yet."

As they went back to making the salad, the garage door opened and Slade and Rossen came in and within minutes Kit, Rossen's wife appeared with their three year old and baby. Kit put the baby down out of the way and then helped three year old Mimi into a high chair and gave her a potato peeler and a carrot to work on. Slade looked out the window to where Michael and Isabel were still deep in conversation and said, "Isn't that the new guy you were telling us about? He finally accepted an invitation to dinner?"

Joey smiled guiltily. "He didn't have much choice. I sorted of dragged him. He and Isabel seemed to know each other though. He called her Carrie when she first walked in. We sent him to help her in hopes she can encourage him to mingle a little more."

Slade chuckled. "You sent a man with my wife to encourage him to mingle. Geez thanks, Joey."

"Oh, Isabel worships you. Knock it off. Plus you've been recruited to the 'help Michael find his smile consortium' as well. Get out there and start looking for it. I think you'll really like him. He grows on you."

Slade went out the patio door and Rossen teased Joey, "Poor guy. Between you and Mother, he doesn't have a prayer."

"On the contrary." Joey smiled up at him. "He's got tons of prayers. You better pray for him, too. He's in worse shape now than when he got here. And he was haggard then."

Slade came back in momentarily and he and Rossen set the table as Rob walked in from the garage. It was only about ten minutes later that Isabel came in to retrieve a huge platter for the grilled salmon. Cooper and Treyne walked in at the last second and as they all sat down, everyone automatically bowed their heads to pray. Joey smiled during the prayer. She'd seen Michael look around blankly before following suit and bowing his head with them, but it was obvious that he wasn't used to the habit.

He was in for a wonderful surprise. She had assumed he wasn't familiar with prayer just simply because he was so troubled. When he figured out what a blessing and comfort talking to God was, his whole life was going to turn around. It was going to be fun to watch.

Chapter 9

It had been a hellacious night and a miserable day when Michael saw Joey coming across the pasture toward his house on horseback, with another saddled horse in tow. He'd heard her talking to the old dog and when she knocked, he had had no intention of answering. But she didn't give up and even when he opened the door to tell her to hit the road, she'd given him no chance. Just pushed her way in and started right in being the busybody that they had joked about, but in retrospect he was incredibly grateful.

She had been the breath of fresh air that he desperately craved just now. A unique blend of spirited efficiency and soft spoken support, she seemed to know just what he needed, almost magically, and by the time they had the cows back in and were headed to her parents' for dinner, he honestly felt like he was up to it for once. The light in his house when she'd opened the drapes, and the physical task of riding and fixing fence, coupled with her sweet, quirky personality had made him feel immensely better.

There had been thirteen people to dinner if you counted the children and in that family the children definitely counted. They were all right there at dinner, either in little chairs right at the table or in someone's arms. He'd never been to a dinner quite like that one, but the sheer numbers had actually made him more comfortable than less. Everyone had greeted him warmly and then simply acted like he belonged there as much as everyone else and he truly did feel like he just fit in.

He'd been floored to look up and see Carrie O'Rourke walk in. Well, he knew her as Carrie O'Rourke, owner of another one of the great Thoroughbred race horse farms in the country, but he'd found that she'd changed her name to Isabel Marsh when she'd married the tall, quiet, dark cowboy he'd met at dinner. She'd always been a nice girl and it had been good to talk to someone who knew somewhat about him, but wouldn't ruin the tenuous new existence he was attempting to carve out for himself here almost two thousand miles from New York City.

And then Kit had appeared and he'd almost felt the hair on the back of his neck stand up. To go to the end of the universe and then have two people that he knew show up within minutes of each other was absolutely enough to make him wonder about Joey's comment earlier that there weren't many coincidences. Especially two of the few truly nice girls that he'd known in his entire life.

With Kit as well, he didn't wonder if she would make a big deal of who he was, although she probably only knew him from his music. As an incredibly popular rising young singing star and studio musician, Kit had recorded many of the songs he'd written for the themes for movies. They had a great respect for each other musically and it was wild to see her here in simply the role of mother to two tiny daughters and the wife of the oldest brother here on this working Wyoming ranch.

They had given him the gift of being included without making a big uncomfortable deal out of it and by the time he and Joey headed out when they were finished, he was happier and more at peace than he'd been in a long, long time.

She'd packed him a container of leftovers and another one of dog food and then when they'd mounted their horses, she'd gone to the main indoor arena and dropped off the saddle she had been riding the old horse that she called

68

Wildfire with. Then she'd legged right back up on the old horse bareback and this time they went back toward his house. Now, riding beside her in the evening quiet he wondered for the first time if he hadn't found the girl he'd been looking for for most of his adult life. Even in the midst of his grief, there was something about her that brought him wonderful, hope inspiring peace.

At his house, she petted the old dog Blue and leaned down to give him a hug. She spoke quietly to him and the old boy was obviously pleased to see her. When Michael took the container of food, thanked her, and started to go in, he noticed she was unsaddling his horse and he turned back.

She slung the saddle down and set it at her feet and then, leading both horses, she said over her shoulder, "I'll put the tack in your garage and these two I'll put here in your pasture. There's plenty of feed and there's a stream that flows through the bottom corner, so you won't need to water them. Someone who rides as well as you do ought to have a horse available and it's not like there aren't enough around here. I'll leave Wildfire as well to keep Jammer company when you aren't riding. As long as you close any gates you open, you should be able to go anywhere you want for miles around unless you see a white bull in a pasture. And there's an indoor and outdoor arena as well."

Surprised, he followed her out to the pasture gate. "You're leaving me your horses? Why would you do that? You don't even know me."

She nodded toward the closest house across the field. "I live over the garage there at Rossen's. It's not like they're going to be hundreds of miles away. I can throw them an apple out my window. And Wildfire is semi retired anyway. Jammer is one of the best cutting horses on the place, so if I need him, I'll come steal him for awhile. In the mean time . . ."

She paused and looked up into his eyes and said quietly, "They will help you, Michael. The outside of a horse really is good for the inside of a man." She reached up and petted Wildfire's kind face. "He got me through my first broken heart and all of the others since then." She smiled, a little embarrassed. "He's a great listener, and he never gives unwanted advice."

Picking up the bridles, she turned and headed back to the saddle she'd set down and picked up the pad and strode into his garage. He followed her with the heavier saddle. Exiting the garage, she turned toward her house and said over her shoulder, "Don't be such a stranger or I'll come be a busybody again."

With that, she ducked through the pasture fence and he couldn't help but watch her walking away. When she disappeared around the corner, he reached up to pet the old horse's head one more time. "Where have you been hiding her all my life, Wildfire? They don't make girls like that back in New York. Do you know that?" He paused for a second, thinking that she was right. The old horse was a good listener. He headed back inside his house, wondering if Joey would change toward him if she knew he was very, very wealthy. He sighed. He would like to think she wouldn't, but so far, that hadn't been his experience with women.

He put the food in the fridge and without turning on any lights, went to sit at the piano and for the first time since his father's death, he started out playing a song that wasn't sad. It was mellow. But it wasn't sad.

For Joey

Chapter 10

For the fifth time, Margot Witter stopped in to Michael Morgan's condo and didn't find him home again. She'd tried early and late and really late and she was beginning to 'wonder what was going on. She went down to his building manager and smiling her biggest enamel capped smile, she asked, "I'm trying to find Michael Morgan and I can't seem to catch him. Do you happen to know when he'll be back?"

Almost lackadaisically, the middle aged man said without looking up, "Michael Morgan." He paused as if thinking. "He's out somewhere. Try his cell phone. If he wants to see you, he will." With that he went back to the paperwork in front of him and Margot grimaced and then went back out to her car.

She had tried Michael's cell phone forty times. He wouldn't pick up and she went straight to voice mail every time. She called his mother. "Marilyn, it's Margot. Have you seen Michael lately? I can't seem to locate him and even my calls are being sent to voice mail."

"Hi, darling. I haven't seen him, but I spoke to him day before yesterday. He didn't mention having to go out of town. Did you try his penthouse? Or the bank? Call his father or Daddy at the bank. They'd know where he is."

Margot small talked for several more minutes and then rang off and then tried to find his father, Daniel''s number. The only one she had in her phone was apparently the wrong number and she kept getting a disconnected signal. She called her secretary and asked her to find it for her and then hung up and called Michael's grandfather at the bank. She

71

hated to do it. Warren Heinz obviously didn't care much for her and never gave her the time of day. "Warren, it's Margot Witter. I'm trying to locate Michael. Do you happen to know where he can be reached?"

"I spoke to him not twenty minutes ago on his cell phone. Have you tried that?"

"Yes, I tried that. I can't seem to get through. He must be having trouble with his phone. Is he out of town? Do you know?"

"I'm sorry; I'm not exactly sure where he is. If I speak to him, I'll tell him you're trying to get hold of him."

She grimaced, but said brightly into the phone, "Yes, do that if you would. I'd love to speak to him. Thank you, Warren. Bye now." Well, that got her nowhere. Warren knew as well as she did that Michael just wasn't taking her calls. But she didn't give up that easily.

Her secretary called back. "Margot, I'm not finding much. Daniel's old house number and his old cell have been disconnected. I can give you his address and you can try his condo. Will that help?"

Margot sighed. "Yes, give it to me. I'll try that." She took down the address and then rang off and handed it to her driver. "Take me here, please. I'm not sure if it will work, but I don't know what else to try."

An hour later, Margot stood before a beautiful condo door with a "For Sale" sign on it. Something was terribly wrong here. She phoned the realtor who was listing the condominium and when she tried to explain that she was trying to find Daniel Morgan, the realtor had no idea who she was talking about. "I'm sorry. You must have the wrong man. The man who owns that condo is Michael Morgan. I don't know of any Daniel Morgan. Are you looking for a higher end condo in that district? I have some other lovely listings as well. I'd be happy to drop by and show them to you."

72

"No, thank you. I'm actually trying to find Michael. You don't by any chance have a number where he can be reached do you?"

"Sure, hon. Let me just scroll down and find it. Hang on. Okay, here it is." Michael's cell phone again. Margot hung up the phone in disgust. Walking back down to the car, she had her driver take her right to Marilyn Morgan's place where she borrowed her phone and dialed Michael's number.

When he picked up a few rings later, she wanted to yell at him, but didn't as he said, "Hello, Mother. What's up? I just talked to you a couple of days ago."

Margot hesitated and then tried to act like she borrowed his mother's phone everyday to call him. "Hey, Michael. It's not your mother, it's Margot. I'm just up here visiting her and borrowed her phone. What are you up to?"

He sounded tired when he answered, "The same old boring stuff. You know me. Why?"

Knowing that this would go nowhere, she asked him outright, "Are you out of town somewhere, Michael? I've been to your house several times. I even went to your father's house and found it was for sale. Is he with you?"

There was a long quiet pause on the other end and finally Michael said, "Yes, I am out of town. And no, he's not with me. Look, Margot, I need to go. It's been good talking to you. Tell Mother hello."

Margot heard the phone go dead as he disconnected and she looked at it and swore. What was going on with him? He'd never been all that enthusiastic with her and she knew that, but she was definitely getting the idea that he wasn't interested at all and that just wasn't an option. He was far too wealthy and way too sexy to simply walk away from.

Turning to Marilyn, she handed her the phone back. "What's going on with him? Has he got another girlfriend all of the sudden? Why won't he even take my calls?"

Marilyn made a little sound with her lips. "Heavens no, Margot. He must just be in the middle of that ridiculous music of his again. Or maybe they're having stockholders' meetings at the bank right now or something. Give him a day or two and try again. He'll be fine. He knows that I think you'd be exquisite with him. A merger between our two families would be perfect."

Margot made a face. She hadn't even spoken to him except for right now in weeks, let alone spent any time with him. That wasn't exactly how "perfect mergers" worked out as far as she knew, but Marilyn had never been one to reason with.

They went out to lunch and then Margot went home and called a private investigator. Something was wrong and she wanted to know what it was. Even though Michael had become a little burnt out lately, he'd never been like this.

For Joey

Chapter 11

Michael slept so well the night after eating with the Rocklands that he half wondered if Joey wasn't right about nutrition being more important, so he got up and ate a decent breakfast sitting beside Blue on the porch watching the sun come up. With that done, he went out and saddled Jammer and took a long, leisurely ride up into the hills behind his house, being careful to shut the gates like Joey had cautioned. At first Blue acted like he wanted to come with, but when Michael rounded the first hill, the old dog turned and headed back home.

When he'd been gone a little more than an hour, Michael topped out on a ridgeline overlooking miles and miles of magnificent mountain ranges piled one on top of the other. Some were still snow capped and the bright white against the deep pines and brilliant green lower down was glorious. He sat the horse and let it have a breather while he looked all around in almost awe. No wonder Joey had been loathe to leave this for Detroit. This was incredible!

After awhile, he went on down the trail on the other side and all told, he rode long enough that Jammer had worked up a sweat and Michael had worked up a respectable appetite by the time he hosed the horse off and put him back in the pasture. As he went to go into his house, he found a glass covered dish sitting on the step with a rock on it.

He looked over across the valley and wondered if this had been Joey or Naomi. Far to the southwest, he glimpsed Joey pushing a herd of cows on horseback and even from this

75

distance, she looked good. Really good. They say that women mature like their mothers. If that was so, then Joey was destined to be healthy and happy and sweet and kind when she was middle aged. Just like she was now.

He'd hoped after the restful night he'd slept all the way through that things were going to be looking up, but it wasn't to be. The next night was one of the most miserable yet and he woke from the empty nightmare bathed in sweat and breathing like a sprinter. He lay there trying to tell himself that there had to be a hereafter.

At dinner the other night when all of them had prayed so faithfully, he'd tried to convince himself that all those intelligent people couldn't be mistaken. There had to be a God and something beyond this existence. But just now, in the black maw of the nothingness, his brain couldn't find the hope that prayer had given him.

Almost desperately, he got out of bed and went in to the piano in the dark and began to play, searching for the respite it would bring. He'd been sitting there for who knew how long when the thought came to him that maybe he was doing this all backward. Maybe pounding out his hurt and sadness and fear was only compounding it. Maybe if he played as if he were already at peace, the peace would come. Anything was worth a try at this point.

He had to focus to make his fingers relax to caress the keys and from time to time he still found himself playing almost with a vengeance, but eventually, the peace did come. It was weird. Sometimes, he almost felt like the peace was a tangible thing that came to him from outside himself, almost like a gift from some unseen power. He had no idea how he got it. All he knew was that he was grateful when it finally released him from that darkness.

At length, he played the final notes, took his foot off the pedal and listened to the last sound die away. Without even

76

thinking about it, he leaned his head back and said, "Thank you." With that, he got up and headed back into his bedroom and as he did so, he saw a shadow move on the deck outside of where Joey had said she lived above the garage. He saw her get up from a deck chair there and go into a sliding glass door and close it behind her.

Apparently she was having trouble sleeping as well. Then he wondered guiltily if he'd woken her up. As he thought about that, he remembered that first day when she'd fallen asleep ten feet from his piano when he'd been playing much less than peacefully and he had to smile in spite of the emotional exhaustion he was feeling. That was one thing about Joey, she did make him smile.

He went back in and laid down, listening to the crickets outside his window and thinking about how good she had looked yesterday when she showed up to be a busybody. She could have walked onto one of the runways back home and then some, only she was far more naturally pretty than those painted and emaciated women. They didn't usually model jeans on those runways, but man, Joey could wear a pair of jeans.

He smiled into the dark and Blue put his head over the edge of the bed and rested it on his hand. "I've got it bad for your owner, Blue. She's the first woman that I think I truly irritate at times, but she's like a breath of fresh air. Fresh Wyoming mountain air." Blue didn't say anything—just thumped his stubby tail on the floor at Michael's words. He was a good listener, too.

It was all he could do to drag himself out of bed the next morning, but Michael was glad he was at least up and showered when Naomi showed up with a plastic covered plate of breakfast and a whole packet full of mail. "The postmaster asked me to give you this. And Joey sent you breakfast. She's worried that you don't know how to cook, but don't worry. I defended you. I bet her you were probably a closet gourmet."

He took the plate and the mail with a humorless laugh. "You'd lose. I honestly don't know how I've survived this long with my cooking skills. I can't fry an egg."

Naomi just smiled. "A lot of people can't fry an egg. Just so you can pour a box of cold cereal. At least you won't starve, but maybe you should start showing up to dinner more often just to be on the safe side."

"Yeah, but if I can't return the favor, I couldn't. It wouldn't be right."

"So, what can you do other than cook? Joey says that you're a ripping musician."

He grinned at her. "Are you in desperate need of a piano player around here?"

She laughed. "Well, no. But music is very important. Is that your only deal? You're not a builder or an accountant or something?"

He shook his head. "I'm worthless. I wield a mean pen. I can write checks and read quarterly reports."

"I don't believe you for a minute. If you can handle Jammer, you can ride well. We certainly need riders around here. And you helped fix fence. Come eat and I promise I'll make you work it off later. You can avoid starvation and stay in shape at the same time." She paused and then asked, "Can I ask you a personal question?"

He hesitated. "I don't know. Do I need to be worried?"

"Actually, you need to be worried if I don't ask. Did you really mean to tell Joey you were gay?"

He was shocked speechless and Naomi laughed. "Can I take that as a no?"

"Definitely a no. She thinks I told her that? What in the world did I say to make her think that?"

"I'm not sure. Something about not liking the New York girls. But maybe you'd better clarify that to her. I mean, she would still treat you the same, but I'd hate for her to think that if it's not true. It can't be good."

He laughed right out loud for the first time in weeks. "I would think not." He shook his head. "I don't think anyone has ever thought that about me before. It's a little deflating, frankly. I must not be as masculine as these Wyoming guys or something."

This time Naomi laughed as she went to leave. "I don't think it had anything to do with being in comparison with the men here. At any rate, Joey was a little disappointed. I think her exact words were, 'What a waste.' That's a good sign, isn't it?"

He smiled and sighed and ran a hand through his hair. "Don't ask me any of the tricky questions right now, Naomi. I'm hopelessly without answers."

She looked at him steadily and gently said, "Every one loses the answers at some time or other, Michael. The good thing is, if we keep trying, we can find them again and then we're stronger for what we've been through. The key is to hang in there."

He considered that for a moment or two. "That is the key, isn't it? I've lost sight of that. Thank goodness for your wisdom. It helps me. Not to mention bringing me food and mail."

"You're welcome, Michael. Have a good day."

Naomi left and Michael sat down on the porch chair and reached to lay a hand on Blue's head, then shook his own head and laughed. "She thinks I told her I was gay. How in the world did I give her that idea? That has to be impressive to a girl, doesn't it?" He rubbed his chin and then got up to go inside, still shaking his head and wondering.

A couple of hours after lunch, he had only been out on Jammer for a mile or so when he came over a hill and found another herd of cows being driven by Joey and one of the younger brothers. When she saw him, she waved, and after a few more minutes when they had the cows inside a new pasture gate, she turned her horse and broke into a lope as she came up the hill toward him. Slowing as she neared, he watched her pale mane bounce gently over her shoulders, thinking again how naturally pretty she was.

This morning, after talking to Naomi, he'd wanted to go find Joey right then to set the record straight. Now, however, he almost wanted to wait and somehow tease her about it. When he realized that, he was pleasantly surprised. It had been a long time since he'd felt like teasing someone. Waiting was probably best anyway, because he had no idea how to broach the subject.

When Joey's horse was finally abreast of him, she looked at him hard before she even said, "Hi". He knew she was wondering why he'd been up playing in the night when, at length, she said, "It's good to see you out again. Rough night?"

He tried to joke it off. "Do I look that bad? What kind of a question is that?"

"Sorry. I just heard you playing and wondered."

"I'm sorry I woke you."

"No, I was already awake. Even across the pasture your music is incredible. I was just worried about you. Did you get your breakfast?"

"Yes, thank you. How long have you been out here?"

"We started early. Why? Do I look tired again?" She put up a gloved hand to brush her hair back.

He grinned at her. "Even tired you look beautiful. Stop fishing for compliments. No, I was just wondering how lazy I had gotten compared to the rest of the world since I came here."

"I thought music was your work. Doesn't working all night make you more dedicated? Not less?"

He shook his head. "I wish. I wasn't exactly making any headway last night. For that matter I haven't made much headway in the bright light of day lately. I think I have an extended case of writer's block."

"Now you're whining."

"You're right. I'm sorry. Where are you two headed next?" He nodded at the brother who was loping up to them.

When the brother got there, he rode up next to Michael and extended his hand. "I'm Treyne. I'm the fourth brother. I'm next after Joey. You must be the Michael from Merv's house. Are you going to help us move this next herd?"

Michael looked from Treyne to Joey. "I don't know. I didn't know what you were doing. I'm a novice, but if you'll tell me what to do, I'll help."

"Good. Three always makes it easier. I'll ride point and open the gates. Just stay behind them with Joey and she'll tell you what to do."

They headed down the hill toward the next pasture of cattle and Michael honestly just had to sit his saddle and let his horse do all the work. He'd never ridden a cutting horse and a couple of times when cows tried to scatter and Jammer went after them, Michael was a little surprised. The horse just exploded sideways underneath him.

They got the cows into the pasture and then Joey ran her horse down the fence line to shut another gate so that they didn't keep on going into the next pasture again. Michael watched her ride and was impressed. She looked like she was an extension of the horse, even when it leaped over the stream that crossed the pasture.

As they headed back, when they approached the ranch, he began to peel off and head to his own house and as Treyne went on ahead, Joey asked, "Are you coming to dinner? I think she's having fried chicken and potato salad and beans."

He considered it and then shook his head. "It sounds wonderful, but I think I'll come another time. Tell her thank you anyway."

She looked at him for just a second and then nodded. "I'll tell her. Have a good night. I hope you can sleep. If you can't, try praying. It really helps. I'll pray for you, too." She spun her horse and headed back to the big arena and he just sat his, watching her go. Maybe he shouldn't tell her that he wasn't gay. Maybe her thinking that would help him keep his head on straight where she was concerned.

He put Jammer away and went inside and after surveying his nearly empty fridge, he decided he'd eat later and went in to work at the piano for awhile. Somehow, he always did better writing right after he was around her. She'd proven to be very inspirational to him.

He'd been playing for over an hour, when he heard a sound and it broke his concentration. Thinking it was Blue scratching to come in the back door, he got up and went in there, but Blue was already inside and there was another plastic covered plate of still warm dinner sitting on his counter. Glancing out the window, he could see her there in the gathering dusk, walking across the field toward her apartment. For someone who thought he preferred men, she was wonderfully thoughtful.

He was able to sleep through the night again.

Chapter 12

The next morning his grandfather called and it was good to hear his voice. More than anything they had been business partners, but it felt wonderful to know he was concerned about him. Very first thing, he asked how Michael was doing and Michael was able to tell him in all honesty that he was better than he'd been. Sleeping well did wonders. Not to mention the real food. Michael told him about the Rocklands and how they had been so good to him and how for some reason, Joey seemed to bring him peace, and he knew his grandfather was truly happy for him.

Warren also told him that Margot had called, trying to find him, and then went on to ask Michael what he thought of some rather higher risk, but potentially higher profit deals the bank had been offered.

Michael shook his head as he walked around the house with the phone. "Warren, I wouldn't do it. Those are just the kinds of risks we've avoided in the past and we've never been sorry. I know profits are down just now. And it's bound to get worse before it gets better with this new president, but that only makes it more imperative to deal conservatively. Right now, we're the strongest bank in the country. I think we should keep it that way. At least that's the way I see it. What do you think?"

"You have echoed my sentiments completely. I only asked because Rollins has been pestering me again and I told him I'd run it by you. I'll let you go. I hope things continue to go well for you there, although we miss you desperately at the bank. You've the lion's share of the business acumen here

I'm afraid. I may have to call you more frequently to offset some of the simple minds I'm dealing with."

Michael smiled. "Call anytime, Warren. And thanks for your patience. I want you to know I appreciate it. I'll be there for the stockholders' meeting next week. Take care."

He got off the phone, wondering if he'd need to get his hair cut before then or if it would be appropriate to attend the meetings with it as long as it was. Then he remembered the Derby. The Kentucky Derby was the first Saturday in May and he had a horse that could very well win it. He'd have to get his hair cut. He didn't want to possibly be immortalized in a million photos with hair that looked a little like Yanni.

He was definitely not looking forward to spending time back in New York, but the horse races actually sounded like fun. He sighed with relief. It would be so good to have some enthusiasm back for a change. It would be even more fun if he could have taken Joey back there with him, but the people here, other than Isabel, didn't have any idea what all he was involved in away from here. He'd have to ask Isabel if she had anything running in the Derby this year.

That night was the first of three bad nights in a row and he didn't even open the drapes during the days between. The horrible dreams of emptiness were bad enough, but then he was exhausted for the rest of the day as well.

Even the music didn't flow when he got up the third night and he ultimately just went outside to sit and watch the stars and wonder if there was a God up there or not. Finally, he thought back to what Joey had said about praying if he couldn't sleep and he had to admit that at this point, he had nothing to lose. He didn't think the nights could get any worse.

He leaned his head back against the chair again and searched the heavens, wondering how you prayed. Did it have to be some set verse like he'd seen in movies or read about in books? Or was it as simple as talking to a really powerful father?

He thought of his own dad and looked up at the stars again and asked, "Where are you, Dad? Are you out there somewhere? You're on the other side now. You know exactly what it's like. Or else you're gone. I wish I could ask you. Which is it? And what do I do here and now?"

That was the first time he'd actually spoken as if to his dad out loud and for some reason it helped. He felt closer to him, even if it was just in his imagination, and he fought to shut the image of the empty gray nothing out of his head forever. One more time he leaned his head back, wondering if he could actually speak out loud to address a God that might not even exist.

Just as he was about to speak, Blue got up from beside his chair and wagging his tail, he walked out into the yard. Wondering what was going on, Michael peered out toward him and realized Joey was coming across the pasture toward him.

On reaching the porch, she dropped quietly into the chair beside him and Blue came back and laid down between them and put his head on his paws. Neither one of them spoke for several minutes and then finally, she softly asked, "Did you try the prayer?"

He was grateful for the dark when he had to admit to her, "I don't know how."

After another few minutes, she asked, "Would you mind if I prayed for you?"

"I would really appreciate it."

"Would you kneel with me?"

"Sure." They both slipped out of the chairs and she came over next to him and bowed her head and he did the same. He was surprised when she started. It was just as if she was speaking to a friend, except that she demonstrated total respect and humility. She prayed for him to find peace of heart and to be able to rest and as she spoke he felt that same unusual strength he'd felt some nights as he played the piano. Miraculously, the anxiousness left over from the empty dreams dissipated like a mist in the night wind and a warm, sweet calm slowly filled his heart.

Lastly, she prayed that he would come to know he was a child of the living God who loved him and watched over him.

At length, when she finished speaking, he echoed her amen and then both of them sat back in the porch chairs without speaking. Michael was so overwhelmed with what had just happened that he didn't know if he could have spoken if he had wanted to. He'd never experienced anything even remotely like this.

After several minutes, Joey stood up and put a hand on his shoulder as she stood for a moment beside his chair. He could tell she wanted to say something, but in the end, she just gave his shoulder a squeeze and walked back into the dark she had appeared out of. Blue went with her for several minutes and then he too emerged out of the shadows and quietly laid back down next to Michael's chair.

Michael sat there for probably another half hour, marveling that finding out that God exists was as simple as speaking to Him and asking for help, only to have the request granted almost immediately. When he began to be uncomfortably chilled, he finally got up and went back into the house.

This time, as he sat down on the piano bench, the music poured from his head and his heart to his fingers and new beautiful harmonies came almost unbidden. By the time the sun came up, he had most of the baseline melodies down for the new movie score he'd been commissioned to do. It was a love story, and he had to wonder if the love themes hadn't come so easily all of the sudden, because of the influence Joey had been having on his life. He'd never felt this way about a girl. He truly respected her even more than he was attracted to her. And that was a lot.

By dawn, the music had been flowing, but physically he was toast and he groaned as he thought about driving into Jackson Hole to catch his plane back to New York for the stockholders meeting. For once, he longed for one of the limousines he had always disdained. It would be great to have a driver and some room to stretch out in this one time.

He packed a minimal carry on, knowing all of his clothes were still hanging in the closet of his condo and was just loading into the funny old car when Joey came by on a horse. If she hadn't been riding he'd have given her a gigantic hug for what she had done for him last night.

As it was, she looked down at him and smiled and said, "You look awful. But the music was incredible! I needed to sleep desperately, but I couldn't stop listening. You're not really planning to drive somewhere as tired as you are, are you?"

He was too tired to smile at her, but he tried. "You're being a busybody again. Leave me alone. I'm too exhausted to defend myself. Do you think I could pay one of your brothers or one of the hands to drive me to the airport? I really am too tired to drive and I need to be alive for this meeting." He yawned and continued, "I'd ask you, but you look as trashed as I am. I'm just far too polite to say so. You notice that I didn't tell you you look awful."

Joey grinned. "Would they have to drive this car?"

Michael rolled his eyes. "I don't care if we take a buckboard as long as I get to the airport by eleven o'clock. You got a problem with Merv's car?"

She laughed. "I'm an automotive engineer with the dream of designing race cars. Off course I have a problem with this car. Go lay down, I'll find you a driver." Her eyes met his quietly for a moment and she asked, "Are you coming back?"

He met her gaze and answered softly but positively, "Yeah. I'm coming back."

Jaclyn M. Hawkes

Chapter 13

It was actually Slade who ended up taking him in Isabel's SUV. Michael had only met him that evening on the deck and at dinner, but he'd liked him right off and knew that if Carrie O'Rourke had married him, he must be a good man. They'd been on the road for about fifteen minutes just shooting the breeze when Slade finally said, "Isabel told me that you're not just a musician. She wanted to know if you have a horse in the Derby next week."

Michael looked over at him. "Yes. Royal Song. I honestly believe we'll win it. Is Isabel running Obsidienne?"

Slade nodded. "She said she's good, but that yours might be better."

Michael had to agree. He hesitated to ask, but he had to know. "How many of your family know my background?"

"Isabel and me. She figured you had your reasons for walking away from it all and that was your own business. She would never betray a confidence. Husbands don't count of course, but she knew I would honor your privacy as well. That being said, sometimes it helps to have a sounding board to bounce things off of.

"Isabel is a good listener and she would understand. She basically went into hiding with Rossen and me on the rodeo circuit when she needed to get away from her real father. That's how we met, in fact. We'd hired her thinking she was a college student." He smiled across the SUV. "I've never been the same since. She saved me from myself."

"I remember when she went missing." Michael was silent for awhile, wondering if he could actually tell this man the reason he'd wanted to walk away from his old life.

Jaclyn M. Hawkes

Finally, he admitted quietly, "My father was my best friend. In my world, sometimes he felt like the only one who was honestly a true friend. He'd survived and still turned out halfway decent and gave me hope." He paused and then almost whispered, "He died a few days before I came here of liver cancer. It was hard because until just recently—really recently, I didn't know for sure if there was a hereafter or if he was just gone. Even knowing there's a hereafter, the loss is still . . . "

He couldn't finish the sentence and just went on. "I know that sounds like a cop out to want to turn my back on the world after losing him, but I just couldn't face everyone and the superficiality of it all anymore. Not for awhile."

Slade didn't say anything and Michael remembered that Naomi had said his family had been killed in a car accident. Finally, without taking his eyes off the road Slade said, "I didn't turn my back on the world, when my father was killed. I turned my back on God. That is far more childish and nonsensical. It took me years to figure it out. I had to find Isabel and then nearly die in a bull riding wreck before it clicked." He paused and then said, "Even now there are days when I still miss them."

"They were killed in a car accident, right?"

In a bitter tone, Slade replied, "A drunk driver. My little sister and my father. Ten years ago this spring."

After a moment of silence, Michael asked, "Was your mother involved as well?"

Again bitterly, Slade answered, "My mother had left long before that. She ran off with the local Baptist preacher. I guess Dad and the preacher's wife should have gotten together and prayed for them or something. That's kind of why I was so ticked at God, I guess."

Michael shook his head and said tiredly, "My dad was much more substantial than my mother as well. When he didn't enjoy her pointless lifestyle, she decided he wasn't
90

much fun. When my dad got sick a year and a half or so ago, he bowed out gracefully. She still doesn't even know he had cancer, let alone that he's dead. She's far more worried about designer shoes."

Slade looked across the truck. "Try not to let it make you bitter at all of them. I'd become almost a woman hater. Until Isabel, the only women in the world that I trusted were Naomi and Joey. Some women aren't worth bothering with, but Isabel is the greatest human being on the planet." He smiled. "I guess I might be a little bit biased."

"She is a wonderful person. She must have been the last single female with substance."

Slade shook his head. "You're forgetting Joey. Joey is definitely a great woman. She is every bit as good and kind as Naomi."

"Why in the world is she still single as beautiful and nice as she is?"

"It's definitely not for lack of opportunity. After I drop you off, I'd be picking up Bryan Cole, the country music star, except that he always rents an exotic sports car to try to win Joey over into marrying him. He's flying in today. He's been after her for more than two years I think.

"And she has a doctor in Jackson who loves her dearly, but knows it's just not there for her. Those are just the two longest love sick men. That doesn't even count the local boys or the one's she left bawling in Michigan after her mission. So far, she's waiting, hoping that someday she'll actually fall in love with one of these guys. Personally, I think she's tired of looking."

"That has to stink watching all the rest of you get married and settle down. She obviously adores all the babies. How old is she anyway?"

"She's only twenty-four. But you know when you hit that point where you're sick of the meat market?" Michael nodded. "She's definitely there. I think she'd love to be done dating. It's just that she has her head on straight and her priorities right and there just aren't a lot of guys that are on par with her. Honestly, most of the men I know who could keep up with her are her brothers. They are a wonderful family. Them taking me under their wing has been an amazing blessing. I honestly don't know what I would have done without them when Dad and Chante' were killed."

Michael smiled. "I know exactly what you mean. You should have seen Joey one day. She walked right into my house and made me take the garbage out. She opened those blinds like a drill sergeant and then tore into the fridge. She was obviously disgusted with me, but she didn't get ornery anyway. She made me go to dinner at Naomi's, but she didn't ever get grouchy with me. I've never met a woman like that."

Slade smiled blandly at him across the truck. "They don't make them like Joey Rockland very often. You ought to try to nab her."

"Me? I'm the least deserving man in the world for a girl like her." He chuckled tiredly. "Not only that, she thinks I told her I'm gay."

Slade busted up. "Gay? She thinks that and you haven't set her straight? Man, you better do something about that."

"I didn't even know until Naomi asked me right out a few days ago. And I haven't had a chance to go there since. You know the funny thing about that? Joey still treats me with absolute respect and kindness. For some reason I wouldn't have thought that. I mean, what beautiful girl watches over a man that she thinks is of questionable persuasion? It kind of warmed my heart. Trashed my ego, but was very heart warming."

"She is one to love unconditionally, but still, man. I can't believe you didn't tell her she misunderstood. That's terrible!"

Michael yawned. "Maybe I should have intimated it years ago. It would have saved a lot of trouble with mercenary women."

Slade laughed again. "No, because if they were only interested in your money they wouldn't care how deviant you were. It would even be worse. You'd just have to deal with mercenary men as well."

"You've got a point." He yawned again. "Do I have time for a nap before we make it to Jackson? My plane leaves at twelve-thirty."

"Probably not. Why are you flying commercial? Do you mind if I ask? Surely you have a plane or two tucked away back there somewhere."

Michael sighed. "I don't. There are several in my family, but for some reason I usually try to just fly like everyone else. I think it's very easy to lose perspective coming from my background. I'm sure my view of the world is still skewed, but I try."

He chuckled. "I can say that, but I came out here in a Ferrari and then parked it in Branden's storage and drove Merv's car. I thought the Ferrari would be over the top here. But I'm not sure what to think about driving Merv's car. I don't think I've ever experienced anything quite like it. Although it did garner me meeting Joey. Maybe I'll keep it forever and booby trap it occasionally so she'll come fix it."

Slade looked across the car at him. "You don't know Joey. Exotic sports cars are her hot button. If you parked a Ferrari in front of your house she'd probably steal the keys and take it for a joy ride."

Michael looked thoughtful when he answered, "Hmm. There's an idea. But wouldn't that just be creating the same problem out here that I tried to leave behind in New York? Someone who liked me for my bottom line and expensive toys?"

"No, of course not. Honestly, I think if Joey had any idea of the kind of money you're involved with, she'd panic and run away from you. She's probably the opposite of mercenary. She just has a weakness for hot cars. We keep accusing Bryan of trying to buy her heart. If she was that way, she'd have married Bryan years ago."

"He's really serious about her then?"

"Hopelessly serious, poor, rich, famous, and sought-after man that he is. Do you know him? You knew Kit, didn't you?"

"Yeah, I wrote several of the songs she has recorded. And yes, I know Bryan. He's actually a really likeable guy. And a great talent. I love his stuff and I'm not even that familiar with country and western."

"We may see him at the airport. It's not a very big place and I think his plane comes in shortly before yours leaves."

Michael closed his eyes and leaned his head back. "I can't blame him. She's definitely a keeper. This country is unreal. I wish I could keep my eyes open to watch it."

When they made it to the airport, Slade shook him to get him to get out of the car, and wouldn't accept payment for bringing him. "Forget it. One of these nights I'll hit you up to babysit or something. Have a good trip."

Michael dragged himself out and into the airport and he did indeed meet Bryan on the way inside. At his gate, he offered an airport employee fifty bucks to make sure he didn't sleep through his boarding call. The young woman smiled at him and refused the money, but promised to wake him anyway, and he was so tired that for once he actually slept on a flight.

Six hours later, once secure inside his condo, he wished he'd stopped to buy milk on the way in. Doc had cleaned his fridge completely out and, in fact, turned it off and he didn't even have bread. He dug out his phone and ordered Chinese from the little place a few blocks down.

Looking around him, for the first time, he noticed just how truly opulent his penthouse condominium really was. Living in the little white house in Wyoming for these last weeks had made him realize that. So then why did that little house feel so much more homey than this elegant home that he'd had for years?

As he undressed and got into the huge shower with three shower heads and a steamer, he had to wonder if peace would come any easier to him here in luxury than it had in a cottage. He thought back to the night before when Joey had shown up literally in the middle of the night to pray for him.

It seemed like it had been days since then, but that sense of peace and surety that someone, somewhere was listening to her and sent comfort to him, was still as vivid as it had been there in the dark on the porch kneeling beside her. She was a wonderful woman, not to mention the frission of attraction he felt even when he only saw her on her horse in the distance.

It had been enlightening to talk to Slade about her during the drive today. It was no wonder she had men traveling half way across the country to try to convince her to marry them. She was a one in millions and millions. New York City felt like a different planet from her right now.

The shower eased away some of the tension from the flight and he was bone tired when he got out and wrapped a towel around his hips. Still thinking about Joey, he threw on some jams and went to the beautiful grand piano that sat in his living room in front of the huge picture windows that looked out over the city.

Even as tired as he was, he wanted to play the song he had written with her in mind after she'd left last night. He played it through and then played it through again, marveling at the beautiful melody that had come so effortlessly after the veritable battle he'd been having lately coming up with anything. She had been wonderful for his productivity as well as everything else.

Standing, he walked to the window and looked out at the city he'd been born in and lived in for twenty-eight years. It was the greatest city in the world. He'd been told that all his life and he truly believed it.

He loved New York. But right now it was too big and busy and impersonal. He felt lost in the masses for some reason. He did want to be a little lost right now, but this sense of being insignificant was too sad. It compounded the grief over losing his dad. Even though no one had known him when he'd gotten to Wyoming, he certainly hadn't felt lost in the masses.

His Chinese came and he ate and then went in and went to bed. He was glad his board meeting wasn't until tomorrow afternoon. He lay down and thought about Joey again and then haltingly slipped back out and knelt beside the bed. He'd never done this before. He really had no idea what he was doing, but he wanted to know this Father the way Joey obviously did. She'd spoken like she was talking to a friend. A very powerful friend. One who had been able to lift the darkness and that fear.

It was strange, but he'd finally recognized it for that. It was a gut deep fear that this was it. That there was no meaning, no point and no forever. It was the most demeaning and discouraging thing he'd ever had to deal with. And it had made his father's death feel unendurable.

Hesitantly, he spoke softly, "Father . . . " Still not sure what to say, he finally just added, "I'm here." After another second, he went on, "And I know that you're there now. Thank you. Thank you for being there. Thank you for helping me. Thank you for knowing that I'm here. Amen." After kneeling there for another few minutes, wondering if he needed to say something else as that sweet, warm easiness filled his bedroom, he got back into his bed. Maybe that's why he'd needed Wyoming. It was easier to believe that he wasn't just one of billions of human beings out there.

Chapter 14

Joey and the others came in for lunch and she was seriously dragging. She looked toward Michael's house and wondered if he was already gone, feeling a little foolish when that thought was such a disappointment to her. That idea made her even more tired, and she wished she had asked him when he was coming back. Thinking about how good he looked, even hammered, she had to stop and remind herself that he didn't necessarily like females and then she felt more foolish than ever.

That afternoon, she threw herself into her work with a vengeance to take her mind off things and when Bryan showed up in the early afternoon in a Porsche Boxter she was caught off guard. She couldn't admit it to him, but she'd completely forgotten he was coming.

He was only staying for a day and then was heading on back home to Alabama, but still. How had she forgotten?

When he asked over dinner why she was so tired, all she said was that she'd had trouble sleeping. She wasn't going to mention that it was because she had this haunted new neighbor that drew her even though he had a thing for men. Bryan would never understand. She didn't even understand. The strangest part about it was that she knew without a doubt that she was helping Michael and that even though he had some world class baggage, he still made her feel more alive than anyone had in forever. What his baggage was she didn't know, but she knew she'd never been around someone more troubled.

Bryan said something to her and she had to pull her mind away from the way Michael had felt under her hand last night when she'd squeezed his shoulder. He was incredibly attractive, and it made her feel stupid. They were at her favorite restaurant in Star Valley and she tried to focus on what Bryan was telling her about the tour he was planning.

He was asking if she wanted to fly out to some of the concerts and she smiled. Of course she'd go. It probably wasn't wise. She knew Bryan liked her far more than she liked him, but she also hated to disappoint him. And it wasn't like there was anyone else pressingly on the horizon. Michael's face popped into her head again and she mentally elbowed herself. *Don't be an idiot.*

After dinner they went to the local American Legion Hall where there was always line dancing on Thursday nights. Her brothers were there as well and even though it was just a bunch of their neighbors with the odd tourist thrown in, it was always fun. Most of the locals had gotten used to seeing Bryan show up from time to time, so it usually wasn't such a big deal as it had been, but the small time bands that played it never quite knew how to handle having a country music superstar in the audience. Sometimes the quality of the music wasn't all that good, but Bryan would laugh good naturedly when somebody really messed up.

Her married brothers and their wives all loved to come and dance and Cooper and Treyne would joke and tease with the single girls they spun around the floor. Even Naomi and Rob at home loved Thursdays because it meant they got all six of the grand kids for the evening. They had always come dancing with them before becoming grandparents, but now they insisted that grandchildren beat the heck out of line dancing.

The band started up a slow song to let everyone rest for a few minutes and Bryan pulled her close with a mellow sigh.

"It's all fun, but holding you is by far the best part of all of this dancing stuff, you know. Are you sure I can't talk you into at least moving to California so I could see you more often?"

Joey smiled up at him, but she said, "Don't you start, Bryan. We're having a good time here. I'm not moving to California. How is your mother doing? She's turning fifty, right?"

The conversation drifted successfully away from their relationship and she was glad. She honestly liked Bryan, and he was fun. She just couldn't marry him.

That night, when he dropped her at her apartment door before going to stay with Cooper and Treyne and the guys in the bunkhouse, he hugged her again and didn't let go right away. She hoped he didn't look down at her with those sad eyes like he did sometimes. She hated that. She couldn't help the way she felt.

He knew she was doing the best she could and he always assured her that he loved her anyway, but sometimes she felt so guilty after he left. He must have known that too, because he pulled back and tried to smile after the long hug. He leaned down and kissed her softly for just a second or two and then smiled again. "Good night, Joey. I still love you. Thanks for letting me come see you again. It was fun."

He turned and walked away and she opened her door and went in with a sigh. This was foolish. She felt like she was toying with him. Even her coming back here after college and her mission was foolish. She'd already met every guy within two hundred miles of the ranch, and they were good, honorable, hard working men for the most part, but the one she was looking for just wasn't here. It wasn't like living and working here was the hot spot for eligible, young, male members of the church. She needed to move away to where there were more men her age. It was just hard to leave. She loved it here.

Stepping over to the window, she watched Bryan walk toward the bunkhouse. He'd joined the church over a year ago. He'd said he didn't do it for her, and she believed him. He was active in his ward in California and he attended wherever he was, when he was on the road.

Every time he came, she wondered if she should break down and marry him. After all, he was a nice, wealthy, fun, happy, handsome man. He had it all. Except for the fireworks. Every time she wondered this, she'd think about her parents and her married brothers and then she knew that she couldn't do it. She did love Bryan. Loved him dearly. But she wasn't in love with him. That was the bottom line.

The next afternoon when he went to leave, he talked about coming back in a few weeks and Joey looked at him earnestly, but she didn't say anything. They'd been over this a hundred times. He still wanted to come and she did have fun with him. He was a big boy. He knew what was going on here, so she let him make the decision. But that didn't stop the wave of guilt that settled over her like the dust from his beautiful little Porsche as he drove off down the gravel lane.

Chapter 15

His grandfather greeted him with a handshake that turned into a hug. That hadn't happened before, but somehow it was exactly what he'd needed. Warren teased him briefly about his hair and then they went to lunch together to talk about the details of the impending meeting. In spite of the huge span of miles between them, for the first time, Michael felt closer to him than ever. He wanted to tell him what he'd found out about God being there, but he felt foolish in a way. It was hard to explain about something as intangible as a feeling.

Their private lunch was interrupted before he got a chance to bring it up when Margot Witter appeared in the restaurant. He had to work not to roll his eyes when she walked over to their table and began to talk to him and he knew that he had to invite her to sit down. At least they had a valid excuse to leave when it was time to head up to their meeting.

As he and Warren got up to go, she said, "Michael, I need to talk to you. Could I meet you after your meeting is over to discuss a few things?"

Glancing up at Warren who simply looked back at him with the decorum of having known this type of thing for sixty something years, Michael graciously agreed, "Certainly. Would my office work?" He glanced at his watch. "Say four o'clock?"

She gave him a wide smile. "That would be perfect. See you then."

He and Warren headed up and even in the elevator his grandfather didn't say anything about her. He must have known that if Michael hadn't done anything stupid with women so far, he wasn't likely to start now. Michael thought back to what Joey had misunderstood when he told her that the New York women weren't his thing. He must have grinned because Warren smiled back at him and asked, "What makes you smile when Margot is pestering you?"

He felt the grin broaden into a full blown smile. "You know the girl I was telling you about over the phone? Joey? Back in Wyoming? She asked me one day why there were no females who had followed me west. I said something about how the New York women just weren't my thing."

He chuckled. "She thinks I was telling her I'm gay." He shook his head and laughed again when Warren looked shocked. "I wouldn't even have known she thought that if her mother hadn't said something." As the elevator door opened on their floor, he laughed again. "She's the first girl I've wanted to be with in who knows how long."

The board meeting went well. There were obviously a few members of the board who weren't happy that Michael wasn't inside the bank on a daily basis, but he and Warren owned a controlling interest so there was nothing they could say.

Rollins was the squeaky wheel again as usual and they politely but firmly told him that no, they wouldn't be taking on any high risk debt at this time, regardless of the profit potential. For the rest of the meeting Rollins sat and glowered, but there was nothing to be done about it. His ideas were not options.

Michael took the time to stay and talk briefly with several of the board members and then glanced at his watch and excused himself. He was a few minutes late and hoped that Margot would have changed her mind and gone already.

She hadn't. She was sitting in the lobby outside his office in a dress that was much too short. One long leg crossed over the other in such a way that it left little question about how much she was wearing underneath. She stood up as he came through and came over and hugged him like they were long lost friends and he rolled his eyes to the receptionist as she did it.

Pushing her away, he continued on into his office and grimaced when Margot shut the door behind them. He went around behind his desk to use it almost as a shield against her, then decided that that hadn't worked well when she came over to it and leaned on it, revealing a generous portion of cleavage in the process.

In a way it helped. He'd been going to stay in New York for the week or so until he left for Kentucky, but as she leaned over the desk, he made an executive decision to go right back to Wyoming as soon as he could round up a plane. He was heading back home to Joey. Two minutes of Margot was more than enough, thank you.

He waited patiently for whatever it was that she needed to speak to him about, but all she did was ask, "Where have you been?" She was still using the whole smile and make sure that he knew she was an attractive female bent, but her words were to the point and he had to respect that. He respected it, he just didn't answer it.

"A board meeting for the bank. I'm sorry I'm late. It went longer than expected."

She wasn't amused. "You know what I meant, Michael. What's going on? Where are you staying and why didn't you tell anyone that your father had passed away? We could have been there for you."

Her question caught him off guard and for just a second the pain in his chest kept him silent. Finally, he said, "I've been out of town, working. And I didn't tell anyone because I wanted to be left alone. Does my mother know he's dead?"

"No." She backed up and sat down in the chair near his desk. "I assumed you would tell her if you wanted her to know. But you could have told me. Surely, you wanted me to know so I could have offered you comfort. We've always been such good friends."

He looked at her without saying anything, wondering how she could have missed the obvious. Finally, he said, "Margot, what was it you needed to talk to me about? I have things I need to do this afternoon."

It was all he could do not to roll his eyes again, when she took on a pout and said, "Michael, don't be mean. I understand that you're unhappy right now. I do. But I miss you. We haven't done anything for ages. Come on and lighten up. Do what you need to do and then let's go do something together. What do you say?"

He went to the file cabinet nearby to retrieve some paperwork he needed to take with him. "I say no, Margot." He picked up some other files from his desk and turned to the door. "It's been good talking with you. Tell Mother hello."

She jumped up and put a hand manicured with long, thick, squared off fingernails on his arm to stop him. "Michael! What do you mean, you say no? I thought we had an understanding."

"Margot, I'm not sure who you made this understanding with, but I wasn't a party to it. And frankly, I'm not interested. Now if you'll excuse me. I need to be leaving." He pulled his arm away from her hand and turned his back on her and began to walk down the hall, but she quickly fell into step with him.

"Why are you being like this, Michael? This isn't like you. You're never mean and short with me."

He pushed the button for the elevator and when it opened almost immediately he stepped in and so did she. When the door closed, he turned to her. "Margot, what is it that you want from me?"

At first she hesitated and then said, "Honestly. Bluntly. I thought we were getting married."

He shook his head. "Honestly. Bluntly. Not in ten thousand years. Sorry. You're not the girl for me, Margot. In fact, there probably isn't a girl for me. In twenty-eight years I've never met anyone I'd care to be with forever, so it's probably hopeless. Marry Mother. She's worth more than me right now anyway. And she's much more suited to you. You can shop together." Her mouth dropped open as the elevator door opened and he stepped out.

He strode across the lobby and out the door and as luck would have it, a cab was just letting a woman out directly ahead. Without a backward glance, he stepped in the open door and shut it as he heard Margot speak his name. He leaned forward and said, "LaGuardia, please."

When the cabbie pulled away, he phoned his grandfather and explained that he was going back to Wyoming and would then go straight to Kentucky. Warren didn't seem surprised. All he said was, "The jet isn't doing anything in the interim. Can I talk you into taking it? It would streamline your travel time and you wouldn't be so tired when you got there. Either place. Just have the pilots spend a few days in Jackson and then take it to Lexington as well. They'd probably love it."

For once, Michael thought the private jet sounded heavenly. He'd be back in Wyoming in half the time and could stay longer before he had to leave as well. "Actually, yes. I'll take you up on that. Could you call them and tell them I'm on my way. But only if neither of them have any pressing prior engagements. Thanks, Warren. And remind me to tell you what I found out about God."

Michael closed his phone and turned back to the cabbie. "Could you take me to the secondary airport south of the main concourse at LaGuardia instead please?"

"Sure thing." The burly African American in the front seat looked at him in the rear view mirror and asked, "So, my man, what did you find out about God? If you don't mind my asking."

Michael leaned back against the seat and closed his eyes. "That He's there. He's really there."

The cabbie gave a huge white smile. "I coulda told you that, man."

Chapter 16

Joey was surprised when she got up Saturday morning to see a little silver Trailblazer parked in front of Michael's house. A day and a half wasn't very long to take a trip to New York City and back. Maybe that wasn't where he'd gone, or maybe it wasn't even him there at the house. It could be the great nephew doctor this time.

She hoped it was Michael. She wasn't going to question why she hoped that, but the day had just gotten more promising. She dressed and went up to her parents' house for breakfast, wondering what time whoever it was had gotten in. She hadn't even heard anyone arrive in the night.

As the family ate, they discussed the day's agenda and Joey tried to focus on what her duties would be and not on wondering who was up at Michael's. She was going to be with Sean checking fences and waterholes over south and east in a little valley. Rob turned to them and asked, "Can you two also go up into the box canyon and check those mares and colts?"

Naomi looked up with a concerned look as he asked it and then said, "Rob, Ruger said he thought that white Rage bull was down in the valley. He saw something white down there and wondered if he'd gone through the fence and gotten out of the upper forty. If he's in the valley, we don't want the kids near there. Do we?"

Finishing a bite of pancake, Rob swallowed. "I saw him and his cows up on top just last night. Ruger must have been mistaken. They should be fine and we haven't checked on those mares in close to two weeks." He turned to Sean and

107

Joey. "Keep your wits about you as you go through there, just in case, but you should be fine. Stay together at any rate."

Naomi listened and then said, "We should get rid of that bull, Rob. I know he's one of our heaviest bulls, but someday he's going to hurt someone or worse. He's already killed one horse. It's not worth the risk. Let's either slaughter him or at least ship him off to some rodeo company. He ought to make a great bullfighting bull."

Rob got up and leaned over to kiss her. "You're right, of course, Mother. His cows are probably already bred this spring anyway. I'll get on the phone tonight and make the arrangements. But today I really do think he's up on top where he's supposed to be."

With breakfast over, everyone went their separate ways and Joey rode out of the valley beside Sean without ever knowing who was in the little house. She was surprised to hear a horse behind them only a few minutes after topping the ridge, and she and Sean pulled up and waited to see who it was.

She couldn't help the little thing her pulse rate did when it was Michael who rode over the hill on Jammer. He stopped when he got to them and Joey knew instantly that he was doing better than he'd been the other night. He still looked tired and maybe a little sad, but most of the haunted look around his eyes was gone. She wondered what had happened while he was traveling to take it away.

Smiling at her, he leaned and offered his hand to Sean. "Have I met you? You guys all look so much alike, but you're a different brother, aren't you? I'm Michael."

Sean looked back and forth between them for just a second and then gave a smile that had Joey worrying as he replied, "No, we haven't met. I'm Sean. Just older than Joey. I'm married to the beautiful red head and have the black and red twins, Eric and Caitlin. It's good to meet you. Have you come to help us check fence?"

Michael looked back over at Joey. "Would you mind if I tagged along? I wanted to ask you some questions sometime. I don't really know what checking fence entails, but I'm a pretty quick study."

Sean flashed Joey another speculative grin and replied, "Ah, fence is a no brainer. In all honesty, cows can get through anything if they really want to, so we're basically just trying to keep it reasonably tight and patching up any major messes. The real key to keeping the cows in is moving them to another pasture before they're out of feed. They're pretty content when their bellies are full. Mostly, I just have to babysit Joey for the day. And I can use all the help with that I can get."

She rolled her eyes and stage whispered to Michael. "Mom named him Sean because he was so full of blarney. Don't encourage it. Are you back already? You haven't been all the way to New York and back this fast, have you?"

They started their horses moving as Michael replied, "I was hoping to undo the jet lag from the first trip by turning around and coming right back. Unfortunately, I don't think it really works that way. But I'm back. For a few days at least. I have to leave again in about a week for a little while. It's funny. New York feels differently after having lived out here for a few weeks." He grinned at her. "There are a lot of people in that city."

Laughing at him, she asked, "Do you think?" Studying his face again, she went on, "Did your meeting go well? You look happy. Even tired you look better."

Sean pulled ahead on the narrow trail and Michael hesitated before he said, "The meeting went okay. I am happier. Much happier in fact, but it wasn't the meeting. That's kind of what I wanted to ask you about." He glanced up at Sean's back. "But it can wait."

She met his eyes, wondering what he needed to ask her and nodded. "All right. Did you have breakfast?"

He grinned again. "Does cold cereal count? I had three bowls and it was the healthy kind."

"Just barely. What time did you get in? I didn't even hear you."

"I have no idea. The wee hours sometime. I almost hit a deer and decided to go slower in the dark."

The trail narrowed even further and she let him pull ahead of her and then they rode in silence for awhile. When it widened out again, Sean pulled up and got out a pair of binoculars and began to glass down the fence line to their left and Joey did the same thing on the other side.

After a minute or two of looking, Sean lowered his pair and said. "Anything on that side? I can see a place that needs work over this way. Do you two want to work together on that side and I'll go this way? We'll meet up down where the valley narrows near the gate. Your side is longer, but you can probably walk right down the fence line. This side is thick and I'm going to have to push through."

Joey looked at Michael and he shrugged and said, "Just tell me what to do."

She turned back to Sean. "See you in awhile then. I have the roll of patching wire in my bags. Whistle if you need it." With that, she headed out across the pasture toward the far fence line, picking her way through the trees and brush as she went, with Michael following behind her.

He didn't attempt to talk, even when the way opened up and so they rode in silence for nearly twenty minutes until she came to a spot where one of the fence stays had come undone and she got off and refastened it. Slowly they worked their way down the little valley, sometimes riding, sometimes working side by side on the fence mending, small talking back and forth, but mostly just enjoying the peace and tranquility.

It hadn't even taken them an hour to reach the gate that spanned the narrowest part of the valley where rocky cliffs jutted far out in a natural barrier, so she was surprised when Sean appeared just a minute or two later.

He glanced again from her to Michael and she had to wonder what he was thinking with that far too innocent look on his face, but she didn't say anything. Sean looked at his watch. "That part of the fence was actually in great shape. We're way ahead of where I thought we'd be. Can the two of you run up to the box canyon and look at those mares and I'll head over to Sweet Creek and go up that rim and work? When you guys come back out, you can go down the east side and then we'll follow it around and meet back at the northwest corner or where ever we get to."

Joey nodded. "That'll work. Take some wire with you." She dug in her saddle bag and unwound a portion of the roll she carried and handed it across to him. "I've got my phone, although it won't work until we get back out of the canyon if you need more. See ya."

Sean headed up a small trail back up the center of the valley at a lope and Joey got down to open the barbed wire gate. Over her shoulder to Michael, she said, "There's a possibility that there may be a rogue bull in this pasture. If you see something white, say something quick because he'll come after us and he means business. He's supposed to be up on the rim." She nodded up the steep cliff face above the gate. "Dad saw him up there last night, but Ruger thought he saw him down here. I'm sure my dad's right, but on the off chance that we see him, run. And I mean run. They didn't name him Rage for fun."

She held the gate wide and Michael went through with both horses and walked several feet in so she could get the gate closed as Michael said, "You're not on Wildfire today."

"No. He's too old to ride much. He's really mostly retired."

Once it was shut securely, she took her horse's reins to get back on. She had one foot in the stirrup and a hand on the horn and was swinging up when something roared out of the

111

thick brush beside them making the most ungodly noise Joey had ever heard. She'd heard the bulls fighting in the pastures and she knew exactly what it was, even though her back was to him. She turned her head just in time to see the Rage bull hit her and her horse with the force of a freight train.

As he hit them, he threw his head and pain exploded in her hamstring and hip as she flew over the horse's back and hit the rocky cliff ahead of them with her shoulder first. She hit hard enough to knock the wind out of her and pain filled her chest as well, as she frantically tried to claw her way up the rocks. She heard her horse make a horrible noise filled with pain and fear and tried to turn around to see where Michael and Jammer had ended up.

The small space between the steep sides of the canyon was filled with the raging bull and both plunging horses and dust billowed from underneath all of the scrambling hooves. At first she couldn't tell where Michael was.

Then the dust cleared enough for her to see him still astride Jammer, fighting his head and trying to back him away from where the bull had knocked her horse completely off its feet and was slamming it into the ground and pounding it with both his head and hooves while the horse screamed in terror.

In turning, she lost her tenuous hold on the rocks of the hillside and slid back down into the dust, almost back under the feet of the raging bull. The bull turned from the horse instantly and in looking toward her, it knocked her flying with its head and she hit the rocks again, this time with the side of her head.

It dazed her and she couldn't quite get her body to do what she was trying to make it do while she was aware of the seething violence that was going on around her. She paused for a split second to try and get a breath and strong arms caught her from behind and literally threw her up the side of the cliff face onto a small ledge several feet off the ground and then Michael scrambled up behind her.

She landed like a ragdoll and just laid there until she realized that the bull was actually trying to climb the cliff after them. When his head and a huge, cloven hoof came over the lip of the rock ledge almost into her face, she shied back instinctively and tried to drag herself upright to move higher into the rocks. Michael lunged toward her and half tackled her as he swept her higher up the broken cliff face.

They landed in a heap on a strip of dirt that was safely above the bull's reach, no matter how many times he bellowed and ran at the cliff below them. They didn't move for a moment or two, each of them too stunned by what had just happened in a matter of a few seconds. She could hear the bull still raging down there, but her horse had quit making any sounds and she feared for what she would see when she looked over.

Her head rang and throbbed and as she was finally able to take in a deep breath, it hurt so much that it brought tears to her eyes. Rolling over off of her face, she winced when she tried to move her leg where the bull had hit her the first time. She groaned and pushed her hair out of her eyes and looked up to see Michael watching her as he held the butt of his left hand against his side where blood smeared his shirt. He was breathing heavily and she wondered how badly he was hurt as well.

She laid her cheek back down on the ground and asked, "Are you okay?"

He nodded. "I'm fine. A little rattled. How are you?"

Hesitantly she admitted, "I . . . I'm not sure. I think I'm fine. Did Jammer get away?"

He leaned and looked over the edge to where the dust was still rising in waves from the fiendish bull below them. "I don't see him. He must have gone on up the canyon. Your horse didn't get away, I'm afraid." She closed her eyes and felt tears seep out of them and slide over her nose and across her cheek bone. That had been a sweet horse.

Jaclyn M. Hawkes

Chapter 17

Michael looked at her laying there face down in the dirt and tried to figure out what had just happened. He'd barely handed her the reins to her bridle when he thought he'd heard something in the brush. Turning his head left and right, he'd expected to see a deer emerge out of the thick stuff that grew between the narrow canyon walls, but instead he turned his head back toward Joey just in time to see a wall of white come crashing through the undergrowth on the other side of her, bellowing like a raging devil. It had hit Joey in mid air as she went to step into the saddle and then all perdition broke loose in front of him.

In a couple of split seconds, Joey had gone flying twice, her horse was down and dying and Jammer had spooked into full blown panic. Michael had tried to hold on to him, but when he saw the bull knock Joey aside a second time, he flew off his horse and without even thinking ran straight past the bull and literally threw her up the cliff face as he scrambled to get away from the bull as well. The image of its shaggy, curly head made him close his eyes to try to displace it as he could practically feel it's breath on his back again.

Laying here beside her on the narrow gravelly ledge, he put pressure on a cut on the side of his hand as he wondered how to start checking her for injuries without hurting her any more. He should have been the one to open the gate. He hadn't even realized they were at a gate and she was already down off her horse or he would have.

He dug his phone out and wanted to swear when he had no service, and she'd said hers had no service here either.

Sean had to have heard the ruckus and would hopefully either come back for them or go get more help.

Michael glanced again over the edge at the monstrous white raging beast below. Geez, he had never seen anything like this. This bull was crazed. Even now its head was a gory red after crushing the horse below so repeatedly into the rocks. Michael reached and put a gentle hand on Joey's hair and then rolled closer and put an arm around her still shaking shoulders. Her tears were puddling into the sandy dirt below her cheek.

Gently, he asked, "Joey, where are you hurt? What can I do to help you?"

She raised her head and he winced to see that it wasn't just tears that puddled into the dirt. Blood had smeared from a number of small cuts on her head and cheek where she'd hit the rocks. She put up a hand to wipe at her face and it was bloody too from where she'd clawed at the rocks to climb the cliff.

He sat up and tried to look her over. He'd seen the force the bull had hit the back of her left thigh with and he wouldn't be surprised if that leg was broken. Her jeans were stretched tightly over her thigh where it was already starting to swell and he didn't know where to even touch her to help her move.

"Should we try to move you, Joey? Or do you want to just lay there until Sean comes back? Do you think anything is hurt internally? I don't think we should try to get down from here until that bull is long gone."

She groaned again. "Just this morning my parents talked about getting rid of him. We raised him from a baby, but he just keeps getting worse, although he's never been anything like this. I carry a gun in my saddle bags, but there's no way to get down there to get it to shoot him. Can we even get to the saddle bags? I don't want to look."

"No. Don't. Can you move your leg at all? Is it broken? Tell me how to help you."

She gingerly rolled onto her right hip and then over onto her back and he could see the pain in her eyes. "I don't think it's broken. I don't think any of me is broken except my head. He really slammed it into the rocks. Can I just lay here?" She raised an arm to try to put it under her head, but then winced and put it back down to her side.

Scooting over against the rocks behind her, Michael helped her to gently raise her head so she could lay it in his lap. "Is that better or is it going to break your neck off?"

She sighed. "It's better. Talk to me to get my mind off all of this. What did you want to ask me this morning?"

As he smoothed her hair back from her face, she looked up at him with an almost questioning look and he said, "I wanted to ask you something, but maybe I'd better tell you something first."

She only continued to look at him and he gave her a mellow smile. "Your mom told me that you thought I was gay the other day. That I'd told you that. I'm sorry I gave you that impression. I'm really not, I promise. I wasn't saying that I'm not attracted to women. I was just saying that I wasn't attracted to the kind of women I'd known and didn't leave anyone back there who mattered to me."

Tiredly, she replied, "Oh, good. You seemed like far too masculine of a guy to be that way. I'm sorry I misunderstood."

She closed her eyes and he smoothed her hair back one more time and said, "You were good to me anyway. That was kind of you."

Almost dryly, she commented with her eyes still closed, "God doesn't approve of the lifestyle, but He loves gays too, Michael. Why should any of us be any less caring than Him?"

He gently rubbed a spot of crusted dirt off her cheek. "Actually, that's what I wanted to talk to you about. Tell me about God. How did you find out He was really there? And how have you gotten to know Him?"

She opened her eyes and looked up at him and he marveled at how blue her eyes were even when they were full of pain. She was quiet for several seconds and then said, "You know, Michael. I was blessed to be born to parents who knew God and I don't think I ever *found out* He was really there because they never let me forget Him. I knew He was there all along. This might be hard to understand, but I know it's true because I've seen it with my nieces and nephews.

"Babies come from heaven knowing God. It's like the veil between heaven and earth is thinner when they are first born or something. Even until they're two and three and four. They know God because they've been with him. If they are always taught about him they always know and understand. It's only when people aren't taught that they forget whose children they really are. I've always known. There hasn't been a day of my life that I haven't known He was there watching over me."

She looked up at him and another single tear escaped. "I'm so sorry you haven't had that. It must have been hard at times."

He sighed and leaned back against the rock face behind him and closed his eyes as well, as he thought about how he'd struggled when his father was dying and once he was gone. It was such a stroke of luck that he'd come here of all places afterward. Just as he thought that, he knew positively that it hadn't been luck at all. That there weren't many coincidences. As he realized, he actually got goose bumps, and then that same warm, sweet peace that he'd begun to understand was how this God communicated.

He felt her move on his lap and then a gentle hand wiped away the moisture that embarrassed him on his eyelashes. He blinked and rubbed his eyes. "Sorry." He let his breath out in a rush.

The same gentle hand that needed comfort far more than he did cupped his cheek for just a moment. "It's okay, Michael. Mourning is human. But you're not supposed to do it alone. Even Blue knows that."

He opened his eyes and looked at her again and knew he'd never be the same after having met Joey Rockland. Softly he admitted what had been haunting him for weeks, "It was my dad. He was my best friend." He rubbed his eyes and sighed and reached for her hand that rested on his leg beside her. "You can't imagine how hard it is to not know if there's a hereafter. It was killing me."

Squeezing his hand gently, she said, "God knew you were struggling, Michael. I hope that's why He sent you to us. I hope He was able to trust that we would help you. But if it hadn't been us, He would have sent someone else. He knows you and what makes you happy and what breaks your heart and what your dreams are and your fears. He absolutely knows us. It's just up to us to come to Him sometimes."

After a minute, he let go of her hand and reached to smooth the grimace of pain that wrinkled her forehead. "It's funny. I'm twenty-eight years old and feel like I'm just beginning to understand what I'm doing here. Or maybe it's not even that far. Maybe I'm just figuring out that I don't understand the point of any of this whole life thing at all. I feel like I'm in intellectual preschool all of the sudden."

"You need to give yourself more credit, Michael. Just the fact that you needed to know shows how discerning you are." She struggled to roll slightly and groaned. "I wish that bull would be quiet. He's ruining a very nice conversation."

The attempt to brush off how much she was hurting wasn't lost on him and although it had only been a few minutes, he knew Sean would have been back by now if he'd heard what was going on. There was a chance that he would have gone straight back to the ranch, but it was doubtful. If he'd heard, he probably would have at least tried to check on them.

Joey must have been reading his thoughts because she said, "I hate to tell you this, but I don't think Sean knows anything happened. He'd have been back long ago. I'm afraid we're either in for a long wait if that darn bull won't go away or a long walk if he does. Sean won't start to worry for awhile."

Michael smiled and eased her forehead again. "You're not really up to a long walk anyway, are you?"

Attempting to turn over again, she tried to smile and said tiredly, "I'm okay. You didn't know you were going to have such an exciting day today, did you? I'll bet you ate your cold cereal thinking you'd have a leisurely horseback ride."

"You would bet wrong, girl. I came all the way from New York City to talk to you. Ever since the other night when you prayed and I felt so much better, I've wanted to understand better. I want to know everything you know."

She gave him that weak smile again. "There are those who think I'm a dumb blonde. It might only take seven minutes to tell you everything I know."

Picking up a lock of her soft, pale hair, he shook his head. "No one who knows you thinks you're a ditz. If anyone thinks that it's just because you're so pretty that they don't think you could be smart."

"You don't have to give me any bologna just because I'm hurt, Michael. And it's my brothers who think I'm dingy sometimes. I accidentally made what they euphemistically called Salty Jell-O one time and will never live it down until the day I die."

"Salty Jell-O?" He chuckled. "I don't even cook and that still sounds impossible. I'll bet it was a riot growing up with that many brothers. You're the only girl right?"

"And the only mechanic. Something got turned around somewhere. Mom says I've needed to take things apart and fix them since I was six months old." Joey turned again slightly and beads of sweat stood out on her upper lip. "Do you think you could help me move or sit up or something? I need to adjust something. I wish I'd been able to grab my saddle bags. I have all kinds of stuff in there I'd like to get my hands on right now."

Slipping out from under her head, he knelt in front of her and reached to take her hands. "Tell where to help you. Should I pull or lift?"

"Pull. Just go slow." He did as she asked and she slowly tried to sit up, but her left hip and thigh were obviously too painful. Her foot started to shake and she stopped, half reclining, leaning on both arms. "I'm sorry, Michael. I can't do it. I'll have to lie back down. Let me just sit here like this for a minute."

Unsure of what to do to help her, he wished he'd worn a heavy coat or something he could pillow her with. Sitting back down, he turned toward her. "Here, try to lean against me and then when it gets too bad I'll help you move again. The bull sounds like he's winding down. If he ever wanders off, I'll go down and bring you your saddle bags and go get help."

She laid her head against his chest and sighed as she tried to relax. "Don't leave me. Dad and the guys will come."

He could hear the pain in her voice and put a gentle arm around her and started to knead the top of her shoulder where she was so tense. "This time, you talk to me to get your mind off the pain. Tell me about growing up on a huge ranch in Wyoming. Where did you go to school?"

For more than an hour he asked her questions and smiled at her stories of growing up in the middle of all those brothers. The bull finally left and when they could hear him bellowing far up the valley, Michael climbed down and wrestled her saddle bags free and brought them back up to her, trying to avoid the subject of her dead horse lying below them. After he'd helped her open her water bottle, and wash down some ibuprofen and shared her squashed sandwiches, he went to climb down again to begin the long walk home and she once more almost begged him not to leave her.

He sat back down and let her lay against him again, but he tried to reason with her, "Joey, it's still early afternoon. They might not know we're here for hours and you need medical attention. Let's get you some real pain medicine and have that leg x-rayed. Hadn't I better go now so we're not trying to figure out how to get you out of here in the dark?"

Without opening her eyes, she softly said, "They'll come."

He sighed and pulled her closer without bumping her leg and started to gently massage her head and neck and upper back where the pain made her so tense. "Okay. We'll wait together. Can you tell me where it hurts and I'll rub it." She winced when he hit a cut on her head. "Or not rub it. Sorry. Should I just leave you alone?"

"No. Please don't stop." She shook her head against his chest. "Your touch helps."

Settling more comfortably against the rock at his back, he thought, *You're right. Touching you helps.* She gave him hope and peace and enthusiasm. He hadn't felt that overwhelming sadness once all day, not even when they were talking about his father. He'd felt sad, but it had mellowed to a bittersweet sadness that remembered the good things about his dad more than his death.

Michael leaned his cheek against Joey's silky hair and enjoyed the warmth of her breath against his shirt. Even after riding horses and fixing fence and being tossed by a bull, she smelled like vanilla and jasmine. As she lay there and he touched her, he could hear the harmonies to her song playing in his head. There was something about her that just made the music come to him. Especially when she was so hurt, and felt so fragile here in his arms.

Twining his fingers through her hair, he tugged on it gently and whispered, "I'm so sorry I didn't open that gate for you."

Giving a minimal head shake without opening her eyes, she said, "Don't Michael. It's bad enough without that. My dad is going to be sick about this. He would never have sent us in here if he really thought something like this would happen. When he gets here, help me act like it's no big deal. He'll never forgive himself as it is."

"I am sorry. So much of this life is new to me that I always let you lead off, but I was a lazy gentleman to let you get it. Please forgive me."

Tiredly, she said, "You're forgiven. Where did you learn to ride so well?"

"I belong to a polo team back in the city. I learned to ride well without even realizing it."

"You do ride well." She sounded absolutely sleepy. "I wonder if Jammer's okay. I hope so."

"I'll bet he's fine. He was out of there as soon as I jumped off."

She raised her head to look up at him. "You jumped off? I thought you'd been knocked off. What did you jump off for?"

He pulled her head back against his chest. "Joey, you were falling right underneath that bull. He wanted to kill you. And you were still dazed from him knocking your head into the rock. Did you expect me to sit there and watch?"

"I knew that you'd saved my life, but I didn't realize you came into that mess on purpose just for me. Thank you. I would probably be down there with that poor horse if you hadn't."

He stroked her hair with his hand. "Shh, Joey. Don't think about it. Let's think about food. When we get back I'm going to eat three more bowls of cereal."

She laughed half-heartedly. "Are you starving? There's more food in my bags. Some granola bars and licorice I think.

Jaclyn M. Hawkes

And probably some beef jerky and Jolly Ranchers. Mom thinks it's funny that we all like Jolly Ranchers and that we love to joke around, so she always buys them for us. She must not get out much. She's pretty easily entertained."

"Beef jerky sounds like ambrosia right how." He dug into the bag and surfaced with the jerky. "Would you care to dine with me, mademoiselle?"

She shook her head once against his chest and tried to adjust her position again, but there was obviously nowhere she could escape the pain and his heart went out to her even more. He gently asked, "What do you need, Jo?"

"Uhh, morphine. Sorry I'm being so whiny. I'm not usually like this, I promise."

He pushed up the sleeve of her button down and stroked the skin of her arm and said, "I don't have any morphine, but I can tell you what helped my dad at the end when the pain was so bad. They encouraged him to try to imagine himself somewhere he loved to be, far away from the pain and to focus on what was there and what he loved about that place. At first I thought they were nuts, but it helped between doses. Touch helped, too. Touch releases endorphins."

Nodding slightly against him, she said, "Okay, I'm going to imagine that I'm sitting on the porch of my parents' house watching a thunderstorm rumble down the canyon at dusk."

Lifting her arm, he turned it so he could stroke the skin on the inside. "And what do you love about watching thunderstorms there?"

She sighed. "I love it all. The smell of the rain, the booms of the thunder as it rolls all the way down the gorge, crashing and echoing back and forth against the canyon walls. The flashes of lightning against those gorgeous dark clouds that hang right down into our valley and shroud the mountains. At sunset the clouds are bright pink and then turn purple and lavender and mauve. I love the way your skin feels so alive and sensitive when the lightning hits. I love it when my
124

whole family is out there together watching from rocking chairs pulled up under the porch eaves. I'll bet that sounds loony to you, but I really love it. Beautiful storms are one of my favorite gifts from our Father in Heaven."

Softly, he replied, "It doesn't sound loony. More like poetic. Now I can't wait for a thunderstorm here. Did it help you forget what all hurts?"

After a short pause, she sounded a little surprised when she said, "Yeah. It really did. That's amazing."

He smiled and put his chin back against her hair. "Where else would you imagine yourself?"

She shook her head against his chest. "I'm tired, Michael. Would you take a turn? Tell me where you'd go."

"Hmm, let me see. I'd go sailing out on a crystal blue ocean in the Caribbean where the sand is so white that you can see the bottom even under sixty feet of water. The waves are brilliant turquoise and the surf is white against them where it bubbles up onto the sand and the sails are that same pristine white against the bright sea and sky. Then the trees and plants are emerald green and the sky is a blue that goes on forever. You can hear the sea birds cry as they wheel across that endless blue on the crisp ocean breezes that taste of salt and sea and exotic flowers. The flowers are incredible and you can smell them even clear out on the water. The whole world there smells like Hibiscus.

When he left off, she yawned and said softly, "That sounds like heaven. I think I can smell tropical flowers. Tell me another one. Please."

He nodded and started to think where else he would go when she relaxed in his arms and he knew she'd finally gone to sleep. He looked down and then touched one finely arched blonde eye brow and whispered, "I'd go to a secluded valley in the tops of the mountains in Wyoming with a beautiful blonde enchantress who smells like Jasmine and vanilla. I'd hold her in my arms and look out over the ranges that glow

125

green at their bases and white at their peaks and listen to her tell me about the things she loves and what she believes— what she feels passionately about. And I'd breathe in the smell of her skin and the sweet smell of sage and wonder if I'd finally come home."

Chapter 18

She'd been sleeping for about forty minutes when he began to hear something and he listened intently, wondering if the bull had come back. It was Joey's father and brothers and they trotted up the little canyon in a tight cavalcade of seven horsemen. All of them with rifles either in their hands or in scabbards attached to their saddles.

When they got close to the gate, Michael put a hand over Joey's ear and whistled softly. All of them looked up the rugged cliffs on the canyon wall to where they sat. Getting down to open the gate for them, Sean looked up in shock when he saw the broken and bloody horse and saddle stomped into the rocks below them.

Rob himself came up the rocks with Sean and Rossen while the others stood guard and he winced when he saw his beautiful daughter lying there injured and scratched and cut up. He leaned down and touched her gently on the cheek and asked, "How bad is she? Is she asleep or unconscious?"

In a low voice, Michael told them what had happened and how the bull had stayed around for hours bellowing and thrashing the brush all around them. "He went somewhere up the canyon an hour or two ago, but Joey didn't want me to try to walk out. She knew you would come. But I don't think she can ride. Her leg is too painful to even bend."

Rob shook his head. "We called the search and rescue helicopter to stand by when we couldn't raise you on Joey's phone." He looked at Sean. "Can you call the helicopter in on your satellite phone? Maybe they can land in that clearing just below here. If not we'll have to carry her further down.

Then call Mother and have her head to the hospital. While we're waiting, we'll go shoot that . . . " He didn't finish his sentence and Michael wondered what he'd have called the killer bull if Michael hadn't been there.

Only several minutes later Michael heard the bull bellow again and then he heard a single gun shot and then nothing. Joey jumped at the rifle report and then slowly opened her eyes to look up at him. All she said before she closed her eyes again was, "I knew they'd come."

The seven riflemen filed back down the canyon with Jammer in tow and Joey woke up to smile bravely at all of them as they helped her out of Michael's arms and carefully passed her down the rocks strategically away from the horse below. He had to smile when Sean complained about how heavy she was and Cooper called her a fat lard and made a big show of struggling not to drop her.

When she was safely at the bottom, they fashioned a sling of sorts out of several metallic emergency blankets and then carried her to the clearing where the valley opened up just below. Michael watched her face as they went, knowing that she was in a lot more pain than she was letting on.

In the clearing, they gently set her down on a thick patch of grass and then Michael was at a loss as to what was going on when all seven of them crouched down in a circle around her and put their hands on her head. He stood to the side feeling conspicuously like an outsider when they talked quietly for a moment, then Sean put something on her hair and Rob said some kind of a prayer over her with all of them standing in.

When they finished, tears rolled down her cheeks and he wondered if they had somehow hurt her leg again. He wanted to go to her but didn't feel like it was his place and he was grateful when she caught his eye and smiled at him through her tears.

They only had to wait a few minutes before the helicopter flew in to pick her up, during which time Michael stood quietly to the side and watched these men caring for their sister and daughter. He'd known at that first dinner that they were tight, but watching them now was almost mind boggling.

All of them except Slade looked remarkably like Rob and though Joey was more like Naomi, she had the same blonde hair and dark skin they all had and it was like watching a small battalion of bodyguards with her. They teased her mercilessly, but the respect was unmistakable and it made him respect all of them that much more in return.

When the helicopter landed, two men jumped out and began to help load her into the patient toboggan. Michael was surprised that she appeared to know one of them and the man leaned down and put a gentle hand to her cheek as he talked to her.

Michael was still wondering what the feeling was that he'd experienced when the EMT had touched her so tenderly as Slade came up to him and told him he needed to go in the chopper with them. Michael didn't know what was going on, but he climbed in the chopper and buckled in and it lifted off almost immediately.

As he was climbing in, the man who had touched Joey's cheek was giving her a shot that he hoped was a pain killer. He and Rob and the other EMT buckled into seats with Joey right in front of Michael and as they flew, she looked at Michael and smiled in spite of the pain he could see in her face. She reached up and took his hand and held it tensely, then closed her eyes.

He rubbed his thumb over the back of her hand and looked up to find Rob and the EMTs watching him closely. Between the seven Rocklands and then these two, he was feeling decidedly like it would be death by firing squad at any moment if he made a wrong move toward her.

He almost let go of her hand just because he didn't want to cause any trouble for her. He was only a neighbor who had happened to be there when she got hurt and had then attempted to help her. And he'd done his level best to try to protect her. It wasn't like he was making any inappropriate claims here. He wanted to say these thoughts out loud to her dad and the others, but he was still inordinately pleased when she held tightly to his hand during the entire flight over the mountains and into Jackson Hole.

Naomi met them at the emergency entrance as they wheeled her in and as she went past him, Naomi squeezed Michael's arm and then they hustled away with Joey

Once inside the hospital as Michael went into a curtained cubical with an older doctor, he could hear Joey in the one next door talking to the EMT who had given her the shot in the helicopter and Michael began to figure out that the EMT wasn't actually an EMT, but was her doctor friend. She was half whining when Michael heard her say, "I love you dearly, Seth, but I still don't want you to examine my hamstring. We're too good of friends."

He heard the doctor reply, "I'm a doctor, Joey and you're hurt. We'll keep you covered up. Stop whining and don't tell me that you love me if you won't marry me. It's mean."

Joey made a sound of outrage. "You just cut my favorite pair of jeans! It's taken me years to break these babies in! Send in Dr. Allen. He's been working on me since I was born. You can read the x-ray."

"Dr. Allen is a pediatrician, Joey. You're twenty-four years old. Be quiet, this is going to hurt."

He heard her groan and then say, "Michal is twenty-eight and Dr. Allen is working on him. And how come I have to wait for a plastic surgeon when he doesn't have to?"

Her doctor, Seth, replied patiently, "He's cut on his hand, not his face."

Michael could hear the sound of scissors again and then he heard Naomi say almost reverently, "Oh, Joey."

Joey replied, "I'm okay, Mom. Honest. Would you ask Dr. Allen to come in here and send Seth out? Wow, Seth, whatever you just put in that IV feels really warm; what was it?"

"I'm Dr. Weston, not Seth to you right now. Especially if you won't marry me. It was a sedative to chill you out. Go to sleep and let me look at you."

Her voice sounded mellower almost instantly, "Someday you're going to thank me for not marrying you when the right Mrs. Weston comes along. You're hurting me."

The doctor was apologetic. "Sorry. I have to get the dirt and rocks out. I may have found Mrs. Weston actually. There's this great new first grade teacher over in Thayne."

"Oh, Seth that's wonderful! Really? You found her?"

"No, I just wanted to see your reaction when you're drugged. Dang it. You really aren't ever going to tell me yes, are you?"

Sleepily, Joey apologized, "I'm so sorry, but no. I shouldn't marry you when I'm not in love with you."

Gently Dr. Weston said, "I know, Joey. I'm just teasing you. Is the pain under control? I'm sending you to radiology."

"I'm fine. Thank you for helping me. I feel so much better. Sorry I was a pill."

Her doctor chuckled. "It's okay. Go to sleep and they'll bring you right back to me. Don't flash anyone in the hall."

She sounded like a little girl as she assured him, "I won't. I promise. Do I still have to get stitches?"

Michael heard them push her out into the hall and he looked up at the smiling Dr. Allen as he was stitching up the cut in his hand and asked, "Has she always been like that?"

"Since the day she was born. She ought to marry him. He knows how to handle her and he's a good man." He finished the last stitch, tied it off and clipped it. "Keep this dry for a couple of days and I'll see you in ten days to remove them. If they get inflamed come back in." He taped over them and then reached to shake Michael's other hand. "It was good to meet you Michael. Thanks for saving her. We're glad you were there. This country would never get over being without Joey Rockland."

Michael shook his head. "No, I imagine not. Thanks again."

Dr. Allen pulled back the curtain between the two cubicles. "You can just wait for them there in the chair. They shouldn't be long. You live out at the ranch with them, don't you?"

Nodding, Michael answered as Joey's doctor friend Seth looked over at him, "In Merv Harris' house."

The sharp looking young doctor stepped across and shook his hand. "Seth Weston. Yes, thank you for helping her. She and I are friends from awhile back."

Michael grinned. "I gathered that. Do you really want to marry her?"

The young physician smiled as he wrote on the chart in his hand. "Oh, I'd marry her in a heart beat. She's a wonderful girl, but she isn't interested. No, it really would be a mistake. I was just teasing her to get her mind off her leg. It had to have been killing her. She's black and blue clear to her knee. Where are you from?"

"New York City."

"You the nephew?"

"The nephew's friend."

Dr. Weston nodded. "Merv was a good man. Keep taking care of her if she'll let you. I'll be right back."

As the young man walked out, Michael leaned back against the wall in the chair. He'd taken care of her today, but she'd been the one to take care of him all the rest of the time. She was the one to be able to help him get away from the gray

132

emptiness and understand God was there, and he'd do anything in his power to try to repay that, but that wasn't something he could explain to these doctors.

After just a few more minutes, they wheeled her back in, dead asleep on the gurney in a hospital gown. Rob and Naomi were with her and as another doctor came in and began to clean up the cuts on her face and head to begin stitching them, Naomi came over to Michael and he stood up. As she embraced him, tears came to her eyes and she whispered, "They told me what happened. I'm so grateful that you're both okay. I'm sorry you ended up in that mess, but thank you for saving her."

He hugged her back, surprised that hugging her was immensely more comfortable than hugging his own mother. "You're welcome. I'm sure she'd have made it up the hill even if I hadn't been there, but I'm glad I could help. She's an amazingly tough young woman, Naomi." He knew he was trying to reassure himself as well as her as they waited for the x-ray to reveal if Joey's femur was broken. Either way she was going to be laid up for awhile and he knew it.

Naomi pulled back and wiped her eyes. "She is. And she'll be fine. But I'm still so glad you were there."

Dr Weston came back in carrying the packet of x-rays and hung two of them up against the light on the wall. "I don't think her leg is broken, but it's terribly contused, and her hip was badly sprained when the bull hit her. All of those tendons and ligaments were pulled and strained and she's going to be extremely sore for awhile." He turned to Rob and Naomi. "These stitches should just take another minute. Do you want me to admit her and we'll take care of her here for a day or two, or do you want to take her home and baby her?"

Naomi asked, "What do you think is best?"

"Honestly, you'd be the best medicine if you're able to help her around. She'd rest better at home and you are the queen of mothering." He smiled at Naomi. "The only benefit to having her here is a moveable bed and lots of help taking care of her. All she needs medically for a few days is pain medicine and to stay off it as much as possible. She's going to hate crutches, but there's no help for it. After a few weeks we'll consider some rehab. And he'll take those stitches out of her face in probably five days. She's in great shape and it should heal quickly."

Naomi nodded thoughtfully. "I'll take her then." She looked over at Michael. "Can you help me get her into the Suburban while Rob runs to the office?"

Michael replied to this woman he'd grown in such a short time to respect remarkably, "You two just tell me what to do."

"Can you try to wake her up while I call home and tell them we're coming?" Turning to Dr. Weston she asked, "Would she be more comfortable lying in the back, do you suppose? What's going to be best for her leg?"

After thinking for a moment, he replied, "I'd guess the back. I'll have a nurse round up some pillows for you."

As the plastic surgeon finished with her, Michael went to Joey and began to talk to her. She only sighed and turned her head and he touched her on the shoulder and kept trying. Dr. Weston came to stand beside him and took the IV out of her arm and taped a bandage over the site. When Michael brushed her hair back from her face, she finally opened her sleepy blue eyes and looked up at him and smiled. "Hello, Michael." She looked over at Dr. Weston and smiled at him, too. "Hey, Seth. What do you two want?"

Dr. Weston replied. "I'm sending you home. Your leg isn't broken. How are you feeling? You up to a ride in the Suburban?"

"Sure, I'm fine."

She closed her eyes and was instantly back to sleep and Dr. Weston murmured, "The sedative certainly worked. Let her sleep until we're ready to move her from the gurney to the truck." He looked up. "Oh, good. Here are the pillows."

134

Michael and Naomi both took an armful of pillows and headed outside and placed them in the back of the Suburban where Naomi had pulled it up to the doors and laid the seats flat. Back inside Dr. Weston gave Naomi a handful of papers and a small pill bottle with some white tablets, then with the help of two nurses they wheeled the bed outside to the waiting truck.

Joey was having trouble waking up and they weren't sure how it would be easiest to get her in. Finally, Michael put an arm carefully under her legs and shoulders and gently picked her up, blankets and all. She opened her eyes and held onto him around his neck as he gingerly sat down in the rear of the SUV and then scooted forward to help her in, with Naomi and Dr. Weston watching. Once she was far enough in that she could stretch out reasonably well, he pulled the pillows into place and went to set her down on them.

She grimaced as he tried to ease her onto the pillows. Holding her breath, she attempted to help him and he could see the pain come up in her eyes and said, "Tell me what to do, Joey. Where will you be the most comfortable?"

She sighed. "I'm sorry. I'm not sure. Just don't put me down on my hip."

He reached and tried to help her down onto the other hip and she gasped again. "Sorry, that's just killing me."

Dr. Weston leaned in and asked Michael, "She's okay there on your lap. Could you stand to ride like that for sixty miles? That way you wouldn't have to hurt her when you pick her back up at the house."

Michael looked down at her. "Are you okay like this if I just stay back here with you? Are you too uncomfortable?"

She shook her head. "I'm fine, but I'm too heavy. Just set me down and I'll be okay. I'll squish you if you have to sit like that the whole way."

Michael looked up at her parents and Dr. Weston. "Go ahead and close the door. I'll be fine. Let's just get her home."

Dr. Weston looked in and met his eyes for a moment and then said, "Take care of her." For a second or two Michael didn't know how to respond to the warm brown eyes that were handing over the guard and he finally nodded without saying anything. Before he'd felt like Dr. Weston didn't trust him, but just now he knew he was being offered her guardianship and he took it willingly, although he regretted hurting this man's feelings. He obviously did love Joey a great deal.

With the door shut behind them, Michael rested her good hip on his legs and reached to pack pillows around her to support her during the trip. Rob and Naomi got in and started up and Michael leaned his back against the seat back behind and pulled Joey closer into his arms. He raised one knee and put a pillow on it to cradle her head and she sighed as she closed her eyes again and went back to her sedated sleep almost instantly. Rob drove away from the hospital as Michael reached down and pulled Joey's hair away from her face and neck, wishing he could do more to help her be comfortable.

Naomi turned the radio on low and Rob drove fast on the straight flat stretches, glancing backwards at the two of them from time to time as Michael tried to cushion Joey from the bumps and turns as best he could. She only woke up a handful of times on the entire trip and when she did, after the second it took her every time to figure out where she was, she invariably smiled up at him.

When they hit the gravel road, she woke up again and grimaced just for a second before giving the gentle smile. He smiled back down at her. "Good morning, sleepy head. How are you doing?"

She tried to move a little and he pulled her up tighter against him to try to ease her as she answered, "I'm fine, thanks. Just a little stiff. Am I killing you?"

He ignored her question as he glimpsed the pain in her eyes when she struggled to move and he knew she would say

136

she was fine even if she was miserable. Brushing her hair back gently again, he told her, "You can be honest with me, Joey. Tell me what to do to make you comfortable."

She sighed and leaned her head on his shoulder. "I'm sorry, Michael. Honestly, I feel lousy, but I hate to whine. Do you think you could touch me again and talk to me like you did this afternoon? You helped me so much. Tell me another place you'd go to imagine yourself away from here."

After thinking about that for a minute, he ran a hand up her arm and said, "There's a place in upstate New York that I love. It's a horse farm with beautiful rolling green fields and white rail fences. The pastures are full of sleek mares with foals that buck and pester their mothers and run and then go back to them and nurse and lay down to sleep every bit as hard as they play. After awhile, they get back up and buck and play again, knowing they were born to run—to be the most beautiful athletes in the world. To someday race for the roses against other sleek, shiny, racy horses that were born to run as well."

He rubbed her shoulder and upper arm as he continued, "At dawn the sun comes up and burns the mist off the grass, just like it does here in Wyoming. That pure yellow light that slants sideways and reveals the dew drops on the grass and dust motes in the alleyways of the barns. In the evening, the light changes again to make the pastures glow emerald and the horses glisten as they graze in the glory of the sunset.

"And then, when the sun has gone down, the whole world mellows and softens and the peace that settles in with the purple shadows is almost tangible. It slowly fills in all the hollows and valleys like lavender smoke that sinks and thickens until finally, sunset fades to dusk that fades to twilight and finally fades to night. Black velvet night that hides the owls and the nighthawks and the white tail deer that sneak out among the horses to feed.

"In the fall the leaves change overnight on the first frost and the whole world turns brilliant red and orange and gold.

The days turn brisk and the nights are crisp and cold and the fruit in the orchards ripens. You can smell it in the air.

"Even in the winter there, it's like a Christmas postcard with the snow covered hills and red barns and horse drawn sleighs. In the winter you can smell the wood smoke from fireplaces and the horses grow shaggy and look like a calendar of some wild island in Europe. Their manes fall over their faces and their fetlocks look like the Budweiser Clydesdales."

He gently rubbed the crease on her brow and her temple before he went on, "Then, just when you can't face any more snow, the sun comes out and melts it all away and the hillsides get that hint of green that grows and deepens as the buds on the trees swell. Then one day, they burst into miles of sweet blossoms as the pastures below them glow emerald green once more, and the mares drop their foals and it starts all over again."

He stopped talking, thinking she had fallen asleep, but she sighed and snuggled into his neck and whispered without opening her eyes, "I've never known anyone who can describe something like you, Michael. You have an incredible gift. I love it when you tell me."

Leaning his cheek on her soft hair, he asked, "But did it help you forget feeling lousy?"

"Absolutely. Thank you."

He gently touched the backs of her fingers with his. "You're welcome."

Chapter 19

Joey woke up in the middle of the night, wondering for just a second where she was and why everything hurt so badly. It all came rushing back and she groaned as she tried to sit up in bed and reach for the pain pills her mother had set on the bedside table of her old room in her parents' house. She was groggy and clumsy and she accidentally knocked the pill bottle over. It rolled off the table and onto the floor.

She couldn't even turn over to look at it, let alone reach for it and she sighed as she leaned back against the pillows, wondering if she could stand the pain for awhile longer or if she should call out for her mother and drag her out of bed. Her mom had spent the entire evening waiting on Joey, hand and foot, and Joey knew she'd finally gone off to bed tired to the bone after such a stressful day.

Just when she'd decided that the pain was overwhelming and she had to wake her mother, she heard something and looked toward the door to see Cooper poke his head in and whisper, "You up, Jo? Was that you I heard groaning?" He advanced into the room, and came to sit on the edge of her bed. "What do you need? Or are you just being a baby?"

"Help me turn over, Coop. Just a little. I think I'm beached and I'm dying. Could you hand me that pill bottle I knocked off?"

He gently rolled her about an eighth turn, being careful not to bump her thigh and hip as he gave an exaggerated grunt and teased her, "Holy beluga! I'll say beached! You weigh like a ton! What did you eat at that hospital? It's no wonder you can't roll. You are going on a *die utt*!"

Retrieving the pill bottle, he shook one out and handed it to her and then held the cup with the bendy straw for her so she could swallow it. "Hadn't you better eat something with that? These things make you slathering drunk, you know. You were practically swooning over Michael when he carried you in. It was so embarrassing."

"Oh, stop. I was not. He's just a very good nurse and I appreciated it. But yes, I'd better have a bite of something with it. Medicine sort of affects me double. Didn't Mom leave some grapes there in a bowl?"

Picking up the bunch of grapes, he held them above her face and let her bite one right off of the bunch. "Look at you. You think you're one of those fancy Roman Emperors. You probably want me to find one of those palm fronds to come and fan you with, too. Don't you? Hey, I could probably come up with some sage brush. That would work."

"Cooper, quit torturing me. I'm sick. I have a gargantuan boo boo."

He held the grapes again. "So what is this guy like? Mom thinks he's a hero, but I think Dad is wondering. I think he's worrying that you're going to fall in love with a pretty boy non-member from clear across the world. You're not dumb enough to really do that, are you?"

Joey sighed, grateful for the darkness. "I don't even really know him, Coop. He's only been here a few weeks and he's pretty private. And no, I'm not going to fall in love with a non-member."

She paused as she remembered how good he had been to her through the whole long painful day yesterday. "But honestly, he's very sweet. He was so careful with me when I was miserable. He talked to me to help me get my mind off of how much I hurt, and he held me the whole way home from the hospital so that my leg didn't throb so much. That couldn't have been much fun as tall as I am. But he never complained once."

"That's just because you'd flattened the air right out of him and he couldn't get a breath to say hellup, I can't, gasp, breathe." Cooper was mimicking the sloth on Ice Age as he teased her and he made her laugh there in the dark.

"Don't make me laugh, Coop. It hurts. Give me back the grapes. Are you going to the singles ward in Jackson tomorrow?"

"No. Treyne and I and Lee are going to the employee branch at Jackson Lake Lodge at nine to meet girls. Why?"

"Just wondered. Why don't you invite him? That's why he came with me yesterday. He wanted to ask me about God."

Cooper gave her more grapes. "Heck, no! I'm not going to church with someone that beeyooteeful! The girls won't even notice me. Make Mom take him. She's the one who thinks he's marbelous."

Joey shook her head. "No, he won't want to go to the family ward. The branch would be better. He'd feel less conspicuous with the younger singles, even if he is gorgeous. And you're every bit as gorgeous as he is. Plus you have all that personality that he doesn't. The girls aren't going to ignore you."

"Me thinketh that the invalid doth protest too loudly."

"That's not exactly the way the quote goes, Coop, but I get your drift. He is very handsome, isn't he?"

"I am *not* answering that. Especially not after you thinking he liked men. How could you think something like that? He's as not that way as they come."

She yawned and defended herself, "I thought he told me that. Not that he seemed like it. So, will you take him to church?"

"You're too late. Isabel and Slade already made arrangements for him to go with them. He apparently knew Isabel before. Did you know that? And he actually wrote some of Kit's songs. Kit and Rossen and the girls are going to ride with them. He'll either join or become a monk after attending with Mimi and Gracie and Cody. Mormons can be monks too, you know."

"The joke was Buddhist, not monks, Coop."

"Really?" He gave her more grapes. "But monks have those great long hoodies. You like him, Joey. Your voice is completely different when you talk to him. Or about him. And you let him hug you all the way home and you liked it. Something's weird here."

There was a long silence before she said in almost disbelief, "I did like it, didn't I?" They both thought about that for a few seconds and then she said confidently, "It had to be the medicine. I'm not that way."

"What about when we got to you yesterday? You'd fallen asleep in his arms and you hadn't had any medicine."

"I was pretty hammered, Coop. And I'd had Ibuprofen. You can't count that. It wouldn't be fair."

"Okay, but what about last night? Even once you were home, you didn't want him to leave."

"Pain medicine. That doesn't count either."

"No way. You gotta count one of them. That's too easy."

"No. I refuse to be railroaded here. Nothing I do counts until I'm completely drug free."

"Okay, but the *only* reason I'm letting you get away with this is because I refuse to be a party to you becoming an old maid. And if you marry him, I get all the credit. But no marriage until he's officially baptized." He gave her more grapes and then got up. "If you get beached again, call my cell. Mom's tired. Is your phone where you can reach it?"

"Yes, thanks."

"No problem."

"Love you, Coop."

"Love you too, my little beluga."

For Joey

Chapter 20

Clicking on the light over his piano music, Michael settled himself on his piano bench and began to play. It was four o'clock in the morning, but he wasn't awake because he was sad or having the nightmare. Tonight he couldn't sleep because he was thinking about the beautiful, blonde tomboy who was over there recuperating at her mother's place after being nearly killed by a bull yesterday.

He thought back to his posh, New York lifestyle and shook his head at the massive paradigm shift that had occurred in his life in the last weeks. He shook his head to himself at the thought of a shaggy, curly headed Charolais monster bull attacking Margot on Fifth Avenue.

As his thoughts went back to Joey and how good she had felt in his arms yesterday, both in the canyon and in the Suburban, the strangest thing happened to the music. The depth of feeling and the expression became surreal and the dynamics took on a spirit of their own as the clearest and purest harmonies poured out of him. The melody that was as graceful and delicate as a ballerina danced lightly from the keys under his hands and the sweetness of the sound was as near as he'd ever come to expressing pure emotion. Pure peace and joy.

He sat at the bench and played until the need to honor her with sound and rhythm and feeling exhausted him again and he got up and went outside and sat on his little porch and looked across the valley toward her. She was over there. Torn and bruised and sore, but sweet and kind and generous

143

and honest. There wasn't a sneaking, conniving, underhanded bone in her body and the more he was around her, the more he liked and respected her and wanted to be around her.

He enjoyed her and wanted to know more about her and wanted to understand what she understood and what made her tick and what she loved and what her goals and hopes and dreams were and what her struggles were and . . . He wanted it all.

Getting up, he went back inside, searching his feelings as he went. This was the closest he'd ever come to honestly falling in love in his life and it was incredibly nice and incredibly disturbing at the same time. They couldn't have been more different, but their friendship had been comfortable from literally the first meeting when she'd fallen asleep on his couch, tired and hungry and damp from the rain. Even then she had been beautiful and fascinating. Even then she'd had the most amazing, sweet, warm, comfortable spirit about her and he must have recognized that even as emotionally tired as he'd been then.

Getting back into bed, he compared how he'd felt driving here to how he felt now and the change was nothing short of miraculous. He still missed his dad desperately, but now he realized it had been so much more than just his father's death. It had been a draining combination of grief and being spiritually bereft and royally burnt out with society. The three of them had been a disaster for him. She'd helped him deal with the loss of his father and introduced him to God and made him know that high society and worldly women with an eye on his fortune would only suck his life out.

Her and Blue and Naomi. Even the others here had helped him to be able to see himself and his life more clearly. The people here had a way of lifting him while they accepted him unconditionally. It brought the best out in him and he'd been able to relax and let his guard down among them. The two who knew who he was and what his life was really like, treated him just like everyone else did and he had found this place to be more comfortable than anywhere he'd ever been.

He turned over and gathered his pillow into his arms. He was going to call Doc tomorrow and ask him if he'd be willing to sell him this place. That was after he'd gone to see how he could help Joey and gone to church for the first time in his life. He wanted to learn all he could about God. He had to make up for a lot of lost time.

He also had to make up for years of missing out on being with a truly nice girl. He'd been about four when he'd caught on to the cynicism of his father about females. It wasn't that his dad had taught him not to like girls. Just not to trust them. And Michael had consistently learned that his father had been right. Without fail, the ones who had pursued him hadn't been trustworthy.

The saddest part of it was that even his own mother had helped to cement that impression for him. In a way it was good. He'd made it through until he was twenty-eight and could meet Joey without turning out like a lot of the other guys he'd grown up in the same circles with.

There was almost no one who lived all that respectably in his estimation. Rich boys tended to be lazy and self-indulgent and make stupid decisions about things like women and drugs and politics. That was probably why his father had ended up his best friend in the first place.

His father had tried all along to tell him that because he'd been born into a long line of incredibly wealthy families more was required of him and not less. His father had encouraged him to see his families' wealth as a legacy to be taken care of and guarded and enhanced instead of squandered and wasted on loose women and addictive habits. Sure he'd had his share of expensive toys, but even at that he'd learned moderation. He smiled into the dark. He drove a Ferrari, but at least he only had one and he'd had it for four years.

As he drifted off to sleep he thought about Joey again. She'd probably love that car. She'd look really good in it.

****

Joey was awake and had been helped into the great room and settled on the couch so she could be a part of breakfast, when Michael knocked on the door and walked in looking like a million bucks the next morning with Blue at his heels. He was in a suit, tie, and Italian shoes, and that haunted look was all but gone from his eyes as he stepped in and came straight toward her lying on the couch. Crouching down next to her, he studied her face for a second before he asked, "How are you?"

She put up a hand to her hair, wishing she'd been up to a shower before he saw her. "I'm fine, thanks. You look very nice. How's the hand?"

He glanced at the stitches in the edge of his hand, but only shrugged and asked her, "How did you do last night? Were you able to rest at all?"

Wondering whether to be honest or not, she smiled. "I slept fine as long as that sedative Seth gave me had me knocked loopy. I take it that you're headed out to church. I wish I were going with. Have you eaten?"

"Yes, I have, Mother." He smiled at her. "And no I didn't feed Blue a Pop Tart. I brought him to you. He's helped put me back together some and I figured you were in worse shape than me now and better have him back."

She searched his eyes for a minute, put her hand on top of his and then said quietly, "You do look much better, Michael. And after this morning, you'll be even better. Enjoy the Spirit that you'll feel there. It will fill up the cracks in your armor." He only looked at her and she wasn't at all surprised that he knew what she meant.

He squeezed her hand as he stood back up. "I wish you were going with as well. Can I come see you this afternoon?"

"Absolutely. I want to hear all about church. Have you been much before?"

He shook his head. "Never. I'm as heathen as they come, I'm sorry to say. I hope I can figure out how to behave."

Joey rolled her eyes. "You may not have attended church, Michael, but you can't fool me. You have too nice a spirit about you. Hurry and grab something else to eat. My mother made this breakfast thing that is to die for. And watch out for the stink bugs."

His eyes narrowed, questioning as Naomi came over to him and handed him a plate with a cheery, "Good morning, Michael." Naomi gave Joey a severe look, but then to Michael she said, "Ask Sean. He'll tell you about the stink bugs. The blonde one is the one you really have to watch out for."

Joey laughed. "Mother, I can't believe you. Where is your lecture about being Christ-like?"

"I'll give you the lecture later. Right now we have to help Michael be prepared so he can have a good experience." Turning back to Michael, she said, "Don't worry, the others will run interference for you. I'll bring you a glass of milk. Sit down in the chair right here."

Joey cracked up again as Michael obediently sat and then looked around at all the breakfast hubbub. Everyone had come, including a couple of the ranch hands and they had all transformed from belted, booted, jeans wearing ranchers into the neatly dressed and pressed churchgoers that they were. But it was still quite an energetic gathering.

There were four high chairs and both the big dining tables were filled, and although they were all dressed up, there was still a great deal of hilarity going on. Cooper tended to carry a wave of humorous energy with him everywhere he went, not to mention the rest of the bunch. It was pretty plain that Michael wasn't used to the way the Rocklands got ready to go to church.

When he looked over at her again, she assured him, "It isn't always this crazy, I promise. But on Sundays usually everyone shows up for breakfast. Mom says that it's easier for her to cook for everyone so they can focus on finding all the little missing shoes and brain squeezers."

Again, Michael gave her a lost look and she went on, "Those cute little headbands the babies have on." She nodded toward the four little girls in the gathering. "They tend to get ripped off and left lying wherever the little beauty queens get tired of wearing them. Are there no little girls in your family?"

"Joey, I was the only child of two only children. There are no little anything in my family."

"I'm so sorry. You'd better marry someone with a bunch of family to make up for it then. You're in for a huge treat. They are the most fun you can imagine. You're handling all of this quite well, under the circumstances."

He gave her a weak smile. "Which is good, because I thought I was going to get shot yesterday for letting you get hurt on my watch. You should have seen your brothers and your dad ride up with all those rifles. It was like a John Wayne movie on steroids. And your Dr. Weston and Dr. Allen weren't very thrilled with me either."

"Sorry, they can be a little intimidating I'm told. But I never question whether they love me."

"No. I wouldn't question that either. But I'm surprised anyone from school ever dared to ask you out."

"Don't worry. I had tons of brothers that all had friends. I thought it was a smorgasbord." He looked at her and she smiled. "Should I not have admitted that?"

Michael grinned. "Honesty is always good, I guess. You probably didn't get a whole lot of privacy. I'll bet the whole county knew when you kissed someone."

"Oh, now kissing was a whole different issue. They honestly didn't dare kiss me. Usually that was okay, but every once in while I wanted someone to kiss me and it was the pits. Do you want some more breakfast?"

148

He glanced down at his empty plate. "No, I'm fine thanks. You were right, it was great. I've never met anyone like your mom. I wish I had. I might have had a better attitude about women." She had to smile at that and he back pedaled, "You know what I mean, don't you?"

"Yes, actually. She is the best. She's my hero. She loves everyone and it's completely sincere. She even loves the ones who are hard to love and it works miracles. But you don't want to tick her off. She's no marshmallow. Under that sweet smile there's steel."

"You're not trying to tell me that she wants to shoot me too, are you?"

"Heavens no. I'm just saying that she washed our mouths out with soap if we cussed and you're in more trouble than you can ever imagine if you're caught lying. You'd be better off to admit that you robbed a bank than lied to my mom."

Just then Naomi came over to him and handed him another plate of her breakfast casserole. "Why are you looking so guilty, Michael? You'd better hurry; you need to leave in just a few minutes." Then she turned to Joey. "Do you need help turning, honey? Or are you doing okay?"

"I'm good, Mom. Thanks." Naomi left and Joey smiled up at Michael. "I think she just busted you for something. You can never fool my mother either."

He chewed a bite and then said, "You're making me paranoid. Is there anything I need to know before I go?"

"Just that you look great and that you're a child of God. He'll take care of the rest."

"I'm not going to have to tell all my sins, or smoke anything or something?"

Joey laughed. "That's all we need is someone smoking in church. Now that'd be something the congregation would never forget! You're fine, Michael. And your sins are between you and Heavenly Father. Don't worry.

149

"That's easy for you to say. Now I'm paranoid again."
He got up and reached down for her hand. "Hurry and get
better so you can come to church with me and tutor me. This
is all new to me and I need instruction."

Joey shook her head. "Michael, don't you usually try to
follow your conscience?"

"Yes, why?"

"Then it's not all new to you. Your conscience is
Heavenly Father's Spirit helping you to make the right
decisions. You're going to find that He is a god of logic and
reasoning and order, and it all makes sense and goes right
along with your conscience. You're obviously a good person.
All of the good, right things you've done in your life are part
of following God. Just because you haven't yet studied
formal religion doesn't mean that you haven't been good.
You just need to understand the big picture. It'll come. Just
listen to that feeling. Sweet and warm and peaceful is right,
and anxious and worried is wrong. Just listen."

He squeezed her hand. "I will. See you in awhile."

Chapter 21

Joey had gotten a little behind on the pain medicine and she was struggling while she waited for the medicine to take effect, when they all came piling back in almost four hours later. Michael came straight over to her again and looked at her before asking, "Did you not take your medicine soon enough?"

She was reclining on the couch and shook her head with a tired smile. "I fell asleep and didn't realize. How did you do? Any smoking?"

He smiled back at her. "No smoking. Did you try to make your mind take you someplace out of the pain?"

"No." She tried to smile at him again, but it didn't work very well. "I needed this eloquent man to coach me, but he was off with the stink bugs. How did that go, by the way?"

"Oh, I was fine. The stink bugs were apparently only interested in Treyne and Cooper, and they were someplace else. Let me go see if your mom needs my help. If not, I'll come talk to you." He went over and talked to Naomi and then came back. Slipping off his jacket, he gently lifted Joey's head, sat down, then let her lay her head on him as he began to smooth her hair back and rub her forehead. "Ruger and Marti are helping her cook. If I rub your head will that help?"

"Yes, thank you." They sat there in silence for several minutes while he soothed her head and finally she said, "If you want to talk about church or have any questions, will you just ask? Otherwise I'll leave you alone and assume that it's private. What are they cooking?"

He answered absently mindedly, "I think she said rack of lamb." He ran his fingers through her hair for a few minutes and she tried to focus on his touch and not the pain. She turned her head gingerly and he rubbed the other side and finally said, "There was a lesson today on something called the plan of salvation. Do you know what that means?"

"Yes." For a few more minutes he was quiet and then he asked, "Is there anywhere I could get any books or information on what they were talking about?"

"Sure. I'll ask Mom to get you some and you can go on the official website. It's mormon.org. It's way user friendly. Or any of my family would have some. It's a very intriguing concept, isn't it?"

He nodded and after a few more minutes, murmured almost to himself, "There aren't many coincidences, are there?"

****

Within about twenty minutes, she had fallen asleep as he massaged her hair and he leaned his head back and went over what he'd heard and seen that day at church and with her family. It had all been thoroughly thought provoking and he needed some time to mull it around in his head.

He knew little about the Mormons other than their ads about the family and indeed this whole family seemed like a living Mormon ad. He'd heard the rumors about them being a cult, but even without a thriving skepticism about the press, he'd have known the rumors were false after the last weeks of having lived here in this valley. These people were good, kind, hardworking, clean living people and had been a good enough example to him that all he wanted was more information.

Naomi came over to him and asked if he wanted to come eat with them. He didn't want to offend them, but he also needed to think about things for awhile and he didn't want to disturb Joey, who had finally found some relief from her pain on his lap. He decided to be honest with Naomi. "Naomi, would you be offended if I just stayed where I was? I don't want to wake her and I wouldn't mind some time thinking."

"We won't be offended." She smiled. "But Cooper will probably start to tease you. Thank you for helping her rest."

Michael stayed where he was and watched and listened to the whole group of them eating and he thought about what he was learning and about what he was feeling toward this girl laying here hurt. He felt his paradigm shift even further. He wished his own family life could have been more like this. He would have felt so differently about so many things.

An hour and a half later, Sunday dinner was long over, the leftovers put away and the dishes done when Joey stirred and grimaced in her sleep. She slowly opened her brilliant eyes and gave him that sweet, tired smile that he was getting attached to. It was so weird that he could sit here with her so comfortably, when usually he worked to stay as far out of arm's reach as possible from women.

He was comfortable, in spite of the whole family being right here with them and it blew his mind a little, actually. It was so unlike him, but it felt perfect.

She woke up and he knew she needed to move again to relieve the stiffness and he tried to help her roll slightly and stretch. Finally, she asked, "Are we making you stiff as well?"

"I'm fine. Tell me what to do."

She sighed. "I don't know. My back is so tired, but I can't really sit up. How long have I been laying here on you? What time is it?"

He wasn't concerned about the time. "I'm not sure." He reached for her hands. "Can you half sit up and just lean on me like we did yesterday out there? Or will Cooper tease us both?"

"I'm sure he'll tease us." She let him pull her up to lean on his chest. "But it's not like he wouldn't tease us anyway." She took his left arm and looked at his watch. "You've been

153

sitting here for two hours holding me, Michael. Aren't you dying by now? You're probably bored out of your mind."

He touched a strand of her hair and gently tugged on it and said mildly, "I'm busy, leave me alone."

At that, she rolled her head slightly back and looked up at him, and he looked down at her steadily. Finally, she asked quietly, "What's going on, Michael? What are you thinking?"

How could he answer that when he didn't know the answer to the first question and didn't dare tell her the answer to the second? Finally, he said, "Peace. Peace is going on. And it's the most amazing feeling I've ever had. Are you comfortable?"

She nodded, barely. "Yeah."

"Good. Because I don't want you to go anywhere right now."

Her eyes were big as she laid there against him and he hoped he wasn't making her worried. Finally, she rolled back into him and snuggled against him. He pulled her closer into his arms and forgot about everything else in his life except this girl who made him feel stronger and breathed against his skin.

A few minutes later, he knew she'd gone back to sleep, so he leaned his head back onto the couch and closed his eyes as well. He would gladly hold her like this forever. He didn't understand how he was feeling, and he had no idea what to do about it, but the feeling was warm and sweet and peaceful, so it had to be right. That was enough for him to know.

He held her like that, helping her to move occasionally, for another few hours, not even glancing at his watch for fear that he'd feel obligated to go. Finally, as Sean and Lexie and their twins came in and began to help Naomi begin cooking, when Joey woke up again, he looked down into her big eyes and reached for her hand. He wound his fingers through hers for a few seconds and softly rubbed the back of her hand with his thumb.

She was watching him quietly and he touched her cheek tenderly with one finger and then gently pushed away from her, let himself out the doors to the deck and headed on home. It was a good thing that Joey wasn't one of those pushy types who demanded answers, because he didn't have a clue what was going on here. It was probably also a good thing he was leaving in a few days for Kentucky. He was losing his head over this sweet, tall, blonde mountain girl.

Letting himself into his house, he tossed his jacket over the couch, went to the piano and sat down and let the music flow. It happened again. Being with her inspired him every time. There was something about her that cleared all the lead out of his brain.

He'd been playing for more than an hour when he thought he heard something and got up and went into the kitchen to let Blue in. He was already in again and there was another covered plate of food sitting on his counter. He picked up the plate, reached for a fork and went to the kitchen table, prayed and then dug into the marvelous hot food.

There was definitely something to be said for being part of a family.

Jaclyn M. Hawkes

Chapter 22

The next morning, he let them all head out of the house to start their day's work before he wandered over to Naomi's house. She was just helping Joey out of the shower and when Joey struggled into the great room on her crutches, she looked damp and sore and adorable.

Michael helped her to get down onto the couch where she could actually stand to bend her hip a little more this morning and she half laid against his chest like she had yesterday afternoon. Naomi had made sure that her pain pill had had plenty of time to start working before letting her try to shower and Joey went to sleep on him again within minutes. He was fine enough with just holding her while she slept that he was still trying to figure out what he was thinking or feeling about her when Naomi came in with a basket of laundry, sat across from them and began to fold it.

Naomi and Michael small talked back and forth for a few minutes and then Naomi said casually, "Joey said you wanted something to read about the plan of salvation. There's a lot of material I could get you. Tell me what part of the plan of salvation you most want to know about."

She was looking at him steadily with blue eyes that were so like Joey's and he decided to level with her, knowing that this woman truly wanted to help him. "Naomi, I'm twenty-eight years old and have muddled through those years as best I could with a belief that I have a responsibility to be a productive, honorable, moral member of society who helped others where I could and tried to follow my conscience. I was an only child with a wonderful father and grandfathers who

157

muddled through with that same value system, and a mother and grandmothers who were frankly more caught up in looking good at the country club. God wasn't an issue to any of them until my father became ill with liver cancer about eighteen months ago."

He ran a hand through his hair and sighed and went on, "At that point, the golden rule just wasn't enough anymore. My father was my greatest confidant and friend in the world and neither one of us knew how to help him beyond what modern medicine had to offer. Even more troubling was the idea that when he died, he was just done. Gone. A flame that would go out and become non-existent. And we both knew he was dying. We couldn't stop it."

There was a long pause while he struggled to know what to say next. "His death a few days before I got here was devastating. It's taken me weeks to realize that it was more than just his death, but you saw what kind of shape I was in when I arrived here. I hate to even admit what a mess I was. I couldn't sleep and was exhausted and couldn't wake up because I couldn't face getting on with my life." He smiled at her sadly. "Thank goodness for sweet, old Blue and that Merv's car broke down that day. I don't know how I'd have made it through without all of you. Thank you. You are definitely angels and have changed my life."

He gently smoothed Joey's hair back from her face as she slept against him and said softly, "Now I know that God is there and watching over me. But I have a whole lifetime of learning to make up for. And I guess that's my biggest need right now. I want to know where my father is. I mean, I want to understand it all in time. I want to know what your family knows that helps them to bypass all of the garbage of society and focus on whatever it is that makes everyone here so happy and satisfied. You guys positively glow.

"But very first I need to know about my dad. I need to know where he is and that he's okay and that it's not too late for him to find out. Is he damned forever for dying before he really knew about God?   He'd begun to search almost frantically there at the end, and I think he had begun to figure it out, but he got so weak.   And honestly, I was too caught up in facing his death and struggling just to keep on dealing with commitments when I was too sad to get out of bed in the morning to even help him in his quest for the truth."

He faced Naomi sadly. "I just didn't understand, Naomi. I didn't figure out that God was the key to it all until one night in the middle of the night Joey came over and prayed for me in the dark on my porch.   Even then I didn't understand what was going on. I've been a fool and I know it now.   At least now I know that He's a loving God who will help to pick up the pieces of us foolish mortals, but I need to know."

Naomi smiled at him and said, "Let's start with reassuring you that it's not too late for your father. He's gone on to the other side and is being taught all the truths that he was looking for at the end.   If his heart is good and if he's honestly willing to be obedient, then he just needs to learn it all on that side of death, just like you'll learn it all here. That's why God has a prophet on the earth, Michael. Because He knows that we *need* to know his plan."

Michael leaned his head back against the couch and looked up at the ceiling. He blew his breath out with a long sigh and then didn't say anything as Naomi got up and went into another room and came back with a book with two men on the front.

She handed it to him and said, "Page through this while she's sleeping, Michael. Then when she wakes up, ask her whatever questions you have.   She probably knows more about the gospel than I do, although she might accidentally talk too fast when she gets excited. She served an eighteen month mission to Michigan and has only been home about sixteen months. The pain medicine slows her down a little,

159

Jaclyn M. Hawkes

but she's still brighter than I'll ever be. And she has that wonderful, peaceful, patient personality that is so reassuring without pressuring you. She can wait until you ask before she offers. That's a marvelous trait. You'll never feel like she's intruding."

Naomi picked up her folded laundry and went to leave and added, "And if you're not comfortable talking with Joey about something, Rob and all of the boys served missions too. And Slade, Isabel, Kit, Lexie, and Marti have all joined the church in the last four or five years. You can ask one of them for a convert's point of view. Of course, I'm available whenever as well. Any one of us would love to help you." With that, she went into the laundry room off the kitchen and Michael began to look through the binder.

He was deep into studying it, when Joey moved against his chest and opened her eyes. After glancing down at her, he went back to his book and she just watched him quietly for several more minutes before he looked down at her again. Her blue eyes were clear and bright and completely unfathomable as she watched him and he had to ask, "What are you thinking inside that pretty head?"

She yawned and said, "Mmm, my brain is off. Sorry, the medicine puts it in hibernation mode. You weren't hoping for anything terribly brilliant, I hope."

Studying her face for a minute, he realized that for the first time since he'd met her, he didn't think she was being forthright with him and he asked her outright, "Are you hedging?"

At least she was honest about not being honest. "Yes, but only because I'm not sure what my thoughts are right now. I think you scramble my brain."

At that he had to smile at her. "You're on Percocet and *I* scramble your brain? How does that work?"

"If I knew that, I could have answered your question. What are you thinking?"
160

He reached down and smoothed a finger along her fine eyebrow and smiled and said, "Uh, my brain is off."

She met his eyes and said evenly, "That wasn't very nice."

Putting up a hand in self defense, he said, "Hey, my brain is at least as scrambled as yours and mine wasn't nearly as brilliant as yours in the first place."

"Why is your brain scrambled?"

He raised an eyebrow and grinned, "You know, I've been asking myself that for weeks now. It has something to do with the way you treat me, and the way your jeans fit. But in all honesty, this has never happened to me before, so I'm a little lost here." Her look widened into surprise at his words. "Hey, you asked what I was thinking."

"I've been sleeping on you and I'm wearing my dad's sweats, so then what?"

Grinning again, he said, "Wow, you mean you look even better than this sometimes? I'll be looking forward to that."

"Oh, stop. What are you going to do today?"

"Well, let's see. I believe my list was visit the neighbor girl, find the meaning of the universe, eat lunch, and write music. I've been working on the first two, so I'm about to the lunch part. He shrugged his shoulders and looked at her innocently. "Brain's still scrambled, that's what's so puzzling. But it's not like sweats could hide your figure. Even hurt, you're a knockout."

Joey rolled her eyes. "That's what's wrong. I've been cutting off the oxygen to your brain. I'm always a mess when you see me."

Are you hungry? I make a mean Lean Cuisine. Well, I make about four mean Lean Cuisines. They aren't very filling."

She groaned. "I think I need to give you another lecture about nutrition. You don't have Pop Tarts for dessert, do you? Can we eat lunch here?"

"Sure, but I'm beginning to feel like a mooch. My

personal creed dictates that I have to feed you occasionally or I have to stop eating here."

"Could you put your personal creed on hold for a moment? Do you remember that when I nearly got you killed yesterday you were fixing fence with me? Then you saved my life. Doesn't that count for earning lunch? Where did you find the meaning of the universe? I didn't even realize it was missing."

He waved the Teach My Gospel book. "I've been reading up while you slept. Do you realize that John the Baptist himself came and restored this priesthood? I'm not sure how you pronounce it."

Before Joey could answer that, Naomi came in and sat in the chair beside them. "Is anyone in here ready for lunch? I don't think anyone is coming in except us. Can we just have hot beef sandwiches?"

Joey looked at Michael. "What'll it be? Four rubber frozen entrees or Wyoming beef?"

Looking from one to the other, Naomi got back up. "I'll start making the sandwiches. Do you like green salad, Michael?"

"I like anything, especially if it's not frozen."

He gently scooted out from where Joey was leaning on him and went into the kitchen where Naomi looked at him and commented, "I thought you said you didn't cook."

"Every one of your sons help with the meals. I figure I'd better start somewhere. Can I just stir something? I promise I won't wreck it. There's just no way that I can sit there and wait for you to serve us."

She came over to him and handed him a potato peeler and a cucumber. "This is a vegetable peeler. And this is a cucumber."

Taking the cucumber from her, he laughed. "I said I couldn't fry an egg, Naomi. Not that I was a quadriplegic. What else do you want in your salad?"

She came over and put an arm around his waist and laughed. "I'm sorry. I thought you were serious that you were culinary challenged."

"Well, I actually made it all the way through college without having to hire a cook. I can peel a cucumber. Just don't ask me about something exotic like a tomato."

Joey piped up from the couch sleepily. "Give it up, Mother. He told me I was a knockout in Dad's sweats. I think he's suffering from me laying on him too long. His smart alec control switch has gone haywire."

"Well, sweetie. You really are a knockout, even in sweats. You can't fault him there. He's not blind."

At that Joey struggled to lean up and look over the back of the couch toward her mother. "Oh, that's just great! He's contagious." She lay back down as the other two laughed.

Jaclyn M. Hawkes

For Joey

Chapter 23

After lunch, Michael sat down in front of the couch with his back against it and opened the Teach My Gospel book back up and with Joey laying above him and looking over his shoulder; they spent most of the afternoon pouring over the basics of the principles of the church. As the others started coming in, he got up and slipped back out the patio doors and went home to finish the last item on his list—taking advantage of the creativity that spending time with Joey gave him. He wasn't surprised when someone brought him a plate again.

At ten-forty-five, he got up from the piano and went in to get ready for bed. As he knelt to pray, he was once again amazed and grateful that he could lie down and know that he'd be able to rest without having any nightmares and even the grief was mellowing now.

The horrible images and anxiousness had been replaced by wonder about the greatness of God, and some other emotion that was warm and sweet about his beautiful neighbor. Climbing into the plain old double bed, he reached a hand out in the dark to pat the old dog's head that he knew would be there. Joey probably did need Blue now more than he did, but he was a wonderful companion.

By the next morning when he got to Naomi's house, Joey was actually sitting slightly upright in a recliner and Michael walked in and gave her a high five. "Look at you! Are you as better as you look?"

"Either that or I accidentally took a double dose of pain medicine. Are you as better as you look?"

Jaclyn M. Hawkes

It was said in a teasing tone of voice, but he knew she was honestly asking and answered, "Either that or I accidentally took a double dose of Wyoming." He sat down across from her. "I'm good, Joey. Amazingly good for how unbelievably bad I've been. Thank you for helping me."

"You can't blame me for how good you look. To use your own words, even depressed you're a knock out. That has nothing to do with me."

"Now look who's being a smart alec. What are you going to do today?"

"I don't know, but something. Lying flat is making me crazy. Would you be willing to play my mom's piano for me sometime today? How is composing coming? Have you still got your writer's block?"

Wondering if he dared to tell her that she inspired him, he looked over at her. "I'm doing better actually. In fact, lately I've been on a roll. I have more than half the movie score I've been working on finished. Hopefully, the rest will keep coming. It's so weird. A few weeks back the only thing that seemed to come together were either the sad scenes, or the tense or angry ones. Now I can't seem to hear the negative melodies and the happy music is coming miraculously."

He could have told her that the love scenes actually came to him when she was right beside him, but he didn't think that would be all that great of an idea. Yesterday she'd looked a little panicky just because he'd told her the way her jeans fit scrambled his brain.

"So, can you play some of it for me?" She sighed. "You wouldn't believe how much I've missed hearing you play since I got hurt. At my apartment I could hear you at night, but here it's too far away."

He met her eyes and nodded. "I could do that. After all, you're the one who somehow broke my writer's block. I'm not sure how it works, but I owe a lot of what I've been able

166

to accomplish to you." He got up and went to Naomi's piano and began to adjust the bench.

Maybe it was knowing she loved his music that affected his heart so much. Back home his mother and Margot and their other New York friends considered his music an amusing hobby or something. None of them recognized that it was his life's passion, and certainly none of them wanted to be bothered to listen to him play for hours at a time. He'd learned over time not to even consider trying to work at his compositions unless he was alone because no one would take him seriously.

Here, from that very first day, he'd known that she loved his music and that it evoked strong emotions in her. At any rate, she had been the one who mentioned that writing late had counted as basically working overtime. Never once had she intimated that writing music wasn't a real occupation. It was incredibly refreshing to know that she took his life's work seriously and believed he was gifted.

He didn't have to wonder what to play for her. She had been the inspiration for several pieces, but the one he played was the one he'd begun to hear in his head almost the first time he laid eyes on her. It was the love theme for the movie score, but to him it would always be Joey's song. As he began to play, he glanced up at her from time to time and he could almost see her relax into the music. The slight grimace between her brows from the pain that she'd had for days now eased, and she leaned her head back and closed her eyes to listen.

When he paused between songs, she leaned up and opened her eyes and smiled at him quietly when he looked over at her and then leaned back again for the next one.

He played through several songs, subtly watching her as he did and tears escaped her eyes and slipped down her cheeks when he played the song he'd been playing that first day she'd come to his house. As he continued, he thought back to that day. He'd been such a wreck then. Emotionally, he'd been drained beyond belief and completely spiritually bankrupt. It hurt just thinking about his struggle at that time.

He'd come an amazingly long way since then, guided almost entirely by her and this good family that seemed to know instinctively that he had been in desperate need of both guidance and unconditional acceptance without anyone even being aware of his money.

Isabel knew his situation, and Branden knew about his car, which wasn't that big of deal; lots of people had a weakness for exotic cars. But so far, other than Isabel telling Slade about him, if anyone else knew who he was, they weren't mentioning it or acting like it. At least they weren't sucking up to him like everyone back home that he met or who knew him did. It was heavenly to be simply befriended and respected as a musician and neighbor.

Glancing over at Joey again, he felt a twinge of guilt that he hadn't told her in detail what he had been doing back home on the bank board. He didn't think she even knew his last name, but there hadn't been a way to say anything that wouldn't have made him seem like he was trying to impress her anyway. And what did it matter? He'd already decided he wasn't ever going to move back to New York City on a permanent basis and he'd arranged to buy the little white cottage from Doc as soon as the paperwork could be finalized.

He'd agreed to stay on the bank board and to a few other responsibilities, but only things that he could fly in and out for or do from here without much more than a fax and computer and a good shipping service. He'd have to find a notary public at some point for some of his needs, but that would come.

Right now, he was far more concerned with what to do with his feelings for the leggy blonde there in the chair than what he needed to do about the bank. For most of his life, his father had been counseling him to be cautious about relationships both because of the responsibility involved with the fortunes that he would end up managing, and the tendency of humans to do anything to get their hands on that kind of money.

The result had been that Michael had learned to be both cynical and more than a little stand-offish about females once he had gotten over the initial fascination with girls as a young teenage boy. That skepticism had stood him in good stead over the years and he'd learned his lesson of caution well. Now he had no idea what to do about the way Joey drew him.

She was so different than any other woman he had ever met. She had this indescribable innate sense of self that gave her almost an air of supreme self confidence. But it wasn't an arrogant pridefulness. It was more an under spoken sense that she knew who she was and exactly what she was capable of and was completely at ease with it without saying a word. It demanded complete respect. There was none of the suggestive flirtatiousness or even that harsh need to prove how powerful she was that some women displayed.

At the same time, she had the most wonderful, sweet spirit about her. There was no other way to describe it. Even her drop dead beauty and the fluid grace she moved with didn't hide the instinctive kindness of her heart and the graciousness of her attitude. She was a server to the core.

Watching her now, listening there on the chair, he had to wonder again how she had managed to preserve her sweet personality through twenty-four years of dealing with reality and even more surprising, how she had remained single the way her whole countenance glowed. These country boys were fools to have not staked their claim long ago.

With these thoughts in mind, he honestly had no idea what to do about her. At first, he had wondered if his attraction was simply that he was so vulnerable just now with what was going on in his life. He had expected that initial fascination to wane when he felt stronger and got to know her better.

Just the opposite had happened and for the first time in his life, he truly wondered if he had found a woman that he could consider being with for the rest of his life. For the rest of eternity if what he was learning from these good people turned out to be as right as it seemed to be.

That thought was earth shaking after feeling as cynical and jaded as he'd felt for as many years as he had. He had truly given up on the whole idea of marriage as not worth the hassle years ago. He remembered just how sad and discouraged that had made him at the time and realized now that that had contributed greatly to the sense of being burned out that stole all of his energy. Losing sight of any point in his existence had drained his enthusiasm to the bone.

Now, wondering if he was honestly falling in love with a girl who was definitely worth the hassle and the risk, was frankly uncharted territory for him. For once the hyper in control Michael Morgan who handled whatever he had to, always, was at a loss. This feeling was all new to him and the only thing that kept him from being skittish about it was her counsel to listen to the Spirit when it was warm and sweet and peaceful. That, and the fact that the attraction was huge. It was a good thing she brought the warm, sweet peace, because walking away from her would have been the hardest thing he'd ever done if he'd felt that he had to.

He knew exactly when she fell asleep, and he had to smile again at the memory of that first day that she'd listened. She'd been so embarrassed and so sweetly complimentary at the same time. It had been incredible to have her tell him that his work was searingly evocative.

He stopped playing for her and began to play about her, letting the creative river that she always brought him flow and wishing he'd brought at least some staff paper with him.
170

There was a new melody that danced in his mind after admitting mentally that he was actually thinking about forever. It was a luxury he'd never allowed himself before and it brought an amazing flood of happy energy.

Naomi was somewhere working here in the house, he'd heard her coming and going from time to time and he went in search of her and borrowed some paper and a pencil and went back to the piano. This new song wasn't something he needed for the movie score, but he had to write it down anyway. After fiddling with it for another half hour, he took his work back over and sat down on the floor again in front of Joey's chair to work on the coffee table. Here, he could even smell her and the jasmine and vanilla spurred his creative juices even further. By the time he heard her stir and then felt her gentle touch on his shoulder, he had most of the melody down and was working on the harmonies and dynamics.

At her touch, he turned and looked at her and was still amazed at the brilliant blue of her eyes. Lately, there was something else there in her eyes that both added to the sweet energy and almost frightened him at the same time. Sometimes when he looked at her, he saw blue sparks at the back of her eyes and her look had a heady intensity that made his heart beat faster.

He looked away, telling himself it was just her pain medicine and that when she felt better, the sparks would disappear. At least that was an easy way to tell himself she wasn't feeling the same things he was and that he didn't need to fear this strange frission that arced between them like an electrical current. With his eyes back on what he was writing, he asked, "How did you sleep? Did I bother you too much?"

"Heavens no. You're like having my own private hypnotist when you play. Your music is fantastic. It makes me wish I wasn't drugged and would never fall asleep for fear that I'll miss something."

He looked up and smiled. "Oh, you missed something. That unentertaining stage where I figure out which chord or rhythm or embellishment I want and play it over and over again until I get it right. It's awful. Even Blue covers his ears."

She rolled up on her side with a small grimace. "What time is it? How long did I sleep?"

"Eleven twenty. You've been asleep a couple of hours." He stood up and offered her a hand to help her move around so that she wasn't so stiff. "What time will your family come in for lunch?"

"Thank you. I don't think they'll be coming in today. I think they're all clear over on the north end. They have to trailer over there and there's not time to come back for lunch."

Pulling the recliner lever slowly, she tried to sit more upright and Michael offered her a hand again. "What are you doing? How can I help you?"

Taking his hand and letting him pull her up to stand beside him, she let her breath out with a sigh. "Can you miraculously unbruise this hip? I've never been down like this in my life. It's making me crazy. Being down and bored is bad enough. Being a little out of it from the medicine is worse. I'm so glad you're here to entertain me. I'd be climbing the walls without you."

She was standing mostly on just her one leg and she swayed slightly so he put an arm around her waist to steady her. "Easy. I haven't done much. Are you going somewhere? Or are you just switching to the couch?"

"I'm going somewhere. Even if it's just up and down the room here for a minute. I have to stand up. Would you hand me those crutches? Thanks. Are you hungry yet?" She began to walk gingerly toward the windows that looked out over the deck and the valley, using her crutches and hesitantly putting her sore leg down and putting weight on it gently.

Not sure whether to follow her or let her go on her own, he answered, "No, I'm not hungry. Are you? Do you want me to bring you something?"

Standing at the window, she said, "Do you know what I really want? Trout almandine from this fancy little restaurant in Jackson and then frozen chocolate covered mint Oreos and a big glass of milk before I go back outside and get on a horse again and go to work. Could you bring me those things, please?"

She turned and smiled at him. "I know. I know. I'm starting to get whiny. I'll quit. Have you got a full afternoon? Or can you stay here with me and do something incredibly dynamic like watch a movie or play Scrabble? I have to entertain myself, or I'm going to go out and see if I can fold myself into a car and drive somewhere. Which, in all honesty, I'm not up to yet. Cars are very therapeutic, you know."

He wished he had the Ferrari close enough to let it take her mind off her infirmities. From what he'd heard, she would love it. "As long as I can write during your naps, and your mother doesn't get sick of me, I can do whatever I want this afternoon. But I'm a lousy Scrabble player. I have to warn you. I can never come up with those great words."

Turning back to hobble toward him, she laughed and said, "My dad came up with majorette one time. He got like twelve hundred points on one word. We've never heard the end of it. He was positively gloating. Even Cooper hasn't been able to top that one. Would you do me a favor? Go down the hall to my mom's office and see if she's ready to eat yet. I shouldn't have talked about trout almandine. Now I'm starving. Actually, maybe I'll come with you. I can't face sitting back down yet."

Just as they began to amble down the hall, Naomi came around the bend. "Did I hear you say trout almandine? That sounds marvelous! I wish we had trout around. I'd make some. We'll have to see if one of the guys can be talked into going fishing soon."

Joey laughed. "That ought to be pretty tricky. Anyone of them would drop everything and go in a heartbeat. It's getting them to stop fishing that I have trouble with. What else do we have for lunch? Anything Michael can peel so that he feels needed? Or how about just having the Oreos?"

Naomi rolled her eyes at Michael. "No Oreos. At least not mint covered ones. I haven't been able to find those this side of Salt Lake for awhile now. How about shrimp with lemon pasta? Michael could stir it."

He looked from one to the other of them and chuckled. "Just for that, I'm going to take a culinary arts course and wear a ridiculous hat into your kitchen. Tell me what to do. Shrimp and lemons are my specialty."

Joey looked at him. "Really?"

"No, but how can you mess up lemon juice? I'll figure it out. Bring it on. I'm from the coast, you know. Shrimp love me to eat them." He picked up the vegetable peeler. "Do you use this to peel them?"

Joey looked at Naomi and laughed. "I haven't laid against him once today, Mom. This is not my fault. I didn't cut off the oxygen to his brain. I promise."

With Joey lounging nearby, he and Naomi cooked and they ate. Then he pushed the coffee table right over against the couch so she could stretch out and still reach the Scrabble board and he sat next to her on the floor again. He tried to spell several made up words and proper nouns and Joey called him on it every time. Then he got mountaineer with a triple word score and she wouldn't even acknowledge his exuberant high five and victory cat call. "You wouldn't cheat on someone who is taking narcotics would you? How did you do that?"

"Hey, you're the one who set me up. I had five E's. Of course, you knew that because you can see all of my letters

174

just as well as I can see yours. By the way, you could spell Michael won right here on this A if you had another two letters."

She leaned over his shoulder and laughed. "With a Z and an A and a J? How does that work? And I could still win. Just because you're sixty two points ahead is nothing."

He dumped the last two letters out of the bag. "I don't think so. You'd better get rid of those Z and J, or they'll count against you." For another ten minutes he tried to help her come up with about sixteen made up words that included her Z and J and they finally gave up in fits of laughter.

Joey conceded gracefully. "Okay, you won. But I demand a rematch when I'm not taking Percocet. I refuse to be beaten this badly. My reputation will never be the same. And don't you dare tell Cooper. Are you up for a movie? You can pick since you just massacred me."

"Actually, I'll let you pick since I just massacred you. What are you in the mood for?"

She gave him a sleepy smile. "You're gonna let me pick, huh? Let's see. How about something serious and dramatic? I'll give you a choice. Glass Bottom Boat or Roman Holiday."

"I've never seen either one of those, so you'll have to choose."

"Oh, Michael. You've never seen Glass Bottom Boat? You've never lived. It's the funniest classic Doris Day in the world."

"I thought you said serious and dramatic."

She laughed. "Did I look serious and dramatic when I said that?"

"Well, no. Where do I find Glass Bottom Boat?"

He put the movie in, pulled the drapes on the big picture windows and then came over toward the couch and was just trying to decide where to sit when she asked, "Can I lean against you again? Will you care if I cut off the oxygen to your brain?"

Sitting down next to her, he pulled her up against him gently so she could relax without straining her hip. Pulling her close, he smiled down at her. "No oxygen is perfect." She looked up at him with those lethal eyes again and it was all he could do not to bend his head and kiss her and he knew she was perfectly aware of it.

After she finally looked away, it took him a second to remember to start the movie, and even then he couldn't focus on it for anything. He rubbed a hand up her arm and wound a strand of her hair through his fingers and then played with it, wishing that he'd kissed her. He should have. Life was too short to feel this kind of regret.

The movie had only been playing for a half hour or so when she sighed, and turned her face away from the TV and into his neck. He had yet to begin to catch the story line and pulled her even closer and breathed in jasmine and vanilla. She felt really good here in his arms. It was heartbreaking that she'd been hurt, but he was enjoying helping her recuperate immensely.

For the first time, he was wishing he didn't have to go to Lexington to the Kentucky Derby on Thursday. Wishing she was up to going with him, he knew he couldn't really back out on this one and breathed deeply against her hair. It was just as well, probably. Slade had said she would likely panic and run away from him if she knew what he was worth. Knowing that he was far more serious about pursuing a relationship with her than with any other woman in his life, the last thing Michael wanted was for her to run away from him.

He'd have to find a way to gently break her into the idea that he wasn't just a musician. Hopefully, she wouldn't think he had been lying to her.

He looked down at her with a sad half smile. In case things went south, as a last resort there was always the Ferrari.

When he knew she was asleep, he clicked off the remote and then just sat there with her in the relative dimness near the TV, thinking. It did look like a funny Doris Day movie, but he wasn't really in the mood for funny. It was nicer just to sit here in the quiet and think about all the things he was finding that he knew nothing about, even though he was twenty-eight years old.

Studying the book Naomi had given him about the church was wonderfully intriguing, and even finding out who Doris Day was was a discovery, but nothing compared to finding out how nice it was to actually want to be with Joey. He wound another strand of hair through his fingers. She was by far the most thought provoking thing that had ever happened to him.

He'd picked up his paper and was working on his composition again when Naomi came back in and came over to him and looked down at Joey. After a minute, she shook her head, smiled up at Michael and went into the kitchen to start dinner.

He was still there with Joey in his arms when the whole troop of them came back in in their riding gear, tired, dusty, and teasing each other. Michael was obviously fair game as they all trooped over to look down at Joey just as Naomi had. After several of them shook their heads in seeming disbelief, Michael finally had to ask quietly, "What? Why are you all shaking your heads like that?"

Cooper laughed and said, "We've just never seen Joey act all snuggly. She's usually the cool one. There are men the world over who have just tried to hug her, but she has some serious personal space. No one gets this close to Joey. Well, Blue, but he doesn't really count. He's a dog."

The others laughed as they all moved off except Rossen, who still stood beside them looking down this time at Michael. Michael looked up and met his eyes evenly and at length Rossen said, "You treat her like a queen, Michael. I like you, but you treat her like a queen."

He walked into the kitchen with the others and Michael almost started to sweat a little. That tall, soft spoken, mellow engineer would have put the fear of God into him if it hadn't already been there. He was glad he could meet those quiet blue eyes honestly, knowing that he had only the best intentions as far as this little sister was concerned. Joey had joked about them protecting her, but he'd never been so subtly, but thoroughly warned in his life.

As the others joked and laughed in the adjoining kitchen, Joey slowly came awake. It took her a minute this time before she raised her tired, striking eyes to his and he looked down into them, wondering if he dared to kiss her like he wanted to with her whole family and then some hanging out nearby. Finally, he just stroked her lower lip with the pad of his thumb and looked back into her eyes and he knew again that she knew exactly what he was thinking. It was almost uncanny how she seemed to read his thoughts every once in awhile.

He glanced up to find Rossen watching him and he made an executive decision to wait to kiss her. She glanced up too, and then looked back at him and he expected her to smile, but she never did. Just kept looking at him with that startling blue intensity.

When the others began to take their seats, Michael gently touched her lip one more time. "Are you up to trying to sit at the table with them tonight? We'll pull a chair up and pad you with pillows if you want to try."

"I don't know that I can actually do it, but let me try. I'd love to be there even for a few minutes. Are you leaving again?" He nodded. "You're welcome here, Michael. You know that by now, don't you?"

"Yes, I do. It's not that I'm not welcome. It's that I still don't know how to accept that hospitality. I've never been around anyone like you guys. I'm still trying to figure out my role here. I know I need to feel like I've earned my welcome and so far, I've only taken, not given back. That's not me. I don't believe in that sort of thing, but like I said, I write music and read quarterly reports. There's not much need for that type of thing around here."

She just looked at him steadily and finally said okay and left it at that. He looked down at her mouth again and then gently scooted away from her so he could stand and give her his hands to help her up. When she was standing, he handed her her crutches and then helped her to the table where Naomi met them with a couple of pillows. Once she was seated as well as she could be, Michael slipped out the patio door to where Blue waited for him patiently. Reaching down to pat the sweet, aged dog, he said, "Come on, old man. Let's go home."

Jaclyn M. Hawkes

Chapter 24

The next morning when there was a loud pounding on his door at five thirty, he was glad he hadn't stayed up half the night writing. He dragged himself out of bed and to the door where he didn't worry too much about who was on the other side because Blue was standing in front of it, wagging his tail. When he opened it, he wondered for a second if he should have worried. There on his porch were Rossen, Ruger, Sean and Cooper, all dressed in boots and spurs and chaps and looking at him like he was a complete slacker in his pajama bottoms.

Sean grinned at him and Michael couldn't help smiling tiredly back. "What?"

Sean was also the one who answered him, "Joey said we were to haul your butt out with us this morning to vaccinate calves. But you'd better at least put a shirt on. It can get a little brisk here in the early mornings. A shirt and some spurs." He handed him a covered plate. "She sent this for you as well. We'll have your horse ready. Get your duds on."

Michael laughed and turned back to his room to get his "duds" while the four of them trooped off his porch toward the garage and pasture. Indeed, by the time he was dressed they had Jammer saddled and ready to go. Unsure of just what this day had in store for him, he wolfed down the breakfast she'd sent, then grabbed a water bottle and a couple of apples and put them into a jacket he shrugged on as he went out the door to join them.

As they trotted their horses across the pasture beside her parents' house, he saw her standing there in the window in the gray light before the sun had made it up over the

181

mountains. She waved a crutch at them and whistled and Blue cut from their little cavalcade and headed for Joey at a jog.

Even though he probably would have rather stayed and spent the day with Joey again, he was frankly thrilled to be included this morning. He had no idea what vaccinating calves entailed, but it felt good to be a part of it anyway. He truly did want to be able to feel welcome, but he'd been serious about not being just a taker.

Not only that, but he knew that if he ever really did make it to forever with Joey, she came as a package deal. He wanted these good men who were her brothers to know that he was as willing as any of them to do his share and work as hard as the next guy at this family enterprise. All of his life he'd done his work intellectually, but it was actually very fulfilling to think that he'd be doing physical work alongside these men for the day.

He knew he was a crack rider and he was grateful for that by about an hour into their morning. As good as he was, he was having to work to keep up with these men who could ride as well as he could and handle a rope at the same time. Because he didn't rope, he and Jammer were the ones sent into the milling herd of cows and calves to separate a pair at a time for the brothers to catch and restrain to vaccinate. Once they had the calf caught, the work went fast, which was good, because about every fourth cow tried to charge one of them to rescue her baby.

Jammer knew exactly what he was doing and there were times that Michael figured out what the horse was going to do next just before he was nearly unseated as Jammer spun and dodged after the cow. At the other end of the herd, Michael could see Rob and Treyne and Slade and two of the hands doing the same thing they were doing, and it was fascinating to watch in the few moments that he dared look away from what he was doing to see all of it.

182

They finished that herd by about ten o'clock and Michael dug out one of his apples and ate it as they headed out to another pasture to do it all over again. As they got there, another hand met them with a string of fresh horses and as Michael switched his saddle and turned Jammer over to the young man, he felt like he'd just stepped out of some great old western movie.

He felt even more like that at noon when Slade began to show him the rudiments of throwing a rope while they waited for whoever it was that was bringing them lunch. Michael was at first completely mystified at how Slade could throw that huge loop and have it catch what he was throwing it at. But it wasn't very long before he began to figure out that if he held his hands the way he was shown and threw the way Slade instructed him, that it wasn't as much of a miracle as it seemed. He still never caught what he was aiming at, but at least he could begin to understand how it was done.

As Slade showed him, they talked quietly about the Kentucky Derby and when Michael told him about his grandfather's jet waiting for him at the Jackson Hole airport and asked him if he and Isabel wanted to fly to Lexington with him, Slade accepted with a smile. "Sure we'll fly with you. It'll be a great opportunity to pick your brain about your race strategy and see if we can get an inside tip about how to win this thing on Saturday."

Michael smiled at that. "You and I both know that Eli Johnson doesn't need an inside tip when it comes to racehorse training. No one is better than Eli. But then neither does my man. Barring any bad luck, crooked headers in the gates, slippery holes in the track and jockey errors, this is going to come down to which horse truly has the best heart. And both of us have great hearted horses. I think the Sheik has an exceptional horse as well. It's going to be a wonderful race."

Slade nodded and threw the rope again. "That is why we do what we do, isn't it?"

At six o'clock that night, three spent horses and four huge herds of cows later, when Michael dragged back into the main ranch yard with the rest of the riders, he had a whole new appreciation for the kind of shape these guys were in and for the lifestyle they led. He also didn't hesitate to stay and eat with the family when Sean grinned and said, "Well, Brother Michael, you've definitely earned your dinner tonight. You'd better stay or Joey will have our heads and Mother will be offended."

He offered Michael his hand. "You did well out there today. Joey told me you could ride and I knew she'd left you Jammer, but I had to see it to believe it, I guess. Where did a New York city slicker learn to ride a cutting horse like that?"

"Actually, I've never ridden a cutting horse before coming here, but a Polo pony in the heat of the game is similar. Beside you guys it seems almost a little silly or childish or something, but I did learn to at least stay on."

Sean laughed and slapped the dust from his jeans with a coiled rope. "We're gonna have you team roping in no time. You'll never be the same after you catch that first set of heels. It's positively addicting."

Stretching his back, Michael admitted, "I have absolutely no idea what you're talking about, but unless it involves illegal substances, I'm game to try whatever it is."

Rossen came over and slapped Michael on the shoulder. "You're gonna love it and Joey's gonna kill us, 'cause then you'll want to spend all your time roping. Of course, you'll have to get darn good before you can out rope her, but women have to stress over something. Maybe you two could team rope together. Then she wouldn't mind us taking you away from her."

Michael wasn't sure how to answer that and simply walked into the house with the rest of them. He went straight over to Joey and squatted down in front of her to ask her how she was feeling. He looked at her for a second, trying to get a take on how she was doing and she looked back at him and smiled and asked, "How did you do out there today? Do you finally feel like you can eat with us without fussing?" She reached and wiped at the dust on his cheek.

"I'm not sure how I did, but I had a good time. I'm definitely not used to being in the saddle for almost twelve hours a day and I'm going to be miserable tomorrow, but it was fascinating. How did you do? Is the hip bending any better?"

She nodded half-heartedly. "It's getting a little better all the time. I'm fine, but I really missed you today. I almost wished I hadn't asked them to haul you along with them, but I want you to feel free to be welcome, too." She shrugged. "It's a toss up I guess. At any rate, I'm really glad to see you back here all in one piece. It can be a long day vaccinating. Are you going to stay for dinner this time?"

"Absolutely. Can I help you to the table? Were you able to sit last night to eat?"

"For a few minutes." She sighed. "It's still ridiculously sore. I have a whole new appreciation for having been healthy and pain free my whole life. That opposition in all things deal, I guess." She offered him her hand and he stood to pull her to her feet and then put an arm around her to steady her while he helped her get her crutches under her.

At the table, he helped her to get as comfortable as possible, padded by pillows, as her brothers and the others stood by and watched. Once she was settled, he sat down next to her and they quickly said a prayer over the food and started in. Michael watched her face while she attempted to eat and when just a few minutes into the meal, he knew she was struggling, he got up again and helped her back into the overstuffed recliner and then brought her her plate and set her drink down beside her. Naomi brought her own plate and came and sat with her. Michael went back to his plate at the table and hurried to finish.

When they were done, he took his plate and followed the others to the sink and loaded his dishes into the dishwasher like everyone else did and then went in to sit next to Joey again while Naomi took her and Joey's plates to the kitchen. He could tell Joey wasn't feeling too hot and checked to see if she needed more pain medicine and then went and got it for her when Joey admitted to being miserable.

Coming back, he sat next to her on the couch and pulled her to lean on him without even asking her about it first. He knew he was able to help her relax and it was exactly where he wanted her anyway. When she was there, he gently brushed her hair back from her face and asked, "Where would you take yourself tonight, Joey, to take yourself out of the pain?"

She took a big breath and released it and then thought quietly for a second. "I think tonight I'd go to the pond in the dark in the rain. We have a hot mineral spring here that Dad piped into a pond when we were little and it stays warm and marvelous all year long. No moss or fish or anything live in it because it's too warm and so it's just this clean, sandy bottom and clear water.

"It's heavenly. Especially in the dark and the rain. It's great when it's raining because the air is cool and the rain is cool and then the water is like a hot tub. The mineral water makes you buoyant and it's . . . Well, it's hard to explain, but it's incredibly nice. I keep wondering if it would ease some of the pressure of lying on this hip. Maybe tomorrow I'll try it if I can get down there. You should go out there if you really are sore. The mineral water is wonderfully therapeutic."

He grinned. "I'm definitely sore. But it's not as much where you'd think. My low back and my knees are what got so tired. I had no idea ranch work was that way. Your brothers are machines."

Laying there on his chest, she smiled. "They are, aren't they? There are days when they work me under the table, but they're the best. Both figuratively and in the record books. Rossen and Slade are both world champions. Rossen in roping and Slade was all around cowboy. He'd have been roping and all around too except that he nearly got killed by a bull that year and had to take a few months off. At any rate, they are the best of the best. And the others are nearly as good. Have they started teaching you to rope yet?"

"Today, actually. At lunch. Sean said I'd never be the same after heeling, whatever that means, and Rossen said you were as good as they are. Is that true?"

She shook her head against him, but he could hear the smile in her voice. "No, of course not. I don't think I could ever be. They're so much bigger and stronger than I am, but it was kind of them to tell you that. I can hold my own when we're vaccinating or branding, but that's all. I've never competed like they do."

He looked down into her face at that. "That surprises me. I would have thought you'd be right in the thick of things competing with them. No?"

His question made her look a little sheepish and he had to wonder what she was going to tell him. With a little shrug she said, "Well, roping is mostly just the cowboys. There are women occasionally, but it's a guy thing. I used to hang with them when I was younger, but then it got to be a pain dealing with all those men. You wouldn't believe how they show off when there's a female around. It got a little over the top."

She paused and then smiled. "Rossen had to break up a couple of fights and he recommended that I might be more comfortable in the stands with Mom. He was right and since then I only rope when it's just our own guys. I don't know if you've noticed, but Rossen has this way about him that kind of makes you stand up and listen. He's pretty soft spoken, and he doesn't say anything very often, but when he does, you know it's wise advice. I haven't questioned him since I was about five."

Michael thought back to the night before when Rossen had warned him to treat her like a queen. Yeah, you definitely had to stand up and listen. Even though he was soft spoken, you didn't question that he was powerful under that easy demeanor. Powerful and wise.

Joey was definitely right. Michael didn't question the fact that Joey could cause a ruckus among a bunch of cowboys either. He smiled at the thought of them actually fist fighting over her. This certainly wasn't the country club back in New York City. He smoothed the hair back from her face and said, "I think I would have liked to have seen the cowboys fighting over you. I'll bet it was a rush, huh?"

She turned and looked up at his grin with a look of disbelief. "Michael . . . Now you're sounding like a guy."

"Which is good, isn't it? Especially after what you used to think of me?"

"No." She shook her head again. "You never seem just like one of the guys. Enjoying a fight doesn't seem like you. And it wasn't a rush. It was awful! I've never been so embarrassed. They were heathens."

"That would be smitten heathens, I believe." She rolled her eyes and turned into him and he put his arm around her snuggly. "You can't blame the poor guys, Joey. They probably couldn't help themselves."

At that, she changed the subject. "Are you going out with them again tomorrow? Did they get all the vaccinating done?"

"Rossen said they aren't done, but they're going to run the cows that are closer in somewhere and put them through a chute. I'm not sure what he meant by that, but that's the plan. I actually have to go out of town again tomorrow afternoon for a couple of days. And apparently Slade and Isabel are traveling tomorrow as well. We're going to ride in to the airport together."

She nodded and spoke against him, "Isabel raises Thoroughbreds out in California. They have a horse running in the Kentucky Derby on Saturday. They think it has a good chance of winning. They're going to Lexington for the race. You should see this ridiculous hat she'll be wearing."

Blandly, he commented, "I'd guess every horse owner or trainer who ever entered that race thought that their horse had a good chance of winning. Otherwise they wouldn't enter, would they?"

"No, I suppose not." She paused and thought about it for a moment. "One of these days I'm going to get a horrendous hat and go back there with them. I usually hate all those crowds, but I'll bet it's a lot better in real life than it is on TV. I'd like to go a few days early so I could watch them actually getting the horses there and used to the place. It seems wild how they fly the horses in and everything. I'll bet security is unreal there. Have you ever wanted to see something like that?"

Completely at a loss as to how to answer that, Michael simply nodded and touched a strand of her hair. He wished he knew how to broach the subject of his horse farm with her. For some reason, he was loathe to even mention it. And the rest of the life he'd as good as left behind when he came here. It had been five weeks since he'd been here, but New York felt like a lifetime away from this time and place and this beautiful girl snuggled against him.

Finally, he admitted, "I've been to the Kentucky Derby, and you're right. Everyone should see it in their lives, but it's blown out of proportion, as far as I'm concerned. Yes, it's the greatest Thoroughbred race horses in the world, but sometimes it seems like all those masses of people have forgotten that it's a horse race and not the social event of the year. To a lot of people it's about being seen at the same venue as Michael Jordan and Kim Kardashian, not about the most incredible animal athletes on the planet."

She pulled away from him and looked up into his face. "Geez, you sound disgusted, Michael. Whatever made you so bitter about Michael Jordan and Kim Kardashian?"

He shook his head and pulled her close again. "Sorry. I didn't mean to sound that way. Forgive me. I must just be tired." He ran a hand up her back gently. "I should probably go. I haven't so much as sat down at my piano bench today. I need to go home and get busy before I'm too tired to focus." He said the words, but he didn't want to leave in the slightest and Joey didn't appear too anxious to move out of his arms.

Instead of moving, she sighed against him and the feel of her breath against his neck made the thought of leaving even less urgent than it had been. Neither one of them said anything and as her brothers and the others finished cleaning up dinner and began to all go their several separate ways, Michael worried again about how he was going to tell her he wasn't just a musician. Naomi was the last one in the great room with them and as she finished what she was doing and wiped her hands on a dish towel, she came over to stand beside them and asked Michael, "Is she asleep?"

At her words, Joey leaned her head back and looked up at her mother. "I'm not asleep, Mom. Did you need something?"

"No, sweetie, I just wondered about helping you lie down. Call me if you need me. I'll just be in reading with your father." She looked up at Michael. "They said you did a great job out there today. Most people would be exhausted after a day like that. Thank you for helping them. And for coming to dinner. It was good to have you stay. Good night."

"Good night, Naomi. Thank you for making me welcome. Dinner was wonderful. The whole day was. And completely off the record, I am more than exhausted. Your sons are machines. You should be incredibly proud of them. They're good men. All of them."

She beamed at that. "Thank you. I agree with you. All of my children are wonderful people, but it's always marvelous to hear it. And I won't breathe a word about how tired you are." She squeezed his shoulder as she went out of the room.

Chapter 25

Alone in the great room, the silence after the recent organized chaos felt loud in his ears. His mind was humming trying to figure out how to tell her more about himself without messing it up or sounding like a stuffed shirt. And with wondering if it was ethical to kiss a girl who was hurt this badly and taking pain medicine. He wished he wasn't leaving tomorrow and that he wouldn't be gone for quite so long when he did.

He thought back to the night before when Cooper had commented that Joey wasn't usually snuggly. Was she letting him hold her like this just because she was a little out of it because of the Percocet, or was it there a reason she let him get closer than other guys in her life?

He was no closer to figuring out any of the answers when she rolled back and looked up at him. After watching him for a second, she asked, "You're very quiet. What goes on inside that head?"

He took her hand and wove his fingers through hers and admitted, "I'm just trying to figure out what to do about you, Joey. You know how men are supposed to have their lives all neatly compartmentalized? I don't have a compartment that fits you. I had no idea that I'd find something like you in Wyoming and I'm not sure where to store you." He smiled at her. "So now what do I do?"

"What do you mean, something like me?"

Choosing not to answer that question, he asked one of his own. "Cooper and your brothers last night were surprised that you let me hold you like this. They said you usually have some serious personal space where guys are concerned. So, I'm curious. Why do you let me into your space?"

She looked honestly confused about that and then replied, "I don't know the answer to that, Michael. Out there on that cliff, I was struggling and I needed help and it just happened and I felt okay about it. I still feel okay about it. I'm not sure why. Actually, I love it." She paused as she considered her words and then said, "This is going to sound crazy, but it has something to do with your music. Don't ask me to explain it, because I couldn't, but for some reason I trust you more than most guys. I have from the very first. How weird is that?" After another second she asked, "Does it bother you? Me letting you into my space?"

He traced her eyebrow with his fingertip and shrugged. "I was being honest about not knowing what to do with you, Joey. Of course holding you doesn't bother me. Just the opposite. I'd be here twenty four seven if I could.

"The fact that I feel this way does trouble me. To say that I have serious personal space where women are concerned would be the understatement of the century. I'm afraid I don't just have serious personal space, but could almost be considered anti-social toward them. I never trust women. I haven't for years. I had to learn that the hard way. It's no wonder you thought I was gay. I guess that's better than thinking I'm a woman hater. That's probably what most of them think. But I've trusted you from the start as well. You're very different than any of the other women I've been around much." He smiled almost sadly. "You don't bother me. You scare me."

After seriously studying him for a few seconds, she shook her head. "I'm sorry, but I don't believe anything in the world scares you, Michael. At first nothing could scare you because you just didn't care one way or another. Now that you aren't so down, you're too in control to be frightened of anything, aren't you? And what could be scary about me? I'm just a Wyoming farm girl. What you see is what you get.

"I've tried the city, I've tried the glamour, and I've tried the career thing. And all of them are okay, but they're not really me. I've even tried the 'find someone I wanted to be with forever' thing, and decided I must be too picky. I've come full circle and am home again. This is where I'm happiest. There's nothing scary about me or here. Boring is probably a better adjective."

Michael laughed out loud at her. "Oh, you think so, huh? I hate to be so honest, but you frighten the dickens out of me. Boring." He shook his head and chuckled softly. "You're very entertaining when you're refreshingly clueless."

She wasn't smiling when she looked back at him. "Now you're being mean, Michael. Being a farm girl doesn't necessarily mean I'm clueless. I've had other options. I just didn't choose them. It was a conscious decision to come back here. I'm not uneducated and backward. I'm just not as happy somewhere else as I am here."

"I can understand that. I'm the same way. Why do you think I asked Doc if he'd sell me Merv's house? There's no place in the world like this valley." He put a soothing hand to her cheek. "Easy, Joey. I wasn't slamming you. I love the fact that you're so down to earth. That's what sets you apart. That's what's so appealing. That's what's so scary. Refreshing isn't a bad thing. It's great. I just never thought I'd end up here."

Still looking skeptical, she asked, "Where is here, Michael? Are we talking Wyoming? Or are we talking in my personal space?"

He shook his head. "Neither. We're talking out of my comfort zone. That's all. Settle down, baby sister. I was trying to tell you that I think I'm falling in love with you, not that you're a hick."

Her eyes got wide at that and she hesitated, "I don't know if you should joke about something like that, Michael. Now I'm the one who's frightened."

"No." He shook his head and looked at her mouth and touched it gently with his fingertip. "I don't believe you, either, Joey. You're too solidly sure of who you are to be frightened by me. And I'm not joking. Not in the slightest."

The striking blue eyes met his darker blue ones and held and then she looked down and rolled back into him. He pulled her closer and held on and leaned his face against her shining hair. At least she hadn't panicked and booted him out. For a minute there, he'd wondered. He ran a finger along her collarbone and then rubbed the little bone behind her ear and felt her almost melt against him. Maybe he shouldn't have said anything to her, but he wanted her to have a little bit of an inkling of how he was feeling before he flew out of here tomorrow.

For a long time he just held her quietly. She must have fallen asleep again and finally he decided he really did need to get home before he fell asleep as well. It didn't take a rocket scientist to know that Naomi and Rob wouldn't be amused. For that matter, Joey herself wouldn't be at all happy with him either.

He brushed her hair back from her face and was just about to whisper her name when she looked up at him and he realized she hadn't been sleeping at all. For some reason that surprised him. What had she been thinking, laying here so quietly for so long? He wished he could read her mind the way he knew she could read his occasionally.

He put a hand into her golden hair, wrapped it around his fingers and asked, "You okay? You were so quiet I thought you'd gone to sleep."

"I'm fine. Just thoughtful." He stroked the little bone behind her ear again and she went on, "I think I know what you mean about not knowing what to do about me."

"Why's that?"

"Mmm. I just do." She changed the subject and asked, "How is your studying about the plan of salvation going?"

194

"Well. I haven't spent enough time studying, but what I'm learning is all good. Although it feels like the more I understand, the more I realize I have a long way to go. Do you ever really know all of it, even after being a missionary?"

"Yes and no. I know God's plan, but I'm still always learning new details I didn't fully understand. I'm sure it will always be that way. But don't let it bog you down. The idea is to embrace truth and keep on seeking for it. There are a few key concepts that are the foundation and then the rest is just steadily moving forward. Line upon line, precept upon precept. Consistently and persistently. It's not a sprint; it's finishing the race on God's team. True Christianity is mostly an attitude I think."

Softly, he asked, "All of life is mostly an attitude isn't it?"

She was watching him as she considered that. "Mmm, yeah, I think you're right. I hadn't ever thought of it that way." She was still thoughtful and he wished he could look inside her head as she looked back at him.

He tried not to focus on her mouth as he said, "I need to go home, Joey. It's getting late and we're both tired. You're parents are going to be sick to death of me."

She sighed. "I know you need to go. I just don't want you to. When are you going to be back?"

"Monday afternoon sometime. I'll bet you're up and riding around by then."

Her breath came out in another sigh as he stroked the small bone of her ear again. "I hope so. Maybe I can have my head together better by the time you get back."

Pushing his fingers into her hair, he gently closed them and said quietly, "I think your head is together just fine now. I wish I was going to be here with you on Sunday to go to church with you."

Those honest eyes promised him. "Next week. Bank on it. But there will be a ward near wherever you are. Just get on line and you can find one. There are wards all over the world. It's very reassuring."

195

On thinking about that, she was right. Knowing God was this organized was very reassuring.

He was having a hard time keeping his own head together when she looked at him like that. Didn't she realize that there was no way he could resist her when he could see those blue sparks?

Absently mindedly, he said, "I'll find a ward." He pulled her closer and gave up trying not to focus on her mouth. In almost a trance, he lowered his head, watching her sparking eyes until his lips touched hers and he closed his eyes to focus on the feel of her mouth under his. Man, he'd wanted this for weeks it seemed. He kissed her slowly and gently and then regretfully raised his head. He really didn't want to stop yet, but he didn't want to scare her either.

He ran a thumb along her jaw line and took a deep breath. "Kick me out of here, Joey, or I'm going to have to kiss you some more and your brothers will be after me."

She didn't give him the smile he was hoping for; just looked back at him with those lethal eyes and he wasn't sure what to think. The blue sparks were still smoldering and he leaned down and kissed her again gently and then carefully moved to stand up and offered her his hand. Once she was on her feet, he put an arm around her again, but before he got around to handing her her crutches he drew her against him tightly and kissed her again. This time with more of the need he was feeling.

When she gently but firmly pushed him away, he sighed and ran a hand through his hair. She smiled shyly up at him and he laughed when she said, "Uh, Michael. You're in my personal space."

Shaking his head, his voice was low and almost husky when he teased her, "And you have great personal space." He gently pushed a strand of her hair back from her cheek. "Where are you heading? Can I help you get there?"

"No, I'll be fine, thanks. I'll walk you to the door. Well,

maybe I'll hobble you to the door, but you know what I mean."

He smiled and put a hand to the small of her back. "Don't. I appreciate the thought, but really I'd rather know that you don't have to walk further with your crutches for me. I can see myself out fine." He touched her on the cheek. "Sleep well, I'll come and tell you good bye before I leave tomorrow."

He'd have pulled away and walked out the door, but she was still leaning on him and there was no way he was pushing her away from him. Finally, she looked up at him again and he met her eyes for a long moment, glanced down at her mouth again and then reluctantly pulled his eyes away and looked back up. "Good night, Joey."

"Good night."

All the way across the little valley to his house with Blue at his heels, he thought about how it had felt to kiss her. He couldn't believe the way she had helped his heart to go from shattered to pieces a few weeks ago to happier than he ever remembered feeling just now. Kissing her almost made him feel guilty about not missing his dad at the moment. He shook his head as he walked. His dad would have been thrilled for him. He didn't doubt that for a second. His dad would have adored her.

Back at home, his piano fairly called to him and another song flowed almost effortlessly. Her kiss had been the most inspirational of all. She had been the best thing that ever happened to him as far as his music and just about everything else in his life to date. He didn't ever remember feeling this way and looking forward to the future with such hope as he did now. It was a great feeling.

When he finally made it to his bedroom, he knelt and thanked God for the blessing of Joey in his life. He'd never been this grateful for anything and he laid down, exhausted physically and blessedly at peace in his heart. Drifting off, he let himself think about her kiss. She definitely had some awesome personal space.

Jaclyn M. Hawkes

Chapter 26

Even the sunshine dimmed when Michael drove away with Slade and Isabel in his rented Trailblazer and it started to rain within the hour. Joey was frankly a little depressed that he was gone and couldn't face lying around without his peaceful company nearby. She tried to settle in and read and when that didn't work she put in a movie.

Her mother must have known she was at a loose end as she came out with her purse and her car keys because she took one look at Joey and said, "Are you up to riding in the car at all? I have to run into town and mail some things and pick up a few groceries. We could pack you in pillows."

Gratefully, Joey accepted, "I would love to get out of this house, Mother. It's silly, but Michael leaving has depressed the heck out of me."

Her mother looked at her, but didn't say anything and Joey was actually a little surprised. She'd expected her to say something about the fact that Joey had become better friends, faster, with this non-member easterner than she ever had with any other guy friend in her life. It was enough to make her think twice herself and the whole time they were driving over the rough gravel road before they made it to the pavement, Joey thought about what was going on with him and didn't even have to work to keep her mind off the pain from the bumps.

She had no idea what was wise or prudent, she only knew that from the first moment she had heard his music he had done something to her heart that had never happened before. At first glance, she felt like she should be worried, because after all, she didn't know him well. After all these weeks, she still didn't even know his last name other than his pseudonym.

And he wasn't a member. That fact alone should have made her hesitant, but the spirit she felt when she was with him overcame any worries she had. That sweet, warm peace that he brought with him helped her to know that Heavenly Father was okay with their friendship and that was enough for her. She'd enjoy him as she waited to see just what was unfolding here. She was hoping the reason she felt at peace was because he was going to be a member soon and it would be a non issue.

Last night, even as tired as she'd been, sleep had been long in coming. She hadn't been able to get her mind off of how nice it had been when he'd kissed her. She didn't often kiss her guy friends and even when she did, it was invariably an obligatory quick peck after a date of some kind. Kissing someone because she really wanted to kiss them had been foreign to her—until last night with Michael.

With him it had been the most amazing sweet need until he finally did kiss her and then she almost felt silly about how let down she was when he told her good night and went home, even when she was the one who had ended the kiss.

How comfortable they were together was positively incredible to her. Even that first day when she'd fixed his car and fallen asleep on his couch had been uncanny. There was something about him that truly did make her trust him with a gut deep sureness, in spite of how sad he had been when she'd met him. Who knows? Maybe it was because he had been so sad that she was drawn to him.

All she knew was that he made her feel more deeply and more poignantly and more surely than any human being on the planet ever had and she couldn't help the way she felt about him, baggage or no. He was more than talented and smart and good looking. He fascinated her at the same time that he brought this unreal sense of rightness to her very soul that had been missing so achingly this last little while since she'd felt like it was time to settle down.

She'd been thinking about him the whole trip in to town and she was surprised to realize that they were already in Hollister and her mother was getting out of the car in the lot between the post office and the little grocery store there. Joey stayed in the car as her mother went first to mail her letters and then headed into the store. Even though she hadn't been inside for an overly long time, Joey still had to get out of the Grand Cherokee and stand beside it on her crutches to get the pressure off her hip and thigh for a few minutes.

She was still standing there when she was amazed to see a stretch limo cruise down the little country highway and pull into the parking lot beside her. A uniformed chauffer got out and opened the door and a beautiful dark haired woman looking like she had just walked out of a glamour magazine stepped out and went into the post office while the driver waited behind like a Royal Canadian Mountie. Joey looked on and almost shook her head. She had never seen anything like this in Hollister, Wyoming in her life!

The woman was only in the post office for a couple of minutes and when she came out there was no doubt that she wasn't happy about something. She fairly stomped back to the pompous car. As the driver opened the door for her, she glanced up and noticed Joey standing with her crutches next to the car and she switched gears and came over to Joey and said, "Excuse me. You wouldn't happen to be a local would you?"

Joey nodded. "I am. Did you need something?"

"Yes, actually. Could you tell me? Has there recently been a very wealthy banker named Morgan from back east move here? Tall, with short dark hair. Drives a black Ferrari. Would you know of him?"

Shaking her head, Joey assured her, "I'm sorry. No new wealthy bankers in Ferrari's. Someone like that would stand out like a sore thumb here and I'd definitely have at least heard of him. Have you lost one?" Joey smiled, but the woman didn't think she was very funny and didn't even answer as she was handed back into her fancy limousine.

When her mother came back out with her groceries and Joey struggled back into the car, she laughed about the stretch limo in their little town. "What in the world do you suppose she was thinking, looking here for someone like that?" Laughing again, she added, "And she definitely wasn't happy to have lost the guy. I wonder if she was his wife or something and the man ran out on her. She didn't look like she was used to not getting her own way. I almost felt sorry for her; poor, rich, glamour girl that she was."

Her mother only looked at her a little strangely again and Joey wondered what was on her mother's mind to make her so quiet this morning.

Chapter 27

Kentucky Derby day at the Rockland Ranch had taken on a carnival atmosphere ever since Slade had found and married Isabel. She still owned half of the California horse farm that regularly had horses in this type of big races and this year the party atmosphere was over the top because her horse Obsidienne was the favorite to win.

Cooper had gotten totally into the spirit of the thing and was sporting this ridiculous huge musketeer hat with a flowing white feather that completely blocked everyone's view of the television whenever he jumped up to get anything and Sean and Lexie each wore crazy hats of their own. Even Rob was walking around wearing a chef's hat, which didn't really work for the Kentucky Derby, but it made everyone laugh when he went through anyway.

Joey had been given the big overstuffed recliner and had been outfitted with about four pillows in case her hip got uncomfortable before the big race and there were all kinds of party foods being passed around as if it were a super bowl party. It was nearly an hour before the race was to begin and they were all watching the pre-race hoopla where the sports commentators went over every possible little detail about the horses and their jockeys and trainers and owners. Any little tidbit that could potentially make a story was explored while they went back and forth between the horses, the celebrities present, and the current odds for each horse as the numbers changed on the boards.

Several times Isabel and Slade were shown in their box in the stands as the announcers made a big deal of how Isabel had disappeared a couple of years earlier to escape her abusive father and his mafia ties and had shown up several months later with a new name and a World Champion All Around Cowboy husband who just happened to look like the Marlboro man. The Rocklands all cheered at this and Joey cracked up when she saw Isabel looking positively Queen Elisabethish in an outlandish floppy hat with a whole bird's nest on it. Isabel's tease about being a member of the Stupid Hat Club at the big races had long been a joke around the Rockland family.

There were two other horses that appeared to be the main competition for Isabel's horse. One was a seven and half million dollar gray owned by some Arabian sheik that had been flown over from the Persian Gulf on its own personal Leer jet and the other was a stud colt owned by a banking magnate from somewhere in Upstate New York. As they told the stories of these three top horses and showed the owners and trainers and respective jockeys, Joey nearly sat upright when they showed the banker from New York. It was obviously a distance shot and was somewhat grainy, but it was astounding how much the man looked like Michael.

Just when she had been going to comment on it, Cooper piped up, "Wow, did you see that guy? He could be Michael's twin if he grew his hair out a few inches. He looks just like him."

Naomi walked closer to the TV to see what they were commenting on, but when she was too late and they had gone on to another story Rob assured her, "Don't worry, Mother. I'm sure they'll show him another forty times before we finally get to post time. He really did look remarkably like Michael, though. I wonder if they could be related. They are both from New York state."

Everyone laughed and Ruger asked, "Dad, do you remember how many million people live in New York City alone. Isn't it like nine million? I doubt they are related."

"You never know. Especially not in a state like New York. You never know about anything in a place like that."

The laughter and teasing went on, but every time they showed the clean cut New York banker there were comments about how much he looked like Michael. He was even named Michael something or other and Joey watched with interest as they discussed this gorgeous New Yorker who was a major stockholder of one of the most financially stable banks in the country. He was apparently considered a most eligible bachelor, but was singularly private, which only made him tend to be more appealing to the press that loved a good juicy story.

At one point the commentator speculated about what socialites the handsome young mega millionaire was seeing at the time and Joey rolled her eyes, remembering Michael's cynical comment about Michael Jordan and Kim Kardashian. When the very next segment was indeed on Kim Kardashian, what hat she was wearing and who she was with, Joey knew that Michael had indeed been right about society having lost sight of the purpose of the whole event.

They eventually made it to post time and as the bugle sounded and the sleek, racy horses paraded past with their jockeys aboard and the red coated pony riders, the excitement in the room ratcheted up to fever pitch. Joey always tried to see if she could pick the winner from the way the horses behaved here with the pony horses and she had been relatively accurate at it in races past. She truly hoped Isabel's horse would win, even though she had owned the horse that won it only two years prior and in a way that seemed almost selfish.

Still, it would be so cool to win it again. Especially with a rare filly that could compete with the big boys. Even as Joey thought that, she had to wonder if a big chestnut stud colt wouldn't have otherwise been her pick. He was raising a bit of a ruckus, but still had a focus that was impressive.

As they finally lunged out of the gates at the start of the race, Joey noticed that the big chestnut colt she had picked at the parade got bumped as it came out and literally went to its knees before regaining its footing and following the rest of the pack down the track. Sadly, today wouldn't be that colt's day, but she didn't worry about it as she tried to follow Isabel's horse's progress as it came around the long track there in Lexington, Kentucky.

Coming into the back stretch, Isabel's horse was in the lead and Joey cheered along with all the others in the room for it to win. Surprisingly, the closest challenger that was fast closing the gap was the big chestnut that had gone to its knees out of the gates. Joey couldn't help herself. Even though it was Isabel's horse that was slowly being overtaken, Joey had to secretly root for this great chestnut horse that had the heart to overcome such a fall and still come around to win one of the greatest horse races in the world. The two sleek and athletic horses ran neck and neck for a number of lengths as they neared the finish line, but at seemingly the last minute, the big hearted chestnut pulled ahead to win the run for the roses by a head.

The entire room erupted into a huge groan of disgust and though Joey was disappointed for Isabel and Slade, she had to admire the desire that the winning horse had demonstrated to overcome such odds.

They watched as the spent horses galloped the track and then met up with the pony horses again. The winning horse was lathered and obviously tired, but the proud carriage of its head said it all as it was brought back to the winner's circle to be draped with the blanket of flowers and stand for the win pictures as the owner and trainers made their way toward the huge silver trophy in the circle down on the track.

For some reason, Joey hadn't realized that the big chestnut was the stud colt owned by the clean cut New York banker. As he was heading down to accept the trophy, the newscasters were going into more detail about the mega millionaire financier, his incredible record as the leader of both a huge and profitable banking institution as well as the sole heir to not one but two of the wealthiest families in the country. They went on to talk about his Thoroughbred farm that consistently produced some of the finest racers in the country and as he and his triple crown hopeful race horse made their way through, cameras were zooming in on him from every possible angle and Joey commented, "His likeness to Michael really is uncanny, isn't it?"

She had to almost feel sorry for the guy. He obviously wasn't enjoying the cameras being shoved into his face and at one point he actually had to put up an arm to deflect a flashbulb that appeared to practically hit him as the photographer went to get the picture.

As he put up the arm, the stitches that had been taken in the heel of his hand were directly in front of the camera and were unmistakable, even in the crush of the moment, and Joey made a strangled cry when she realized that it was, in fact, Michael she was watching on TV. There was no way there were two men who looked that much alike, and had the exact same shaped cuts on their left hands.

It was Michael all right. Her Michael. Soft spoken, sad, musician Michael. The man who held her when she hurt, and played his piano for her, and had gotten that very cut in the act of saving her life. The same Michael who beat her at scrabble and talked to her about God, and had made her heart race and her spirit dance when he had kissed her two nights ago.

She watched in a suffocating daze as he accepted the trophy with a tight smile that didn't reach his eyes, and then she couldn't see anymore because there were these awkward, painful drops coming out of her own eyes and blurring her vision. Hauling her crutches up off the floor beside her, she struggled to her feet and made her way to her old bedroom as the rest of her family watched her go in silent pity that only made her cry harder.

In her room, she collapsed painfully onto the bed, wondering what in the world had just happened. How could he be a banking magnate? One of the wealthiest men in the country. Eligible bachelor of the century. He was a pianist for crying out loud! A beautiful, sweet, kind, sad pianist. He ate frozen rubber entrees and hoarked her dog and drove Merv's old car. How had this happened?

For the first time in her life she had honestly begun to wonder if she had found him. She hadn't found anything! She turned her face into the pillow so the others wouldn't hear her sobbing. How had this happened?

She was hurt, and then furious, and then amazed, and then just incredibly, incredibly hurt again. Lying there, she began to see things more clearly. She'd been such a sucker. Such a small town, naive sucker. He'd never lied to her, he'd just never told her anything at all. She hadn't even known his last name.

The woman in the limo hadn't been crazy. It had been Joey who had been crazy to be so clueless as to not even realize one little bit that she had just been taken for a royal ride. He'd even teased about her being clueless. He'd probably laughed all the way to Lexington on his private jet. He had said he wasn't calling her a hick.

She buried her face deeper and cried harder than ever, wishing she could burrow right into the pillow and disappear. Nothing had ever hurt like being so betrayed by the one she had trusted the most. How had this happened?

When she was finally too worn out to cry anymore, she laid there and wondered why God had let her feel so good about him. Why had she felt so comfortable when all kinds of warnings should have been going off in her head and heart? She thought back over the weeks that Michael had been here and couldn't even begin to equate the haunted man who had shown up here back in March with the center of the media circus she had seen on TV. How had all of this happened?

Some time later, Cooper knocked on her door and poked his head in. "Mom said to tell you dinner is ready."

Joey rolled over and shook her head. "I'm still full from all the buffalo wings during the Derby. Tell her I don't really feel like eating, but thank you."

He watched her for a few seconds and then turned and ducked out the door and she rolled back over and buried her head again. How had she been so stupid?

She finally truly got to sleep after hours of troubled cat naps and intermittent waking to relive the heart breaking revelation about Michael and what he really was, but then a sudden rain storm woke her back up. Sighing, she tried to sit up. The long hours of tossing and turning had her hip and back tied in knots. She struggled to stand up and went to the window to watch the rain come down in sheets out in the blackness, hating the fact that she still needed strong pain medicine.

On an impulse, she pulled on a pair of shorts and a t-shirt and sandals, threw on her old raincoat and quietly let herself out the French doors to the deck. Maybe the hot mineral water would loosen up the throbbing ache and help her to finally rest without resorting to more narcotics. She slogged through the rain with her crutches and was glad she could pretend that the stupid tears that ran down her face were merely wayward rain drops. Even alone, she was embarrassed that she had been such a fool about him.

You'd have thought by the time she had made it through college, served a mission and dated as many men as she had that she'd have figured out how to avoid being taken in like this, but you'd have been wrong. The rubber tips of her crutches slipped in the wet grass at the bank of the pond and she set them aside and carefully hobbled down into the water without them.

She'd been right about the buoyancy of the mineral water soothing the strain on her hip. Almost immediately the ache that dogged her whether she was sitting, standing or lying down, eased and she breathed a long sigh of relief as she turned her teary face to the sky and let the rain and the pain mix in total indistinguishable darkness.

When the heat of the mineral water became too much, she kicked with her good leg and laid over on her back to float and let the chill of the rain and the soft night wind cool her. The sound of the raindrops hitting the water and the steamy mist that rose to waft off into the night soothed her heart and her mind and by the time her hip quit hurting so badly, she felt like she could go back in and sleep. She let the heat build and then got out and back into her rain coat. Slowly, she made her way back up and into her parents' home and went back to bed. This time to finally be able to rest.

It was Cooper again who cheerily blew a blubbery reveille the next morning with his lips. She couldn't help but smile at him when she pried her eyes open, even though little droplets of spit were flying in every direction from his wake up call. When he saw her waking, he asked, "Are you coming in to the singles ward with us, or staying and going with Mom and Dad?"

Joey groaned. "The singles ward. What time is it?"

He blew another off key mock bugle. "Time to get going. We're outta here in forty minutes, with or without any mermaids." He set her sandy sandals inside the bedroom door. "D'you go down to the pond in the night in the rain?"

"Yeah." She sighed as she struggled to sit upright. "I couldn't sleep for anything last night. The mineral water really helped. I'm sick to death of feeling so groggy from the painkillers."

"Well, just so you don't embarrass the rest of us by snoring in church. Seth called to see if you were coming. I'll try to save you some breakfast if you hurry." He went back out the door and as she struggled out of bed and to the shower she thought about Dr. Seth Weston. She sighed. She wasn't in love with Seth, but the whole fireworks thing had backfired with a vengeance. Maybe she should take another shot with Seth and the feelings would eventually come. He was a good man and she respected him. Maybe that was enough.

As she limped into the chapel with her crutches for sacrament meeting he came up to her and looked at her for a long moment before he said, "I guess I don't need to ask how you're doing. Are you okay?"

He made her smile for the first time in almost a whole day. "Are you telling me that I look awful, Seth? Because that's what it sounds like."

Looking properly guilty, he smiled back at her. "Sorry. You just don't look like you feel that great. Can I sit here with you guys or are you fellowshipping someone today?"

"We were saving this seat for you, actually." He helped her to gingerly sit down on the padded bench and then sat beside her and she asked, "Do I still need to come back in for an appointment tomorrow? Or can I just tell you it's still ridiculously sore, and call it good?"

He was looking at her again and then said, "Come in and get checked, but it would appear it's not just your hip that's out of sorts here today. Are you just discouraged about being injured? Or are you as unhappy as you look?"

She dropped her eyes and nudged him with her shoulder. "Don't analyze me, Dr. Weston. It will make me even worse. Can't you just be Seth right now and tell me something interesting about how your week went?"

"It was Seth asking that question, actually. My week went well. I'm so busy right now that I can't seem to take time for a lunch, but that's good I suppose. I'd rather that than be twiddling my thumbs. How did your week go?"

That question made her stop and think for a minute. She wondered how to answer it because she knew he was still in love with her and would be hurt to know that she'd finally fallen for someone and it wasn't him. At length, she simply said, "It was just a week, Seth. Nothing more, nothing less. I'm sorry I'm not overly enthusiastic. I'll do better next week. I promise."

The first counselor went to the microphone to start the meeting and they quit talking to listen. As Joey sat beside Seth for the duration of the meeting, she tried to listen to the speakers and at the same time, figure out what made her not fall for this nice, kind, handsome LDS man beside her, but then be so drawn to a haunted non-member who had needed a hair cut. There was no logic to it at all as far as she could see.

After the meeting, Seth walked her to the parking lot and left her there with her brothers after telling her goodbye and she remembered why she had begun to try to stay away from him. It wasn't that she disliked him. She liked him a lot. It was that she knew her lack of emotion toward him hurt him and she could read it in his eyes. It made her almost ashamed and she hesitated to try one more time with him. She didn't think one more try would change the way she felt about him. It would only hurt him worse and that wasn't very fair to him.

At home, while she was still wondering what to do about Seth, Bryan called. He was on tour just now and had a concert in Salt Lake City in a couple days and then another one in Denver two days later. He wanted to know if he could come and get her for the concert in Salt Lake.

She told him what had happened and that she wasn't terribly mobile, and he first was disappointed that she hadn't told him she was hurt, and then reasoned that since she couldn't work anyway, she should come hang out with him and let him baby her. He promised to put her in a cushy seat somewhere for the concert where she wouldn't have to deal with the crowds at all and if she was up to it, he'd take her to Denver with him as well.

Surprisingly, she took him up on it. What he said made sense. If she couldn't work anyway, what was the point in sitting around here moping and feeling like a doormat?

He promised to be there around noon the next day to get her and she got off the phone feeling a touch guilty for encouraging him, but still glad that maybe he could help take her mind off of Michael. She still couldn't believe she had been such a sucker.

Chapter 28

Michael picked up his bag, thanked the pilots warmly, told them to head on back to New York and followed Slade and Isabel off of his grandfather's jet that had just landed in Jackson Hole. He walked down the short set of stairs, looked all around at the glorious mountains, and took a deep breath of Wyoming air. It was good to be home. He couldn't wait to get back and see Joey. It felt like it had been weeks since he'd left her four days ago.

Rossen met them in his pickup to take them home and as they piled in and got underway, Michael asked him how Joey was doing. Her tall, soft spoken brother with that exact same color of sun streaked blonde hair looked across the truck at him and said casually, "Oh, she's fine. Except for crying most of the last two days."

Slade and Isabel both leaned forward in the back seat and Michael looked across the truck in concern and asked earnestly, "What happened? Is she okay? Why has she been crying?"

Rossen didn't take his eyes off the road as he said in an off-handed way, "Uh, well. She was watching the Kentucky Derby and found out that this guy who she had fallen for, hadn't been all that straight forward with her. It pretty much just wiped her out."

Michael leaned back in his seat and ran a frustrated hand through his hair with a sigh. "I was afraid of that. I shouldn't even have gone. I just didn't want to let Drew down and all the guys who have worked so hard. Not going felt like blowing off all of their effort. I should have told her something, I just didn't know what to say."

Looking across the truck cab, Rossen nodded. "I can understand that, Michael. But Joey can't. I'm not sure what she's thinking, but I'm going to venture a guess that it runs along the lines of you basically lied to get close to her and she trusted you. Know what I mean?"

"No." Michael paused and then added sadly, "Yes. But I haven't lied to her. I haven't. But what was I supposed to do? Tell her that it's of utmost importance to me that everyone be thoroughly aware that I have a lot of money and a big, fancy horse farm?"

He shook his head and looked out the window and said softly, "It was incredibly nice to be befriended because I was a human being and not because I was Michael Morgan, the heir to the fortune."

Shaking his head, Rossen said, "That friendship hasn't changed, Michael. She's not the kind of girl who loves conditionally. But, she doesn't believe you befriended her because she's a one in a million. Right now, I'm betting she thinks she's just another one of a myriad of women to you and didn't warrant details. I'll bet she doesn't understand that you were being unmaterialistic. I'll bet she just thinks that you were toying and that she didn't matter enough for you to be honest with her. That to you, it was none of her business, and that what she knew or felt wasn't even an issue."

"Which isn't true at all."

Rossen shrugged. "Prove it."

They rode in silence for a few minutes and then Rossen turned the radio on low and mentioned, "That's another thing. She's sore and discouraged and let Bryan Cole talk her into coming to get her to take her to a couple of his concerts. He's due to show up there just about the time we are and then they're heading to Salt Lake and then Denver."

In a tone that totally belied the word, Michael replied, "Great."

Rossen pulled his truck up to Michael's house first and as he let him out, they locked glances and then Rossen said, "Good luck. You're gonna need it." He gave Michael a grin and pulled away again to take Slade and Isabel home. Michael didn't even put his bag in his house before he strode off across the pasture to find Joey.

She was leaving her mom's house and by the time Michael realized where she was, Bryan was helping her into the passenger seat of a sleek, low slung Mustang GT in the gravel road in front. As Bryan shut the door for her and came around to the other side, he noticed Michael striding up and said, "Hey, Joseph. What are you doing here? Or is it Michael? I was watching the Kentucky Derby and was surprised to see you. What should I call you anyway?"

Michael was focused on the tall blonde who was inside the car and said absently mindedly. "Michael. Joseph is just what I write the music under." He strode to the passenger door and opened it and then crouched down next to Joey. Bryan got in the driver's side and looked over at Michael in surprise as Michael met Joey's eyes for a long moment and then said quietly, "I missed you. How are you feeling?"

Acting as if there wasn't hurt and distrust etched into her eyes, she calmly and coolly answered, "I'm fine, Michael. Congratulations on your Derby win. Your horse was beautiful."

"Thanks. When are you coming home?"

She was still coolly polite when she told him, "I'm not sure."

Not knowing what to say to her and wishing Bryan Cole would dry up and disappear instead of sitting there watching this, Michael reached in and put a gentle hand on her cheek. He almost wondered if she was going to flinch and he knew she didn't pull away only because she didn't want to make a scene. Wishing he could tell her a thousand things, he settled for a simple, intense, almost tender, "Hurry." Her brilliant

217

blue eyes narrowed as she tried to understand and after a long, steady look he leaned in and ever so softly kissed her. "Hurry."

Across the car, Bryan cleared his throat loudly and Michael dragged his eyes away from Joey's to look at him. "What?"

Bryan's gaze was icy. "What do you think? I thought we were friends. Get out of my car."

Michael looked back at Joey and one more time he said, "Hurry." He squeezed her hand and then stood up and carefully shut the door, never taking his eyes off hers. Bryan started up the engine, put the car into gear and nearly ran over Michael's foot as he dug out with the glass packs rumbling deafeningly.

Michael didn't really blame him. He'd have been furious in Bryan's shoes, but Joey needed to know where Michael stood without any question. He watched the car drive away in a cloud of dust and when it was gone over the rise, he turned to head back to his house.

Hearing a sound, he glanced up to see Cooper standing on the porch a few feet away, grinning from ear to ear. "Holy cannoli, Michael. You're lucky he didn't punch you right in the mouth before he tried to drive over you. Or would that be right in the kisser? Nothing like staking a claim."

Michael gave him half of a smile. "Mind your own business, Coop. It's not polite to watch people kiss."

Cooper cracked up and retorted, "It's a heck of a lot more polite than kissing another guy's date inside his own car. Gees, you got a lot of . . . I'm not even sure what you got a lot of, but that's more guts than is healthy. That kind of thing will get you in trouble."

"Getting into trouble with the guy isn't my concern. It's getting out of trouble with the girl that I'm worried about." With that he headed back across the pasture to go unpack his stuff. Man, it was awful to watch her drive away with another man. He'd have to see if Naomi knew how long she'd be gone.

****

Bryan had driven for more than ten miles before he finally slowed down a little and commented sarcastically, "That was a touching little scene. So what's going on with you and Michael, or Joseph, or whoever he is?"

Looking out the window with bleary eyes, Joey tried to sound nonchalant, "Nothing is going on with Michael. I hardly know the man."

"He kisses you and you hardly know the man? How does that work?"

Joey sighed. She really wasn't in the mood for this right now. "Bryan, quit. You're mad at him and taking it out on me and I don't deserve this. I really do hardly know the man."

"You let him kiss you, Joey. Sitting beside me in my own car. Is there something I should know here? He's obviously kissed you before, hasn't he?"

She turned to him and said gently, "Bryan, I've always been honest with you. Always. But whether I've kissed another guy or not is not really any of your business. Is it?"

"Oh, so you won't deny kissing him even though you supposedly don't know him?"

Sadly, Joey admitted, "I thought I knew him, Bryan. I was just really badly mistaken. Do you think we can talk about something else? Because if you're going to continue to grill me about him and be angry with me for that touching little scene, you can just take me back home. It was him, not me, and short of slapping the guy, there wasn't much I could have done about it. I never dreamed he was going to do that. There is nothing between us. Frankly, I'm surprised he even came back to Wyoming. We're obviously not his usual stomping ground. Cut me some slack."

Hardly mollified, Bryan looked over at her and she met his eyes. "Why is he at your house? He was at the airport the last time I was here too. How long has he had a thing for you?"

Joey smiled sadly. "He's buying a house nearby that used to be one of our ranch hand's. I'm not sure why he was at my house, and he doesn't have a thing for me. Trust me. I'm just a girl he'd like to toy with. But you know me well enough to know that I'm nobody's toy. Now, can we change the subject?"

Pulling up at the junction to the paved highway, Bryan looked over at her and studied her. Finally, he pulled out onto the highway and said, "I'm sorry I got upset at you. That just took me by surprise a little." He reached across the car and took her hand. "I'm also sorry you got so hurt. Do you feel as lousy as you look like you feel?"

Trying to smile at him, she answered, "You're about the sixteenth person who has told me I look awful this week, but thank you for your concern. And yeah, I feel as lousy as I look." She didn't tell him she felt a lot lousier in her heart than in her hip.

"That got a little twisted in the telling. You know you're exquisite always. Especially to me. I'm your number one connoisseur. Remember? I was just trying to ask you how you were feeling."

She squeezed his hand. "No. Don't remind me that I feel lousy. Let's talk about something else and I'll try to forget it. Are you going to let me drive this baby?"

The tall, good looking country music star at her side grinned at her. "If you behave yourself, we'll see. But you have to keep your lips away from any other men than me or we have no deal, Miss Andretti. You think you're up to it?"

"No, but I'd really like to give it a shot anyway."

Chapter 29

Michael stood up and wiped the sweat off his brow with a sleeve, glad that he'd kept up a simple exercise regime since he'd been here or he'd have had to lie down and collapse. Rubbing the hand that he'd just smashed in the metal gate and wanting to swear, he knew he needed to keep his mind off of Joey and more on the task at hand or he was going to get killed working with these crazy Rockland brothers. She'd only been gone for four days, but coupled with the days he had been gone to Kentucky, it felt more like a month. He kept picturing her driving away in Bryan's Mustang and it was killing him.

He looked over to where Sean stood at the other end of the chute with a plastic sleeve all the way up his arm and even tired and lonely, he had to smile. It had been the longest four days of his life, but he'd never, ever forget it. The brothers had apparently inducted him into the brotherhood ever since that first day Joey had asked them to haul his butt out with them to vaccinate calves. Since then they'd had him branding, tagging, doctoring, and today had been the pinnacle of the deal as he'd been recruited to help them pregnancy check cows.

Talk about your initiation. He was afraid his business man's mind would be scarred forever. He'd had no idea that stuff like this was part of the production of beef, but he knew he would certainly never look at a filet mignon the same again in his life.

They ran the last cow through the squeeze chute at six-thirty p.m. and then hustled back up to Naomi and Rob's house to eat before they were hosting something called a

Jackpot. Michael wasn't entirely sure he understood what was going to happen here tonight, but all six of the brothers and even Rob had been coaching him in his roping for three days now and he hoped he could make a halfway decent showing of himself when it came his turn to try to catch his steer's head.

He was going to be roping with Sean tonight and whatever happened he knew Sean would be okay with it, but he really wanted to do well. He was more uptight about this than he ever remembered being even through any of his polo matches. This had been the most exhausting, and interesting, and lonely four days of his life.

****

Even though the concert had kept them up until the wee hours the night before, there came a knock on Joey's hotel room door at a little before nine. Her hip was better than it had been, but it was still a struggle to get around and it took her a minute to make it to her hotel room door. It was Bryan, coming to see if she was ready for breakfast. He greeted her with a smile, but he was still watching her with that same careful attention he'd been giving her since he'd picked her up three days before. It was almost starting to make her worry and she wondered what he was thinking when he looked at her like that.

Escorting her down to the elegant main restaurant, the maître d seated them discreetly at the back and out of the way where they wouldn't be so likely to be interrupted by one of Bryan's fans. After the server had taken their order and left, Bryan was back to his pensive study of her and finally, she asked him outright, "What's going on, Bryan? Why have you been looking at me so intently this whole trip? What are you thinking?"

He leaned back in his chair and gave her his easy going signature smile, but it didn't really convince her. Reaching across the table, he took her hand and began to play with the little sterling silver CTR ring that she wore on her right pinkie. In his adorable, slow, south Alabama drawl he tried to tease her, "I always look at you intently, Joey. You know that. It comes with the territory of being such a fantastic beauty. You should be used to it by now."

She eyed him skeptically. "Be honest, Bryan. What's going on? Is something wrong?"

A young woman brought them their drinks and he began to absently mindedly toy with his orange juice as he quietly said, "Yeah, there's something wrong, babe. But so far, I can't quite figure out what it is. This whole time, I've been trying to decide whether it's just that you're hurt and feel lousy, or if I'm correct in wondering where in tarnation your smile has gone." He gave her a sad smile and then went back to turning his glass in slow circles in the moisture that was wicking off of it. "You wanna talk about it? I'm a heck of a listener."

She looked down and shook her head. "You are a great listener, Bryan. And I'm sorry I haven't been more energetic. Please don't take my lack of enthusiasm personally. I must still be tired from my last week. I'm not the sitting around type and this whole deal has depressed the spirit right out of me. I'll do better. I promise."

"Is it only being so banged up, Joey? Because you're not whining. You're just not smiling. What happened to my 'tell it like it is and then soften the blow with a heart stopping smile' girl? What are you so unhappy about?"

She thought about that and what to say to this man who had stuck with her even when she'd tried to tell him that she didn't think she'd ever fall in love with him and marry him. She had always tried to be honest with him, but this was the first time there had actually been a guy that she thought she *could* fall in love with. And she'd messed this one royally.

She blew a stray tendril of hair out of her face with her bottom lip. Yeah, she'd almost inadvertently become a toy

223

and it had banged her up badly. She just couldn't admit to Bryan that it had been her heart that had been banged up the most and that it was a gorgeous and ridiculously wealthy New York banker who had done the worst damage and not a mad bull.

Turning back to Bryan she gave him the brightest smile she could muster. "It's just been a rough several days, Bryan. But that's no reason not to smile, is it? You'll have to remind me that I'm more durable than this." She squeezed his hand. "I'll resolve here and now to do better at smiling. Deal?"

He put his fist up and she met it with hers. "That sounds more like the Joey I know. Are you up to driving to the airport?"

"You just give me the keys and watch."

Chapter 30

Michael neatly caught his and Sean's first steer out, but then he completely missed the second one. They were waiting quietly for the team ahead of them to rope a third time when he heard the unmistakable rumble of the glass packs on Bryan's Mustang. He looked over to see the sweet racy car pull up in front of Rossen's house where Joey lived over the garage and for a second Michael forgot that he was just about to rope again. He saw Bryan come around and open the passenger door and then help Joey out.

She wasn't using her crutches, but she was still limping miserably and he wanted to go straight to her and see what he could do to help her, but that was a little out of the question right now. Even if he left the other ropers hanging, he would be likely to get that punch in the mouth from Bryan that Cooper had been teasing him about.

The steer ahead of them was released and the team ropers burst from the box and raced down the arena. Michael reluctantly pulled his eyes away from where Joey was slowly climbing the stairs to her apartment door with Bryan close beside her to watch the ropers close in on their steer. The header caught the horns, but the heeler only caught one hind foot as Michael and Sean rode their horses into the box and turned them and backed them into the corners.

****

Joey was tired to the bone as she dragged herself up the stairway to her apartment. She should have realized that no

225

matter how much Bryan could baby her, she hadn't really been up to a road trip just now. Driving into the valley, she had tried her best not to wonder what Michael was up to and she'd managed to keep him off of her mind pretty well until they'd rounded the bend and she saw his little white house.

Now, dragging herself up the stairs, when she glanced over at the jackpot roping that was going on in the big outdoor arena, she was absolutely surprised to realize that the tall, dark haired roper who was just now loading into the box with Sean, was none other than Michael. He had said Slade had started showing him how to hold a rope, but could he really be competing in a jackpot already?

She paused with her hand on the door knob to watch as they steadied their horses and called for the steer. Michael and Jammer stood in the box at attention like they'd done this a thousand times and when Michael nodded his head and the steer plunged out of the chute, she caught herself holding her breath. They left the box at a run and as Jammer bore down on the steer, Michael swung and cleanly caught the steer's head and then he pulled his horse around short and hauled on the steer to set it up for Sean to rope its feet. In mere seconds, the steer was stretched between the two ropers and the orange flag was down.

It was all Joey could do not to stare open mouthed at what Michael had just done right in front of her eyes. She'd heard of a quick study before, but holy cow! No one learned to rope like that this fast!

When the judge dropped the timing flag, Michael eased Jammer forward and glanced up at her just as Bryan put a hand to the small of her back and finished pushing her door open. He ushered her inside where she gratefully sank onto her couch and gingerly stretched out full length with a long sigh and admitted, "The concerts were great Bryan and I had a wonderful time. But oh, it's good to be home. I'm sorry I didn't realize I wasn't up to this."

He set her bag on the floor next to her bedroom door and then sat in the chair next to her. "I'm still glad you came, although I'm sorry it was too much for you. I wish you could be with me all the time on the road. Maybe you can take a day or two to just veg and relax."

With a tired smile, she admitted, "I might have to. Who knew one little bull could turn me into a marshmallow?"

Leaning forward on his chair he teased her in his southern drawl. "You are the hottest marshmallow I've ever known. If I leave you alone, do you think you can rest?"

Trying not to yawn, she assured him, "Yes, but what are you going to do? When do you have to leave?"

"Late. But you don't need to entertain me. You need to relax. I'll go out and watch your brothers and that Romeo composer slash rich person of yours." He picked up the throw from the back of the couch and gently draped it over her. "Do you want me to bring you anything?"

She shook her head tiredly. "Just news that my brothers all ripped up out there."

"With your brothers, that's a no brainer." He went to the door and said over his shoulder, "I have my cell phone if you need anything."

She had fallen fast asleep when her phone rang and she answered it groggily, wondering what Bryan had decided he needed.

It wasn't Bryan's voice, but Sean's that came over the line. "Hey, Joey. I'm assuming you're home since Bryan is hanging out watching us. I'm going to rope in a second. Look out the window."

Still half asleep, she said blandly, "If you're trying to get me to watch Michael rope, I already saw him. You were just getting into the box when I came up my stairs. And yes, he's amazing. Was there anything else you needed?"

"Nope. Just to welcome you home. We missed you. Did you finally tell Bryan you'd marry him?"

"What do you think? I'll look out the window. See ya."

"See ya."

Even though it was stupid, she did go to the window and she was amazed all over again. He really shouldn't have been able to rope like that this quickly. Even her brothers, as good as they were, hadn't picked it up anywhere near this fast. She watched the way he moved and appreciated the way his shirt bulged over the muscles in his arms and chest and then gave herself a mental shake and went back to the couch.

That had been foolish. It wasn't like she needed any encouragement in the infatuation department. Even half way across the arena from her he looked good. Really, really good. Dang.

She pulled a throw pillow over her eyes. Stupid, hot shot banker anyway. Who did he think he was playing with people's emotions? Half of the fatigue from this trip was due to him kissing her and asking her in that sexy, intense voice to hurry. How the heck was she supposed to take that? She'd spent a good portion of her energy trying to remind herself that he'd acted that way before she'd found out who he really was, too. It wasn't like she really mattered to him.

At a little before eleven, Bryan came back with Rossen to tell her he was leaving. She was still dead tired and about half asleep when he hugged her at the door to tell her goodbye. He kissed her once, gently and then looked at her like he was trying to read her mind. She hoped he couldn't. She'd been dreaming of Michael and even though she hadn't planned it, she still felt guilty and foolish. Finally, Bryan pulled her into a tight hug and just held her for a minute or two, and then kissed her again and went out the door and down the steps.

Rossen was still standing on the balcony outside looking out across the valley and she picked up the throw and limped out to stand beside him as they heard Bryan start up the 'stang and pull away with the glass packs rumbling. Rossen grinned at her in the dark and asked quietly, "Did he buy it or is it a rental?"

She smiled tiredly. "I have no idea, but it was really fun. Although I felt too lousy to fully enjoy it."

"Even I could have told you you were too hammered for a road trip. Why did you go? I thought you've been trying to wean him."

How to answer that question? She was still trying to figure out what to say when he said, "Never mind. I know why you went, but it won't work. All you'll do is give them both heart burn. You're never going to fall out of love with Michael and you're never going to fall in love with Bryan. You might as well give it up."

"You're depressing the heck out of me. You can stop anytime. At least let me be deluded so I can have hope. What all happened here? Other than Michael appearing to be a prodigy as a roper. Did you guys get the fence done over on Poison Creek?"

Ignoring her question about the fence, he went back to her reference to Michael. "He's unreal. I've never seen anything like it. Slade showed him some basics the other day and it was like he analytically studied how to move and after only a few tries, he's been catching them relatively consistently. You were wrong about him, you know."

She sighed tiredly. "I know, Rossen. Trust me. I know. But I honestly felt okay about him. I never dreamed he was playing me like that. You live and learn, I guess."

"That's what I mean. You were wrong to think he was toying with you."

She rolled her eyes at him. "Oh, sure, Rossen. That's why he was so brutally upfront with me the whole time. See, even you've been taken in by him. And you usually have killer judgment in people. He can be very convincing." She changed the subject. "What is everyone doing tomorrow? Is there something I can do to help without being very mobile? Just hanging out is driving me crazy, but I'm ridiculously sore."

Rossen turned to look at her and then said, "Joey, if he had waltzed in here and announced that he was filthy, stinking rich and a New York jetsetter and had a big, slick Thoroughbred farm that would produce this year's Kentucky Derby winner, you wouldn't have given him the time of day. And even if he hadn't been so emotionally thrashed when he got here, he would never have acted that way. It's just not him. He's as down to earth as they come. So don't be so quick to judge him. That's not your place anyway."

She heard him through and then turned to lean against the rail and look out over the valley again without saying anything. It was easy for him to excuse Michael's subterfuge. He hadn't been the one made a complete fool of. And he certainly hadn't been the one laying in Michael's arms and beginning to feel the way she had. Even just thinking about it made her feel foolish and she asked herself for the thousandth time how she ever let herself get that attached to him when she didn't even know him.

And how was she supposed to not judge him, when she was the one who had made such a gargantuan misstep in assuming he was what he appeared to be? She was the one left feeling so hurt and vulnerable. She was the one who had needed to use better judgment. You had to judge someone at least a little in order to use your head when you made decisions like whether to trust them or not, didn't you?

Too tired and discouraged to have this discussion that she didn't even want to be having in the first place, she sat down on the porch swing that hung from the roof of her balcony and tried to pass the whole thing off as no big deal. "Okay, I won't judge him. Do you need any babysitting? I could do that. How about taking Kit off for a romantical getaway and leaving the girls with me. They'd make me forget my hind leg."

He took her throw and tucked it around her gently. "Give it up, Jo. You and I both know it's not your hind leg you're trying to forget. And you're right. I am a good judge of character. And I think he's a good man. An honest man. Don't be so pig headed that you screw up the rest of your mortality."

She laughed softly. "Pig headed? I've never been pig headed in my life."

"Pig headed, bull headed, stubborn as a mule. You call it what you like, just don't let it get in the way of being happy. Speaking of which. I do believe that here he comes now. He must have heard the 'stang leave." Rossen stood behind her swing with a hand on her shoulder and watched Michael appear out of the shadows of the pasture. When Michael ducked through the fence and began to climb the stairs, Rossen leaned down and whispered in her ear, "Don't be pig headed." With that he headed back downstairs to his own house, nodding to Michael as he passed him on the way.

****

When Michael finally heard Bryan's car rumble off, he stepped off the porch where he'd been sitting and headed across the pasture to check on Joey. He'd tried to be discreet for her and Bryan's sake, but he wanted to talk to her tonight, even if it was almost eleven o'clock at night. Passing Rossen on her stairs, he knew unequivocally that Rossen was on his team. It was just Joey now who didn't trust him. But remembering the hurt he'd seen in her eyes the other day when she was leaving with Bryan, he knew earning that trust back was the biggest project he'd ever taken on in his life.

He squared his shoulders. It was going to take some doing, but failing wasn't an option. These more than eight

231

days of being away from her had helped him to see some things very clearly. Mainly that he needed Joey Rockland in his life for the rest of forever. She was the best thing that had ever happened to him. Now he just needed to return the favor.

Approaching her, he tried to see her eyes as he crouched down beside the swing she sat on, but it was hard to see her expression in the dark. Unable to know what she was thinking for sure, he reached up to touch her cheek. "Hey, Joey. How was your trip?"

She pulled her face away from him and looked out toward his house. "It was fine, thanks."

Sitting down beside her, he reached over and took her hand. "I missed you. Where did you go?"

She gently, but firmly pulled her hand away. "Salt Lake and then Denver."

"How were you? Have you healed enough for you to be comfortable on a trip like that?"

After hesitating for a second, she said one word, "No."

"How is it?

She shrugged. "I'll live."

Turning toward her, he asked, "Do I get the distinct impression that you're not talking to me?"

She answered without looking at him. "I've just answered five questions. I'd call that talking."

He shook his head. "I'd call that answering. Don't you even care what I've been doing or how I've been?"

"I'm sorry. I got the distinct impression that details about your life aren't really any of my business."

Gently, he said, "Well, you got the wrong impression then. It was never that it wasn't your business. It was just that it didn't matter."

She didn't answer that for several minutes and then she said softly, "It did matter, Michael. Maybe in your world it's

232

not a big deal, but here being honorable matters. Leaving me in the dark about who you really are wasn't honorable."

He took her hand again. "No, Joey. You know exactly who I really am. In fact, you know far more about me *really* than almost anyone on the planet. In spite of what you think, I prefer to be private. What you heard on TV by some hot shot news caster has nothing to do with who I really am. They don't know anything about me, *really*. And I'd like to think that here is my world now. I live here now. And I don't have any plans to change that."

She tried to pull her hand away again, but he resisted and she sighed and said, "Look, Michael. I'm too tired to argue. I understand, and I'll honor your privacy. Let's call it a night, huh? There's not a lot of point in having this discussion. In the morning when we aren't tired it won't even matter what I know or don't know."

"Are you still mad at me?"

She shook her head and said sadly, "I was never mad at you, Michael. You have the right to all the privacy you want."

He turned toward her and took her other hand as well. "Then what are you at me?"

This time when she answered there was resignation in her voice. "Just tired, Michael. It's been a long day. I just need to go in and go back to bed."

Knowing he'd discouraged her made him so regret not finding a way to tell her a little more about himself. He gently rubbed the backs of her hands with his thumbs. "Are you still on pain medication?"

"Just over the counter stuff now. It doesn't work as well, but I hate to take the hard stuff. It skews my brain."

Standing up, he pulled her gently to her feet and then put an arm around her to help her in. "Come on. I'll help you in. What else can I do for you? Do you need anything?"

She shook her head again. "I don't need anything."

At the door, when she would have gone straight in, he tugged on her arm to stop her and when she turned to see what he wanted, he wrapped her in a gentle hug. Laying his head against her silky hair, he said, "Can I apologize to you?"

She let him hug her, but she didn't relax into it and she certainly wasn't hugging him back. She looked up at him and said, "You don't need to apologize, Michael. I told you I understand. I'm sorry I didn't understand sooner. I'll be more discerning in the future, I promise."

When she was through speaking, he studied her face there in the dark and then put his head down and went to kiss her, but she neatly sidestepped him and turned toward her door. She hardly looked back when she said, "Good night, Michael."

At first, he wanted to keep hold of her hands and stop her, but decided against it. He did hold one hand long enough to reach up with the other one to gently touch her lower lip. "Good night, Joey. I hope you can sleep well. I'll see you tomorrow."

She went in and he stood there for a second wondering if he'd made any headway or if she was still convinced that he had been toying with her.

****

Joey got undressed and ready for bed and even as she was brushing her teeth her lip still tingled where he had touched her and it made her mad. She was twenty-four years old, for crying out loud. You'd think she could have enough self control not to let her heart react when she knew he probably had lines of girls waiting to get his attention.

She laid her tired body down and prayed that way, wishing she wasn't still too sore to kneel. She knew God would understand, but it still felt strange to her. As she laid there and waited for sleep to claim her mind, she thought back to how he had looked tonight roping with her brothers. The shorter dark, sleek hair drew her and his muscular build coupled with that almost feline grace was incredibly sexy.

He seemed to fit in so well here with her brothers. She almost wished she was just another one of the guys and that falling in love with him wasn't an issue. It would be so much simpler to be able to just be friends like they could without worrying about whether he was being emotionally honest or not.

He had fit right in and he had looked so good. That self confidence was lethal and his incredible natural athleticism was magnetic. It was no wonder she was attracted in spite of her logical lectures to herself to keep her emotional distance. It was nearly impossible to resist him when he was that fascinating.

Struggling to turn over, she tried to remind herself that his gentle concern for how she was feeling and his attempt to help her out any way she needed was not to be taken at face value. He had been all solicitous before she found out he wasn't being forthright as well and it hurt all over again when she remembered how she had come to lean on him before she had known. For awhile there, she had felt so special and so well cared for. How had she been so gullible as that?

As she vacillated between remembering how good he had made her feel and then feeling foolish by turn, she wished sleep would bring its welcome respite from her thoughts. The trip with Bryan had been too much, but it really had helped to take her mind elsewhere. Tomorrow she'd have to find something else to occupy her thoughts or she'd be an emotional wreck just like she was tonight.

Jaclyn M. Hawkes

Chapter 31

After a restless night, Joey was up and hobbling across to her mother's house for breakfast, talking herself into letting life fall back into the lonely but safe rut it had been in before a hunky New Yorker had shown up. By the time she reached the patio doors from the deck, she was relatively confident that she could resist anything Michael could throw at her right up until she opened the door and walked inside.

The first thing she saw was Michael standing in the kitchen with a pancake turner in one hand and Rossen and Kit's six month old daughter Gracie in the other arm. He was letting her play with his face with her hands and both of them were obviously delighted with each other. Gracie would laugh and pat him and he couldn't hide the fact that he was completely enamored with the beautiful little girl with the dark hair that almost matched his own.

Joey suddenly found it hard to breathe. She had thought he was attractive before, but nothing was as devastating as watching how gentle and sweet he was with this trusting little baby. He fairly glowed as he talked and smiled at her and Joey was fascinated, knowing that he'd said he'd never been around a child in his life, let alone a baby.

Without realizing it, she had stopped dead in her tracks and when Michael glanced up, he met her gaze. The impact of him looking at her shook her out of her daze. She turned abruptly around to escape from the incredibly compelling scene of how fascinating he was with the dark haired baby and headed for the exact same door she'd come into just moments before. Rossen stepped in front of her as she hobbled toward it and she was forced to face him and answer him when he looked at her and whispered, "Chicken?"

She knew he meant it as a challenge, but she didn't hesitate for a second when she whispered back, "Heck, yes! Tell Mom I decided to just grab a bite at home."

Putting a hand on her arm as she went to step out the door, he said, "Joey, it's not like you to be afraid of him."

She shook her head. "It's not him I'm afraid of, Rossen. It's me. I'll see you later." With that she slipped back out the French doors and headed across the pasture.

She hadn't even made it a quarter of the way across when she realized Michael had come out the door and was bent on catching up to her. There was no way she could evade him limping as she was and she stopped and waited for him, trying to keep her heart rate steady, but it was impossible. He strode up to her in his boots and faded jeans and it was all she could do to look at him as if nothing was going on. As he reached her, he put a gentle hand on her arm and studied her for a second in a way that made her want to squirm and then he finally said, "Good morning. Are you feeling better?"

"Yes, thank you. How are you?"

"I'm good, Joey." His deep blue eyes were still watching her intently and she tried to shrug his hand off and turn to walk back to her house, but he didn't let her go. She looked back up at him as he asked, "Is something wrong? Why did you walk in and then turn right back around to leave? Did you forget something? Can I go get it for you so you don't have to walk all that way?"

Shaking her head, she tried to sound off hand as she replied, "No, I'm just not all that hungry this morning. I decided I'd skip breakfast with the family and just snack later in the morning."

After another second of looking at her, he dropped the hand from her arm and asked her point blank, "You're leaving because I'm there, aren't you?"

Wishing desperately that she could have denied it, she knew she could never lie to him and she finally nodded and looked down and admitted, "Yeah, I guess I am. Sorry."

He caught her arm again. "Don't go. They're your family. You go on in. I'll leave. If my being there makes you uncomfortable it should be you who stays, not me. I'm sorry I made you feel like you had to go." He met her eyes sadly and then went to turn away toward his little white house and she caught his arm this time.

Chiding herself for causing him to feel like he wasn't welcome, she knew instantly that he needed to be able to be with her family no matter how it made her struggle to see him. "No! Michael, no. You're welcome here. We both are. I'm just being childish. Please forgive me. Come back and we'll both go in and have breakfast. It's not a big deal. Really."

For several seconds he didn't say anything, just looked at her and then he finally nodded and they both turned back toward her parents', walking in silence, side by side, as she tried to convince herself that her words were true, and that this wasn't a big deal. He waited patiently without touching her as she struggled up the deck steps and then he held the door for her.

On the way inside, Rossen was watching them and she decided to do her best to act like nothing was going on at all as she went into the kitchen and picked up the pancake turner Michael had been wielding just moments before. Standing on one leg, she nonchalantly began to flip the pancakes and then started opening the cans of orange juice that sat thawing on the counter, waiting to be made. Michael had followed her in and when she couldn't budge the top of one of the cans she turned to him and asked him to help her with it as if they made breakfast together every morning as a matter of course.

He helped fix the meal, but the happy smile she'd seen when he'd been holding Gracie never resurfaced and she silently cussed herself for taking that happiness from him even though it had been inadvertent. So he had toyed with her emotions, that was no reason to deny him being part of a family that he had never had the good fortune to experience back home in New York. Especially not right now when he was just discovering that he truly was a child of God.

She thought back to how haunted he had been when he'd come here and how much her family had helped him and she wanted to kick herself for being so weak and adolescent. From here on out she was going to be more careful to make sure that he never felt unwelcome, no matter how hard it was to see him. She knew in her heart that that was what Jesus would do whether it ripped her emotions to pieces or not, and she made an extra effort to be more upbeat and cheerful to him.

It seemed to work. By the time the breakfast dishes were done and put away, his marvelous smile was back and she was surprised that even she had been able to lighten up and been able to more than just pretend to enjoy being there.

****

When Michael had looked up to see her staring at him that morning and then she had abruptly turned around and walked out, it had killed him. He'd known instantly that she was leaving because he was there and he'd also known instantly that he couldn't continue to enjoy being welcomed into her family if he made her stay away. It had made him unbelievably sad. He was having a ball being welcomed into the fold the way he had been.

Then when he'd followed her out to the pasture, already mentally gearing up to become a recluse in Merv's house again if he had to, he'd been able to watch the different emotions sweep across her face as they talked there. She cared for him. He knew that both from the friendship they had found before the Kentucky Derby and from watching the

240

expressions on her face. And although she had changed drastically toward him when she'd found out that he wasn't just a pianist, he had to hold out hope that he could overcome her distrust somehow.

He had to hope. Now that he'd found a girl like her existed, he wasn't going to give up on trying to win her over until the day he died. He had nothing to lose and everything to gain. As he stood there beside her in the pasture and watched her decide to welcome him into her family, in spite of the fact that her first inclination was to get away from him, he was incredibly grateful. For two reasons. He didn't want to have to stay away from this wonderful family. He had come to love them dearly in the weeks he'd been here. And he needed to be around her to be able to win her trust back. There was no other way that he could think of and he had to succeed. He'd never felt as strongly about anything in his life.

She hadn't wanted to welcome him. He was bright enough to realize that, but it was proof of what a kind person she was that she would welcome him anyway. He hoped that deep inside she really did want to be with him. He honestly thought that.

It wasn't that she didn't care for him. It was that she was trying to protect herself from what she believed to be a wealthy, big city playboy who used people. He knew that wasn't the way he was, and he had to hope that a woman as intuitive as she was could sense that his heart truly was good, even if he was wealthy but hadn't mentioned it. He had to hope, and with that hope, he was willing to take any breaks she was willing to give him, knowing he would meet her far more than half way, if he needed to.

He was still willing to do whatever it took to be able to spend time with her, when he saw her come out onto her deck at almost eleven that night to listen to him playing. He played for nearly an hour and then went over to talk to her before she went back inside.

Two weeks ago she had promised she would go to church with him to help him learn about God and he was going to hold her to that promise. That was one area that he knew without a doubt she would help him with and he was going to take full advantage of it.

Walking through the darkness of the pasture, he climbed her stairway and quietly sat down on the deck chair next to her, not saying anything at first.

She was the one to break the silence. "What are you up to, Michael? Why did you only play for such a short time?"

Deciding to lay his cards right out on the table, he replied, "I needed to come over and find out what your plans are for church tomorrow. You are still planning to help me learn more about God tomorrow, aren't you? I was worried you wouldn't want to because I didn't tell you about my background. Although, you did promise me."

She turned and looked at him in the dark and then gave an almost inaudible sigh before she said, "Of course, I'll help you anyway I can, Michael. What would you rather? We can go into the regular family ward with my parents and married siblings or we can go to the local singles ward or even the ward that is just the seasonal resort employees up at Jackson Lake Lodge. What would you prefer?"

After finding her, he had absolutely no interest in meeting any singles. He wished he dared to tell her that, but he had no idea how to bring it up, so he just said, "How about the family ward? That's where I've gone the last couple of times and it's been great."

"That's fine, but Michael, the whole idea behind singles wards is so that single people can meet other single people with good values in the hope of finding the right one and eventually settling down. If you're really serious about following God's will, marriage is important. Maybe we should take you to the singles ward."

She had made it easier to tell her than he'd thought it would be. Deciding that he needed to always be up front with her in the hopes that someday she would choose to believe him, he said softly, "Joey, I'm twenty-eight years old. Honestly, I'd actually given up on the idea of ever finding someone I wanted to be with for the rest of my life. You can't imagine how discouraging that was. Sometimes I had a hard time figuring out what the point of existing at all was. Since coming here, not only have I found you, but now the rest of my life isn't anywhere near long enough.

"I want the whole enchilada. Temple marriage, sealed family, time and all eternity. The whole thing with you. I know you probably don't want to hear that from me right now, but I honestly am a big enough boy to know that I don't want a singles ward. I'll go with you if you really have your heart set on meeting some single guys, but don't plan to go on my account."

As he spoke, she turned to look at him in obvious surprise and then turned away again. When he finished, she sat very still for a couple of long moments. Then, finally, she whispered simply, "The family ward is fine. We need to leave at about nine-thirty-five."

They sat in silence for several minutes and then she said, "You've been studying then."

"Yeah."

"That's good."

Wishing he could reach over and take her hand, he replied, "Yeah, it's good."

After another few minutes, she said softly, "It's all true, Michael."

It took him a second to swallow the lump that rose in his throat and be able to answer just as softly, "I know."

Finally, he did reach across and take her hand and said, "You've changed my life, Joey. But then you already know

243

that. Thank you." They sat in silence that was at once incredibly peaceful and singularly poignant. At length, he raised her hand to his mouth and gently kissed it and then stood up to go. "Good night, Joey. I'm so glad you can forgive me enough to still take me to church. I'll see you in the morning. Sleep well."

Chapter 32

He'd dropped several bombshells and then quietly kissed her hand, got up and disappeared into the dark of the pasture. Joey sat there in stunned silence.

She was still too confused to even know what to think when she heard him begin to play again. He always played beautiful, peaceful songs at night when she was listening now, and it was sweetly reassuring to know he wasn't haunted anymore, but tonight she had no idea what to think about him. He'd almost sounded like he was telling her he wanted to be with her forever, and he'd sounded so sincere that it was difficult to remember that he'd been playing her for a fool for those weeks, especially with his evocative music drifting across on the misty night wind.

She softly touched where he'd kissed her hand. Wouldn't it have been nice if he really meant it?

She got up with a sigh, remembering again how much it had hurt to find out he hadn't been honest with her. She shouldn't let her mind wander like that. It was a recipe for heartache. Again.

Pausing at the door to listen for just another moment, she sighed one more time. He was an amazing man. She really wished he'd been more honorable with her.

Back inside, she opened her bedroom window so she could still hear his night music and then prayed and laid down, wondering if she should shut it again so that she didn't always dream of him. When he'd come here, he was the one who was haunted, but the last little while, he did the haunting and she was at a total loss as to how to escape him.

Jaclyn M. Hawkes

She laid there and enjoyed the music. It wasn't like shutting the window would shut off her mind, anyway.

The next morning he appeared at her parents' house dressed to kill again, and she marveled at how he could go from working with the guys in his jeans, to Armani and Italian leather effortlessly. He took off his jacket, rolled up his shirt sleeves over brown, muscled forearms and stood beside her to fry hash browns and slice cantaloupe off the rind. She was hard put to remember what she was supposed to be doing while she could smell his aftershave.

All during church she had to keep reminding herself that he had only been toying with her as he sat beside her and soaked up the lessons like a sponge, taking occasional notes and asking insightful questions.

After the meetings, the missionaries pulled him aside and asked about teaching him again and Joey was surprised at that. She hadn't even realized he'd been meeting with them while she had been gone with Bryan. She looked at him as he picked up Slade's son, Cody, and cuddled him, and she wondered what else she had been missing.

They made the appointment to meet at Rossen's house just downstairs from Joey's apartment on Wednesday and she was inordinately pleased when, after it was made and they were walking to the parking lot, Michael turned to her and asked her if she would be willing to sit in with them. She agreed, even though she wondered if it was wise. She told herself it had nothing to do with how she felt about Michael, it was simply building the kingdom and, after all, it was her responsibility.

Her leg was much better, but it was still miserably sore. The three hours of church and the drive to and from were really more than she was up to and she climbed her stairs wearily afterward. Slipping out of her dress, she lay down on her bed and then called her mom and told her she was honestly too sore to come to eat and not to expect her.
246

Forty minutes later, when Joey heard someone on her stairs, then heard her apartment door open, she knew Cooper must be bringing her a plate from her mom. She struggled up, threw on a robe and limped out to thank him. It wasn't Cooper.

She walked into her living room and realized it was Michael and Blue who stood in her kitchen with a covered dish. Groaning, she brushed back her wild hair, looked down at her robe and then to Michael's half smile, and wished she'd dressed before coming out. She always seemed to be at her worst when he saw her. Blue greeted her warmly, and she leaned down to pet his sweet old head as he wagged his whole back end at her. She knew Michael needed him worse than her, but sometimes she really missed his unconditional devotion.

Michael put the plate on the counter and came around the end of the cabinet toward her. "Church was too much?" His deep, gentle voice held a note of genuine concern and it made her emotional. She nodded wordlessly and met his eyes, wishing with all her heart that she could ask him to hold her and talk to her to help her get the throbbing ache under control—but she knew that was all in the past in a more naive and clueless place.

She sighed, and went to a cupboard and shook out some ibuprofen and poured herself a tall glass of milk to wash it down with, trying all the while not to meet his eyes that were as sad as hers were. Somehow she knew he was thinking the exact same thing she was and if she acknowledged it, she would break right down and cry again in front of him, which she was determined not to do. She'd cried more in the last week than she'd cried in her life and the last thing she wanted was him to see it.

Knowing the tears were inevitable, she turned back toward her room and said over her shoulder, "Thank you for bringing that to me. I appreciate it. I'll come back in a few minutes when the medicine has kicked in and eat it."

"Sure." He said the one word, but kept looking at her. She didn't know what to do about leaving him standing there, but she didn't want him to see her cry from the pain in her hip and the ache in her heart. She went back into her bedroom, pushed the door partially closed and gingerly sat back down on her bed as she heard him close her outer door. With the click of the latch, she let down her guard and turned her face into her pillow and let the tears come.

A minute later, when Blue pushed his nose into her hand, she had never been more grateful. "Oh, Blue. I'm so glad he left you. How did you know I needed a buddy just now? Huh, old man?" He sniffed at her face and then reached and licked at the tears and she tried to smile at him. "Your mistress is an idiot, Blue. I didn't even see this one coming." He just wagged again and laid his muzzle on the bed beside her.

****

Leaving her sore and sad and alone at her apartment was incredibly hard, but Michael didn't know what else to do. He would have given about anything to have been able to hold her through it, but he knew she wouldn't let him. On an impulse, he stopped and knocked on Rossen and Kit's door on his way out.

When Rossen opened the door, he gave Michael a brilliant smile and said, "Hey! Come on in. What are you up to, Michael?"

Michael just shook his head, not sure what to say and finally settled for, "No, I'm just heading home, but thanks. Actually, I took a plate to Joey for your mom and uh . . . " He hesitated and then went on, "Maybe you could go up and check on her. She didn't look so good, but I'm not really the one she wants around her right now."

Rossen glanced up at her door and then nodded. "Sure, I'll go check on her. Head on home and I'll touch base with you later. Thanks for stopping to tell me." As Michael went to leave, Rossen shut his door behind him and went toward Joey's stairway. Michael headed across to his house, praying for her this time like he knew she had probably been praying for him the whole time.

****

When she heard her door open again, Joey tried to dry her tears as she wondered if Michael had come back or if someone else had come in. There came a knock at her bedroom door, then Rossen poked his head in and spoke softly, "Jo, you awake?"

She rolled carefully to look up at him, wishing it wasn't so obvious that she was having an emotional meltdown. He came over and sat on the edge of her bed and asked gently, "Is this about Michael or is your hip really this sore?"

She sighed and rolled back onto her stomach. "The hip is still really sore, but it's not that. I must just be tired. I'll be fine after a nap."

"Are you ever just going to answer me honestly about him? You and I are friends, aren't we? You can trust me with a confidence. And after all, the guy did risk his life to save you."

"I can't bear to be honest. It makes me feel like such a fool. And he would have risked his life to save anyone. That's just the kind of guy he is."

He put a hand on her back. "If you know that, then why do you have such a hard time believing that he wasn't using you?"

She looked back up at him, wondering why he could even question that. "That's kind of a no brainer, isn't it? You saw how we were before he went to Kentucky. I was

249

honestly beginning to wonder if I'd finally found him. I thought I felt so good about him." She put her face back down on her hands. "I was such a clueless idiot. How did I ever sucker into trusting him? I didn't even know his last name."

"I think you have it backwards, Joey. If you did feel good about him, why have you decided now that the Holy Ghost was wrong? So he didn't broadcast that he's wealthy. So what. It's not like he's a fast and loose playboy. Trust yourself here. He just went out of here worried sick about you, but he knew you wouldn't accept any help from him."

Sighing, she turned over and pulled her pillows up behind her and tried to sit up. "I know you believe what you're saying Rossen, but the fact of the matter is that I didn't matter enough to warrant any information at all. We just had different perspectives about what was going on. I understand that. I'm just having a bit of an issue getting past my feelings. Give me some time. I'll figure it out and I'll be fine. I'm not too proud to admit I was a fool. I can work to fix it. I've just never been on this end before. How bad is that? I know now that I haven't been empathetic enough with some of the guys who fell for me. In a way, maybe this is good for me."

Rossen shook his head. "Joey, you're not making sense. It's not like you to discount what the Spirit is telling you. What's up with that?"

Closing her eyes against the tears again, she said, "I just misread things, Rossen. I heard what I wanted to hear from the Spirit, obviously."

"Well, if you did, then we all are. Because every single one of us trusts him. Except you. Even Mom trusts him."

"You know that Mom loves everyone."

"Loves. Not trusts. There's a big difference."

"And I did trust him, Rossen, but it was a mistake. My life was safe with him. My heart wasn't. I understand that now and I'll come to terms with it and be fine. Just give me a little time."

This time Rossen sighed. "Okay, Joey. But keep praying about it, please. I think if you'll give him the benefit of the doubt, you'll find that your heart is safe. I haven't seen so much as a phone call to or from another woman. He's not toying. I honestly believe that. If I thought he was I'd make him miserable, but I truly don't." He paused and gave her shoulder a squeeze. "And I'm pretty protective of my baby sister. You should know that by now."

Wiping at her tears, she laughed in spite of herself. "Don't remind me. I thought I was going to be sweet sixty before anyone dared to kiss me."

She sat up and put her legs over the side of the bed and Rossen gave her a smile. "You'll thank me when you're older and wiser. When you've eaten come on down. Don't sit up here and bawl alone. Kit would be so offended if she found out."

"Actually, can I nap again first? Then I promise I'll come down."

He headed for the door. "Okay, but no bawling. It makes your nose run and your eyes red and you look like such a sissy."

She rolled her eyes. "I'm supposed to be a sissy. You guys keep forgetting that."

"Oh. That's right. Sorry. See ya in awhile."

Jaclyn M. Hawkes

Chapter 33

By Wednesday night, Joey had begun to suspect a conspiracy. By Thursday night, she was sure of it, and it was incredibly hard to keep her head straight. Every single day that week, she had mysteriously found herself somehow thrown together with Michael.

On Monday when she had asked what she could do to help, in spite of her bum leg, her mother had suggested doing the grocery shopping. Joey had agreed, but Michael had been the one sent in to help her.

She'd gotten through that relatively unscathed only to find herself in charge of dinner with him on Tuesday. He'd obviously decided that he needed to learn to cook right alongside the rest of the brothers and was taking that task very seriously as he stood beside her and mixed meatloaf as she added ingredients. She could smell his aftershave again and nearly added twice as many bread crumbs as she meant to before she caught herself. The whole time she was cooking she had been caught between his lethal physical attraction and the painful truth about how little she had meant to him.

Wednesday morning she had begrudgingly agreed to help in Naomi's office, a task she hated, when Michael appeared and said, "Apparently you need some help fixing the printer."

Joey looked up skeptically. "I do? I wasn't even aware it was on the blink." She rolled her chair from in front of the computer to the printer and found that the printer was indeed completely incommunicado. "Huh? Mother didn't mention it earlier. I wouldn't have been so loathe to work in here if I'd known I had to fix something. Can you check and see that it's plugged in correctly for me? Both to the power and to the computer?"

She rolled her chair back out of the way and he climbed under the big desk to check the connections as he asked her, "Is working in the office not high on your list of preferences?"

"It's okay if I can design something with wheels. But spreadsheets and taxes and some of the government reports that have to be filed bore me to tears." The machine made a whirring sound and started to print out a sheet but stopped mid-page. "There, something was working there for a second. What were you doing just then?"

He raised his head up from under the desk. "Everything is plugged in right. I think there must be a short. I'm the opposite of you. Spreadsheets are fine; just don't ask me to muddle through a repair."

"Then why did you get sent in here?"

Looking honestly confused about that, he replied, "I have no idea. Your dad just asked me."

For two hours they worked on the electronics there in the office and had actually toasted the entire system for a time before they got everything working correctly. The short was in the surge protector clear under the desk where she couldn't begin to get to it as sore as she was and she was incredibly grateful for Michael's help by the time they got the system up and running again. She also felt like she was hopelessly caught on a thoroughly draining emotional roller coaster.

Thursday afternoon she had another doctor's appointment with Seth and somehow she ended up riding into the clinic in Jackson Hole in her little SUV with Michael behind the wheel. Everyone else was mysteriously tied up with other tasks and Michael needed to ship some things from the airport anyway.

There was a horrible wreck on the outskirts of Jackson and as they drove past the crumpled bodies of the cars, she commented sadly, "It's such a shame that cars can still be that

254

mangled in a wreck. We have the technology to design every single car more safely, but all the car companies aren't on board yet about using it. We can actually design cars that crush right where we want them to instead of into the passengers. It would save millions of lives if it were implemented more."

Michael turned to look across the car at her. "You can really do that? So they give at certain places and keep the people inside safer?"

She nodded. "It costs a little more to do, but would be so worth it. Most people just don't know it can be done or they would be outraged."

"Wow, I had no idea. Could you go ahead and design it? Get it on paper and I'll have someone get it to the different car companies. If they won't agree to buy it from you, I'll help you start up a car company of your own. It would be worth it to save lives." He turned his attention back to the road nonchalantly, but she was staring across the car at him in amazement. It was a total wake up call again about just how wealthy and powerful he was. They both were still thoughtful when he dropped her at Seth's office for her appointment a few minutes later.

She was thoroughly convinced that for some reason, he or her family was throwing her and Michael together on purpose, but she went along with him without comment because it honestly was a relief to have someone else drive on long trips as sore as she was. Moreover, it wasn't like she could forget him, even if she wasn't working or riding beside him.

The haunting had become a constant bittersweet pain she had no idea how to manage, but knew she couldn't make everyone else in the family miserable over it as well. All she could do was try to choose happy and smile, in spite of her personal heartbreak, to try to escape her family's pity. She also decided she needed to do a little conspiring on her own, even though she wasn't sure if it was him or them.

She got just the chance when on the way out of the doctor's office, Michael pulled into the lot behind Brandon's shop and handed her a set of keys that had a little black race horse emblem on them. She just looked at them blankly for a second, wondering what he wanted her to do with them and then Brandon came out and opened the big shop doors of his storage building. He walked inside and pulled a canvas cover off of a shiny black low slung car in the dim interior.

When Joey realized that Michael had handed her the keys to his Ferrari, she couldn't help the smile that spread across her face from ear to ear and turned to him. "Really? You're going to turn me loose with your car?"

"Your brothers said they thought you could handle it. Knock yourself out. Well, don't really knock yourself out. Be careful, but she's all yours for . . . " He glanced down at his watch. "Forty-five minutes before we're going to meet them all at Mert's for dinner."

She had leaned across the car and hugged him before she even realized it, then got out as quickly as her bum hind leg would carry her, and went into the shop and almost reverently got into the car. She just sat there for a minute or two, looking around at the sleek controls and noticing that even after all these weeks, the interior of the car smelled like Michael.

She buckled in, started it up, and slowly rolled it out of the shop into the brilliant May sunshine, reveling in the racy lines that glistened in the light. She drove it around the back lot a few times, getting a feel for it and then with a laugh she couldn't help, she squealed it out of the lot and headed for the long, flat straightaway south of town.

****

When Joey lit up like a county fair when he handed her his keys, Michael wondered if she was finally going to start taking down the brick wall she'd carefully erected between them after the Kentucky Derby. Seeing her smile made him want to hand her the keys permanently. Then, when she went screaming out of the parking lot and reached about sixty miles an hour in like four seconds, he began to wonder if he hadn't made a big mistake. When she hit the outskirts of town and opened the car up wide open, he began to flat out worry.

Sean had told him Joey had been to both a race car driving course and a stunt driving school, courtesy of her parents, when they'd figured out that her burn for racy cars wasn't going away any time soon. Michael didn't necessarily worry about her wrecking, but if she got caught going that fast by a state trooper she'd go straight to jail without passing go. He sat in her SUV wondering what to do now that he'd handed her the keys.

After sitting there for a few minutes, he went and got his mail and then bought a paper, hoping he could read and not worry about her getting busted on his watch. It worked pretty well until he watched a Lincoln County Sheriff car cruise by and head down the same highway she had disappeared on south of town. Just several minutes later he heard a siren and looked up to see his low, lean black car out on the flat, straight highway barreling back toward town, going about mach fifty, with the officer doing his best to catch her, siren on and lights flashing.

Michael swore before he caught himself and glanced down at his watch. Oh, this was just great! And they were supposed to meet her whole family in like five minutes for dinner. This time the John Wayne cavalcade just might really shoot him.

He watched as she pulled over and had to step out of the car, and was sick when he realized she'd been handcuffed and put into the back seat of the patrol car and taken away, while his car sat forlornly at the side of the road, no doubt about to be impounded and hauled away.

Within only a couple of minutes his phone rang and he answered to hear Naomi's much less than happy voice explain that Joey had been arrested. In the most disgusted voice he'd ever heard Naomi use she went on, "And I'm not bailing her out of jail. I told all my kids years ago that if they ever got arrested, they hadn't better call me to come get them! You got her into this one, Michael. You can bail her out. And while you're at it, you can call her dad and brothers and break the news to them." Naomi practically hung up on him and Michael soberly closed his phone and resolutely started up Joey's SUV and headed toward Mert's. He might as well tell them in person and get the thing over with.

The guys were late and he spent another ten minutes rehearsing in his head how he was going to tell them he'd been responsible in a way for getting Joey arrested. There was no way to sugar coat it much and by the time three trucks pulled into Mert's parking lot, he was practically sweating bullets.

He ran a hand through his hair and got out of the car and as they gathered around him, he began to give them an explanation of what had happened. To his surprise, none of then appeared too terribly concerned. In fact, Sean was hard put to conceal a wide grin and he began to wonder what they thought was so funny.

He still hadn't clued in that he'd been had until a few minutes later when Joey cruised up in his car with Naomi in the passenger seat, both of them grinning like they'd won the lottery and the rest of the family busted up laughing. Joey pulled up beside him and revved the engine as she rolled down the window and smiled at him. "Hey, Michael! This is a great car! Why in the world are you storing it at Branden's?" If she hadn't looked so deliriously happy, he'd have wanted to throttle her. Maybe he still did.

They all busted up again at his expense when about two minutes later, not one, but two sheriff department vehicles pulled up and parked. The officers got out and came over to where he was standing next to the Ferrari and extended their hands. "You must be Michael. It's good to meet you. Welcome to Lincoln County." They slapped him on the back and headed into Mert's, wondering aloud what the special was today.

Michael looked at the officers walking away from him, and then at the Rockland brothers who were still chuckling at him, and then at Joey as she eased the Ferrari into a parking space between a sheriff's car and a truck with a load of hay and two dogs in it and he shook his head and laughed. He couldn't even believe how laid back this place was. They'd gotten him good this time.

Going to the Ferrari, he opened Naomi's door and she got out, flashing him a huge smile. "Sorry about that, Michael. But it was a good one. I couldn't help but go along with it. You kind of set yourself up for this one. Jerry is our home teacher and Wade is on the school board with Rob. They've known Joey since she was born and she always calls to let them know when she's driving fast out south of town. She just asked them to help her tease you."

"Jerry and Wade are the officers, I take it."

Naomi laughed again. "Joey is like a daughter to both of them. It came in quite handy this evening."

"Quite." He went around to Joey's side of the car. She was still smiling and he asked, "Are you going to get out so I can start to lecture you about scaring years off of a guy's life or what?"

She laughed and held his keys out to him, but then she grimaced. "I'd get out if I thought I could. I may be permanently embedded. I drove it about twice as long as I should have and I think rigormortis has set in. It might take all of you to get me out."

Touching a button at the side of the seat to let it back as far as it could go, he smiled at her and said, "How do I know that this isn't just a ploy to stay in the car? Give me your hand." It took her a minute to swing her left leg out of the car and he could tell by the look on her face that just that little

259

movement was killing her. Reaching for both of her hands, he gently almost lifted her out and then put a steadying arm around her as she slowly straightened. He saw her clench her teeth and chided her gently, "Joey, why did you do this to yourself? You can drive the car anytime. You didn't need to drive it until it killed you."

Blowing out a breath, she tried to smile. "I didn't realize or I wouldn't have. I got a bit caught up in the car, I guess." He was surprised when she leaned her head right into his chest and just rested for a minute or two. Finally, she asked, "If I take something for the pain, will you drive home again? I know that sounds like a marshmallow, but I don't think I'm up to it."

"Of course." He wanted to pull her in close and support her with both arms, but he was afraid if he tried she would tell him he was in her personal space and pull away and he really didn't want her to do that. Even holding her a little was heavenly after more than two weeks of her staying away from him.

When she finally raised her head, she mumbled a thank you and went to step away. Her left leg buckled and she would have fallen if he hadn't still had hold of her. She looked up, embarrassed and he didn't hesitate to wrap his arm firmly around her as he helped her away from the car toward the entrance of the little diner. "Sorry, Michael. I had no idea it would make me this stiff. I'll be okay in a minute, I'm sure. I just need to stand up and walk around on it a little maybe. Go on inside with the others. Mert makes a killer Chicken Royale on Thursdays."

Ignoring her, he kept his arm around her as she stepped up onto the sidewalk and then he asked, "Would it help to walk out here for a minute before we go in? Won't sitting down at the table be just as bad as the car right now? Or should we just get something to go and I'll let you lie down in the back and take you home right now?"

260

Shaking her head, she said, "Just let me walk for a second. We can't take it and go. Mert would be offended. And aren't the others taking you line dancing? We can't go home until you've tried it. It's really fun and they'll tease me forever if I make you take me."

He looked down at her wondering if she had lost her mind. "Joey, I'm not going to make you hang out when you don't feel good just so I can try some dance. Don't be ridiculous. And I'm sure this Mert would understand."

Squaring her shoulders, she shook her head again and turned resolutely for the door. "No, I'm fine now. Let's go in." Her leg buckled again just then, belying her words, but he chose not to mention it and instead kept his arm around her as they went in the door and went to where the others were gathered around a huge table that had been made by pushing several others together.

Rossen glanced up and met his eyes and then automatically got up and went somewhere and came back with several of the little ruffled pads that lined the seats of the diner's chairs. As Joey went to sit down they carefully padded all around her hip and thigh.

Michael crouched down beside her and asked, "Where is your medicine? I'll get it for you."

Leaning carefully back against the chair, she gave him a grateful look. "It's in my purse in my car. Don't worry about it. I'll go out and get it in a second. Just let me sit for a minute."

He stood up and went back out to the car and brought her purse back in to her, shaking his head at her and wondering if she truly thought he wouldn't go get her medicine for her. He knew she was tough, but she needed to get more used to the way he wanted to serve her. Handing her the purse, he sat in the seat they'd left empty beside her and then took the pill bottle from her to open it when it stuck as she tried.

261

It even stuck when he went to open it and he was glad in a way because he had seen a hint of rebellion come up in her eyes when he'd taken it from her. He handed it back to her wordlessly and watched as she took two of the white tablets with her water. Looking around, he wondered why no one had any menus.

About thirty seconds later he chuckled when a teenaged girl began to bring in plates and put them in front of everyone. He'd forgotten that Thursday was some killer chicken thing. Apparently the locals didn't need menus at Mert's either.

Joey was right. The chicken was marvelous and he made a mental note to stop at Mert's anytime he needed to come through town in the future. He watched Joey and was relieved when about twenty minutes into the meal the little grimace of pain between her eyebrows finally eased and her posture relaxed. He could almost see her mellow as her medicine kicked in.

She still stood up and stretched from time to time and when she went to walk into the restroom, he would have escorted her except for the look she gave him when he stood up as she did. He watched her limp away, hoping her leg was working better than it had when she'd climbed out of the car and he was relieved to see Isabel slip out of her seat and casually walk in the direction of the restroom with her. The way this family took care of each other was uncanny, but he loved it.

Chapter 34

With dinner over, as Rob and Naomi loaded the children into various car seats to return to the ranch, Michael loaded Joey back into her SUV to take her home as well, but she was having none of it. She insisted he take them to the log American Legion Hall down the street next to Branden's shop while Sean drove the Ferrari. In the parking lot that was fast filling up, he turned and looked at her and asked "Why are you doing this, Joey? This is illogical and foolish. If this is just for me, I'm offended. I want to take you home to bed."

She raised her eyebrows at him and he didn't even crack a smile at her teasing. "You know what I mean. Why are we doing this?"

"Oh, settle down, Herman. I feel much better now with the Percocet and I'll be fine watching everyone. Quit hovering and hand me that car blanket, would you? I'll use it for padding on whatever chair I'll use as my throne. No one can move to Wyoming without learning to line dance. The dancing police would come and then think of the mess we'd be in."

Reaching for the blanket in the back seat, he said, "Oh, I'm sure you'd handle them as neatly as you handled the deputies tonight. The dancing police probably eat out of your hand, just like all the others."

She took the blanket and smiled up at him. "I'll take that as a compliment, thank you. Would you mind helping me out again? I think this time I may have partial paralysis."

He handed her out of the car and did a double take when she wavered when she went to step away. Steadying her as he shut the car door, he said, "Whoa, Herman. I think you've had a little too much Chicken Royale or else those Percocet were extra potent. I don't believe you can walk a straight line just now." He put a snug arm around her again. "Do you usually take two?"

Shaking her head, she leaned into him. "Not usually. I was just dying in there. I feel much better now. Girls cannot be called Herman, by the way."

"What? Will the name police show up?" She laughed and he had to wonder just for a second if she was completely there mentally with that much medicine in her. She was heading away from the door when he steered her back around. "Come on, Lucille. Dancing is this way. I am not letting you dance with anyone but your brothers in this condition."

She yawned. "Oh, Lucille. That's awful. I'm fine. Truly. I'm not really up to dancing tonight anyway except for a slow song or two maybe. Just park me somewhere. Someone will come entertain me."

That's just what he was afraid of. And when several men gathered around her as soon as she was seated, he was irritated immediately. As he let Treyne haul him off into the line, he glanced back at her, hoping she was with it enough to fend off anyone who got too friendly. The first slow song he went and gently, but firmly, pulled her away from the handful of men who were vying for her attention. She was still a little tipsy and he held her tighter than he would have otherwise and looked down into her face. "How are you doing, Jo? You didn't just agree to marry any of those guys while you're dancing under the influence, did you?"

She leaned into him with a sigh. "I don't think so. What? Now are you worried about the marriage police?" She lifted her hand off his shoulder and half waved it. "Ah, I can

264

handle the marriage police too, if I have to. Are you having fun? Isn't line dancing great?"

"No, I'm worrying about you and your mob of admirers. Some of those guys don't look all that respectable."

Shaking her head, she assured him, "Don't worry. They all know that Sean and Ruger would kill them if they insulted me. Lighten up, DeVerl."

That made him laugh right out loud and he pulled her close and said, "Now why didn't I think of DeVerl when I was choosing a pseudonym? Ruger would kill them as well? I can see Sean raining all over them, but I didn't know Ruger was a heathen as well."

"Oh, my. You should have seen him before Marti settled him down. Talk about your heathens." She leaned her head against his shoulder and after a minute added, "I guess compared to most guys he's a saint, but he's got a much shorter fuse than my dad or Rossen. Honestly, you don't want to get any of them hot. They're all mellow, but if someone really did insult me it would be bad."

Resting his cheek against her hair, he thought about the day she'd gotten hurt by the bull. "I can only imagine. How is the leg feeling now? Are you still so sore?"

She barely shook her head. "I'm fine, but you might be right. I'm not sure I could walk a straight line. It's a good thing I don't have to try to stand up on my own just now."

"Well, I've tried line dancing now, so tell me when you're ready to go home and we'll leave."

She pulled back and looked up at him. "You know, Michael. There are some very pretty, very nice young women here tonight. You're not paying them much attention."

"What are you talking about? I'm giving you my complete attention. What more do you want?" Her eyes got big and he pulled her back in close. "Just tell me when you want to go, Joey. I don't have the need to deal with any other pretty, nice girls tonight."

****

When the song ended, he took her back to her throne and went back to line dancing, but he kept his eye on her the whole time and she had no idea how to take his half smart alecky comments. When the next slow song started, he came and got her again and this time she was more than a little worried when he took her in his arms.

She knew she really was a little over medicated, but she was still not sure how to feel when he pulled her close and rested his cheek against her hair again. Part of her knew he was just being neighborly and watching out for her almost like one of her brothers, but the part of her that was connected to her heart was both happy to be here in his arms and worried to death about how much she liked it.

There was this nasty little voice in her brain that was nagging at her to use her head and not open herself back up to the hurt she'd been trying to drown ever since the day of the Kentucky Derby. All she had to do was remember how she had felt when she'd realized that race horse owner was Michael and she got her resolve back to keep her distance. Unfortunately, between the medicine and his close proximity, her memory was ridiculously short-lived.

During the fifth slow song, when she realized she was thoroughly enjoying being there in his arms and that Cooper would say she was embarrassing them by swooning over Michael, she decided it was definitely time she headed for home. The problem was the only one from the Rockland ranch who wasn't there with either a date or a wife, was Michael—who she aught to be avoiding. For a second she considered driving and then nixed that thought. There was no way she should be behind the wheel.

For Joey

There was a particularly attentive guy hanging around her and she was contemplating asking him to take her when Michael steered her to the door after the dance instead of to her throne. Even though she'd already decided to go, she rebelled at his attempting to take her without even clearing it with her first and she put the brakes on. "Where do you think you're taking me, Michael Morgan? The night just got started. Take me back to my chair."

He stopped and looked down at her. "Joey, do you remember how much you hated it when the ropers got into a fist fight over you?" She nodded. "Well, you're gonna cause another one if I don't get you out of here. Not only that, but you're practically melting out on the dance floor. It's time, Bertha. Do you need me to go get Rossen to second the opinion?"

She sighed and shook her head. "No, you're right, but Bertha? I feel like I've instantly gained two hundred pounds. Please not Bertha. I should grab my car blanket off my chair before I go."

"Stay here." He parked her on an out of the way chair near the door. "I'll go get your car blanket. Don't go anywhere." As he ducked back into the crowd, she looked around tiredly. Who did he think was going to get into a fist fight? It was a good thing to go home though and she knew it. The medicine was making her positively dopey.

It seemed like he'd been gone a long time and she was just about to go back and look for him when one of the other men who had been hanging around her approached. "So this is where you got to. I've been looking for you. It's a slow song, so I'm sure you'll be able to handle it. After all, you've been dancing the slow ones with that foreigner."

Michael appeared at her elbow before she could answer and the man gave him a scowl and growled, "Look, buddy. You don't own her. This dance is mine. Go find your own partner."

267

Joey looked blankly from one to the other and then said to the man, "Actually, you're right, he doesn't own me, but I did come with him. Would you excuse us please? He's going to take me home to bed. I mean he's going to take me home and then he's going to go to his own home while I go to my own home . . . "

Michael rolled his eyes and put an arm around her. "Come on, Esmeralda. Enough of the explanations. You're burying us."

She let him lead her outside, but then she turned to him. "I wasn't burying us. I wanted to make sure he didn't think we were doing something inapropiate... inapopriat... inapopriate."

Helping her into her SUV, as he buckled her in and then tucked her car blanket around her, he said, "I know what you mean, Joey. He doesn't think you're inappropriate. He thinks you're drunk and he hopes that will make you inappropriate."

"Michael!"

He went around and got into the driver's seat and then said, "I'm a guy, Joey. Not all of us think that way, but I know what he was thinking. It's a good thing we're taking you home."

"But, I'm not drunk. I've never so much as tasted alcohol in my life."

"No, honey, you're not drunk. But you took too much pain medicine. Either way, you're not really up to making that great of decisions right now. At least you won't be hung over in the morning. I've never tried that either, but I've heard it's awful."

She sighed and leaned her head back against the head rest and asked, "Alcohol or being hung over?"

Looking across the car at her, he had this confused look that made her laugh as he questioned, "What?"

"Have you never tried alcohol or being hung over?"

"Uh, well. I can't say I've never tried alcohol. But I can

say that after trying it, I didn't like it and don't drink. But of course I've never been hung over. That would only be stupid, wouldn't it?"

"That is so cool."

Again, he looked confused. "What's cool?"

"That you knew not to drink even before you knew about the Word of Wisdom."

"You lost me, Joey. What's the Word of Wisdom?"

She yawned and closed her eyes. "Can I tell you in the morning? I'm really tired."

"Go to sleep, Penelope. I'll have you back home in a few minutes."

Without opening her eyes she said, "Thank you, Cuthbert."

****

He almost busted up when she called him Cuthbert, but he managed to contain himself. When he pulled into the ranch yard, he decided to take her to her mom's house. Even if he was able to wake her up enough to get her into her apartment, he couldn't help her into her bedroom and he wanted to make sure she made it to bed okay. Naomi would be able to help her.

As he roused her to get her to walk inside, she turned to him. "Michael, we forgot to put your beautiful car away."

"Sean said he'd do it. Come on, Willameena. Let's get you to bed."

She was obviously half asleep when just as Naomi opened the door to let them in, she said dreamily, "Willameena is a nice name, isn't it?"

Naomi looked from Joey to Michael and then back again in concern and Michael assured her, "She took two Percocet. Can she stay with you tonight? I wasn't sure I could get her into her apartment very well."

269

Slowly shaking her head, Joey said, "I'm fine, Mom. Really. Just a little tired is all. Michael is a great dancer. Although he told some guy he was taking me home to bed."

Michael hurried to back pedal as Naomi's eyebrows shot up. "No, Joey was trying to tell some guy that I wasn't taking her home to bed, but I'm afraid she pretty well buried us. Hopefully he won't repeat what she said. Otherwise both of our reputations are toasted. Can you see now why I brought her to you?"

"Yes, I believe I can. You didn't let her drive anything like this did you?"

"No!"

"Oh, good. It'd be a shame to have her really get arrested after teasing you so well tonight. Thank you for bringing her."

"No problem. Goodnight, Joey. I love you."

"I love you too, Michael."

Naomi looked at the two of them like they'd lost their minds and Michael winked at her and whispered, "She won't remember she said that in the morning, but you're my witness if I ever need to blackmail her."

Whispering back, Naomi said, "Yes, I suppose I am. Do you think that means that she really does love you, or she really doesn't?"

He shrugged and laughed. "I have no idea, but I'm going with does. Do you need any help?"

"No. We'll be fine. Thanks again. Good night, Michael. I love you."

"I love you too, Naomi."

He chuckled all the way to his house. If the brothers ever got hold of that one, Joey was a goner.

Chapter 35

In fact, Joey didn't remember what she'd said to him when she woke up late at her mom's house Friday morning. She didn't remember much of anything and she asked her mom as she came in, "How did I come to have a sleep over with you again? I can't even remember how that happened."

Her mom gave her a mellow almost mysterious smile. "Michael was a little worried about you making it to bed okay and thought maybe he'd better bring you here. You were pretty tired."

At the smile, Joey began to worry a bit. "What? Why are you smiling like that?"

Naomi shook her head. "You were a little out of it."

"What do you mean, out of it?"

"Oh, just out of it." She changed the subject and asked about something else and Joey had to wonder what she wasn't saying. All Joey could remember was dancing close with Michael and having an almost slow motion mental tug of war about trying not to enjoy it too much.

This morning, last night was all a little blurry except for the sweet, warmth she remembered feeling when he was taking such kind care of her. In the cold, hard light of day, free of any pain medication, she knew last night had been foolish. She should never have let him dance with her. It was almost a little frightening how easily she had slipped back into being so comfortable with him. She chalked it up to taking too much pain medicine and then committed to keeping her distance from him better.

If she were wise, she wouldn't spend any time with him at all. It put her right back on that slippery slope to being clueless, and if she slid again, her heart would hurt even more than on derby day. She had to purposely remind herself that she hadn't warranted him even leveling with her before she could make herself stop day dreaming about him. She could add great dancer to the list of attributes she was working on ignoring about him.

It wasn't just her family that was making it hard to keep her mind off of him. That Friday morning she was running errands for her mom when she walked out of the post office to find the stretch limo in the parking lot again. Feeling instantly guilty for having unknowingly lied to this woman before and then ridiculously jealous, she walked over to the car and as the driver opened the door for the glamorous female in the back seat, Joey addressed her. "Excuse me. You don't know me, but I owe you an apology. I honestly didn't mean to lie to you before. Michael Morgan does live here. I just didn't realize he was who you were looking for last time. Please forgive me."

The woman stepped out of the luxurious car and turned to her, all smiles. "Michael is here? You know where he is?"

"Yes, he's here. I'm sorry, I didn't realize he was a banker then. He lives a ways out of town on a private road, but I'm going there right now. You could follow me."

At this, the woman looked Joey up and down and the smiles clouded up a bit. "You're going to his house right now? What, do you work for him or something?"

Joey tried to stifle her irritation at the woman. "No. Nothing like that. I'm just a neighbor who lives on the same road."

"Oh. Pardon my assumption. Yes, we'd certainly appreciate it if you'd direct us. Thank you." The smiles were

272

back as the woman spoke to the driver and got back into her car. All the way home, Joey did battle with herself, at once wishing she hadn't volunteered anything about him, and then telling herself that his friends were none of her business, and she'd be wise if she distanced herself from him completely. At any rate, she had been obligated to apologize for inadvertently misleading the woman. She hadn't meant to, but she had still lied to her.

Once at the ranch, she led them to her parents' house, knowing Michael was out moving cows with Sean and Ruger, and that they would show up for lunch there momentarily. This time, as the chauffer handed the woman out of the car on the gravel drive in front of the house, she offered her hand to Joey. "I'm Margot Witter, by the way. Thank you for directing me. Now, where does he live?"

Feeling almost fatalistic, Joey instructed, "Come with me." Limping into the house, she continued as she walked across the great room to the French doors of the deck. "He's not here at the moment, but keep your eyes in that direction and he should appear within a few minutes with my brothers." She nodded toward the west fields. "In fact, there they come now."

Margot followed her to the windows and looked out. After a minute, she said, "I'm sorry, I don't see him. Where are you saying? All I see are those men on horses."

Joey glanced out to where the three of them were approaching. "He's the dark haired one. Can I get you something to drink? A soda or some lemonade?"

The glamorous woman from New York turned to her. "I'm sorry. There's been a misunderstanding. I was looking for a different Michael Morgan. He's a business man. Not a cowboy. He's recently moved here somewhere. I know his mail is coming to Hollister. I just don't know where he is out here exactly. I'm sorry to have bothered you."

She turned to go back to the door and Joey was almost tempted to let her go, but said, "Banker, raises race horses, gifted musician, disgustingly wealthy?"

Margot turned back around in surprise and Joey nodded out the window to where the three horsemen pulled up at the hitch rail at the side of the yard. Michael dismounted, tossed his reins over the rail and took off his hat to slap it against his pant leg at the dust. He tossed it over his saddle horn and in one smooth motion he reached behind his neck and pulled his shirt off over his head. He tossed it over the saddle too and then leaned into the sprinkler that was watering the lawn beside them to douse his head and torso in the spray. He stood back up and shook his head, sending water droplets flying like ten thousand diamonds in the midday sun.

The water glistened off the muscles of his chest and shoulders, making him look like a bronze graven image of a mythical god and time seemed to pause as Joey watched him. How in the world was she supposed to keep her distance from something as beautiful as that?

Laughing at something Sean said, he retrieved his shirt and turned toward the stairs to the deck, completely oblivious to the fact that he was absolutely fascinating to the women inside the window.

Joey didn't realize she'd stopped breathing until she heard Margot breathe out a very unladylike expletive in complete disbelief beside her. Margot's voice was almost reverent as she continued. "I can't even believe what I'm seeing. It really is Michael. It really is."

Dragging her eyes away from the vision that was striding across the deck toward them, Joey turned back to Margot, both saddened and grateful for the little wake up call that Michael really was a New York financial tycoon. She walked into the kitchen with a sigh. "Yeah, it's him. Have you eaten? They're just coming in for lunch. Would you like to join them?" She reached into the oven to remove the baked pasta her mother had made earlier, and replace it with foil wrapped garlic bread.

By the time he came in the door, Michael had his shirt back on. He was still laughing when he walked in and stopped abruptly in surprise when he saw Margot. She almost ran to him and went to hug him, but he came out of his shock just in time to intercept her and keep her at arms length. He looked from her to Joey in confusion as Margot stuck out a pouty lip. He pushed her away and asked hesitantly, "Margot, how did you get here? Where did you come from?"

Joey tried to be completely occupied in the kitchen as Margot said, "Your neighbor here brought me. I'd met her the last time I came out looking for you, but at that time she didn't know who you were. And it's no wonder. What are you doing out here? Playing cowboys and Indians? I almost didn't recognize you. You're a hard man to find."

Sean and Ruger looked on interestly as Joey fought to remain aloof from it all as she set the table and put the last touches on lunch. She finally did look up and Michael gave her a disgusted look as he pulled an apple out of the basket on the counter. "That would be because I didn't want to be found, Margot. Why else would I not return all the calls? I'm not playing anything. I live here. This is my life now and I love it."

Margot's pout became more pronounced. "Now you're being rude, Michael, right in front of all these people. That's not like you. Aren't you even glad to see me?"

Michael glanced around at the others and then almost glared at Joey. "Thanks. Thanks a lot." Turning back to Margot, he said, "I'm sorry, Margot, but I'm not glad to see you." He continued, but he was looking at Joey again as he went on, "I wanted to be able to stay here without anyone back there finding out where I am." With the apple in his hand, he turned back to the door and said over his shoulder, "I'll be over on Columbine Creek. I'll see you guys later."

Before he made it out the door, Margot swept across the room to confront him. "Michael Morgan, don't you dare walk out that door! I've come all the way from New York twice to see you!"

He shook his head and said in disgust, "That's unfortunate, Margot, but I'm leaving anyway. Say hello to Mother for me."

"Michael, if you leave like this, I swear, I'll tell Shannon Bronson exactly where you are!"

At that, Michael turned back around, but this time, the disgusted tone was softened in his voice. Again, he was talking to Margot, but looking at Joey. "Please don't. I have a great life here now, Margot. I'm happy. I've gotten to know God, and I've finally found the girl I want to be with forever. And even though she won't have me right now, I'm going to stay here and keep working on her, hoping and praying that someday she'll change her mind and consent to marry me. I'm at peace here, Margot. It feels like I've come home. I don't mean to be rude, but go home and leave me alone. I'm not the man for you, I'm sorry."

With that, he strode out the door and down to his horse, where he mounted and kicked it up to a high lope on the trail directly away from the little white house. They all watched him in silence until he disappeared over the rise. When Joey glanced over, Sean and Ruger were watching her and she turned away to take the bread out of the oven. Margot stayed staring out the window and finally said almost to herself, "What woman in the world wouldn't have him? He's wealthy and gorgeous and the most decent human being I know. He doesn't even drink, and has this antiquated idea about saving himself for his wife. Who wouldn't have him?"

She shook her head sadly as she walked back over to the front door, almost in a daze and let herself out. Joey's eyes followed her as she made her way to the stretch limo and the driver handed her back in. As the long car pulled away, she turned back to the lunch she had been about to serve, but she couldn't face Sean's and Ruger's knowing gazes and without a word, left them to eat and went out the door Michael had gone through.

Walking across the pasture, she didn't even notice when Blue pushed his nose into her hand. She was too busy trying to figure out what Michael had been saying back there. Try as she might, she couldn't figure it out. She let herself into her apartment, completely at a loss as to what had just happened.

Even though she hadn't eaten any lunch, she couldn't face going up to dinner and settled for a frozen entre'. As she got it out of the freezer, she noticed it was a Lean Cuisine and was more mixed up than ever when even a TV dinner made her focus on him. Holy moly, this felt almost impossible. Talk about your haunted.

She turned on her TV, something she rarely did, to try to take her mind off of him as she ate and afterwards she settled in with a good book, but it was hopeless. More than an hour later she'd only made it through six pages. Giving it up, she put the book aside and took a long bath. As the sun went down, she and Blue went out to go for a walk.

Only half way up the rise behind her house, she realized her hip wasn't up to this, and also that her family had all gathered around the fire pit on the trail on the other side of her parents' house to roast marshmallows and listen to Kit sing. From where Joey was, she could see and hear, but she didn't have to necessarily socialize. It was perfect.

She settled down onto a flat rock on the hillside and leaned back to try to relax her hip, grateful for the relative cover of darkness. If they all realized she was up here and struggling, her brothers would come and try to help her down and tonight she just wanted not to be noticed. She still hadn't figured out how to take what Michael had said that afternoon. By now everyone would have heard about it and honestly, she wasn't really up to facing them.

Sitting on her rock listening, there was something different tonight about Kit's music. On nights like tonight, her family occasionally sang along, but there was something else. A subtle harmony she had never heard before. A deep, mellow voice blended softly with Kit's there in the mauve gray twilight and instinctively Joey knew it was Michael.

She'd never heard him sing before and the effect of his voice was as evocative as his piano music had been that first time. Not searingly so like then, but incredibly sexy and compelling. The soul deep pain he'd come here to survive was gone and had been replaced with a comfortable, sweet, warm peace that came through in his harmony. Truly, music was this man's gift.

His music reached across the little valley to her as it always did, drawing her like the Pied Piper more than ever, until she either had to give up and give in to its pull on her heart, or leave now and get away from the emotions she had begun to fear were going to drown her. Even with all of her resolve to resist this man, she was more fascinated by him than ever. Sometimes she felt like she was beyond haunted and if she were honest, it scared her to death. She thought back to how much her heart had hurt that derby day and the thought of that pain deepening day in and day out made her wonder how she was ever going to survive him. She didn't think her heart was up to this.

Hobbling down the slope in the dark, she slid the last few feet to the bottom and then limped to her SUV, got in and drove away. She had no idea where she was going, and she probably wasn't really up to this, but hanging out being hypnotized into hopeless infatuation was beyond foolish.

Turning the little truck northward, she took a scenic highway that wound in and out of the river bottom like a silver ribbon laced among the huge trees. She rolled the windows all down and let the night wind blow through. Maybe it would miraculously clear these feelings from her heart and these thoughts from her head. Maybe they could waft off like the mist that rose from the river there in the light of the moon that danced in and out of the ragged clouds. Anything was worth a try. Tonight she felt like she was drowning.

She drove until her hip and pelvis burned, then turned to head for home. Almost subconsciously she began to pray aloud as she cruised along. Never in her life had she struggled like this. As she wound back south along the highway, she poured out her heart and her thoughts to God, trying to find the fine line she had somehow lost track of that balanced what she wanted, what she thought was wise, and what she felt like her Father in Heaven had in mind for her.

Her whole life she'd trusted that they would all come together someday for her, but lately she'd lost faith in that for some reason. She told Him honestly of her dreams and her fears and even how she felt it was so unfair that she feel so strongly about someone and then find she'd been naive and gullible. She told Him how she didn't feel like she deserved to be so hurt when she'd always tried so hard to be a good person.

It was easier to drive and talk to Him there in the misty dark. For some reason, this whole mess made a little more sense as she talked it all out. At length, she was still incredibly lost as to how to deal with all of it, but at least she still knew that God was there and watching over her and that He had it all under control, despite the fact that she couldn't quite see how it was going to work out at this point in time. He would help her be strong enough to handle whatever she needed to, and He would help her figure out how to cope with this hurt and disillusionment.

She finally just committed to trying harder to walk by faith and to not worry so much about it. It felt incredibly good to let go of that struggle and strain, at least for the time being.

At two in the morning she pulled back into her parking spot and then groaned as she shut off the car and opened her door to get out. The drive had helped her heart, but her body was thoroughly hammered. She put the seat back and slowly slid her leg over and carefully rested the weight on the ground as she tried to muster the fortitude she was going to need to get herself and her hip and thigh up those stairs to bed. Just now that seemed like more than she was up to.

It was strange, but she knew he was there before he materialized out the darkness from the pasture. He came up to the door of her SUV and crouched down beside her and even in the dark she could see the concern in his eyes. He didn't ask where she'd been, just if she was okay, and she was sore enough that she shook her head with a tired smile. "Actually, no. You're looking like an angel of mercy to me just now. Would you mind helping me stand up?"

He took both of her hands and lifted as she slowly stood up straight. Feeling him put an arm around her and even leaning into his chest for a minute to ease the pain only felt right. After her long drive and talk with God, she was able to bypass the stress of feeling like she should stay away from him and was simply grateful for his strength as he helped her out and up the stairs to her house. At the door, he didn't let go right away and she was glad. She'd have never made it in tonight without him.

She turned her face toward him and he put both arms around her and pulled her into a warm, comfortable, sweet hug. She let herself relax against him just for a few minutes as she breathed in his smell against his neck. Holy moly he smelled good. And felt like heaven. She had missed this so much it almost made her feel weepy. It must have just been that she was so tired.

280

Taking a deep, shuddering breath, she finally looked up at him, grateful that so much of the confusion about how she felt and what she should do and what he wanted from her had dissipated during her prayerful drive. Just now none of that mattered. At the moment she only had the emotional energy to make it up one more step and eventually to bed. The rest she was giving over to God to figure out. Her little brain had no answers tonight.

Michael looked down at her, still with that concern, and she couldn't help looking into those midnight blue eyes and thinking that they were incredibly intriguing. She'd only made it to intriguing when he bent his head to kiss her.

There was a small alarm beeping somewhere in the deepest recesses of her tired brain, but the pain and fatigue had buried it enough that she was hard put to even hear it, let alone heed it. She stood there in his arms and kissed him back, enjoying it enough that when he finally pulled back, she was unabashedly disappointed and dropped her hands from around his neck with a small sigh. She'd have been perfectly content to stay there for a little while, but she wasn't going to admit that to him.

She went to turn away and open her door, but he stopped her with a gentle hand on her arm and she looked back up at him. He didn't really say anything, just stood there looking at her and she met his eyes, wondering if it was going to be hard to face him tomorrow and not really even caring. Tonight it was just nice to be able to be with him and still enjoy the warm, sweet peace that lingered after her talk with her Father in Heaven.

Just as she was thinking that, Michael gently touched her face and said, "If you can't sleep, try praying. It really helps. A wise and beautiful woman told me that once and changed my life forever. I'll be praying for you. I hope you feel better tomorrow." He leaned to kiss her one more time and then gave her the most unfathomable look before he turned and

281

walked back down her stairs to ghost off into the darkness of the pasture.

She was still standing there, touching her lips and thinking about his kiss when she heard the sound of his piano drifting softly on the night wind. It was that same captivating harmony he always played when she heard him begin and it was the final touch to the spell of this night. For the first time in weeks, she laid down to sleep at peace.

Chapter 36

That peace lasted all the way through both Saturday and Sunday and when the missionaries challenged Michael to get baptized on Sunday afternoon and he accepted without hesitation, Joey was honestly wondering if maybe she had been wrong about him. How could he be less than honorable when he positively glowed?

She'd been praying about him like she'd promised Rossen, and at worst, the peace of heart she felt about Michael confused her. At best, she was almost beginning to wonder if he wasn't serious when he acted like he honestly loved her. He still looked at her with that look that tended to make her heart do funny things and Rossen had been right. Michael wasn't so much as taking phone calls from any females in New York or anywhere else that she was aware of.

All of those feelings of peace came to a screeching halt on Monday morning. She and Michael had been cleaning up her mother's kitchen after breakfast and then they were going to drive into town together to run errands. They were all but finished when Michael did indeed take a phone call from New York.

His cell phone hadn't rung much. Joey didn't even recognize its ring as he fished it out of his pocket while he wiped down the countertops beside where she was loading the dishwasher. She could tell right away it was a business call as she heard him talking about an upcoming bank board meeting.

After a few minutes, she heard him say, "No, I'm sorry, Rollins, but Warren believes that type of investment is too risky and I agree with him. I always have. Yes, I know most banks are involved with that type of thing, but frankly we aren't interested. I believe that's one of the reasons we're considered to be the strongest bank in the nation. Yes, there are potentially higher profits, but the risk is too great and there's a definite question of ethics. Yes, ethics. Buying sub-prime mortgages, knowing we can dump them on the backs of the taxpayers isn't ethical, even if it's legal and extremely profitable."

At this point, Joey could tell he was becoming a bit disgusted, but he remained cool and professional to the core as he calmly went on, "I'm sorry that you feel that way, Rollins, but you'll have to invest in another bank if that's what you want. Yes, I know you've considerable stocks. Yes, I know you're one of the biggest shareholders besides Warren and me. Look, Carl, if this is this big of deal to you, I'll buy you out right now if the FTC will okay it. Yes, at market value. It's up to you.

"Fine, have your man call and I'll set it up with my accounting people. I'm sorry it's come down to this. We'll certainly miss you, but it's important that you're happy with how your holdings are being handled. I'm sure this will be for the best. Have a good day, Rollins."

Michael closed his phone and went back to wiping the counter, but Joey just stood looking at him, trying to wrap her brain around what she had just been hearing. If she understood correctly, he had just spent who knew how much money? Millions, probably. Maybe a gob of millions, on an off the cuff phone call.

His nonchalance over the whole thing blew her completely out of the water. She started the dishwasher and in an absolute mental turmoil, she turned and walked out the front door, unable to even comprehend what she had just heard. Let alone deal with it.

She was limping along the main road when Michael pulled up beside her in Merv's car. Without preamble, and in a no-nonsense tone of voice, he said, "Get in."

Obediently, she got in, her mind still blown enough that she had no idea what she should be doing anyway. They drove in silence for a few minutes before she finally said, "We need to take my SUV." He just looked across at her and she added, "I have to pick up a whole cut and wrapped beef. It won't fit here in Merv's car. And I need my purse."

Michael abruptly swerved to the side of the gravel road and turned around so fast that the little car slid in the gravel as he pulled back out. At that, she turned to look at him again. She'd seen him sad, and tired, and happy, and concerned, and probably even silly, but she'd never seen him mad before. He hadn't been upset in the kitchen and she wondered what had happened and asked, "What?

Tersely he returned, "What, what?"

"What's wrong, what? Why are you driving like this?"

"I'm driving fine." He pulled in beside her SUV and stopped fast enough to throw her forward into her seat belt, got out and came around to open her door and help her out. Joey was still so blown away over his phone conversation that she just obediently switched vehicles and climbed back in, did up her seat belt and they headed down the gravel road again with Michael only marginally driving less angry than he'd been in his own car.

Finally, she glanced across the car at him and said, "Michael, stop being childish and tell me what's wrong before you take a turn too fast and kill us both. What's going on? You were fine ten minutes ago. Do you want me to drive?"

He pulled the car to another abrupt stop between Sean's house and the pond, shut off the engine and turned toward her. "Childish? You stomp out of your mom's house like a two year old and I'm the one who's childish?"

She was a little taken aback at the amount of feeling behind his comment, but she gamely went on. "This is about

285

me walking out at my parents? I didn't stomp. I'm not even angry. What is up with you?"

"What is up with me is that, Joey, there's no way to win with you. I can't even take a simple phone call without freaking you out. What is it you want from me?"

This time she finally did get a little testy. "You call that a simple phone call?"

She rolled her eyes and turned to look out the window, but then turned back when he exploded. "Yes, it was a simple phone call! So I have money. So what! Quit being an idiot about it! Most of the time you're a pretty decent Christian, but about this you're prejudiced and bigoted and judgmental! Let God judge me!"

"You think I'm judging you? You think this is about Christianity? Oh, Michael, get a grip. Yeah, I was kind of freaked out. But your money is none of my business. Which is good because I can't even comprehend how much you have. And quit raising your voice or I'm going to get out of this car and go home. I've done nothing to warrant this tirade."

"Oh, honey. I haven't even gotten started. For weeks you've been punishing me for the fact that I was born into wealth and no matter what I do to downplay that, it's never enough for you."

At that, Joey opened the door and got out and began to walk toward her house, but he got out and came after her. She spun on him, still a little confused about how her being shell shocked about his buying a gazillion dollars worth of bank shares had started all this.

Striving for calm she didn't feel, she said, "Michael, I haven't been punishing you. And it certainly isn't because you're wealthy. Being wealthy doesn't bother me. Well, the scope of your wealth blows me completely away. But what are you talking about me punishing you?"

286

"What would you call the difference in the way you treated me before I went to Kentucky and since then, if it's not punishment?"

The ripping emotion of that painful afternoon came back to her in a single heart beat. She dropped her eyes and turned away from him and began to walk back up the road again, but he followed her and caught her arm.

She tried to draw away and keep walking, but he pulled her to a stop and she turned to look up at him and said tiredly, "Try self-preservation, Michael. It had nothing to do with money. It was simply that I didn't even warrant honesty from a basically honest guy. And I'm not punishing anybody. I just won't be your toy. I'm sorry."

She pulled her arm away and turned to walk again, grateful that they'd finally gotten through that with some modicum of grace.

A few steps later he caught her arm again. "Honesty? Toy? Joey, what are you talking about? How can you accuse me of being dishonest? I've never lied to you. And how have I treated you like a toy?"

With a sigh, Joey turned back to him. "You're right, Michael. You didn't lie. I didn't merit any information at all. I got your first name and a pseudonym. It took me awhile to figure out that you had your own personal joke about telling people you were Joe Blow.

"It would have been really funny, except that the joke was on me. Full disclosure wasn't even an issue. It's okay, Michael. I understand. You have the right to keep your life your life. I was just a little confused for a minute there. Clueless, just like you intimated. Don't worry about it. I'll get over it. But I won't be a toy."

This time he let her walk several steps away before he stopped her. He went right around in front of her and took both of her shoulders in his hands and when she looked up at him, the anger was gone when he said, "I'm not toying, Joey.

I've been here for months and other than at church, or the grocery store or something, I haven't even spoken to another woman. I'm not toying."

She wasn't sure how to take his sudden mood changes this morning and she looked up at him and hesitantly said, "Okay."

"No, Joey. You don't understand. I'm really not toying. I know what I want now, Joey. And I believe it's what you want too. And I'm going to be patient until you clue in that I'm okay, and a nice guy, and can be trusted, and am moral, and ethical, and unmaterialistic."

"You drive a Ferrari, Michael."

He looked straight up and shook his head. "No, I store a Ferrari. And you love it! So knock it off! I've driven that stupid car of Merv's this whole time just to prove to you that money isn't a big deal, and you know it. And storing a Ferrari doesn't necessarily make me materialistic. But that's not the issue, remember? You just said this wasn't about money."

"What isn't about money? I don't even understand why you're so angry with me right now."

"Well, I don't understand why you got so upset in the kitchen."

She pushed a hand through her hair for a moment and blew a breath out. "It's all just a little hard for me to comprehend sometimes, Michael. I'm sorry. I'm working on it. I've just never dreamed of anyone spending that kind of money so off handedly. It's hard to wrap my brain around."

"It's just money, Joey. It needed to be done. He's been giving us garbage over not double dipping for years now. It'll be more than a relief to get him off our backs and move on without him. If the FTC will even let me buy it. They may say we can't do it."

"Meaning that you'll be deemed too powerful if you own too much."

He looked at her warily. "Something like that, yeah."

"It's okay, Michael. You don't have to worry about freaking me out again."

"Why's that?"

She shrugged, suddenly tired. "I don't know. I'll just decide not to be freaked out. Let's go get the errands done."

"It's all just that simple? You're just going to decide? Why didn't you decide that a long time ago?"

"I only got freaked out ten minutes ago, Michael. Chill out."

"So then why didn't you just decide not to be so upset at me after the Kentucky Derby?"

At that she looked up at him to see if he was being serious. He was, and it killed her in one glance. He really, truly thought that her falling for him when he didn't care enough to tell her anything, wasn't much of a big deal. She turned away from him, unable to even face him as much as it still hurt. He had no idea how much she cared apparently.

Maybe that was a good thing. At least it let her save face a little that he didn't know how deeply she felt about him. Striving to joke about it, she said, "I guess I should have, Michael. I'm sorry. We could have put all of this behind us and been living happily ever after by now."

She walked back to her SUV and climbed into the driver's seat, determined to make it through this trip into Hollister without breaking down and sobbing like a baby.

Geez, she'd almost done it again! She was such an idiot! Just this last couple of days she'd actually been wondering if maybe he didn't truly like her a little after all. Let alone thinking just now that he was trying to tell her he was serious about her. How could she be so foolish? She was still as much of a lame brain as she'd been before that stupid Kentucky Derby!

At the guardhouse, one of the security guys said there was someone there who wanted to talk to Michael. He'd been hanging around for a half hour or so, but they hadn't let him in because they hadn't been able to reach Michael to okay it. Joey coasted the SUV through the gate and stopped to let the guy talk to him. Michael rolled the window down as a slick, almost effeminate looking man approached and Michael asked him, "Did you need something?"

The man beamed at Michael through the window. "Yes, Mr. Morgan, I'm privileged to offer you a wonderful opportunity!" He stuck out a hand and said, "Gerard Mince. I'm from Get Real Productions, based out of California. I'm sure you've heard of us! My boss has sent me to offer you the chance to be the star of the next blockbuster reality show about the ultimate eligible bachelor! We would pay all of the expenses, of course, and you'd get to be filmed with twenty of the most beautiful young women in the world who would all be vying to win your hand in marriage! It will be the hit of the year! The decade! You'll be even more famous than you are already! Isn't that an absolutely fantastic idea?"

Michael didn't even answer the guy as he rolled up the window and nodded on down the road and Joey pulled out, more than a little floored at the brazenness of it all. She wondered how in the world they had found him and then she remembered that she'd literally hand delivered Margot just a couple of days before. Margot must have told them where to find him. Joey glanced across the car at him, feeling guilty for having been the one to subject him to that right here at his home.

Driving on, it only punctuated what Michael had brought out earlier. Her naive dreams about him were more ridiculously idiotic than ever. He was one of the most eligible men in not just the U.S., but in the whole world. And he probably didn't really mean to toy with her, but then he couldn't help the circumstances he was in either.

290

Chapter 37

Michael went to bed early that night without ever touching his piano. It had taken him a good portion of the afternoon to realize he'd somehow made Joey close up like a flower in the dark. She had gamely pasted on a smile that had actually fooled him for awhile. He'd gone over their conversation a thousand times in his head and for the life of him, he couldn't figure out what he'd said that had made her so unhappy.

They'd talked about money and he'd tried to tell her in a roundabout way that he loved her. Then they'd talked about how she could just decide not to let things bother her and it was somewhere in there that she'd gotten upset with him, but he couldn't really pin down what he'd said or done.

Then they'd met that clown from some reality show. The timing couldn't have been more disastrous. He could have reached out the window and choked the guy! It had been all down hill from there and Michael hadn't been the least bit surprised when she'd gotten back into her little truck and disappeared again as soon as dinner was over. The dinner that she hadn't so much as even spoken during, let alone cracked a smile. Her sparkle had gone out like a candle in an arctic gale and he was completely at a loss as to what to do about it.

Then when she'd finally come home and limped up her stairs, he had seen Rossen go up and even he came back down just a few minutes later. Michael knew that if Rossen had struck out on talking to her that he didn't have a chance.

He'd had to settle for sending Blue over and then watching for her and praying for her from a distance.

How had this friendship gotten this tanked in the first place? In the beginning it had come effortlessly. And then he hadn't even been looking for a relationship. Now, when he didn't think he could possibly live without her, it wasn't coming at all. He turned over for the fortieth time and hauled his pillow under his cheek and then sat straight up in bed when he heard the unmistakable rumble of the glass packs on Bryan Cole's Mustang. Oh, that was all he needed just now! How had Bryan known that Joey was desperately unhappy? She must have called him.

****

Joey had heard the glass packs too, and had had a restless night, wondering how she was going to juggle Bryan right now when she was depressed worse than ever. Thank goodness Blue had shown up last night after she'd gotten home from her drive. His unconditional devotion was priceless at a time like this. As she was doing her hair there came a knock at her door and she opened it to see Bryan's handsome face smiling back at her. Looking at him, she decided maybe this wouldn't be too bad. At least he would help take her mind off Michael.

That had been a good theory. Right up until he brought her a CD from a movie score he had just recorded back in LA. He handed it to her with about a half sad smile and said, "I have to hand it to him. Your song is incredible."

Not understanding, she just looked at Bryan until he leaned in close to point out that the CD he had just handed her was composed by none other than Joseph Michael Blouet and that the love theme for the movie was titled, "For Joey".

Bryan gave her that little smile again. "Didn't you know he wrote it for you?" Joey shook her head in disbelief. "It's actually a beautiful song. You're going to love it. The other songs for this movie are excellent too, dang it. He's an incredible talent. I'm singing some of them, so I brought it to you."

Joey tried to hide her shock as she spent the balance of the day with Bryan. How in the world was she supposed to take Michael openly naming a love theme for her?

Bryan only stayed the day and then he had to head back out on his tour, and though he had been a welcome distraction, she wasn't sad to see him go. She always enjoyed him, but she hated to see that shadow in his eyes. He perpetually smiled, but it was awful to know she was hurting him.

After he left, she put the CD in to listen to it and was amazed to find that the beautiful song Michael always played after he spent time with her was the one he'd dedicated to her on the CD. All of the songs on it were ones she'd heard him play over the months he'd been here, and when she listened to the lyrics, she recognized the eloquent man she had fallen in love with when he had helped her mind take her out of the pain.

For a few minutes, she let herself be carried away with the words that only made Michael's music more evocative, and then she realized this was simply going to make her obsessed even further, and turned it off. She would be wise if she remembered that he had always been eloquent, even when he had not offered any details about who he really was while she had been snuggled against him for all that time before Kentucky.

Although the CD had been intended as a wonderful gift, in a way, it made the heartache worse. Hearing Michael's music and acknowledging his talent only made trying to exorcise him out of her heart all the harder.

That night Michael haunted her dreams until she woke up exhausted and discouraged to the point of honestly wondering if she just needed to move away from the valley for awhile until she could get a handle on her heartache. Living here beside him, every time she saw him he made her pulse jump and when she didn't see him, she wondered what he was up to and her pulse jumped anyway.

Inevitably there followed that heart wrenching, sickening reality check—that hole she got in her stomach when she remembered she hadn't really meant enough to him to merit being told even the vaguest details, and the ache in her chest that was almost physical.

She hated the fact that since he had come here she had gone from a relatively confident, happy, hopeful young woman, to having to face the fact that, in reality, she hadn't truly measured up enough to matter when she'd wanted it most. It made her feel like such an undesirable fool. Clueless, just like he'd intimated.

Still wondering if she needed to just get away, the next morning she tried to ride a horse for the first time since her run in with the bull, and she was pleasantly surprised to find that, although it was painful, she could handle it for a short ride. Being able to ride again would help. At least she wouldn't be just hanging around, pining like some lovesick country bumpkin, while she worked up the initiative to leave everyone she loved to protect her heart and self esteem.

She took Wildfire since he was sweet and old and mellow, and rode bareback. As she came back and rode to put him back in Michael's pasture, Michael came out of his house and walked over to the gate. Both thrilled to see him and disgusted that she was so thrilled to see him, she wondered if he knew that she was just now trying to figure out how to get off of Wildfire after stiffening up on her ride.

Still sitting up on the mellow horse, she looked down at Michael and in an attempt to simply be polite, asked, "What are you up to, Michael?"

For a second he studied her and then asked, "Can you get off? How is the hip and leg?"

She had to laugh self-consciously and she laid forward over Wildfire's mane. "I'm not sure. Don't watch while I try. It might not be pretty." Still laying forward, she lifted her right leg and slid it over Wildfire's rump and then was immensely relieved as Michael stepped forward to catch her as she slid off, wondering if her left leg would hold up at all as she came down on it. She'd have felt like even more of an idiot if she'd landed in a heap at his feet.

The leg buckled and she would have fallen except for Michael's hands at her waist. She just stood there for a second and then gingerly tried to turn around and was surprised when Michael didn't step back and give her some room. She looked up at him, questioning and wasn't sure what to think about the way he was looking at her as he asked gently, "Are you okay?"

His extremely close proximity was disconcerting and she looked down before she could answer. Being near him was so nice and so troubling at the same time. She loved it and yet knew that if she was smart, she really would move away from here and stay where she couldn't get any more vulnerable than she already was. Which was certainly way too much already. Still without daring to look at him, she nodded, then she said, "Yeah, I'm okay. Just let me stand here for a second and I'll be fine."

In the silkiest and sexiest low voice she could have possibly imagined, he returned, "I've got forever, Joey. I've set aside eternity for you, so take as long as you want."

Wondering if she'd heard him right, she looked up so fast that her hair caught on his collar because he was standing so close. He met her eyes calmly as he reached up to smooth the strands back beside her cheek while she studied him. At length, she looked down, disgusted with her heart for pounding so when he had to be just teasing her. She tried to back off, but her leg buckled again and he caught her one more time. This time he pulled her against him and when she looked up at him in confusion, he leaned down and kissed her before she even realized what he was going to do.

She was at once stunned yet instinctively drawn to him. It was incredibly nice. His warm, firm mouth against hers was the most heavenly feeling she had ever known and her whole universe moved into alignment and the stars held completely still as she kissed him back, breathing against his mouth and feeling his heart beat against hers just for a moment. She was basking in the strength of him as he held her and leaned into the sweet, old horse, thoroughly enjoying being held captive and reveling in knowing that he wanted this as much as she did.

Wishing with all her heart that she could just keep kissing him back and enjoy this time here in his arms, she knew it would break her heart later and at length she pushed against his chest.

Even though she was the one to end the kiss, it was awful when he finally pulled away. Maddeningly frustrated, she said the words she knew she needed to, "Don't Michael. You shouldn't joke like that."

Without giving an inch, he continued to hold her hostage against the old horse as that same, lethal voice said, "I'm not joking in the slightest, Joey." His voice became even more dangerous when he encouraged her huskily. "Stop pushing me away. Literally and figuratively. At least let me hold you when you'll fall down if I let go. There aren't many coincidences, Joey. Us being here together certainly isn't one. And I think deep down you know that, don't you?"

For Joey

His breath in her ear, on top of what he was saying, was making her brain short-circuit and she was frankly amazed that she could think at all with him so close that she could feel his thighs against hers and smell his aftershave. The little warning signal beeping in her head was colliding with the blood rushing to her heart. Both of them were being drowned out by the all out mutiny of her body. She felt herself melt into him, even as she wanted to run away from how much she knew this was going to hurt when she came to her senses.

At least half of her brain chose to stick with her and she tried to lean back as she replied sadly and a little breathlessly, "Don't toy, Michael. I'm not up to it just now, okay?"

He didn't answer her and when she finally looked up at him, she forgot to push back as he kissed her again, this time hard and fast. Raising his head, his voice was no longer silky, but intense when he swore and then said, "What is it going to take for you to trust me, Joey? What have I ever done to give you the impression I'm toying with you?"

Almost angrily he half snapped, "I am not toying, Joey Rockland! I've never in my life been more sincere. I love you and want to be with you forever and ever and ever. I'm not toying! I don't even know how to toy. I don't know why you have to assume that just because I'm more than a musician I can't be honorable. I'm not some womanizer with ten thousand girls all over the country like you seem to think. There's only you. From that first moment I got up from my piano bench to realize that an exhausted, exquisite angel had appeared in my house and fallen asleep on my couch, there's only been you."

He paused and kissed her more gently for several seconds and added softly, "Even before that there was only you, I just didn't know that a woman as incredible as you even existed and had given up on them all. Remember that

297

there was nobody I cared to tell that I was leaving New York and you thought I was telling you I was gay?" He watched her again and then lowered his head to her mouth one more time.

At length, he pulled her tighter against him and spoke quietly against her hair with that same low, sexy voice, "I'm not toying, Joey. I'm simply madly, hopelessly in love with you and want to hold you, and kiss away your pain and your fear and your distrust. I want that girl back who walked into my house and made me take out the garbage and eat better just because I was a human being and she was a disciple of Christ. The one who trusted me to let me hold her when she didn't feel good, even when I invaded her personal space. The one who made me laugh and gave me hope and helped me to know that I'm a child of God. I fell hopelessly in love with her and for the first time in my life I felt like I'd come home."

He reached up and stroked the little bone behind her ear before he quietly asked, "Why did you take her away, Joey? I didn't deserve that, did I? Have I really been that horrible and untrustworthy? Do I really deserve this cold shoulder just because I'm not only a musician?"

Looking into his eyes and hearing what he was saying in such a velvet tone of voice had her completely at a loss. She had no idea what to think about what was going on here, and all semblance of intelligent judgment had gone out the window with his touch on the skin behind her ear. Emotionally she was scrambling to try to understand why he would be saying all these things to her, and there was this fundamentally disconcerting battle going on between her head and her heart and her intuition. It didn't help when he continued to search her eyes and plead silkily, "Come on, Joey. Listen for that sweet, warm peace that you taught me. Listen to the Spirit. He'll tell you that you can trust me. Just listen."

298

They stood there like that, with his deep blue eyes looking into hers until she was more mixed up than she could even imagine. She felt like she was drowning, and while she wanted to trust this rushing current of emotion, she was more afraid than she'd ever been in her life.

She wanted to trust him, but she'd done that before and been bitterly hurt to know that he hadn't been at all honest with her. She tried to do as he was asking and listen for that peace, but as close as he was, all she could hear was that her body craved him with a need she knew could leave her charred in its wake if she let it. Still searching his eyes, she wanted more than ever in her life to push aside her good judgment and believe what he was saying.

The intensity of the moment grew and seemed to take on a life of its own. Then, instantly, the spell was shattered with the ringing of his cell phone.

In a split second, reality came crashing in like a tidal wave, and she saw that he knew it too, as she turned away and edged her body out from between him and the horse. Feeling hot tears well into her eyes, she opened the gate and led Wildfire in and as the gate clanged shut behind her, she heard Michael sigh and answer his phone.

She could hear him talking as she unbuckled the old horse's halter. It was another conversation about the upcoming bank board of director's meeting and she was glad he was too preoccupied to notice the tears dripping down her face as she walked away from him across the pasture. It had been a great little fantasy there for a moment. A really tempting great little fantasy.

As she neared Rossen's house, she could see him and Sean pulling into the driveway in Rossen's truck. She couldn't bear to face them as emotional as she was at the moment. Instead, she opened the door to her SUV, got in and gave them a half-hearted wave as she pulled out and down the gravel drive. She knew she'd have to face their questions sometime, but it would have to be when she wouldn't embarrass herself to death with uncontrollable tears.

Jaclyn M. Hawkes

Chapter 38

Frustrated beyond belief, Michael watched Joey drive off down the lane in a cloud of dust before he could catch her. They'd been so close! So close to finally getting past that nasty, impenetrable brick wall she'd built up between them! He had seen her heart there in her eyes. She did love him. But he'd also seen the distrust and fear there in her eyes and he wished for the ten thousandth time that he'd just found a way to at least hint about his background before he'd gone to Kentucky. They had been so close!

That was the problem with loving a truly strong charactered woman. The very character strength that he respected and loved was what he couldn't get past to make her believe he honestly loved her.

He wanted to swear like a sailor and instead, had to feign cheerfulness, as Rossen and Sean piled out of Rossen's truck and greeted him. Glancing at his watch, he realized he needed to leave for the airport within the hour if he was going to make his plane and that made him swear in actuality. Somehow he knew he wouldn't be seeing Joey drive back in here in the next hour. He'd seen the determined set to her shoulders as she'd struggled to get into the driver's seat. For all he knew she was more distrustful of him than ever. A call from New York was the last thing he'd needed right then. He looked down at the cell phone in his hand, wanting to throw it.

****

Joey drove until she was shaky from not eating and her leg screamed for relief. She parked the SUV and got out and walked until she could stand to drive some more and then got back in and pulled away again. She was even having trouble praying today, she was so upset. She would have given anything to believe what Michael had been telling her, but the obvious reality of, well, reality just couldn't let her go there. It would be insane to even hope that he might be seriously reserving eternity for her.

Not only could she not believe that Michael would choose her forever out of all the women who had to be waiting for a simple chance at him, but knowing how he had blown off giving her any details all those weeks ago made it only too painfully obvious that they had different ideas of what toying was.

When she still hadn't gotten the tears under control at seven o'clock that night, she pulled into a little local hotel, got a room and then called her mom to tell her she'd decided to take a little road trip. Hanging up, she knew she hadn't fooled her mother. She knew darn well that Joey was a wreck, but at least her mom hadn't asked about it right now.

A night at a hotel and the long drive home would give her a chance to figure this all out in her head. At least she dearly hoped so. At the very minimum, she could maybe find some peace of mind like the last time she'd driven away her struggles. If not, she truly would have to leave home. She couldn't live like this. It was killing her.

She showered and laid on the bed, fervently wishing she could have kept driving. She could think so much more clearly behind the wheel, but her body was far too sore to face the road again. There was just no way.

Laying there, she let the tears come again, wishing she had been able to order room service so she wouldn't have to face anyone with such puffy eyes tonight. Holy moly, she was being a baby! Six months ago, she'd have never dreamed she could get this upset over a guy.

She'd wanted real emotion. We'll, she'd more than gotten what she'd asked for. This real emotion was killing her and she knew that one way or another, she had to get a handle on her life. She had two choices. She had to finally get control of her heart, or get away from Michael, and the ugly truth was, getting control of her heart wasn't working. Controlling her heart where he was concerned truly felt beyond her. It was sadly obvious which one it was going to have to be. She was going to have to leave.

Facing the reality that she needed to leave her home brought on a whole new spate of heartbreak she didn't feel up to right now. She prayed again, this time for strength, and then pep talked herself that she was strong enough. She had to be. She gingerly turned over to try to begin dealing with what had to be done in a more adult manner.

Hunger was what made her finally get up and pull her hair into a pony tail and go in search of food. Enough was enough. She didn't have to be miserably sad because she had to leave home, and hungry as well.

She was just letting herself back into the hotel room when her cell phone rang. She glanced at it, loathe to have to speak to anyone, but it was her mom. She knew she was probably worrying and praying for her and Joey took the call, trying to sound cheerful. "Hi, Mom. What's up?"

She had never been so grateful for her good mother in her life when her mother answered, "Joey, I've been thinking about you all evening and I just wanted to make sure that you remembered who you are."

It sounded strange, but instantly Joey knew exactly what her mother meant. It had nothing to do with being a Rockland, and everything to do with being a daughter of God. Remembering who she was hit with such a force that for a moment Joey was too emotional to speak.

That was it. That was the answer to all of this. It was that simple. It was really that simple.

Finally, she said tearfully, "Thanks, Mom. That's exactly what I needed to hear right now."

All her mother said in reply was, "Don't forget. Don't ever forget. I love you, Joey. I have complete faith that you're going to get through this beautifully. Bye, sweetie."

"I love you, too, Mom. Thank you. Bye."

Her mother's intuitive phone call had been a mildly earth shaking epiphany. In this whole emotional battlefield she'd lost sight of that most important detail. She was a beloved daughter of the living God. Not only did that mean she was absolutely worthy of any man on the planet, whether he was ridiculously wealthy or not. But it also meant she'd forgotten again that God was watching over her and loved her and would guide her to the right course of action to get through this, if she'd only let Him.

Knowing that surviving falling in love with Michael still might not be easy, but that at least she would be doing what her Heavenly Father deemed best, Joey carefully hit her knees, grateful beyond belief for loving parents, both heavenly and mortal. Somehow, it was all going to be okay.

The peace that came from her prayers was nothing short of miraculous. As she stiffly got up, she wondered how she had gotten so caught up in her emotions that she had forgotten to trust God and His Spirit. She lay back down, pondering what she needed to do the next morning. One thing was sure. She was going to quit trying to second guess God and listen to the Spirit instead of her own, negative head. Trying to think through something as important as eternity was a recipe for disaster. She needed one far more intelligent than herself to be able to guide her through how to handle this.

Through the quiet, thoughtful hours of the night she tried to sort out exactly what she was feeling and hearing and what she should be doing and when she got gut honest with herself, she had to admit that whether she believed Michael was toying or not, she loved him. She faced the fact that he was a good, honorable, kind, hard working man and that she did love him and she should be trying to make him want to stay with her instead of feeling like she needed to walk away from him.

The truth was that he was indeed worth fighting for and that she had nothing to lose. If she fought and lost, she would be no more devastated than if she didn't try and moved away. And if she fought and won, she stood the chance of finding the fireworks and the soul mate she'd so long dreamed of. The bottom line was she needed to get home and do her best to win Michael's commitment.

He had said he wasn't toying. She was going to give him the opportunity to prove whether he was serious or not.

By the time Joey pulled back into her parking space beside Rossen's house the next day she was disgusted that she'd spent so much energy and heartache trying to fight how she had been feeling all this time. Turning everything over to God made her realize that she probably caused herself a ridiculous amount of pain she might have avoided if she'd listened better. She still wasn't sure how it would all work out, but she had faith that God was over all regardless.

Struggling to get out of her SUV, she was brutally sore. And completely at peace with the fact that she was in love with Michael.

Now she just hoped she hadn't burned her bridges with him and that if he had been in love with her, he still was after the way she'd been treating him. She didn't understand why he had done everything he'd done over these months, like not being completely forthright with her, but she did know that the thought of forever with him brought that warm, sweet peace he'd been trying to get her to listen for. In spite of anything else, being with him was the right thing to do—if he'd still have her.

That was a big if, considering.

Not long after she pulled in, Rossen showed up at her door. His nonchalance about visiting her made her wonder how many of the family had been in on sending him to check on her. Knowing he loved her dearly and wanted only the best for her, she broke down and cried again as she recounted the struggle she'd been through to reach the conclusion she finally had.

When she admitted that she'd marry Michael in a heartbeat if he really wanted her, Rossen's whole face lit up as he said, "Finally! It's taken you long enough."

"Don't get too smug, bro." She sniffled. "He may tell me to take a flying leap after what a pain I've been. And I may be completely off base about what he wants from me. We'll just have to wait and see. Did he say how long he was going to be in New York this time?"

"He didn't say." She sighed and tried to move to stretch her miserable hip. Watching her, Rossen suggested, "While he's still out of town, why don't you go in and see a massage therapist? It might help to counteract the self-inflicted misery from driving yourself to agony. I have to go in and pick up some computer parts. I'll even take you."

She gingerly stood up. "I think I'll take you up on that."

Chapter 39

They were three miles from the ranch yard and Joey had just partially reclined her seat in Rossen's truck when they rounded a curve in the road to see a handful of loose cows grazing along the side. Frowning, Rossen said, "That's strange. Dad just came in over this road and didn't mention cows being out. Where the heck did these guys come from?" He slowed down and asked, "Do you see a break in the fence anywhere?"

Joey looked along the fence line ahead left and right and shook her head. "Nothing that I can see."

Rossen was looking in his rearview mirror and said, "It's back there." He pulled the truck around and Joey's stomach clutched when she realized the hole in the fence that had liberated the cows had to have been made by a vehicle plowing through the fence and going down the bank toward the river. Nearly panicking as Rossen gunned his truck back up the road toward the break, she asked, "Who would have been out here? Who went to town today?"

Rossen looked grim as he said, "No one. It had to have been someone coming back from town."

Michael. He was telling her that it was Michael.

Rossen nearly hit the fence as he swerved toward the opening so they could see down the hill and Joey thought she would be sick as she recognized Merv's car rolled down the embankment, tipped precariously on its side. It was wedged against a rock and almost in the river.

Rossen nearly deployed airbags as he slammed on the brakes and threw the truck into park. As he dug behind his

307

seat, through gritted teeth he said, "I don't know why he keeps insisting on driving that stupid car. I kept trying to talk him into getting a more dependable truck. Joey, grab the blankets from behind that side. I've got the first aid kit. I wonder how long he's been here."

With that, he slammed out of the truck and went flying down the steep embankment as Joey dug out the blankets, feeling horribly guilty, and came right behind him. She knew exactly why Michael kept driving Merv's car.

At first she thought Michael was unconscious, but as they struggled to open the driver's side door, he wearily raised a bloody head to them and in a voice that sounded infinitely tired said, "I'm glad you guys are here. I can't move much."

As Rossen tried to get Michael free of the steering wheel and dash, Joey asked him, "What happened?"

He slowly shook his head. "I don't know . . . The steering ." He paused and then continued, "Just went. One minute it was fine . . . and then the car . . . the steering wheel didn't work."

Opening the first aid kit to retrieve something to wipe the blood off his face, she asked, "Where are you hurt?"

"Right leg. I think . . . Not sure what all. I'm a little woozy."

Joey heard Rossen swear viciously from where he was working under the dash after he'd forced the passenger door open. In a terrifyingly calm voice he said, "Joey, he's bleeding badly from somewhere. He'll bleed to death fast if we don't get it stopped. When I push on this seat, see if you can find out where it's coming from."

She scrambled to where he indicated and when he shoved for all he was worth, she saw the thin stream of blood literally shooting from Michael's leg into a sickeningly large black spot under the dash. She drew in a sharp breath and began to pray not to panic and said, "It's just above his knee.

Let me grab the scissors." She frantically cut away the torn leg of Michael's jeans to reveal a deep cut that had hacked the muscle of his thigh and now spurted blood.

Swallowing back a wave of nausea, she instinctively reached and pressed around until the thin stream of his life's blood stopped draining away. "There. I think I've got it stopped! Call for an ambulance! No, the Life Flight! Quick! Sorry, my phone is in your truck."

Michael groaned at where she had her hand deep in the flesh of his thigh as she pleaded, "I'm so sorry, Michael. Please forgive me for hurting you. And for everything else I've pulled lately. And for letting this awful car break down."

Grunting from the exertion of trying to move the mangled seat, Rossen said, "Joey, I can't let go of this to call. Use Michael's. It's probably in his right jean pocket."

Michael tried to reach for it, but was too weak to pull it out where it was stuck in the fold of his pocket. Joey shook her head in near panic and shoved his hand out of the way. After fumbling to get it out without letting go of the bleeder, she was eventually able to wrestle it free. Then her clumsiness with her left hand made her want to scream in frustration. Finally, she was able to make the call and was surprised at how succinctly she was able to communicate the severity of the situation.

With the helicopter enroute, she set the phone aside with the dispatcher still on the line and reached up and touched Michael's cheek and tried to speak in a reassuring voice, "Hang in there, Michael. They're on their way, but it's going to be a minute. Where else are you hurt?"

Michael sighed weakly and then slowly said, "I'm sorry, I have no idea." He reached over and tried to take her hand, but in his weakness he missed and she had to catch his fingers in hers.

Seeing him like this, and knowing it was all her fault made the tears she'd been trying to control spill over her eyes and she whispered, "Michael, I'm so sorry. Please forgive me for making you feel like you have to drive this car, and please forgive me for being such a complete jerk to you. I'm so sorry for everything. Please hang in there with me. I'd be so lost without you."

He looked at her as if he hadn't heard right and was confused. Finally, he weakly asked, "Really?"

She blinked at the tears as she struggled not to sob and nodded. Even as weak as he was, he gave her a gorgeous, tired smile. "I'm lost without you, too." He softly squeezed her fingers and haltingly said, "I do love you, Joey. There's nothing to forgive. It was all my fault for being so cynical in the first place. I should have said something. If I don't bleed to death, will you marry me?"

At that Joey's tears started in earnest. She was crying so hard, she could hardly speak to say, "Yes, and don't you die!" She swallowed hard to try to stem the water works so he wouldn't think he was going to die. "I need you, Michael. Be strong, okay? You're gonna be fine. You're gonna be so fine. Just hang in there."

He leaned his head back and closed his eyes and said softly, "You think I'd die when you finally agree to marry me? No way."

Joey bent forward to ease her hip, tried again to swallow her tears and with a small sob, said, "I'm going to be ticked off at you when you're better for trying to make jokes in this situation. You know the marriage police will probably come for that."

Without opening his eyes, he said slowly, "I'm fine with being arrested by the marriage police as long as I'm with you."

Rossen chuckled from his awkward position beneath the dash and Joey started to cry harder again. Michael opened his eyes and gently touched her cheek. "Don't cry, Joey. We're going to be okay. We really are. We're going to get to that happily ever after yet. Just give me a minute."

310

She looked up and met his eyes and tried not to sob again as she whispered, "You've got forever, Michael. I've set aside eternity for you, so take as long as you want." At that he smiled tiredly as he caressed her cheek and she turned her head and kissed his hand. "Stay with me, Michael. Please stay with me."

His head rolled back, but he whispered softly, "I'm trying, babe."

After awhile, he quit talking to them and she realized he was no longer conscious, but she thought he was still breathing as she struggled to keep the artery in his leg pinched off. The tears wouldn't seem to stop and Rossen kept up an intermittent conversation with her while he struggled to keep the seat from moving.

A highway patrolman reached them before the helicopter did and he helped Rossen to dismantle the seat enough that Michael's body was freed by the time the helicopter set down in the gravel road above them.

Seth had actually ridden in the chopper again and had Joey keep the pressure on as they moved Michael onto the stretcher. She stayed beside them as they struggled up the hill and then loaded into the chopper and took off.

Once they got him stretched out, Joey was shocked to see what a bloody mess he was and how chalky his skin tone was. It was probably a good thing she hadn't been able to see much as they waited because it would have scared her all the more.

Michael came to momentarily as they strapped him in and started an IV and when he saw Seth, he tried to smile and weakly asked, "You're not going to get rid of me while I'm out of it, are you?"

Seth grinned stiffly and replied as he quickly worked, "You just hang in there, man. Joey's happiness is far more important than offing the competition. I'll do my best to keep you all in one piece."

Jaclyn M. Hawkes

Michael only nodded weakly before he drifted out again. Seth frowned intensely and hastily pushed something out of a syringe into Michael's IV. Their conversation and Seth's intense look made Joey so upset that Seth had to encourage her not to cry and to pay attention to what she was doing.

As they flew, Seth finally had her let go of the artery and she was horrified as it began to spurt again. Seth sucked in a breath and quickly clamped it off with some forceps. He continued to hurriedly work over Michael and by the time they landed and had him unloaded, there was a surgical team waiting for them that smoothly transferred him to a waiting gurney. Seth gave her an intense look as if trying to warn her not to get her hopes up and then they hustled Michael away, leaving Joey standing outside the doorway on the helipad by herself.

In the sudden letdown, she felt more fear rise in her again as she looked down at Michael's blood spattered all over her clothes. There was so much! The guilt overwhelmed her and she began to sob again. This was all just because she had been insecure. And the car should have been in better repair. It was all her fault! She would deserve it if he didn't make it after all. And then she and Rossen had almost driven right past where he'd gone off without even seeing the hole in the fence. If it hadn't been for the loose cows . . .

Suddenly crying so hard she could hardly get a breath, she put a hand up to cover her face. He was too good a man for this to happen to and now that he wasn't there to see her fall apart she couldn't hold it back.

She wasn't aware of anything except her fears and worries and the pain in her heart until, finally, a nurse came and helped her inside and to an exam room where she pulled the curtain for the cubicle around her. With a sad shake of her head, she snapped on some rubber gloves and gently began to help Joey clean off the blood that had even spattered onto her face. Joey struggled to stop the tears, but all she

312

could manage for a time was to try to make herself cry as quietly as she could as the nurse mutely helped her.

Once Joey was somewhat cleaner, the nurse offered her a box of tissue and then put a gentle arm around her shoulders and shepherded her through the hallway to a small room nearby where there was a tiny couch, a table and two chairs and a coffee pot. With another look of pity that spoke of the gravity of Michael's condition, the nurse tried unsuccessfully to reassure her and then promised to come tell her as soon as she heard anything and walked out.

Knowing that even the nurse didn't believe Michael was going to make it made the fear and the pain in Joey's heart surge out of control. Why had she wasted their time together? Why had she been so insecure that he had felt he needed to drive an old car just to try to appease her? What was the matter with her? This was all her fault! All of it!

When the self-recrimination felt too overwhelming, she finally collapsed into a heap onto the little couch in inconsolable anguish.

Rossen found her there at some point and sat down next to her to gently rub her on the back. She looked up at him and asked with a shuddering sob, "Have they come back and said anything yet?"

He shook his head with a sad face, but then said mildly, "No, but he's gonna be fine. Seth and God are with him. Quit bawling and start praying. When he finally makes it out of surgery you'll scare him to death with all this hysteria."

That gentle brotherly ribbing was exactly what she needed. Rossen was right. He always was. Seth and God were enough. She started to pray.

Chapter 40

Eighteen hours later, after any number of CT scans, and x-rays, and when Michael was officially out of the woods, she was doing better. His artery had been stitched up by another plastic surgeon and he had been stabilized with several units of blood and was finally resting comfortably in a regular room. Miraculously, Michael was in remarkably good shape and other than the stitches on his thigh and in a few other places, and being terribly weak for awhile, his recovery would be relatively quick.

Naomi had come. She'd brought Joey a change of clothes, some Ibuprofen to help with the ache in her hip that made her feel guilty because Michael was in so much worse shape. Mostly, she brought the moral support Joey needed to quit beating herself up and eventually wrap her mind around it all enough to stop the perpetual tears. Exhausted, both emotionally and physically, Joey had finally fallen asleep in the chair beside Michael's hospital bed.

Sometime in the night a sound woke her, and she fought her way past the overwhelming fatigue to find Michael stirring. Moving to him, she clasped his hand in hers and spoke his name and was rewarded when he opened his tired eyes.

He sounded horribly weak as he whispered her own name, and she couldn't help the tears that filled her eyes as she said, "Michael."

It took her a minute to be able to say more. "I'm so sorry. Please forgive me."

He softly squeezed her hand with his large, brown, calloused one and gave her a hint of a smile and a minimal shake of his head. They just looked into each others eyes for several moments and then she could tell he was struggling to speak. She leaned close as he asked, "Did you really promise me eternity?"

Covering their clasped hands with her other one, she swallowed the lump in her throat and whispered, "Absolutely."

Then she could have smacked him as he gave her a real smile and tiredly said, "I should have crashed that car a long time ago."

She shook her head and tried to sound severe as she said, "Don't joke like that." Then she had to work to keep the emotion under control before she could add, "You almost died."

She swallowed hard to keep her composure and then admitted softly, "I've never been so scared in my life. How are you feeling?"

Still gently smiling, he closed his eyes and she barely heard him say, "Happy." A second later he said, "Incredibly tired. But happy."

He slept most of the next day while they monitored him and then toward evening the sound of his hospital bed moving woke her where she was napping in the chair beside him again. She opened her eyes in the semi darkness to see him sitting up in bed with the head of it raised, watching her, looking more awake and with it than he'd looked since they'd found him after the accident.

As she struggled to wake up herself, he said softly, "You're beautiful when you're tired."

She self-consciously put a hand to her hair that she was sure wasn't really beautiful at this point, returned his studied look and said, "Thank you. You look better. How are you feeling?"

316

He shrugged. "A little tired. How long have I been here?"

"About a day and a half."

He was quiet then for a few minutes as she simply watched him from her chair and she wondered if he was unhappy or just still too thrashed to relax. Finally, she came right out and asked, "Are you okay? Is something wrong?"

He shrugged again, looking at her and then at length asked in a low voice, "Did you really tell me you'd marry me? Or did I dream it?"

Her heart skipped a beat as she wondered if he was regretting having asked her in the desperation of nearly bleeding to death. Hesitantly, she said, "I told you." She paused, watching him, wondering what was coming next.

Several seconds went by while she waited, watching him watch her, holding her breath until finally, he asked her quietly, "Are you going to take it back now that I'm not dying?"

She stood up, paused for a moment to let her bum hip relax and then came over to stand beside his bed in the dimmed lights. "No."

They were still looking at each other almost warily and she had to ask him as well, "Why? Are you having second thoughts now that you're out of the woods?"

He shook his head and gave a short, low, humorless laugh. "Joey, I haven't had a second thought about you since the moment I laid eyes on you. Do you really not know that in your heart by now?"

Timidly, she looked down. "I don't know what to know about you, Michael."

But then she raised her head and looked right at him and said, "Except that I love you. I know that. Somehow, I've always loved you." She held his eyes. "Even before I really knew you, I loved you." She paused again and then admitted softly, "It scares me."

He finally gave her a small, but encouraging tired smile and reached for her hand. He pulled her closer to the elevated head of his bed and asked gently, "Why does that scare you, Joey?"

She shook her head and looked away. "Because you make me feel, Michael. For years I've been waiting for someone to really make me feel something. And then you came and that very first day the emotions were so strong with you. At first it was your sadness, but I'd never felt something so strongly in my life. Then later. As I got closer to you and realized who . . . What you were."

She shook her head again. "You're the only one who can make me feel that much emotion and you were so easy to let into my heart. It makes me feel incredibly vulnerable. You can make me happier than I've ever been, but you can devastate me just as easily."

He nodded and softly said, "Don't you realize it's the same with me? But to me it's a gift. You make everything brighter and crisper and sharper. More alive. You found my soul, Joey. You've made my whole life have meaning. You give me energy and passion and direction. You've inspired me from that very first day."

He paused and rubbed her hand with his thumb and asked gently, "How can I return that? How can I ever make you trust me the same way, Joey? You did at first. How can I get it back? I need you in my life forever and ever and ever. And ever again. Tell me what to do so I can give some of that back."

His eyes searched hers for several seconds. She could see forever there. Leaning over, she kissed his temple and then rested her head carefully against his. "I'm sorry, Michael, but I don't have all the answers. All I know is that I adore you, and it frightens me to the point that I listen to the little devil on my shoulder telling me I mean nothing to you. That I couldn't, coming from your background. Instead of listening

318

to the Spirit that brings that warm, sweet peace. I'm hoping to be able to kick that little devil out of here. You may have to help me. He's been pretty adamant."

He turned his head and whispered against her cheek, almost nuzzling her ear, "I would love to kick him out. But I don't always know what to do to reach you. At first, I thought you could just tell if I treated you well, but that didn't work out. You heard the media instead of my actions. You heard what I didn't say louder than what I did say. I'm so sorry I didn't tell you about my background before I left. At the time, I just wanted to leave it all behind. I didn't mean to hurt you on purpose, I swear. And now I don't know how to make you trust me again. To overcome the hurt. To make you know how vital you are to me."

Feeling guilty again, she barely shook her head against him and admitted, "I'm sorry. I don't know either, Michael. Hearing it helps. And I'm sure commitment will be huge. I just need to know that I matter to you."

Pulling slightly back, he gave her an intense look that almost burned her and said in the most intimate, velvet voice, "Joey Rockland, you matter more than anything. You are my life. If I tell you every day for the rest of eternity and show you with how I treat you until we're old and gray and beyond. If I make sure you know that I worship you, would you marry me and be with me forever?"

She met his look steadily and struggled to control the tears as she answered, "Yes, Michael. I would love to marry you."

"I can't go through the temple for a year, but I promise we'll go as soon as I can, okay?"

Nodding, she whispered, "Of course." He moved closer to the edge of the bed and pulled her tightly into his arms to kiss her, gently, but then after a second, with more of that searing emotion he evoked in her. She knew she'd be feeling this depth of emotion that she'd waited for so long, for the

Jaclyn M. Hawkes

rest of forever with him. It was warm and sweet and peaceful, and she didn't hesitate to kiss him back.

Actually, maybe it was hotter than warm, but it was right and good and felt like eternity.

"Well, it looks like he's going to live, anyway. At least he will if Joey will let him come up for air!" It took a second for her to realize she was hearing Cooper's voice and she slowly pulled back from Michael's arms to turn and blush when she realized three of her brothers and her dad and even Seth were standing just inside the door of Michael's hospital room. Cooper cracked up and said, "Geez, Joey. He's a patient. Try to keep that in mind, would ya!"

Cooper turned to the pretty nurse who walked in just then to begin taking Michael's vitals and gave her his swashbuckling smile and said, "We're gonna need some oxygen here. Do you think you could help us out with that? On second thought, what do you know about kissing? Is there a problem with doing that here in the hospital?"

The nurse raised her eyebrows and then returned the teasing smile. "Are you asking for permission? Or instruction? Or are you just checking for Mr. Morgan's future reference? What do you have in mind?"

Cooper sidled over to her. "I'm thinking that instruction part. Definitely! Have you got a minute?"

The nurse smiled sweetly. "I'm sorry, but Helga Bergdorfel is our kissing instructor and she isn't available at the moment. I could bring you some sugar free Jell-O. Would that help?"

He gave her a heart stopping smile. "Now, if I just happened to pass out right now, you'd have to give me mouth to mouth, right?"

At that moment a tall, heavyset nurse with a graying braid around her head came in with Michael's dinner tray and the pretty, little spitfire nurse that Cooper had been

320

flirting with laughed and said, "Here's Helga now. I'm sure she'd be able to help you out in case of an emergency."

With that, the pretty nurse bustled out the door and the very large nurse turned to Cooper and asked with a deep eastern European accent, "Vut vuz it that you are vontin'?"

Without skipping a beat, Cooper grinned and said, "CPR actually. I think she gave me a cardiac arrest. She was just mentioning that you teach CPR. Is that true?"

The big nurse cracked the merest hint of a smile. "You ah a teasah, I can see. She vill finish her shift at eleven o'clock. You must come back zen."

Cooper wrapped a long arm around her shoulder as she headed out the door, grinned again and said, "Why thank you, Nurse . . . " He glanced down at the name tag attached to her buxom bosom. "Bergdorfel. Is there anything else you could tell me about your very attractive co-worker? I would be willing to make it worth your while." They could hear the big nurse laugh as she and Cooper went down the hall.

With Cooper gone, Seth approached Michael's bed and put some papers down on the tray table. "Coop was right. You look like you're apparently going to live. You might want to wipe that lipstick off before you head out of here, though."

At this, Michael looked at Joey with slightly raised brows. She laughed and said, "I'm not wearing lipstick, Michael. He's just teasing."

Seth chuckled and went on, "Same routine as last time, Romeo, only this is a much bigger owie, so don't push it. Be careful not to tear them. Keep them dry and we'll yank 'em out in ten days. And you're weak as a kitten, so pace yourself. How sore is it? You want something for the pain?"

Michael smiled. "Your bedside manner stinks."

Seth gave a small laugh. "You got my girl. Be glad you made it through surgery. And you've been doing a hack job of taking care of her. She looks thrashed." Seth grinned over at Joey, then continued speaking to Michael. "Better step up the chivalry or the next time I'll remove your gall bladder while you're under. You want this prescription?" He held out the little white notepad.

Michael shook his head. "Just the girl, thanks. I'll do better at keeping her happy."

Seth nodded. "See that you do."

Seth went out the door and Rossen, Treyne and her dad came over to the bed, where Rossen said, "We'll go see if we can keep Cooper out of trouble while you eat. Then are you okay to go?"

Smiling tiredly at him, Michael replied, "Oh, I don't know. The last little while here hasn't been too bad. Maybe I'll stay. Watching Cooper with the nurses might be worth the bad food."

"Yeah, like it's Cooper and not kissing Joey that has kept you entertained. We'll be back with a wheel chair."

"Okay, but Cooper is *not* driving."

Rossen chuckled. "Spoil sport. You have no sense of adventure."

As they all went out the door, Michael murmured, "Just a sense of self-preservation."

Joey laughed and came back over close to him and asked innocently, "Now. Where were we?"

Michael kissed her once before he smiled and said in that lethal, husky voice again, "I believe I was in your personal space. Does that bother you?"

She looked into his eyes and shook her head. "As long as you're okay, I don't even care if the kissing police show up."

Pulling her close again, he said, "It's not the kissing police who worry me. It's that John Wayne cavalcade with all the rifles."

Leaning in, she whispered, "They don't typically allow too many horses into the hospital. I think you're safe with me. At least for the next couple of eternities. Go ahead and kiss me."

The End

About the author

Jaclyn M. Hawkes grew up with 6 sisters, 4 brothers and any number of pets. (It was never boring!) She got a bachelor's degree, had a career and traveled extensively before settling down to her life's work of being the mother of four magnificent and sometimes challenging children. She loves shellfish, meat lover's pizza, the out of doors, the youth, and hearing her children laugh. She and her adorable husband, their younger children, and their happy dog, now live in a mountain valley in northern Utah, where it smells like heaven and kids still move sprinkler pipe.

To learn more about Jaclyn, visit www.jaclynmhawkes.com.

Author's note

So, about that Salty Jello . . . Most people call it Pretzel Salad, and when most people make it, it's one of those lovely Relief Society luncheon kinds of things with fresh fruit and all.

And yes, when I said that Joey would be famous forever, I wasn't kidding. My children will never let me live that one down—ever! First, I'll give the recipe, then after, I'll tell you how NOT to make it famous!

2 C. lightly crushed pretzels
3 T. sugar
1/2 C. butter   Mix and bake in 9x13 5 min. @ 400. Cool

8 oz. cream cheese
1 C. sugar
8 oz. Cool Whip   Beat cream cheese and sugar until fluffy. Fold in Cool Whip. Spread on cooled pretzel crust, sealing edges to pan.

1 (6 oz.) pkg. raspberry Jello
2 C. hot water
12 oz. fresh raspberries
1 (8 oz.) can crushed pineapple   Dissolve Jello in boiling water. Cool slightly until it starts to gel and mix in raspberries. Drain pineapple and add to raspberry mixture. Spread onto Cool Whip mixture. Chill until set. Enjoy.

NOTE: <u>Do Not</u> crush the pretzels in the bag they came in unless you dump out all the salt that has fallen to the bottom of the bag first—unless you want to be really, really famous! (At least it happened at dinner at home and not at some church social! Whew!) Just making memories,

                                    Jaclyn